The Rock & Roll Murders: A Rennie Stride Mystery

Also by Patricia Kennealy Morrison

Strange Days: My Life With and Without Jim Morrison

Rock Chick: A Girl and Her Music
The Jazz & Pop *Writings, 1968 - 1971*

The Books of The Keltiad

The Copper Crown
The Throne of Scone
The Silver Branch
The Hawk's Gray Feather
The Oak Above the Kings
The Hedge of Mist
Blackmantle
The Deer's Cry
Tales of Spiral Castle: Stories of The Keltiad

The Rennie Stride Mysteries: The Rock & Roll Murders

Ungrateful Dead: Murder at the Fillmore
California Screamin': Murder at Monterey Pop
Love Him Madly: Murder at the Whisky
A Hard Slay's Night: Murder at the Albert Hall
Go Ask Malice: Murder at Woodstock
Scareway to Heaven: Murder at the Fillmore East
Daydream Bereaver: Murder on the Good Ship Rock&Roll
Ruby Gruesday: Murder on the Rock Limited (forthcoming)

Daydream Bereaver

Murder on the Good Ship Rock&Roll

Patricia Morrison

Lizard Queen Press

This book is a work of fiction. Although certain real locations, events and public figures are mentioned, all names, characters, places and events described herein are the product of the author's imagination or are used fictitiously. Any resemblance to actual events, places or persons (living or dead) is purely coincidental.

DAYDREAM BEREAVER: Murder on the Good Ship Rock&Roll
 For further information, contact: Lizard Queen Press, 151 1st Avenue, Ste. 120, New York NY 10003.

Jacket art and design by Andrew Przybyszewski
Book interior design by the author
Book produced by Lorrieann Russell and Jesse V. Coffey

Acknowledgments

Full disclosure: I have never been on a cruise ship in my life. In fact, I have never been farther out to sea than the Block Island ferry. As a child, I did go on a school field trip aboard the supercarrier U.S.S. Saratoga (docked at the time), and as a slightly older child, drove a Circle Line tour boat down the Hudson for a minute or two (supervised by the actual driver).

And I was in, or on, one of those scary tiny Sunfish things once, on an upstate New York lake—one of the most frightening experiences of my life, like balancing on a playing card two inches off the water, with a hole in the middle—and I've paddled a Girl Scout canoe on a lake near home. Sum total of my nautical experience.

Nor have I ever scuba-dived, or seen life underwater except on television nature programs, or even so much as put my face in the water since my required college swimming class. And I still cannot swim.

And though I did consult people who have actually been on cruises to the Caribbean, the rest is entirely invented. There *could* be islands like Grand Palm Island and Lion Island, as I built them using Tortola and Mustique as models, among other such places. But I've never been there. And I plan to keep it that way. I've been to Hawaii, and that's as close as I ever want to get.

I hate everything about the tropics: sun, surf, sand, heat, humidity. And bugs. It's odd that I would write a book about all these things I hate. All I can say is that this is what the book wanted. And that's what imagination is for. And God bless the Internet.

For the talented and amazing triumvirate
who make these books possible
and manifest my creative will in the world,
and who are also my dear friends:
Lorrieann Russell; Jesse V. Coffey;
and Andrew Przybyszewski, by whose covers
I am so proud my books are judged.

Go Down Easy, Come Down Hard

Life can be so simple
When you're living in the bricks
But when the street is all you've got
There's nothing left but tricks
Only time will tell
just what the hell
you did to get so scarred
Whatever goes down easy comes down hard

Now gravity's not just a good idea, it happens to be the law
Statute of limitations never ends
Break it, you're gonna get busted worse than anyone ever saw
There's no bail set and no parole and no time for amends
But no sane fool
can bend the rule
was meant to be your guard
Whoever goes down easy comes down hard

[bridge]

Lovers losers keepers winners, seen it all before
Say hello before they go away
Coming in the windowsills and going out the door
None of them have ever planned to stay
Still, luck and fate
can surely mate

It doesn't have to be ill-starred
Whichever side goes easy comes down hard

Black and white and shades of gray and nothing left but blues
Wonder if the work was all in vain
Everything I'm winning here is all that I can lose
Do it right or if it's wrong I'll do it all again
Not engineer
nor scrutineer
I'm hoist with my own petard
Whatever goes down easy comes down hard

Deal me out or deal me in or deal me to a draw
Jack of diamonds up a neighbor's sleeve
I keep my cards close to my vest, I'm cautious to a flaw
The Dealer tells us what was real and what was make-believe
So let me know
what was just for show
and who held the winning card
That life I went down easy, came down hard

~Turk Wayland

Prologue

*T*HE OCEAN LINER *sat at a midtown dock on the Hudson River, as it did every Saturday before she made her weekly shuttle voyage down to the northern Caribbean and back again. She was on the small side, not like the huge Atlantic-crossing ones that were still left – there were fewer and fewer of those every year – but exceptionally beautiful, a "lady" of her type, as sailors said.*

Carrying at capacity some six hundred souls, as the lexicon had it, two thirds passengers, the other third crew, the ship was called the Excalibur, *and the owning company was Sword Lines, sailing out of Southampton; her five sisters were also named after historic famous blades of old* – Curtana, Clarent, Durendal, Tizona, Joyeuse.

But workers had lashed canvas-strip masks to bow and stern, a temporary and humiliating renaming for a week's hired sail; and now the Excalibur, *affectionately known to her crew as Callie, was forced to take to the seas as the Good Ship Rock&Roll.*

In an hour, the tide would start ebbing down the broad, shining main Hudson estuary, the North River as local watermen called it, as distinguished from the East River – the river was all the same, just different arms – and when it did the ship would go with it. Of course, the tugs and her own great engines could take her out of harbor whenever the captain pleased; such vessels were no longer dependent on wind and tide. But the owners of the line were sticklers for tradition: their vessels sailed on the ebb and docked on the flood, and not a moment sooner.

This trip, the Excalibur *had been bought out privately, for a press junket cruise to the Caribbean: the Grand Palm Islands and back again. She was carrying two hundred of rock's most powerful movers and shakers and shapers: critics, editors, photographers, trade writers, record company people, a luminous slate of musicians. All to hear the new music of one of the most popular and famous groups in the world, who were also aboard, and who were, in fact the hosts of this little nautical adventure.*

But though the group may have been popular and famous to a ridiculous extent, it was not one of the best or most artistic groups in the world, as all of them knew well. And that was both the reason for the cruise and the problem with it. And also it was what, directly or indirectly, would lead to murder on the high seas…

One

"THIS IS *SOOOO* STUPID."

Belinda Melbourne, writer on rock matters for such varied journals as the New York Sun-Tribune and the Village Voice and Life magazine, leaned on the rail of the ocean liner next to her good friend and colleague, fellow journalist Rennie Stride, both young women watching with interest as the controlled confusion of imminent departure spread like an oil slick over the pier. She looked wickedly bright-eyed and bushy-tailed, like a clever, pretty squirrel on speed.

Rennie, herself looking sleek and vaguely dangerous, like a bored panther who might do anything for a laugh, raised delicate eyebrows.

"And yet I notice we're both here."

"I said *this* is stupid, not *we're* stupid. Who would be stupid enough to turn down an all-expenses-paid ten-day cruise to the Caribbean and back?"

"Turk. Turk turned it down," said Rennie, smiling. "And we all know how unstupid *he* is. Furthermore, he said—let me make sure I get this right, he hates it when anyone misquotes him—he said that he'd sooner eat his own toes with a nice hollandaise than let himself be trapped at sea aboard a floating tub of hell with critics and label scum and, God save him for his sins, the Weezles."

"Gosh." Belinda shook her head admiringly. "That boy

of yours has such a turn of phrase."

"Doesn't he though. Even for an Oxford-graduate superstud guitar god. But I remind you that you and I and the hundred and ninety-eight others like us are not only trapped aboard this floating tub of hell but we have to kind of, well, not *sing* for our supper, that's the Weezles' job, but at least *listen* for it. Work for our room and board. For *our* sins, we have to listen to our hosts trying to persuade us that they're a real live creative cutting-edge rock and roll band. And not just a tricked-out, made-up, total and hugely successful fabrication."

Belinda grinned. "Talk about ship of fools... I ask you! Is it too late to shout out 'Away all boats and abandon ship!'?"

Rennie rather thought it was, and as if to punctuate her opinion the ship shuddered under them, like a horse vexed by a fly, and began to back out slowly and throbbingly into the Hudson, shoved by feisty little tugboats into a giant aquatic three-point turn.

Belinda looked behind them at the pier, and ahead down the river. "Can't escape now, Strider."

"No... Well, maybe it won't be as bad as we think."

Maybe, she privately considered, it might even not be bad at all, and that wasn't false hope talking. Though possibly it could be worse. It was just—oh man, it was the freakin' *Weezles*, for God's sake! They were a sort of third-generation print-off, illegitimate lovechild of the Beatles and the Monkees, with the Stones as blushing godfathers. If the Beatles were the Fab Four, and the Monkees were the Pre-Fab Four, then the Weezles were the Post-Fab Four. And their success level was beyond all degrees of fab together.

Four cute boys with terrific hair. Great voices. Irresistibly catchy tunes. Millions upon millions of records sold.

Trouble was, it was all bogus, in a seriously non-bogus sort of way. The Weezles had been cold-bloodedly assembled from a talent hunt five years before, like an Erector set, or erection set, a sort of hybrid trans-Atlantic response to the British rock invasion and the American counter-reaction to that. Lead guitarist/vocalist Luke Woods, drummer/vocalist Matt Cutler, bass player/vocalist Brian Moretti and rhythm guitarist/lead vocalist—and designated fan heartthrob—Hoden. No other name, please; just Hoden. Once they'd been put together, their evil overlord manager, Jo Fleet, had sprung them on an unsuspecting world, and the rest was pop history.

They'd all been picked strictly for their cuteness and biddability, not for their musicianship. Which was, at least when they began and except for their uniformly excellent singing voices, insufficient by most genuine rock standards. Oh, they were quite pleasant to listen to, but save for the singularly cognomened and very English Hoden, who was truly talented—though not allowed to use his talent in any real way, and for five years he'd had to pretend he didn't possess it—none of them could play an instrument on a level anywhere *near* matching their almost instantaneous and pretty darn near global fame.

Of course, that hadn't stopped the public from instantly taking them to its heart, if not its actual mind. Such nice clean-cut boys, those Weezles! No swearing or drinking or wenching or drugging, like those awful Rolling Stones! Well, at least none that anyone knew about, anyway.

Who cared that they couldn't play! That's why God made overdubs! And session guys! And lip-synching! They were adorable! They had great hair! They sang simple catchy songs by simply great pop composers with simple slick lyrics that any simpleton could understand! They made tons of money! All the teenies lovedlovedlooooved them! And so did their mothers!

What more could you ask for? What else mattered? And for five years and many millions of people—and many, many gold records, and many more millions of dollars—nothing did.

But a year ago the worms had turned and shown their fangs. And it was Hoden who had rallied the charge. The Weezles were done with fraud, done with being biddable and nice: they were fed up to here with bullies—whether those bullies were the label, the audience, the critics or their own management—and by God they were going to take charge of their own image and their own souls. They were going to play their own music, the way they wanted to, the way they'd always known they could, the way they'd worked their asses off for the past five years to perfect. The way every other band in rock and roll did.

So, between one album and the next, they'd *Sgt. Pepper*-ized themselves. Luke grew a beard, Matt and Brian began sporting droopy mustaches, Hoden let his hair get *really* long, and they'd all begun writing songs like madmen: intricate music with dense, brilliant lyrics like nobody else's. They'd proudly put the new stuff on their last album, released a month ago to instant triple platinum sales. To keep their public and their label's promotion department happy, they'd sprinkled in among the hard stuff a few poppy little bouncetunes coldly calculated to be chart-toppers—a sop to the Philistines—then sat back and eagerly awaited results, knowing they'd done a bang-up job, rightly expectant of being praised by critics and populace alike.

"And you know what happened as well as I do," said Rennie. "Nothing changed. Not a damn thing. Because nobody cared but the band. And a few people like, in all modesty, you and me, who gave them full marks for the breakout. Credit for trying, and credit for what was good."

"Some of it was really good."

"Some of it was *great*. Oh, and we did administer nice sharp smacks upside their head for still pushing the crap, for trying to have it both ways and not cutting loose completely from their bogusness. That's fair, surely."

"They deserved what we said," agreed Belinda. "All of it. But they've been desperate to prove their cred for at least a couple of albums now. You remember it started right after they had that humongous hit with 'All Four Won'. Then they talked Dylan into writing something for them, and nobody ever thought he would, but he did and it turned out to be 'Double Barreled', which blew everybody's mind, and they saw they could be a serious band after all. And then they started writing their own stuff. And then *we* saw they could be a serious band after all. Maybe they always knew that, you know—that they could be serious. Even if most of us didn't. Even if the label knew but didn't care. Their fans didn't give a rat's. Maybe that's why they're so extra-hot to prove themselves now."

"They're not exactly innocent little music-biz virgins,

may I remind you," said Rennie with a knowing glance. "They've been bending over for Jo Fleet, Manager from Hell, for five years now. And by all accounts, both parties have been satisfied with the transaction."

Belinda was laughing. "See, that's where a liberal-arts education comes in so goddamn handy. It teaches even rocknrollers not to make bargains with Satan."

Her friend nodded. Blackpool-born Joslin Fleet, known as Jo to all but his parents, was notorious even in a cutthroat business. He was a rock hyena, no, a whole hyena *pack* all on his own, and he had never troubled to hide his scent upwind as he closed in on his prey, out there on the vast open savannas of rock and roll. Because he knew he was an unstoppable predator and it didn't matter if his prey knew he was coming; they couldn't escape. Sure, he did well for his dozen or so big-name clients, very well indeed, but they all knew the devil's bargain, and the final tab that they had no choice but to sign for: he'd get them what they wanted, and in return they couldn't complain when the hyena jaws clamped down on their own vitals, as sooner or later the jaws always would.

"Can you say 'Faust', boys and girls? Yes, I think you can," said Rennie gleefully. "Really though, they should have known Manager Mephistoph-fleet-les and the label would never let them get away with anything like a higher order of musicmaking. Frankly, I'm amazed they even got to do the Dylan song at all. Fabulously popular and staggeringly commercial was all they were ever supposed to be. And so they have been. And now they're trapped in it."

"And popular and commercial isn't enough for them anymore. Which is why we're all here."

"Uh-*huh*. We the so-called movers and shakers of rock and roll, forced to spend days and nights listening to the Weezles' new music, down to, among, and back from the Grand Palm Islands. And one of those nights to be devoted to witnessing and attesting to the world premiere performance of their new rock opera. With a reprise on the way back. Lord, have mercy."

"And by 'Lord' I take it you don't mean Turk," Belinda chortled. "But comes now 'Paize Lee: The Story of A Little Hippie Girl'! Uninterrupted setting, no distractions. Angels and ministers of grace defend us! They actually plan to use this to get us to rate them right up there with the Airplane and Hendrix and Lionheart and Turnstone and the Dead. Riiiight..."

"It's that uninterrupted no distractions part that's freaking me out," said Rennie darkly. "Do you realize we can't escape, not unless we call for a Navy destroyer to fire across our bow and then trans-ship us like freed hostages? But it's still not too late, maybe. If we jump overboard right now, we can get away before anyone knows we're gone. Look, there's the West Side Highway, not far at all, you can see cars and people. Come on, hold my hand, you won't even feel it when we hit the water. I promise. We could swim to shore, grab a cab and be home in ten minutes. Sodden, but home."

"Oh, I don't think so. If the fall doesn't kill us, then the pollution will. And no cab would pick up two soaked, bedraggled urchins. Cheer up—'Paize Lee' isn't until our second night out. Even though there will be all sorts of music by all sorts of people every single evening and all day long too."

"True..." Rennie brightened a bit. "Maybe we'll all be too seasick by then to even leave our cabins. But marooned in oceanic isolation with fellow rock hacks isn't my idea of perfect bliss, even with a gorgeous Caribbean island and my handsome sexy English fiancé waiting for me at the end of the voyage."

"It's not *just* hacks like us." Belinda paused to admire the double-lattice steel framework of the World Trade Center towers under construction, flinging themselves into the sky north of the Battery. "Weezies also wanted the company of peers. So they invited some. There's a bunch of artists on board you wouldn't think in a million years would be along for this ride. I am expecting *serious* jamming, as they are all expected to play. Plato Lars, Judy Collins, April Rainers, some of the Yardbirds and the Dead and Canned Heat, John Sebastian, Prisca Quarters, David Crosby, he's always up for a boat trip, even Jimi's here—must be that 'free Caribbean cruise' thing."

Rennie nodded sagely. "Not to mention the artistic legitimacy that their presence confers on our hosts. But that's nothing new. They've all been friends for ages, oddly enough. You'll remember Jimi actually opened for the Weezles on that big U.S. tour three years back, and they've been best buds ever since. Same with Crosby and the Dead. Luke dated Judy before Stephen Stills did and April after Hendrix, and Hoden knows the Yardbirds from their Lunnon days. Though I don't think his path and Turk's ever crossed."

She whipped out a small camera and snapped a picture of Belinda with the Statue of Liberty behind her. "I must try to talk to Crosby and April and Plato—they've all been promising me an interview for months, and now I have them cornered. As for the gratis nature of the voyage, it's not as if any of that lot can't afford to pay for a cruise on their own."

"Well, sure," said Belinda. "But free is always nice. Especially when it comes in the form of record-company graft. Or rock-star graft. I do love being modestly corrupted, don't you?"

"I cooperate and rejoice in it," said Rennie primly. "A solid-silver Mark Cross pen from RCA, a gold Tiffany keyring from Columbia, an Italian-leather diary from Atlantic, similar trinkets from other grafters, all for last Christmas. I don't think that compromises my integrity too incredibly much."

"Certainly not. And now this trip. The Weezles' management said so many big names called up wanting in, for whatever reasons, that they had to bring in Pig Blue's outfit to do security. Though why security would be needed on a floating lockbox like this…I mean, it's not as if we're expecting to be boarded by Barbary corsairs or anything, right? They tried to get Ares Sakura first, of course, to handle things, but he was unavailable, as you undoubtedly know. And lest you think it went unnoticed, which it most certainly did *not*, what was that ever so casual mention of your handsome sexy fiancé awaiting you at journey's end all about?"

Rennie's mouth quirked at the lower right corner. "Yes, well, I did know about Ares, and what's more, I know *exactly* where he's being unavailable at the moment. He and Prax went to stay with Turk at his house in the Grand Palm Islands, the little ratbags. You'd think my superstar betrothed and my superstar best friend and her super-rock-bodyguard boyfriend would be a bit more diplomatic and caring of my feelings, but no. Both Lionheart and Evenor are off the road and not recording just now, so the lead guitarist of Lionheart and the lead singer of Evenor and the head of Argus Guardians have been sunning and swimming and eating like kings for the past two weeks, the bastards, while I was stuck in New York and now while I'm stuck on this damn dinghy. But when we get to Palmton I'm jumping ship to join them. They know I'm coming, and they know I'll be cross when I get there."

"Ares has a house in the Grand Palms?"

"He doesn't. Turk does."

"Ah. Your pronouns were a little fuzzy. Okay then, I didn't know *Turk* had a house in the Grand Palms."

"Well, really it's his family who have it, but yeah. As seems to be ever the case with them, they've owned it for like a thousand years. Though in this case only a measly three hundred."

"The house?" asked Belinda, impressed.

"The *island*. It's called Lion Island. Not actually in the Grand Palms but about twenty miles east. Tropical, quite sizable, they own the whole freakin' thing. I don't know much else about it, except there's a mansion, isn't there always with them, and gnarly surf breaks, and some famous kind of local *ham*, if I heard Turk correctly. Oh, and it had real pirates, too, back in the day. One of them was even a distant Turk-ish ancestor. And the Tarrants own it all, and Turk Wayland, or rather Richard Tarrant, twenty-first Marquess of Raxton and future Duke of Locksley, is its crown prince. And before you ask, I've never been."

She stretched elaborately. "Anyway, here we are, and so is everyone else, and it is after all a free junket to the latitudes of palm trees and blue waters, which totally beats a bus trip to, say, the Capitol Theater in horrible old Port Chester to see Traffic, and there are shipboard buffets, mmm, yes, and the Weezles are really quite dealable with for, what, one little mini-gig a day and some mandatory one-on-one interviews? They're always a lot of fun to talk to, though I've only ever spoken to Luke and Matt. How hard can it be? Besides, I used to dance to their singles, you know, back in my college go-go dancing days. I think I'll tell them that, in fact."

Belinda nodded wisely. "Ah, but you're forgetting 'Paize Lee: The Story of A Little Hippie Girl'. Two performances thereof. We may have to mutiny. Where's Fletcher Christian when you really need him?"

As the ship passed under the Verrazano Bridge and began the great sweeping turn for open Atlantic waters, Rennie took a deep breath of salt air, and, suddenly, causelessly cheerful, looked back at the towers of New York rapidly receding astern.

"Oh, I expect we'll survive."

They would, too. Well, most of them.

Two

There being only two hundred passengers on a vessel designed to carry twice as many in spaciousness and luxury, all the posh upper deck suites and outside cabins were in use and nobody had to share if they didn't want to, or be trapped far below in steerage, either – though, on a smallish old-school ship like this, even steerage was still quite nice. It also meant an unprecedented level of attention from cabin staff, who now were on pretty much a one-to-one ratio with the passengers.

Rennie had been entranced with the first sight of her accommodations, up on the second-highest possible deck; most of her close friends were close by. Only the Weezles and their entourage were exalted above her, in splendid isolation on the sun deck that began right behind the Excalibur's bridge. But she wasn't complaining: the suite she'd been assigned to was amazing – a big round bed with a tufted satin headboard, a small but very pretty sitting room with vast chintz-covered armchairs, everything done in shades of blue and cream and fuchsia. Even the bathroom had a vintage look: a terrific old open-floor shower with Pompeii-mosaic tiles, set off by mermaid designs etched into thick frosty Thirties glass.

The cabin was stuffed with bon-voyage flowers, as befitted first-class space on a departing liner. All her preferred blooms: three dozen peonies, her favorite, from

Turk, all pink and white with one splendid dark-crimson blossom tucked away at the heart of them, presumably to apologize for the fight they'd had, though they'd made up in other ways before Turk left; a sofa-sized bolster of white roses from her publisher Oliver Fitzroy; huge puffy blue hydrangeas from Lionheart's manager Francher Green; a sheaf of deep-purple lilacs, sent by her dearest friend superstar Prax McKenna and Prax's boyfriend, bodyguard to the stars Ares Sakura, that was more like your actual lilac *bush.* Plus assorted generic explosions of expensive cellophaned and beribboned flora from assorted friendly or fawning or enemy publicists. It all looked like the hospital room of a terminal patient who didn't yet know she was terminal. But at least it was staggeringly fragrant.

Too bad most of the flowers had probably been sent more out of guilt or apology or flunkeydom than in the genuine spirit of happy sails to you. Turk, Prax, Ares, yes, guilt indeed. Fitz's offering likewise: he was at present off in the South of France with his wife and kiddies, stuffing his greedy face with duck confit and cassoulet and escargots. And her parents and her sister Dana and Dana's family were all merrily tootling around Ireland and apparently couldn't be bothered to send her so much as a shamrock. Everyone was on holiday except Rennie Stride, nobody was working in the whole round world apart from her, oh woe is she.

Rennie grinned, not even buying that herself, and practically inhaled the hyacinths sent by her friend and partner in crime reporting Ken Karper. *If you can actually call this working...* Still, she wouldn't be flinging the posies out the porthole. For the thousandth time, she wished that

Turk had come with her—that was what their fight had been about. Well, not so much a fight as a wrangle. True, he would have had to fly back to New York and then travel all the way back down to where he already was, so that *was* probably dumb, but it would have been so romantic to be with him aboard this groovy ship. It was a pity to waste that groovy round bed on sleeping alone… Still, they would be together again in a mere four days, so she would just have to suck it up and look forward to better nights not too far distant.

When she went to unpack her great-aunt's pleasingly battered Vuitton suitcases, her usual tackle for travel, she found that the steward who had drawn her cabin number had got there first, and all her things were already neatly arranged in drawers or hung equally neatly in the built-in armoire. Well, well. Exactly like being back at Pacings or Cleargrove or Tarrant House. And pretty much every bit as embarrassing. She tried to think if all her underwear had been clean—there wasn't very much of it, either then or now, of course, because there never was and that was the way Turk liked it—then dismissed the thought and pinned a peony behind one ear, just to get into the spirit of the thing. Time to go exploring.

Rennie had never been on an ocean liner before, but she'd packed her Dramamine and had her pressure points memorized, and she figured she could handle it. She'd never been to Lion Island, either, and there probably was precious little that seasick pills or shiatsu could do to help her handle *that*. Which was why she'd also packed *real* drugs. So one way or another she'd be fine. But as she wandered the promenade deck, promenading fit to beat the band, she found herself thinking not about the voyage ahead but about Turk, and where they were with each other since beginning their relationship two and a half years ago.

This was an odd time for them: a couple of months back, expanding their horizons, their mutual commitment and their real estate portfolio alike, they had bought yet *more* property, this time on the north shore of Maui—a house and thirty misty acres of rain forest halfway up the slopes of the hopefully extinct giant volcano Haleakala, between a tiny sleepy village called Makawao and another named, pleasingly poetically, Haiku. They'd rented it while on a week's Hawaiian break after attending Rennie's annulled husband Stephen Lacing's Hong Kong wedding and the band's brief tour of the Far East that had followed, and by the time they had to leave they'd fallen in love with it.

Lionheart had played at the stupendously lavish wedding reception. Turk's idea, perhaps not so surprisingly: a wedding present, or reparations, or atonement, for the mile-wide guilt trip he'd laid on himself for, as he saw it, stealing Rennie away from Stephen and living with her, another man's wife, for two and a half years. Not that anyone but him was seeing it that way: Rennie and Stephen had been separated for almost that long by the time Turk turned up on the scene, and she did not even for a nanosecond consider herself stolen by him. Rather, gifted to him, by her own hand.

But now of course the annulment meant that Stephen and Rennie had, oops, never been married in the first place, which was just plain trippy, so all four of them were technically getting married for the first time, which was just plain weird. But great face and honor accrued all round to Turk's gesture: after all, it wasn't every wedding reception where the band was an internationally famous supergroup who ordinarily pulled down a hundred grand a night, and it had really, *really* pleased Rennie that Turk had been gracious enough to offer it as a wedding gift, without her asking, even. And that Ling and Stephen had been gracious enough to accept.

Stephen's bride, with whom Rennie was on excellent terms, as indeed she still was with Stephen, was a gem expert, so naturally they bonded instantly. Ling-ling de la Fontange was half Chinese, half French, entirely gorgeous—and the daughter of Stephen's father's Asian-area business partner, the president of LacingCo Hong Kong, so it was a business alliance as well as a love match. The two families had been close for decades, so everyone was happy as a lark about it, even Rennie's onetime bane, Marjorie, Stephen's gorgon mother—well, at least once Motherdear, as she liked to be called by her offspring, had gotten into the spirit of the thing, after her initial racist reaction.

Or, more correctly, once she'd realized the many distinct advantages there were—business, financial, dynastic, social, genetic, you name it—to the Lacings enfolding the de la Fontanges even more closely to their pragmatic, San-Francisco-whorehouse-money, old-line-society clan bosom. So Ling, not Rennie, was now going to be the next Lacing matriarch, for which Rennie thanked God on her knees. Or thanked Turk on her knees. Anyway, Ling had already delivered the requisite male heir, so now she could do no wrong in Marjorie's eyes.

Better her than me! I've *only got to be a duchess eventually. Piece of cake by comparison...and wasn't it fun impressing Mothernotsodear with my engagement ring, her grim little surgically lifted jaw positively crashed to the floor—even Ling said it was the biggest and best damn ruby she'd ever seen. Of course Turk would* never *have given me an inferior stone... and it's miles nicer than the rock Stephen gave me, even without all the sexy royal history attached to it...*

After the wedding gig and a massive public Hong Kong concert, and Lionheart's tour of Australia and New Zealand and Japan and Honolulu, Rennie and Turk had gone to Maui to cool out for a week; they'd rented the house and had liked it so much that Turk had purchased it on the spot. Tucked away in cool upland rain forests, with spectacular views over emerald island and sapphire ocean, the place wasn't huge, but it was pure Hawaiian-style, all glass and native wood, airy lanais and breezeways and hidden verandas and secret suntrap courtyards. A massive single-pitched roof overhung the whole main house like a giant sheltering wing—they didn't even have to close the windows in a storm.

It remained entirely as they had bought it; all they'd had done was a paint job and a deep clean. They weren't planning on changing anything else: after last year's epic renovation of three New York brownstones into one, neither of them felt like reliving a major construction experience—especially Rennie, who'd ended up overseeing the New York project when Turk went out on the road.

She'd been a little freaked by the whole thing, and still was, and Turk's instant and impulsive acquisition of the Maui house didn't help. She'd never owned anything before, and now she was becoming a landowner partner on a grand scale—the excessive, or what she saw as excessive, expenditure, cavalierly buying houses whenever one felt like it, made her feel nervous and even guilty. She herself had had a fairly privileged upper-middle-class upbringing that had provided her with a Riverdale domicile and a boarding school/Ivy League education—posh Catholic academy grade school, the same one Caroline Kennedy would later attend, then Emma Willard, Cornell and Columbia—not to mention ballet, riding, ice skating and tennis lessons.

But Turk's level of immediate gratification was something staggeringly different, and proving very hard to get used to, though not for the reasons you might think. Sure, her name was right next to his on the various deeds, but Turk had really paid for the houses, and anyway all the property was considered an investment by and for the Duchy of Locksley. Big things like land and houses made her nervous, and the idea that once Turk had succeeded to the ultimate title she'd be not only a duchess but the chatelaine of six, count 'em, six ancestral Tarrant castles and uncounted other chunks of worldwide real estate was still quietly flipping her out. She was very much aware, of course, of how seriously fortunate she was, and how very, very grateful.

Still, the idea that her life was now pretty much one of never again having to wonder if she could afford anything she really wanted or needed, or even anything she merely expressed an idle desire for, scared the hell out of her.

Nobody in the world could own everything they liked, of course, not even dukes and rock stars, but the Tarrant family, for centuries, had been living their lives not far off that. Turk would buy her anything she wanted, and in addition would provide for and protect her on a truly regal scale—he'd already promised that, and demonstrated that, several times over. But was having it all, or most, really good for you? Surely longing, or planning, or saving, for things you wanted was a healthy thing; otherwise, wouldn't you get jaded and bored and spoiled? That Turk hadn't was a credit to his character and to his upbringing, and presumably she would be able to emulate him in that. If not—well, they would just have to be very, very careful. Especially once the kids started coming: there was no way she was going to breed up spoiled-brat English children, like those horrid kiddies in Victorian books. Though Eton and a pony or two would probably be okay.

But that was well down the road, and in the meantime owning a piece of enchanting, tranquil, backwater Maui felt safe enough—though, worryingly, the island was beginning to get dangerously hip. Several other people they knew were now thinking of buying there as well, or had already purchased property: George Harrison, Janis Joplin, their good friend actress Quinnie Saint Clears and her sculptor husband Rolf Stormgren, Lucian and Lindon Dolabella, the twin lead singers of Bosom Serpent, Rennie's painter friend and former boarding-school roommate Liege Clary Royal, if she could ever manage to uproot herself from her beloved Appalachians.

Even Ares' partner in the celebrity-bodyguard business,

the massive and paradoxically gentle Rhino Kanaloa, who'd been feeling a bit strung out of late, was thinking of returning home to his native East Maui coast and his large Hawaiian family, and Turk was considering asking him to be the permanent resident caretaker of the Haiku house, the way Ares was in Nichols Canyon, or at least that he recommend someone local and reliable.

Yeah, Maui wasn't bad at all, and it could be a lot worse. At least they'd have some cool, fun neighbors—hopefully not too close—and that wasn't even counting the surfers down on the shore or the pot growers and artisans and gurus up in the hills. People drawn, as Turk and Rennie had been, to the *mana* of the land, the ancient spirit power, as well as the natural beauty: not to mention the refreshing fact that nobody local gave a flying fuck about how famous you were, only about how you carried yourself in the world—polite, respectful, careful of others and of the land and ocean.

She was honest enough to admit that, though they never mentioned it to each other, both of them saw the Maui place as a refuge from not only Turk's celebrity but Rennie's notoriety, the backbeat of murder that had been part of their lives from their first night together, part of her life from even before that. If they could find that kind of sanctuary anywhere, surely they could find it there.

Of course, Turk had built yet *another* recording studio, as he did in each of the places he lived and had been doing for years—it was like marking his territory. But it did save a lot of time and money otherwise spent in studios belonging to other people, so it was considered a sound business investment. The property had a couple of cottages tucked away in the trees near a lush ravine, where a stream skipped merrily down the volcano's slope over a series of scenic waterfalls. One cottage held the state-of-the-art studio facilities, and the other, much larger one was a charming guesthouse, and they planned on renting the whole thing out to other bands who wanted tropical grooviness along with their 16-tracks.

Oh, and not forgetting the surf shack down the hill on a reef-infested slice of North Shore beach with prime breaks, to keep Turk happy, and Ares when he visited... She had no idea how long they were likely to remain in possession—Tarrant real estate was usually either profitably flipped soon after purchase or held on to for a few hundred years—but it was pleasant for the moment.

Now, however, there was a new island paradise in a different ocean to contend with, and more Tarrant history that she was about to become part of. Rennie leaned on the rail, gazing astern. The land had vanished. As they'd sailed down New York harbor through the Narrows, she had gazed over to Brooklyn, where she'd been born, where loads of her aunts and uncles and cousins still lived. Family. Family was ohana in Hawaiian, extended family in the wonderful, warm island sense: the Tarrants of Locksley and, yes, Lionheart itself were Turk's ohana, which meant both of them were hers now too, but they were all still working out how it was, well, working out.

The initial tensions with the Tarrants had been resolved happily and in full, thank God—nothing like her travails with the Lacings, and she adored Turk's parents and grandmother, though she sensed there might still be some stiffish moments to come with others of his noble kind to whom he was not related. But from the very start there had been friction between Rennie and the band, or more accurately, between her and lead singer Niles Clay. After she'd helped him out in a murder investigation at the Fillmore East last Christmas, things had improved dramatically in that quarter as well, much to Turk's relief. But it was still iffy, and everyone was being as careful with everyone else as they knew how to be.

At any rate, Lionheart was off the road for now, and she was on her way to meet Turk, and she let her thoughts spin out again as she ambled down the deck, dwelling deliciously on white-sugar Caribbean sands and aquamarine Caribbean waters and a bronzed rock god with, hopefully, very few clothes on and a lot to make up for. Until a familiar voice came cutting through her reverie.

"Stride? That you?"

Rennie spun around, her face flashing instantly into laughter, and then ran into the arms of the person who had spoken. *Talk about* ohana, *man…*

"I knew I'd see you sooner or later, you adorable little rock hack," said Laird Burkhart, lifting her off her feet and kissing her soundly on both cheeks. Suddenly materializing at Rennie's elbow, Belinda looked on, attentive and expectant, all Introduce me *please!*, and Rennie did not fail of courtesy.

"Belinda, this is Laird Burkhart, cute rocker boy. Laird, my friend Belinda Melbourne. Another adorable little rock hack, of course. Linny writes for the Sun-Trib, and Life, and

Creem, buncha other places, lives around the corner from us in the East Village."

Laird and Belinda smiled and shook hands, all while giving each other the reflective—or reflexive—rock and roll onceover. They both seemed intrigued by what they saw, and Rennie inwardly groaned.

"Do you guys know each other from somewhere not rock?" asked Belinda, still deep in meaningful eyelock with Laird. "Only, you called her 'Stride', and nobody does that sort of thing except at school."

Laird grinned. "Well spotted. But really, until we all started calling her 'Stri*der*', under the influence of *The Lord of the Rings*, I've never called her anything else. We met ages ago, in our freshman year at Cornell, second week we were there. Living in hope, I took her to a couple of frat mixers, but she was only sixteen, the precocious little thing, not even close to legal, and so we never so much as smooched. Not that that was ever the vibe with us, really. And then I got this band started."

"And by 'this band' he modestly means Powderhouse Road," said Rennie, and Belinda made an impressed acknowledging face. "I was their first groupie," added Rennie boastfully. "Though not in the usual groupie sense. Back then I was still hanging on to my virginity."

"She gave up just about everything else for us, though," said Laird, laughing. "Sewed stage clothes for us, designed posters, cut our hair, even go-go danced mostly naked for our sets in local roadhouses. Wearing nothing but a black fringed bikini and thigh-high boots. What Hamlet would have worn, if he'd been a go-go chick with a bit of a kink.

The redneck drunks and collegiate drunks alike loved her; I'm sure our seriously lavish tips came about entirely because of her effect on them. And then, when she became this big famous journalist, she wrote about us. Our first professional validation. So we owe it all to her. She even gave us our name."

Rennie waved it away, but you could tell she was gratified he'd mentioned it. "No big inspiration. It was a locally favored makeout place up in the hills, was Powderhouse Road. Not that I'd know personally, you understand."

"Of *course* not, pidge," said Belinda, and turned the renewed force of her huge honey-brown eyes on Laird. "Powderhouse Road…I couldn't remember where I recognized you from."

Laird Burkhart—almost as tall as Turk, and with even longer hair, though not quite as blond—probably hadn't heard that sort of thing too often lately. Powderhouse may have started out local and collegiate in upstate central New York, a folk-blues bar band of the Creedence Clearwater Revival ilk, but, like Rennie herself, they'd made the move to the big city right after graduation. They'd started off doing the Greenwich Village club-scene New York scuffle along with bands like the Young Rascals and the Blues Project, and the Mamas and the Papas before they *were* the Mamas and the Papas, and even Dylan; they'd played the center stage at the Big Magic festival and the auxiliary stage at Monterey Pop, though they'd missed Woodstock, having been touring Europe at the time, and now they were *huge*, coming off their fifth Top-10 single and third gold album.

Rennie could see Laird wasn't sure Belinda wasn't majorly

goofing on him by pretending not to know who he was—which she was, of course, the little flirt. But he took it with a good and intrigued grace, and flirted manfully right back at her.

"What are you doing on this cruise of the damned and the damning, anyway?" asked Rennie. She signaled a steward for drinks, and they all repaired to a trio of cushioned deck chairs. "Nobody told me you were aboard."

"Weezles invited me," said Laird, chivalrously draping the girls in soft plaid blankets and stretching out in a chair between them, draped likewise. "No big secret. We've been thinking of touring together next summer—buses with hot and cold running groupies, huge arenas with rotten sound. Yes, that's right, a total sell-out to Mammon, orchestrated by Ted Tessman and Tontine; we're not proud of ourselves but there it is. Anyway, Hoden thought some of us should come along on this little boat trip to check each other out, see if we were compatible enough to not slit each other's throats with a guitar pick after a week on the road. So Buck and I nobly volunteered."

He waved vaguely aft. "He's around somewhere, is Buck. He'll be so happy to see you. We don't know too many other people on board, and most of the ones we *do* know, we don't much like."

Rennie, who shared his sentiments and said so, was seeing that tour in her head. "Powderpuffs and Weezies out together on the Magic Bus, cutting a swath from coast to coast, right through the unsuspecting heartland, oh yes. Could be very interesting. Apocalyptically American. Alternate-night top billing and opening/closing status, of course."

Laird's grin flashed again. "Of course. And I think a small fleet of very luxury buses, not just one or two. Maybe we'll invite you along to cover it for one of Fitz's big important magazines."

"Hey, if I survive this cruise, a little bus ride across the lower forty-eight with a bunch of insane rocknrollers? Piece of cake."

"Dear girl, I shall hold you to that." Laird looked around curiously. "Where's Turk? Didn't he come with you? After all I've heard about him, from you especially, I've really been wanting to meet him. I only turned you on to him, after all, taking you to that Winter Wonderland thing at Cornell, and you a mere lass of sixteen."

"Not here. As I was telling Belinda, he's already down there, in his family's private little tropical fiefdom. They own this island, near Grand Palm..."

Three

"SOOOOO?" ASKED BELINDA, with a fine careless air that didn't fool anyone. She was gazing speculatively after Laird, who had finally dragged himself away after two hours' conversation and several gin and tonics, and who was, after all, visible from quite a long way off. "He got an old lady?"

Rennie snorted, and pulled her friend out of the deck chair for an idle stroll forward from the stern—and away from Laird.

"Not that I am aware of. At the moment. And I know *exactly* where this is headed, my little heffalump, so don't try that innocent face with me. Don't think I didn't notice you two staring soulfully into each other's eyes, imagining what the other would look like all naked and sweaty and orgasmic. It was amazing how you managed to lock eyes and yet ogle cleavage and package respectively at the same time. You may have been making eye contact, but you were both really thinking of contact somewhere a lot farther south."

Belinda had the grace to blush, but didn't deny it.

"Besides," Rennie continued severely, "aren't you still involved with Diego Hidalgo, and hence off the market? I have a long and very sisterly trip going with Laird. If you just want to fuck him, fine; he can certainly be had, and I'm sure a splendid time will be had by all who *are* had. But if you mess him over I'll have to beat you up. He's a very sweet and very sensitive soul, triple Pisces with some heavy Scorp and Cancer, totally watersign-y—I've known him a long time and I wouldn't like to see him hurt."

"I would *never*!" protested Belinda, wounded, and tossed her long dark mane for emphasis. "You know that. Besides, I broke up with Diego a month ago. For real this time. He's demented. You remember, he threw all my clothes out the window when I told him I wouldn't move to L.A. with him?"

"Oh, right. Yes, that *was* demented. Excessive possessive clothing-based protest does seem to be a pattern with your men—didn't Hacker Bennett nail all your shoes to the floor when you left *him*?"

Belinda shrugged. "Hacker was stoned. Gave me an excuse to go straight to Capezio and buy ten new pairs and then over to Allan Block for some new sandals and those cool T-strappy Mary Janes we like. Diego was just pissed off. Though at least he was chivalrous enough to pay my dry-cleaning bill once I'd rescued all my clobber. Unlike Hacker, who didn't even spring for the shoemaker's bill."

"Allan Block has the best leather," said Rennie dreamily. "That nice thick soft dark-brown latigo stuff—hey, do you like my new cowgirl boots?" She posed her long, elegant legs to show off the gorgeous copper-and-turquoise footwear. "I bought them in Austin when I was down there on Fitz business. I never thought I wanted cowgirl boots until I saw these and lusted for them madly. And then I bought three more pairs. Oh, oh, speaking of lust, look who it is! Yes, surrounded by fifteen worshipful groupies in various stages of heat, it's Hoden Weezle, you betcha. I'd forgotten they had fans along on this barge—there was a contest in Loya Tessman's teenybopper rag. These are the lucky and adoring winners, apparently."

They paused to watch, silently and smirkingly, as Hoden made his way along the deck past them. To his credit, he looked deeply embarrassed at the extent of the accompanying twittering seraglio, and slid his gaze right over the two reporters without meeting their eyes more than glancingly. When the procession had gone by, Belinda returned to their conversation.

"It's very silly to call him that, you know. 'Hoden Weezle', I mean."

"Well, until he deigns to let the rest of the world in on his actual *name*—"

Belinda laughed. "I hear only the lawyers know what his real name is. And are forbidden from disclosing it on pain of instant dismissal, or perhaps beheading. Why does he do that? The name thing, I mean."

Rennie shook her head, still gazing after Hoden and harem. "I have no idea. At least Turk, when he started out doing something similar, had a good reason. Or thought he did."

Well, technically the jury was still out on that, and Rennie herself was jury foreman. Two and a half years back, mere weeks after he and Rennie had gotten together, Turk had been busted on a murder rap—the vicious slaying of superstar singer Tansy Belladonna, one of Rennie and Prax's closest friends and Turk's recent ex—and only then had his deep dark secret emerged. Turk Wayland, English guitar hero and leader of the blues-rock supergroup Lionheart, was really Richard Tarrant, Earl of Saltire, only son and heir of a thousand-year-old name and a three-hundred-year-old dukedom.

Even Rennie, who had moved in with him a mere six weeks before the bust and one week after the murder, hadn't known. She'd had to read about it in the papers like everyone else, and they'd almost broken up over it, so upset had she been that he'd not told her about his noble status—she'd taken his nondisclosure as him not trusting her, which was definitely not the case, or not entirely the case, though you could see where she might think that.

But he'd been proven right, at least about the title part: the publicity had been just as unbearable as he'd known it would be, which was why he'd kept silent in the first place, to protect her as much as to protect himself. For her part, she had stood by him with the loyalty of a swan and the tenacity of a wolverine and the protective fury of a mongoose, and had not only cleared him of the murder charge but had taken two bullets for him, and except for one spectacular breakup and equally spectacular reuniting, they'd lived happily ever after. Still, it had been pretty rugged for a while there.

Now it was even worse, only in a different way, Rennie reflected dismally, as she and Belinda strolled leisurely on. Now Turk, or rather Richard, was the Marquess of Raxton: his grandfather the old Duke had died the previous fall, and his father, himself formerly Lord Raxton, had ascended the ladder of succession to become sixteenth Duke of Locksley. Turk would be duke himself in the fullness of time; and if she married him, *when* she married him—a wedding extravaganza was planned for October and they'd been officially engaged for a year now, hence the ring—she would eventually be his duchess...his first as well as his last.

Rennie came out of her reverie and stopped dead, so fast and hard she left skidmarks on the deck. "I don't *believe* it."

"What?" asked Belinda.

"On your two o'clock. Chunky little bottle blonde. Weezles t-shirt, face like an angry scone. If you want to live, stay behind me."

Belinda looked. "I don't—"

"Oh yes you do. Deranged groupie and well-known slut Samantha Stoyer. She was running around a few months ago with a preposterous trumped-up story about herself and her alleged lurid drugged-out sexcapades with Lionheart in general and Turk in particular."

"Oh, right."

"Right, and that noxious bitch Loya Tessman positively leaped to publish the lies in her Teen Angels asswipe rag. Cleverly phrased to avoid libel, of course. They knew I'd be here, and they inveigled their way onto the cruise just to drive me mad."

"Now that's crazy talk. Loya's husband organized this whole thing; she has as much business being here as you do, Miss Paranoia 1970."

"My point exactly. Even paranoids are right sometimes. And Stoyer probably blowjobbed her way aboard. Though I'm not sure who'd want to be on the receiving end." She stared at Sammi with revulsion undilute. "The common little piece of trash. Maybe she'll fall overboard. And take Messman with her. I can hope, can't I?"

"One can always hope."

After guiding the directionally challenged Belinda ("Port. Starboard. Forward. Aft. Left. Right. Front. Back. Get a grip!") to her stateroom, Rennie went to her own, changed into a handpainted cream and rust silk minidress by one of her favorite designers, a very British little shop in Oxford called Annabelinda, and flounced off to the buffet in the grand salon.

She was loading pasta carbonara onto her plate when she happened to glance up. Reflected in the gold-veined mirror behind the serving station was a terrifying sight: the frizzy hair and little pursed chicken's bum of a mouth and dead-eyed basilisk gaze of Loya Tessman herself. She was glaring at Rennie as if she grudged her right even to share the same ocean, let alone the same ship. If it hadn't been in the mirror, Rennie would doubtless have been turned to stone, so baleful, indeed, was the gaze. As it was, she just smiled sweetly back, which only seemed to annoy Loya even more.

For such a petite woman, Loya Mailing Tessman had vast wildernesses of nastiness inside her, concealed like a septic oil spill within the compass of her small, scrawny, no-tits-to-speak-of body. Yet not concealed at all: common opinion in the rockerverse held her to be a mean, unpleasant, bad-tempered bitchy brunette. She'd started out in the music business straight out of high school, as secretary to a record company president, and had worked her way up; now in her early thirties, she'd become a power in the land, universally detested and universally feared, which was of course why people were so sickeningly nice to her. At least to her face: behind her back they were anything but, and, amazingly, she was completely oblivious to it all. Most people like that generally were, when it came to realizing how they affected others, how affected they were themselves—serious short count on the self-awareness front.

Oh, loads of people sucked up to her, mainly other posers like some of the Max's Kansas City crowd—lesser luminaries like trashcan painter Camden Ransoff, fashion arbiter Valmai Le Vanda, weirdo filmmaker Frink, others of that pretentious ilk. Real talents would have nothing to do with her, except, reluctantly, when they needed the publicity. Her husband, Ted, an unpleasant, tall and somehow also stumpish individual whose neck, if you could call it that, was wider than the head it supported and who spoke mostly in grunts, was said to be deeply fond of her, though you couldn't tell by watching them in public, where they seldom exchanged three words running; there were dark stories that he seriously beat up on her in private. But they'd been married for years, quite successfully by all accounts, and they were both major rock players.

For Ted Tessman headed up Tontine, the hugely powerful booking/p.r. agency that boasted giants like Cold Fire and Prisca Quarters and of course the Weezles among its assets—it had had the Budgies too, right up to their breakup, and Lionheart as well, though Turk was seriously considering bolting—and even star reporters like Rennie occasionally had to kiss his ring to get interviews with his more desirable clients. Tontine was responsible for assembling and supervising probably half the superstar tours in America, and a third of the overseas ones as well; if you were a top band and wanted prime venues with decent opening acts who would neither upstage you with too much excellence nor offend your audience with gross incompetence, or at least dull musicianship, you wouldn't turn up your nose at Tontine running your band, no matter how you might personally feel about Ted and his minions.

For her part, Loya put out a semiliterate teenybopper gushfest called Teen Angels—"put out" being the operative verb, both for the publication itself and its owner's sexual proclivities. Real journalists would hardly term it "published", and Rennie didn't, and real ladies would term her a tramp, and Rennie did. TA, as it was appositely known, was a rag among rags; even Rennie's boss Lord Fitz, the uncrowned king of Tabloidia, had been heard to say he wouldn't use it to line the bottom of a cat-box. But it had a huge circulation amongst its target audience and gave Loya great clout in the biz; and in turn she gave shamelessly preferential treatment to not only the current teen hot favorites but her husband's clients, or acts he liked—read, "had hopes of poaching". Hence the face-friendliness of so many: between them, Ted and Loya could make or break a band as they so chose, and everybody knew it. In fact, together they could rule Hell. And possibly already did.

Rennie and Loya had cordially hated each other's guts from before they had ever even met. Loya had been a great friend and ally of Rennie's late nemesis Devin Sweetzer, who'd managed the equally late Tansy Belladonna and who'd been murdered in his Malibu house the night of Tansy's funeral, after a wake there attended by two hundred people. Including Turk Wayland and Rennie Stride, who had ditched the wake and spent a night of mad passion at Turk's house in the Hollywood Hills; their first of many, as she'd moved in with him the next day, at his invitation. When the big juicy gossipy news had finally broken a few weeks later about their new living arrangements, Loya's jealous, spiteful toxicity had known no bounds, and she'd indulged it in print—a tactical error, as the rockerverse, greatly entertained, had judged it. For the most part Rennie ignored her, figuring she could squash her like a bug if it ever came to it, physically as well as metaphorically, and indeed she was looking forward to that happy day.

So it was to Rennie's vast surprise and even vaster suspicion that Loya sidled up beside her now and actually smiled. Though the alleged smile looked more like that horrible rictus people get when they're in agony from a fox gnawing their vitals out, or dying from cyanide poisoning. But Rennie would never have pegged Loya for a classical Spartan. Still, she briefly wondered where she herself might come by a hungry fox to slip under Loya's dress. Or even cyanide.

"Rennie! It's so *groovy* to see you here. I'm *so* sorry Turk couldn't join us. I just *loved* Lionheart's last album—the new stuff they're doing—that song he wrote for you was so *beautiful* it made me *cry*. Oh my *God*, your *ring*, it's absolutely *GORGEOUS*—" She made a grab for Rennie's left hand, but Rennie snatched her bejeweled mitt away before contact could be made.

How dare you even approach *me, you loathsome little shrew? Considering you published that groupie slut's lies about Turk, what makes you think I won't stick a fish knife in your throat first chance I get?* No, this was just evil and weird, possibly even a hitherto undiscovered sign of the world ending. Loya had actually sounded—sincere. Not even the littlest bit sarcastic, and she wasn't *that* good an actress. But hey, Rennie was game, she'd play along. At least until she could figure out what the freaking hell was going on.

So she put on a saccharinely cooing voice that nauseated even her, to the point where she had to set down the pasta plate, and matched Loya's italicized speech. "Oh, and *yooouuu*, it's so *long* since I've *seen* you, what have you been *doing*, how's that cutie *Ted*?"

Loya simpered and gestured grandly around. "'He's in our suite, he had some little details to take care of. He set up this whole thing, you know."

"I do know. We have him to thank for all this. As we do for so much else, really."

That penetrated even Loya's fabled self-absorption, and she gave Rennie a narrow glance. Rennie smiled back, thinking of all their various past encounters, and reflecting smugly on all the moral stuffing this one was putting into her. But Loya, seemingly, had a bit more on what it pleased her to call her mind: she glanced around the room with what Rennie could only describe as furtiveness, moved closer and spoke in a lowered voice.

"Rennie—do you think I could talk to you privately? Sometime on the cruise, before we get to the Grand Palms?"

Rennie hoped she didn't look as dumbfounded as she felt. "Oh—I guess—yeah, sure. Whenever you like. Is there something—well, wrong?"

For the first time Rennie had ever seen, Loya Tessman unexpectedly looked afraid. Not fear but sheer, stark terror—face like a death's-head, eyes like a frightened horse. And underneath her enemy's sudden pallor, underneath the uncharacteristically heavy makeup, Rennie troublingly discerned slight bruising, a cut lip, purple circles under the eyes. But it was gone in an instant, and Loya smiled her usual little piranha smile.

"Of *course* not, no, what could be *wrong*? But I *would* like to talk. We've never really sat down and *talked*, have we."

"No, we haven't. Now why is that, I wonder." *Well, I don't* really *wonder, do I, no, I don't, because I know damn well why we haven't, and you do too...*

"And we have *so* much to talk *about*. Maybe tomorrow night? After the show. The—*opera*." Loya pronounced the word as if it were a lemon she was forced to suck on, the little pursed mouth looking more like a chicken's bum than ever. "Just us."

Rennie had reclaimed her plate and started to move down the buffet line, heading for the Alaska king crab. "Sure. Fine. That'll be—yeah, fine. I look forward to it."

And, perversely enough, though the words stuck in her throat like fishbones, Rennie did.

Four

AFTER DINING CONVIVIALLY with some colleagues and a couple of musicians, Rennie went for a solo stroll around the ship's main deck, thinking about her encounter with Loya. Something was up, for sure, something nasty; she'd seen it too often not to recognize the signs of fear and abuse when she saw them. But until Tessman told her what was going on, there was nothing she could do, and she certainly didn't care about the dreadful woman enough to do anything about it, because, again, what *could* she do? Who could she go to? She couldn't approach Ted about it, not when he might be the cause of the bruises, and it wasn't her business anyway. Perhaps the promised conversation tomorrow night would fill in the details. So she continued her exploration of the *Excalibur,* poking into the library and the billiards room and the theater where "Paize Lee" would be staged the next night—a gloriously anachronistic Viennese confection of plush seats and mirrors and gilded moldings and crystal chandeliers.

Exiting the theater, she found she wasn't too far from the ship's prow. Coming carefully to the railings, she hooked her arm securely around the metal bars to steady herself and looked at the surrounding seascape. They were well out on the Atlantic by now, a glorious golden evening coming up on sunset, clouds heaped up in the west in purple and pink profusion, cool breeze streaming from the bows on back.

Far below her, where the prow cut hypnotically through the light swell, there were, magically, deep-sea dolphins surfing the foaming bow wave on the starboard side. She watched, charmed, and a few other passengers clustering nearby excitedly pointed down at the leaping sea creatures. Dolphin smile: ever since Agamemnon's fleet had sailed to Troy, it was considered great good luck for a ship to score such an escort. Hadn't worked out so well for Troy, of course, or for Agamemnon either, in the long run…

"You look like a figurehead posing there. All painted and wooden, I mean."

She turned, startled, to see Samantha Stoyer standing not ten feet away. The lumpy blonde was now wearing an unfortunately tight-fitting red Lionheart t-shirt, on which Turk's image had been outlined and haloed in sparkly home-applied rhinestones, and her face as she stared at Rennie was contorted with venom.

"And your point would be…?" asked Rennie politely. *God, it's still so weird seeing his face on other people's tits…a face that has, after all, been on* my *tits, and not printed on cotton either…*

"You have some nerve showing up here, after what I told everybody about your so-called boyfriend and what I did with him. They all read about it and they're all laughing at you. Why don't you just leave him? Or jump over the side. He'd be better off without you either way. He's mine."

Rennie paused for a long, long beat, then calmly raised her voice to public-announcement level. "Everybody turn away. I want no witnesses."

The people who were standing around nearby did

nothing of the sort, of course. Instead, they perked up at the possibility of a really good scene that they could take back home to spread around New York and London and L.A., and Rennie, who knew they would and was in fact counting on it, did not disappoint.

"Oh, I've heard *that* song before, little girl. Well—not so little girl," said Rennie, smiling condescendingly, and flashed Turk's ring to make it sparkle oh so prettily in the light. "The last person who sang it went over the side for real, and is now spending the rest of her life in the nice comfortable psycho ward of a California slammer. I'm sure she'd enjoy some company there to share her hung-up delusions of Turk. *My* Turk. You could compare notes on your non-relationships with your mutual imaginary boyfriend. Who is my actual future and totally *non*imaginary husband. Who gave me this actual nonimaginary ring to prove it. Oh, and who, on the nights you claimed you spent with him, was actually in Hong Kong with me on tour—always check your facts first, Law Number One of Lying and Journalism both. Anyway, I could easily arrange it—a nice little tenancy in Loonyville. Or shall I maybe push *you* over the side? Your head being as large and empty as it is, though, I expect you'd float like flotsam. Or is it jetsam? Trash, in any case."

Sammi huffed off, shoving her way through the other passengers, who were still shamelessly eavesdropping and highly amused at the exchange. Rennie glanced back down at the dolphins, grudging them their serene smiles and simple peace. She was getting better at handling this sort of thing than she had been when she and Turk first fell in love;

back then, groupie challenges had generally resulted in white-hot verbal fury and on occasion nonverbal physical violence. Usually initiated by her, shameful to say. It was still unpleasant, of course, and even now she was trying hard to control both her breathing and her homicidal impulse, but she was learning from Turk to develop a duck's back, let it all slide off. It was hard, though, and it hurt. Or maybe it was more like Prax's theory of the karma mirror, for which rather elegant postulation she had named her first successful band: when wronged, hang up the karma mirror and let it reflect all the crap straight back on its originator. Preferably with a little extra kick, just so they'd *learn* something…

The delighted listeners offered applause and praiseful approval, and Rennie graciously acknowledged the thumbs-ups and cheers by curtseying and then blowing off two mock finger-pistols, smiling as she holstered them. It hadn't really been a fair fight, of course: in a battle of wits, almost anyone who went up against Rennie Stride was only half-armed, and most people in the rockerverse knew and respected that. Not to mention the fact that all the Turkness weighed heavily and exclusively on her side as well. Still, this little exchange would be all over the boat within the hour. She could hardly wait.

Continuing her prowl, she found that several of the artists along for the ride were setting up an ad hoc guitar workshop in the exquisitely mirror-walled and crystal-sconced ballroom, and she detoured to check it out. Perching upon one of the dainty gilt chairs lined up along the wall, Rennie admired Laird Burkhart's beautiful old ivory-inlaid acoustic

Martin, not unlike Turk's own favored one.

"Nice axe you've got there, cutie. A link to days of yore, when men were men and guitars were hollow."

Laird laughed and fiddled with an open tuning. "It's good to get back to that sometimes. I'm sure your old man feels the same way."

"Oh dear Lord, does he ever. He's educated my eye and ear, for sure." She gestured around the theater at the handful of other guitarists, busying themselves just like Laird. "God, what a guy thing! The testosterone in here is sloshing around like the main we're bounding over."

"You little sweet-talker! But Turk should really be here. He'd enjoy this. And he'd wipe the floor with all of us."

"Turk, hell. *Sledger* should be here. You think this is a testosterone fest *now*—she'd take one look at you boys and play you all limp. In every sense."

"So I've heard," said Laird diplomatically, not wishing to badmouth Miss Veronica Lee Cairns to present company, knowing that the two girls were close friends. Instead, he nodded toward the other side of the room. "I see Luke Woods over there. But where's our top-billed host?"

"The monomonikered Hoden? I doubt he'll be mingling with us commoners. Too busy psyching himself up for the premiere of the *parvum opus*."

Laird, a classics major, grinned. "Actually, I was talking to Luke about it earlier—he being the co-composer, you might want to chat with him yourself."

"Might I?" Rennie glanced away, then visibly edited herself, with some delicacy, watching Luke in one of the mirrors. "Yes, I suppose. But—how can I say this—the

Weezles don't, uh, take it *seriously*, do they? I mean, they do know how ridiculous the whole rock opera thing is?"

"Oh yeah. Well, they sort of do. But not entirely. You haven't heard it yet. I have—at least parts of it. You're going to be surprised. In both good ways and bad." He chorded idly, ran a few riffs up and down the neck, and then laid the guitar down across two nearby chairs, regarding Rennie with uncharacteristic seriousness. "So, have you decided to savage them no matter what? You're not even going to give it a fair hearing?"

Rennie looked shocked and hurt. "Hey! I always give *everything* a fair hearing no matter what, and you of all people should know that. I give every single song I hear up to the hook to, well, hook me. By that point I feel I've done my job, and after that it's the artist's fault if they haven't done theirs. Much as I have mocked this 'Paize Lee', I will certainly allow it an honest chance to win my heart and mind. After that, if I have to shoot it in print like a broken-legged racehorse, well, that's the way it is."

Laird picked up his axe again and started to play. "Fair enough."

"If your lips were shut any tighter you'd be a puffer fish. Come *on*, Strider. Give. What's the problem?"

Rennie shot Belinda a dark look. "You're getting to sound like Prax. Obviously I spend too much time around both of you."

"No," said Belinda calmly, "you're just easily read. At least by people who know you and care about you. So? What's going on, my friend?"

"To tell you the truth, I don't know yet." Quickly she filled Belinda in on the encounter with Loya Tessman, and was gratified to see suspicion bloom like a flower. Well, Lin was a reporter, after all, and every bit as narrow-eyed as Rennie herself.

"Oho! I wonder—I've heard a few things about Ted," remarked Belinda after her friend had finished.

"What kind of things?"

"Not very nice things. Things like he beats up on Loya on a regular basis, for one."

Rennie looked suddenly grave. "I've heard that too, and I wouldn't wish it on anyone. Not even her. And why would she be coming to me about something like that? Anyway, I wouldn't put up with that for a millisecond. If Turk ever raised his hand to me, he'd go through the rest of his life without it *and* the arm it was attached to. But of course he never would do such a vile thing, because he is a gentleman through and through. Though occasional light, loving contact below the neck, in the pursuit of mutual and consensual sexual fulfillment, with or without the aid of a finely wielded instrument, absolutely does not count as abuse, as you are yourself well aware of and as we have compared notes on. Kink, yes; abuse, no. Turk did go to Eton, after all. So why does Loya stay with her brutish spouse, if he's into *real* abuse?"

"I think we both know the answer to that. Money and power. Her money, his power."

"Doesn't seem anywhere remotely near good enough." Rennie repositioned herself on the lounge chair, crossing her ankles and turning her face up to the evening breeze, and closed her right hand over her ring. "Thank God I've got something so much better."

They had breakfast the next morning with Buck Lai of Powderhouse Road and Luke Woods, Weezle lead guitarist—the 'they' being Rennie, Belinda, Laird, and Gary Chang, Rennie's newest successor on the San Francisco Clarion rock beat, Stan Hirsch having moved south to the San Diego Mariner, and, after his divorce from Rennie's dear friend Marishka Erzog, gotten engaged to a marine biologist from Iceland named Hild.

"So, was she always like this?" Luke asked, only half-teasingly, gesturing toward Rennie with his fork.

Laird laughed. "You bet! She was poking that pretty little nose of hers into other people's affairs way back when we were all at college together."

Buck leaned forward, whispering mock-confidingly, "It got so bad we finally wrote a song about it, and we serenaded her with it one night on the lawn of her sorority house."

"Sing it now!" Belinda commanded, enchanted. "Both of you."

"Okay, if you insist, but it's much lovelier with the whole of 'House harmonizing. Crosby, Stills, et al., aren't even in it. You'll just have to imagine."

Buck cleared his throat, gave the count to Laird, then both of them launched into a most tuneful rendering of a sprightly ditty.

"Young Rennie Strider
Was always an insider

'Bout business that wasn't her own.
One day we decided
To keep our secrets hided
Sweet Rennie, please leave us ALONE.
She's always platonic
In fact, she's moronic
Her boyfriends they number sixteen
One is a mover,
Another a groover,
And one is fond of pinup queens."

They split into effortless two-part harmony with professional ease, and across the dining room ears swiveled to listen: hell, it wasn't every day you got to hear half of Powderhouse Road a cappella, especially singing doggerel.

"One day Rennie's ass it
Just took off to Paris
And lived in a garret to paint.
Picasso and Dali
And their cousin Molly
Thought Strider was something she ain't.
They all lived together
like birds of a feather
Till Strider came home all alone.
She hung up her brushes
and stopped all her crushes
And sat in the park on a stone.
Now young Rennie Strider
Is just an outsider
Her friends are all grateful as pie
She never gets manic

Though sometimes she'll panic
But mostly she'll just go get high."

They finished on a professionally slowed split-octave note and bowed deeply, acknowledging the applause from all tables. Unruffled, Rennie was laughing as heartily as Belinda, Luke and Gary, who were pretty much on the floor by now, and took a sip of tea.

"Ah yes, I remember it well. And even fondly. But you didn't seriously expect me to be flustered by people who use the word 'hided', did you?"

"We were frat boys, what did you expect?" Buck was grinning broadly. "Our first attempt at topical songwriting. I seem to recall it impressed the hell out of some of your sorority sisters. I got dates on the strength of it for *weeks*."

"Easily swayed, those Greek bimbos. And in spite of that"—she addressed herself imploringly to the other three—"I *still* helped this lot get where they are today. What a fine and outstanding person I must be, to be sure."

"Yes you are. You really—are." Belinda smiled at her friend, and then began peeling and eating a banana in a manner so X-rated that Laird began to get visibly—uncomfortable. She ignored him, however, and eyed Luke Woods across the table.

"Soooo…groovy little rock opera you've got for us all, hey Woodsie? Give 'Tommy' a run for its *recitative*?"

Luke sighed, as one who had been through this before. Many times. "It's not an opera. It's not even a cantata. Neither is 'Tommy'. Pete Townshend has much to answer for."

"But we forgive him much, because he assaulted Abbie Hoffman with his guitar at Woodstock, which was only what we dearly wished we could all have done ourselves. So what *would* you call it, then?"

"It's a musical. Or a song cycle."

Buck laughed. "Like *My Fair Lady*? Or those stodgy German *Lieder* Strider's so fond of? 'Der Erlkönig' and 'Die Winterreise' and 'Die schöne Müllerin'. I remember from Music 101."

"I'll bet you do," said Rennie. "Well, for one thing, 'Der Erlkönig' is *not* stodgy; you'd better not let der König hear you say that—it's one of the creepiest things I've ever heard. But let's just see here, Woodsie: you have lyrics from three years ago that weren't good enough to be B-sides, you have strings and horns and chick backup singers, and you have the title character being sung by no-name hired help. Well, pretentiously named hired help, anyway."

"Penny Serenade, can you believe it," said Luke dispiritedly. "Total airhead. Hasn't got the chops to sing Little Buttercup in a high-school *Pinafore*. We wanted Judy, or Sunny Silver, or Ponica Jacks, but—"

"So why did you—"

"Ted Tessman insisted."

"Screwing her?" asked Belinda, entirely non-judgmentally.

Luke shook his head. "That's what you'd assume, right? But, surprisingly, no. He's got wife Loya along on the cruise, as you know, and he doesn't seem particularly interested in the fair Penny's ostensible charms."

"Maybe wife Loya's screwing her," suggested Laird.

"They're not into that. Well, as far as I know." Luke brightened. "Could be some three-way action, maybe. That, I *wouldn't* be surprised by. Anyway, Strider, you mean old cow, it's not B-side rejects. Hoden wrote some amazing stuff. Powerful stuff. You'll see."

"Why yes, I suppose I will."

"Have you talked to him yet?"

"No, and I'm beginning to think he's avoiding me. Any thoughts on that?"

Luke shook his head. "Honestly, not one. I know he mentioned to me before the cruise that he did want to talk to you particularly. He reads your stuff and respects your take on things. Even when you bash us."

"Well, love hurts, and I only bash the bands I love."

Gary laughed. "And you don't admit the others exist."

"Life is short," agreed Rennie, "and art is fleeting. I haven't got time to take out *all* the rocktrash."

But sometimes, just sometimes, it takes out itself.

Five

"Paize Lee: The Story of a Little Hippie Girl" was lurching into Act IV of VI when Rennie herself lurched out of the theater and slid gasping into a deckchair, comfortably distant from the rail. The clean wind of the ship's passage cooled her flushed face and the oceanic quiet calmed her nausea. And it wasn't seasickness, either; Dramamine couldn't do a thing to sort *this* out.

It was the second night of the cruise. The *Good Ship Rock&Roll* was a day and a half out from its destination port of Palmton, where there would be a two-night hiatus and then the turnaround sailing back to New York, or charter flights home for anyone not up for more sea air. As promised, Rennie and the other journalists aboard were getting all the facetime they wanted with anyone they could get their hands on, doing one interview after another and stockpiling stories for future use—so convenient to have a captive talent pool. All day and far into the night, in venues all over the ship, there had been musical entertainment provided by said talent pool, and much of it had been absolutely superb. And then came along "Paize Lee."

In her desperation, she was trying to clear the present horror out of her ears by putting a favorite Lionheart song on the brain radio, though there wasn't much she could do about the garish sets and godawful costumes that still danced vividly in her sight—they were probably seared forever upon her retinas.

"Holy crap," she said aloud and fervently, flinging her arms wide in an attitude of supplication and addressing the universe at large. "And 'crap' being the operative word… Do you not *feel* for me?"

The universe, unfeeling, made no answer. Well, she had been warned, and by those who obviously knew best. But the guarded tip-off she'd received was as nothing to the scope of the sheer horror she'd just witnessed. Had it been written by Martians, perhaps? Or wombats? Or some other individuals whose native language was other than English and who had never heard of the concept known as narrative flow?

And yet, to be fair, as Luke Woods had protested, there was some very real and very, *very* good music going on here and there in those depths of utter shallow. Four of the songs, all of them written and sung by lead Weezle Hoden, had weight and heft and punch to them—honest-to-God rock and roll songs, and thus completely wasted on this monstrosity. And he'd sung them with his new-found passion and power, the passion and power that the teenyfans didn't understand at *all* and didn't want to hear about, and yet which was now just about the only thing that was keeping him sane.

And even though they had so far on this cruise not spoken a word to each other, Rennie and Hoden, she knew that he knew that it wasn't going to be enough.

She allowed herself to speculate a bit on Hoden as a solo act. Well, unlike Penny, *he* sure had chops enough to make it on his own. He didn't play guitar in Turk's league, of course, but then only about four other human beings on the planet did. Still, he was a capable axeman, not to mention an incredible lead singer and a dynamite songwriter, and if he ever got free rein and the bit between his teeth, he could amaze far tougher audiences than teenies and their mums.

He was never going to get either, though, as least as long as he was under the contractual thumbs of the vile Jo Fleet and the only slightly less vile Jack Holland of Isis Records, as she and Laird and Belinda had sadly concluded. And even if he did break free of his contractual chains, he was going to have to overcome an awful lot of rock snobbery from an awful lot of awful people before getting his rightful due.

The saddest part was that, barring stupendous good luck in changed circumstances, he probably wouldn't ever even be allowed a decent shot. How incomparably fortunate Lionheart had been. Superstardom had been years in coming, but they had refused to whore themselves out to the pop charts to get it and they had patiently done their best work all along, and so they didn't have to be ashamed when finally the laurel crown rightly descended upon their collective brow. What could Hoden possibly do to spring himself from the coils of evil and find similar creative happiness? And could he even maybe take his bandmates with him?

Lost in her contemplation, it was a second or two before Rennie registered the distant sound from up at the bow end as the terrified scream it was, and then after a sickening five-second delay a heavy splash came up from below that seemed more than an errant wave smacking the hull. As she leaped to the rail, already fending off horror in her mind, she was just in time to catch a glimpse of a colorful mass going by in the dark water, swirling swiftly astern before she could manage to get "Man overboard!" out of her mouth.

But her shout was heard, and others too, likewise refugees from the unremitting awfulness going on in the theater, had heard and seen this new, genuine horror and were also frantically yelling, and after what seemed like twenty thousand leagues of open sea the ship slowed to a halt. Rennie stood anxiously amidships with the captain and a small crowd of passengers, while crew members prepared to launch three motorized rescue rafts down the side.

Strangely, no one from the "Paize Lee" audience still in the theater seemed to have heard a thing. Maybe they had all been stupefied by badness, anesthetized deaf, dumb and oblivious—or maybe they were simply too paralytically stoned to move. In spite of the ship's cessation of forward motion, few had yet come out on deck to find out why; the horrified score or so who'd already been out there and still stood watching were the only spectators.

OhGodohGodohGod... Rennie stared through the deck railings, suddenly afraid to go nearer to the edge, and from over by a hanging lifeboat Loya Tessman stared blankly back at her. *Well, looks like we won't be having our little chat tonight, I guess...*

Soon the word had spread, and half the ship was now crowding the deck. After what seemed an eternity of powerful searchlights crisscrossing the black water in the ship's wake, the rafts paused for a few minutes, bobbing in the swell, then came zooming back, something wrapped in a dark blanket aboard the first one. As the craft was hoisted up and the bundled something was lifted hastily out on deck, the blanket fell open, and as desperate artificial respiration was begun all over again, this time administered by the ship's doctor, Rennie got a good look at the puffy, water-blotched face of Samantha Stoyer, shockingly white against the brightly colored Weezles t-shirt she had been wearing.

But the doctor's efforts were as vain as the boat crew's had been, and at last he sat back on his heels and shook his head. The blanket was gently replaced and the body was carried off belowdecks to the tiny refrigerated morgue off the sickbay that stood ready for such sad occurrences. The rear of Sammi's ad hoc cortege was brought up by a now showily weeping Loya, supported by no-neck husband Ted, who looked unusually thoughtful, particularly for him, and to Rennie's surprise, Weezles manager Jo Fleet, Mephistofleetles himself.

As they went by, Rennie quickly faded back into the shadow of the upper deck overhang, less out of respect for the violently dead than out of a sudden, instinctive wish not to be seen, and came up with a soft jolt against someone already standing there, still and quiet, even deeper into the sheltering darkness than she was.

"Well, Rennie Stride," said Hoden Weezle somberly, "here you go again."

"What's the law about people dying at sea?" asked Belinda the next morning.

They were all at the first seating for breakfast, but

nobody seemed particularly hungry. Even Rennie was merely toying with a perfectly ripened Packham pear, her favorite, trying to decide if she was hungry enough to spoil its luscious perfection by actually biting into it. It was as if they were all on speed—revved up, nervy, no appetite, babbling away—except no one was actually speeding. Their brains were all flying dolphin-like through shoals of varied speculation, but nothing else about them was moving: their bodies seemed frozen in place. It was weird; even weirder, drugs didn't seem to help.

Belinda and Laird, who had snuck out of the ballroom very early on, had spent the entire night in Laird's cabin, blissfully ignorant of the somber event that had taken place. They had encountered Rennie on their way to the grand salon for breakfast; she had filled them in immediately on the incident, and now they were all shocked and stunned. Being public at the breakfast table, there had been no opportunity for the girls to privately discuss Laird and Belinda's overnight activities. Indeed, all that suddenly seemed rather less important than it would otherwise have done, in the light of what had happened on deck. Or off deck, as it were.

Rennie had not had a glimpse of Hoden since their brief encounter last night, as Sammi Stoyer's body was carried past them on its way to the ship's morgue. During the wakeful small hours, before she'd fallen fitfully asleep, she had wondered about what Hoden had been doing there, standing in the shadows; but then she'd been standing there herself. In any case, she hadn't seen him this morning, or any other Weezle either; most likely they were all closeted with Jo Fleet, trying to figure out what possible spin they could put on the accident. *If accident it was*... Not to mention she hadn't had a glimpse of Loya Tessman, either. Perhaps Ted was keeping her busy.

Matt Cutler, the Weezles' drummer, had been scheduled to sit with them at breakfast. In the publicist-supervised round-robin mandated by Jo Fleet, the four band members were rotated like tires from table to table at every meal, so everyone on board could later boast of having gotten up close and personal with each Weezle over the cornflakes or club sandwiches or racks of lamb. But he hadn't shown up either, no doubt too busy with his bandmates, discussing the publicity ramifications of Sammi Stoyer's death plunge into the waves the night before.

Well, it made sense for the Weezles to circle the wagons as early as possible; once the ship reached Palmton the next morning, it would be a bit too late. There would probably be no formal musical entertainment that evening, except maybe some ad hoc jams in various staterooms; the captain had announced that the *Excalibur* was in a state of de facto mourning, though the two movie theaters would be showing the scheduled bill for anyone who felt like watching.

Nobody had answered Belinda's question right away. There weren't many other people up this early, or maybe it was just that since word had gone round about Sammi, most of them were too shocked to venture out and were sticking to cabin service—only about ten tables had breakfasters seated round them. Or else they were simply too seasick to move: the swell had risen considerably around dawn, thanks to a distant hurricane, and the *Excalibur* was now pitching impressively through big, rolling waves, taking sheeting veils of water over her bows; not a soul was outside on the drenched and windy decks, and no one would have dreamed of trying—indeed, the captain had forbidden anyone to go out on deck at all, even crewmen.

At any rate, their table had filled up quickly, people nervously seeking the comfort of any random company rather than be forced to eat alone: Belinda, Laird, Rennie, photographer Mitchell Rosevalley (brother of Jay, to whom she'd donated a spare Lionheart motel room at Woodstock), style editor Zsa Zsa ("Call me ZoZo!") Briscoe, and a couple of record company executives who seemed either seasick or stoned, or perhaps both, now sitting at the breakfast board dooming and glooming amongst themselves.

"I'm not sure," said Rennie, after a while. "I suppose we could go ask someone. Like a ship's officer. But right now they're probably all too busy just sailing this tub for us to bother them."

A primly assured voice from across the table. "Actually, each case is regulated according to the registry of the vessel involved, if the death took place on the high seas. Outside the local international limit, that is. Which can be between three and twelve nautical miles, depending on the country adjacent. Did you know, the three-mile limit was originally established as the distance a cannonball could travel when fired from land? Yes!"

They turned their heads as one, like spectators at a tennis match, startled more by who had spoken than by the words themselves. Elegant in lime-colored linen, especially at this ungodly hour of an even ungodlier morning, and twenty years older than the rest of them, ZoZo Briscoe smiled at them from under perfectly trimmed platinum bangs.

"When I was your age and an absolute beginner, I was briefly—mercifully so—a shipping news reporter," she said, reaching for a plate of strawberries and sliced melon. "For my sins, dear children, for my sins. But I do remember the drill. If the death occurs in territorial waters, the relevant nation has jurisdiction. Otherwise, the nation in which the ship is registered is the one concerned. Obviously, we were in international waters when it happened, so it will be a matter for the Palmton police. Where we're putting in anyway."

"Palmton, huh? That's, like, Grand Palm Islands, right?" asked the more awake record company guy, making impressive inroads on a stack of pancakes, not being one to let either tragedy or weather affect his appetite. "That's where we were headed anyway."

Laird nodded patiently. "Right next to the British Virgin Islands and near to the U. S. Virgin Islands, yes. Very convenient," he added, grinning at Rennie.

"Why's that?" asked ZoZo promptly. "Oh no reason," said Rennie even more promptly, and sent a quelling look in Laird's direction.

"Why didn't you want her to know you were deserting the ship at Palmton to go join your magnificent betrothed in his tropical island kingdom?" asked Laird, as they were leaving the grand salon to go out on deck. "Where he rules like something out of H. Rider Haggard, no doubt... Not to mention your best friend forever, Miss Praxedes McKenna, and that grand hunk maleroad of *hers*, Mr. Ares Sakura."

"Uh, exactly *because* of that? I don't want people knowing we're all there, that's the whole point. Turk and I don't generally get bothered by reporters and I don't want to start now."

Laird laughed until he started to cough, and grabbed a glass of water from a nearby table to calm himself.

"I'm sorry, is this Miss Rennie Stride I'm talking to or have I suddenly stepped into an alternate universe? 'Don't generally get bothered by reporters'! Babycakes, you're never anything *but*! What with murders and murder attempts and homicidal tree-hugging drug manufacturers and killer producers and criminally insane publicists and all the rest of the riffraff you continually contend with—I know, I know, it's not your fault—you're *in* the papers more often than you're *writing* for them. And so's his lordship. Come on! Besides, the cops are going to want to talk to you. Not to mention your press colleagues who will jump on us like ducks on a bug as soon as we set our collective foot on the Palmton dock. I bet they've been flying in from all over the globe to get the scoop. Or their revenge on you. Or both."

Rennie gave him a baleful look. "I'm trying not to think of it. So what do I have to do to shut you up? Bribe you?"

Laird was still grinning. "Or you could just kill me."

"Don't even. And *don't* call me 'babycakes'."

"What are you *doooooing*?"

That evening, after a dinner fully as gloomy as breakfast and lunch had been, Belinda and Laird had barged into Rennie's cabin, and had immediately appropriated the bedroom sofa. Now they were helping themselves uninvited to an enormous, overdecorated box of fancy Belgian chocolates—fearfully expensive bon-voyage bonbons, courtesy of Freddy Bellasca, Turk's label president—and watching their friend.

Rennie spared them a glance, trying not to laugh at their identical owlish, entitled expressions as they stuffed their faces with stolen champagne truffles.

"What does it look like I'm doing? I'm packing. We're leaving—I mean debarking, I so love shiptalk—in the morning, remember? Oh, and Freddy sent me those chokkies, by the way—I didn't eat them for fear they were poisoned. Just so you know. *Bon appétit.*"

Ignoring her, Laird reached for two more chocolates, popped one into Belinda's mouth. "No, but what are you *doing*?"

"Since you ask so nicely, I'm arranging my clothes in order of color, lightest to darkest."

Belinda laughed, and lobbed her a stray sandal. "You're such a freak."

"And proud of it, by God."

Rennie stuffed the sandal into the last tiny space in her great-aunt's largest Vuitton suitcase, closed the lid and began filling up the two smaller ones. She was an inveterate overpacker, and not a very neat one at that. *Better to bring something and not use it than not bring it and really need it...but of course I don't expect* them *to understand.* Still, it pleased her to think that Great-aunt Isabel's groovy Louies might have traveled on this very ship, or one not unlike it, four decades back...

"Oh, come on, babe, finish later." Laird pulled the cases out of Rennie's reach. "It's our last night at sea and we all know we'll have cops and press to deal with when we reach Palmton in the morning. Let's go do something *fun*."

"Okay, but only 'cause I'm finished."

Coming out of the movie theater two hours later, where they'd gone to try to forget their worries by watching "Fantasia" but were driven out by the cloud of high-quality pot smoke, giving them a for once unwanted contact high—as if hippopotamus ballerinas weren't trippy enough on their own!—they decided to go for a turn about the deck. Laird gallantly offered an arm to each girl, and they strolled past the swimming pool astern, lighted underwater blue, the water liquidly inviting in its ghostly undulations, and at this hour completely empty.

"Swim?" he asked hopefully.

Belinda looked interested, but Rennie just snorted. "None of us has a swimsuit or even *underwear* on. As you very well know. So it would have to be skinnydipping. As you also very well know."

Laird hooted. "As if I haven't already seen you both without any clothes on! And you me likewise. All that fraternal bareass swimming at the weekend lakeside frat cabin. Not to mention Woodstock. And Peter Tork's pool in Laurel Canyon. But you can't blame a guy for trying. A sexy gorgeous lady on each arm. A rock star's dream."

"Nothing unprecedented for you, my friend. Surprising, really, how often dreams can come true in this brave new rockerverse of ours."

Skirting the pool, they stepped around a dark corner

where a stack of deck chairs barred their way, promptly tripped over an unseen one and came to a sudden and clattering stop. Rennie, who had pitched headlong and was caught just in time by Laird, just as promptly began calling down maledictions on inconsiderate morons and lazy ship's swabs who left empty chairs out right where blameless stoned people would be sure to fall right over them.

But one chair was far from empty, or indeed blameless, and as they noticed, they first stood still and stunned, then approached with rising dread.

Face garishly made up like Paize Lee the Little Hippie Girl's, Day-Glo flowers painted onto her pale cheeks and white Twiggy lines drawn in amongst her lower lashes, wearing Paize Lee's little red hippie dress from the opera's first act, Loya Tessman was stretched out in a chair under the sun canopy beside the pool. As Rennie discovered when she leaned over to give Tessman a piece of her irate mind, Loya hadn't gotten up because she was lashed securely into the chair with the canopy's torn-off cord.

And also because she was very, very dead.

"Strangled," said Belinda in a hoarse whisper. "Apparently with the same kind of cord that was tying her to the chair. I heard the ship's doctor say so when they carried her down to the infirmary. Morgue. I mean the morgue. Where Samantha is." She raised the brandy snifter to her lips again, hands still shaking, and took a huge swallow.

"They're going to want to talk to us even more now," said Rennie matter-of-factly. "The cops in the Grand Palm Islands. Because we found her body. And me on both counts, 'cause I was also nearby when Sammi hit the drink."

"Oh, you do this sort of thing all the time, it's easy for *you*!"

Rennie's voice remained even, and her face was carefully blank. "Yes, I suppose it might look like that. God is, after all, a serial killer."

The three of them were sitting huddled in a corner of the high-ceilinged first-class lounge, like lost children among the mirrors and marble columns of a fairy palace, watched over solicitously by not only the risqué, classically themed wall frescoes but by a bar steward in case they should require restorative alcohol. Which they very well might, and indeed had, several times. There had already been a distinctly unpleasant hour spent talking to the captain, the first officer and the ship's doctor, but nothing could really be done until the ship docked at Palmton in the morning. After examination in situ, Loya's body had been brought down to the morgue to join Sammi Stoyer in cold storage. She was still tied into the chaise, minimally disturbed, with a blanket humanely covering her; the cops would have wanted her kept as is, or was, but it was inconceivable to have left her up on deck. It was only a matter of hours now till they reached port, and the morgue was basically a converted freezer, so probably things wouldn't get too…icky.

"Something's going on here," ventured Laird after a while, looking first at Belinda, then at Rennie.

"You *think*? And yet, apart from homicide, we have no idea what it might be." Rennie took a long hit out of her own snifter. "Not yet, anyway. It's there, though, I know it is. Somewhere in my brain, a small but valiant neuron, crying because it's all alone, struggles heroically to fire a message across the Grand Synapse Canyon. Alas, the distance from rim to rim is greater every day."

"I blame drugs?"

"Nah, intellectual laziness. Or maybe it's me blanking it all out because I'm absolutely freaked and selfishly not wanting it to interfere with my reunion with my honey... You know, our first day at sea, at lunch, Tessman said she needed to talk. To *me*. Whom she never, *ever* talked to."

"And did you?"

"What with one thing and another, we never got around to it. We were supposed to, after 'Paize Lee'. But in all honesty I don't remember even seeing her again after she asked, except when they brought Stoyer back aboard that first night. But she looked really weird when she asked me."

Belinda scoffed. "That was the way she always looked. Like she had a straw up her bum."

"No, this was different. She looked—well, if I didn't how hard as nails she was I'd have said she looked terrified."

"Don't start, Strider," said Laird. "Everything isn't always a mystery and a drama. Though I can see where you might think so, given your track record."

"It's not my fault," said Rennie defensively. "I just happen to be around when things happen."

"Yes, so you keep saying and so we keep hearing. And yet the fact remains that you so often are."

Next morning, between apprehension of talking to the Palmton police and anticipation of seeing Turk, Rennie was up early, if she had ever even really slept at all. All packed from the night before, she had little to do but shower, tuck away the framed photo of Turk from where it stood on the nightstand—it was always the first thing she took out when she traveled and the last thing she put away—and pull on the clothes she'd left out to wear. After that, there was nothing to do, and she stepped out onto the little balcony outside her picture windows.

It was dim and misty, even a bit cool, though with the promise of a warm, clear day to come once the mist burned off. Nobody else was in sight on deck. She turned her gaze across a small bay to where, behind a broad, palm-lined waterfront esplanade and a fringe of working piers on one side, a small, bright city rose up from coral-red brick streets—an enchanting toy town, a dollhouse village.

This was Palmton, the old British-colony capital of the Grand Palm Islands. Blindingly clean, charming white or pastel-colored buildings, some going back to the seventeenth century, were mixed in with a few brand-new high-rises, neat streets bustling in a pleasantly low-key way even at this early hour. Behind the town, green-covered jungly hills loomed, and behind those, some serious mountains, ex-volcanic as were many such in the Caribbean, rose up in front of a bank of high pink-tinged clouds.

There were lots of people on deck now, ship's people doing shippish things. As Rennie watched, the *Excalibur* bumped gently into the Palmton pier and parked itself like an ocean-going limo. First off the aft gangway, in a vain attempt to avoid cameras and other prying eyes, was a body bag strapped securely to a gurney—Sammi, presumably—which was landed, loaded into a waiting ambulance and driven off, escorted by two police cars. And coming up the gangway immediately thereafter was a little knot of policemen—some in handsome tropical uniforms of white shirts, white Bermuda shorts and white pith helmets, some in plainclothes, though still shorts—to inspect Loya Tessman on board before removing her to shore like Sammi.

Rennie glanced to her left and quietly snarled. That side of the pier was crowded with people who didn't look at all as if they had come to greet arriving loved ones: dozens of cameras both still and TV; pushing, shoving, yelling reporters; lines of cops holding it all back. Laird had been right: the international press corps had descended upon pretty little Palmton like a flock of battlefield vultures. It made her ashamed of her profession. And very, very cross with it.

She drew back quickly into her cabin, hoping she hadn't been spotted through someone's telephoto lens. That was some gantlet they were all going to have to run when they left the safety of the ship, and the police would likely grab her as soon as she stepped onto Grand Palm soil and whisk her away, along with Belinda and Laird.

She sighed and brushed her hair off her face. Well, there was no escaping it. Hopefully she'd be allowed to phone Turk over on Lion Island at some point, and he could come and get her. But try as she might, she still could come up with no reason why Sammi and Loya should have been murdered, nothing she could give the cops when they came to ask her, and oh they so would.

Unless it's because of what Loya wanted to talk to me about. But I'll never know now, will I… And I have no idea why anyone would want to kill Stoyer. They'll probably think I did it myself, because the little tramp said she'd slept with Turk and other passengers witnessed our charming encounter. Motive, means, opportunity...been down that road before. But at least now I have a roadmap...

An hour later, squaring her shoulders and lifting her chin and stepping off the forward gangway with her fellow passengers, steeled to face the worst, Rennie took a deep breath as she set foot on the pier, looked up and fell straight and amazedly into Turk Wayland's arms.

Six

"I HAD A FEELING YOU MIGHT LIKE ME to meet you," said Turk, after Rennie's raptures at their surprise reunion were under control. Well, surprise to her, anyway. They were making their hasty, purposeful way across the pier area, away from the main throng behind the barrier; out of the corner of her eye, Rennie noticed Belinda waving excitedly and giving her a double thumbs-up, presumably expressing her approval at seeing Turk there, and she gave a cautious wave back.

"Rather than sending the seaplane to fetch you home, I mean," he continued, surprised that she seemed surprised to see him. "Did you really think I'd let you face that mob alone?"

Rennie felt a great wash of relief and thankfulness flood clear to her toes. *'Home'... Liberation and independence are great, and no way in hell I'd ever give that up, but sometimes, just sometimes, it's really nice to have a big strong guy simply take things out of your hands and enfold you in his manly arms. It's only good, though, if you're capable of dealing with those things yourself, and of doing the same thing for him in return. Otherwise it's all a waste...*

"There's a *seaplane*? Well of course there is..." She instinctively moved closer to him. "I take it you heard what happened, then."

He nodded. "Oh yes. It's been all over the papers and

TV. And so have you, Murder Chick." He tightened his arm around her shoulders and dropped a kiss on the top of her head. "Which is why we're smuggling you out the back way and over to the island. I'm sure you've already noticed, but there's about fifty bloodthirsty members of your tribe, from all corners of the world, waiting to pounce on you for the real, in-depth, exclusive no-detail-spared story as soon as you emerge from the customs hall. Not to mention the coppers, who also want to get their hands on you, so to speak, for pretty much the same reason. So I snuck behind the lines to carry you off, and I can say with complete confidence that you won't be talking to either profession today. Tomorrow will be another story; even *I* can't keep the demanding plod or ambushing reporters away from you indefinitely, and it's probably best to get it over with. But at least you'll be rested and ready to face them."

Rennie glanced back over her shoulder, involuntarily, and saw the baying scrum they had so narrowly escaped.

"How did you manage that? I know you have connections, not to mention powers and abilities, far beyond those of mortal men, but won't I be entering the Grand Palms illegally?"

"Not a bit of it." Turk made her a little bow. "Being the prince of Lion Island has its advantages from time to time. So, shamelessly, I *took* advantage. My father was at Eton with the Grand Palms prime minister, and I at Oxford with said minister's son Nigel, so I rang up and asked if a tiny little minor favor could be done for old family friends and oh yes future owners of Lion Island and powers in these parts the next Duke and Duchess of Locksley. Not to mention the soon-to-be Mr. and Mrs. Turk Wayland, forces of the rockerverse. The P.M. was most sympathetic—said hi to my parents and invited us to dinner. I'll send Nigel thank-you tickets to our next London gig. Anyway, it's hardly as if we're breaking the law: Lion Island has its own immigrations and customs office, because of all the things we bring in and out of there, so you, being my own personal import, can be duly processed and lawfully admitted to the islands. Just in private and just not here."

Rennie made no reply, grateful that he'd pulled such major political strings for her, and also appalled that he had, but she leaned into him again and slid her arm around his waist. Obviously their little wrangle had been long forgotten, in the light of their time apart, as well as more serious events... *Tomorrow, yes, I'll think about all of this tomorrow...thank* you, *Scarlett O'Hara!*

"I'm not the only one that the hacks and the fuzz want to get their paws on," she pointed out as they headed down a smaller connecting pier, at the end of which bobbed a dashing white and blue seaplane, already being loaded with Rennie's luggage by white-jeaned and t-shirted locals.

"That's as may be, but you're the only one I care about. That's why I'm getting you the hell out of here and onto our own turf."

"But Belinda, and Laird, and the Weezles, and Jimi and Crosby and Sebastian and all of them—"

"—will have to fend for themselves," said Turk firmly. "I don't want to have to see or talk to any of them. And I'm sure they'll enjoy every minute."

*

The Lion Islands—all dozen-odd of them, some little more than rocks—sit just off the Anegada Passage, a deep, wide, turbulent stretch of water known locally, and without the least bit of either irony or fondness, as the Oh-My-God-A Passage, in the center of a triangle whose points are the U.S. Virgin Islands, the British Virgin Islands and the British-owned Anguilla. They associate themselves politically with the British-run Grand Palm Islands twenty miles to the west, also in the Passage, and the citizens, though independent as Lion Islanders, also live as British subjects. The islands, usually referred to in the singular, enjoy a sort of protectorate status: not exactly independent—a fact that Rennie often laments, with visions of Turk as U.N. ambassador dancing in her head—but for all practical purposes a Commonwealth member safely under the jurisdiction of Her Majesty's government as represented by the Grand Palms prime minister. Who was, as Turk had mentioned, a longtime friend of the family.

Though under the absolute control of the Duke of Locksley, as owner and governor-general, Lion Island and its tiny adjuncts have an elected officer, the Tenant-in-Chief, to handle the day-to-day civil duties with the help of his own staff, as the Duke spends most of his time in England. Additionally, there are important lesser positions, such as island manager, chief agriculturist, customs controllers and mayors of the various townships and settled areas, which together contribute to the smooth running of the place.

All the islands in that vicinity are racially mixed, for a certain value of "mixed": meaning that, as in most other places in the Caribbean, the indigenous majority is overwhelmingly of color and the ruling minority is predominantly white. The mixing in the Grand Palms, though, as on Lion Island itself, had begun centuries ago, and so by now has achieved a harmony and a balance shared by few other places in the volatile island chain. Oh, there are rumblings of discontent, and occasional outbreaks of protest and even violence, but for the most part the Grand Palms have quietly been moving into true racial equality, mostly because their situation has been a lot more equal all along than that of other Caribbean island nations.

Financial equality, however, has further to go, and the native Grand Palmian population, though wealthier and better situated than the inhabitants of other, more well-known tourist islands, is still in general a great deal poorer than the white minority, to such an extent as makes criminal activity a feasible career choice. Lion Island itself, thankfully, has been spared all this, for a number of excellent reasons, and the Tarrants are devoted to seeing that it stays that way.

Their family compound, Falcons Levels, is set commandingly in lush gardens atop a jungly hill near the island's western end, from which one can see almost the whole of the island, a kidney-shaped emerald blaze about twenty miles long by five at the widest, with tall rocky horns on its south coast enclosing a fine deep harbor where the kidney curves sharply in. A spine of rough ex-volcanic peaks four thousand feet high bisects the island lengthwise; otherwise, it is edged with sandy beaches and fringed almost completely with offshore coral reefs, more like shoals, that extend far out to sea. Hidden in the dense rainforests, colorfully painted houses are dotted around, spreading out from Lion Town, the charming capital settlement set on the harbor shore, and climbing up the hill slopes behind. At five thousand souls, Lion Town is the largest of only half a dozen villages on the island; all are clustered on the western and southern end—the eastern half and north shore are uninhabited. Jungles and rainforests predominate; cleared fields for crops and pastures for large herds of dairy cattle patchwork the landscape.

"Wow."

Rennie, peering down from the seaplane's window, was nose-against-the-glass, and as they went by not all that far above, Turk, smiling at her excitement, pointed out the main house and town buildings to her, before they touched down in Lion Bay and taxied to the dock. They were met by a cheerful island official, black, who turned out to be the Tenant-in-Chief himself, and who greeted them with casual delight, formally welcoming Rennie to the Lion Islands and zipping her through passport control and customs in about thirty seconds. An equally cheerful estate driver, white, was waiting outside with a Jeep, and after another delighted welcome, loaded Rennie's bags, Rennie herself and Turk into the vehicle, and ferried them all up twisting roads into the hills.

"I see nobody really cares all that much that their rightful prince walks among them," she remarked after a few minutes, trying not to look over the terrifying edges of the unguardrailed hairpin road and the sheer thousand-foot drops beyond. "Nobody's particularly reverential to see you: no bows, no curtsies, no peasants tugging their forelocks…"

Turk laughed. "You don't know it yet, but you should be deeply flattered that Christophen—the Tenant, Christophen Hilling—came to meet you. But everybody here wants to meet you. As for the forelock-tugging, we don't go in for that. Nor do we do the lordship and ladyship thing. When I get that from anyone, I know I'm in trouble. Even the Duke is just 'Mister Duke.' You'll be 'Miss', at least until they feel comfortable with you, then it'll be 'Miss Rennie'. 'Mister Richard' is what I get if I'm lucky—these days it's just as often 'Yo Turk!' And I'm good with it either way, believe me, though from that faint sneer upon your exquisite countenance perhaps you think it's all too plantation-style for your comfort. Well, madam, it's not like that at all. I've spent holidays here since I was a tot in nappies. I know everybody and their family and family history, and they know me and mine. It's very different to what it's like at Cleargrove or Locksley."

"So it would seem."

As they pulled up in front of the big white house that crowned the hill, the double front doors swung open, and a young man with skin the color of polished bronze stood there glaring at them both.

"Took your own sweet time getting back, didn't you," he said in a deep, island-accented voice. Rennie stared as Turk and the stranger held a mock-twangling silence, then they both burst out laughing and punched each other's arms. Still smiling, the stranger looked pointedly, and admiringly, at Rennie.

"So? Introduce me to your bonny woman, brother."

Turk put an arm around each of them. "Rennie, may

I present one of my oldest, dearest friends in the world, Phanuel Shine. He runs this place. Phan, this is Rennie Stride, the future Lady Raxton. She runs my heart."

Rennie blushed, smiled and took the proffered hand in hers. "I've heard a lot about you, Phanuel."

"Likewise." He raised her hand to his lips and bowed deeply. "Welcome to Falcons Levels, m'lady."

"And that's the last time you'll be getting that from him," said Turk comfortably.

"Fine with me."

After washing her face and changing into tiny white denim cut-off shorts, bare feet and a colorful fringed Ukrainian scarf from Eko on Second Avenue tied in a triangle over her breasts, and getting outside a bit of breakfast, Rennie was given the grand tour. Falcons Levels was bigger than it had looked from the air: long and low and light, it had a sizable center section of cozily elegant common rooms and half a dozen wings leading off in several different directions on several different planes and in several different architectural styles, all snugly nestled into the hillside.

Much of the house was an ancient fortress built of the island's tough native volcanic rock, while much of the rest was light-colored coquina stone quarried from the reefs—tiny compressed shells bound with coral that made easily cuttable textured blocks. A largish addition was white-brick Georgian, still other parts made of beautifully silvered and weathered Balinese teak or local pine—all a patchwork dating from various decades of assorted centuries, yet all comprising a somehow harmonious and organic whole that looked as if it had sprung fully grown from the hill.

From the main rear terrace, a long easy flight of broad switchbacked steps, with a crushed-clamshell path for golf carts running alongside, led down the hill to a cove with gold sand and clear green water. There was an eternity pool on three levels, easy of access from most rooms, for those who felt inclined for a swim but too lazy to schlep all the way down to the beach—they could dive straight in almost from their bedrooms. The house was open to the tradewinds and incredible views of neighboring islands through French doors, sliding doors, colonnades, breezeways and windows, though, it being the Caribbean, all such were prudently fitted with hurricane-resistant shutters and battens; the rather shabby, chintz-heavy furniture within was pleasant and comfortable, a far cry from posh. Typically English upper-class décor, as Rennie knew by now: not at all how people imagined the upper-class English to typically live, though the Tarrants fit the stereotype in more than one of their domiciles.

They dined that night with Prax and Ares, who had been lazing down on the beach, and who had fallen joyfully upon Rennie when they golf-carted back up to the house. They were also joined by Phanuel and his Grenadian wife, Marigo, whom Turk was reluctantly allowing to do the general cooking. Tonight, though, in honor of his lady's arrival, his lordship had prepared the meal himself: all local produce from the island—citrus-glazed roast pork with coconut rice pilaf, soup bowls made from small loaves of hollowed-out bread, filled with tiny whole shrimp and langoustine tails in a thick, spicy Caribbean sauce. Turk being a skilled chef, it was all delicious, and everyone tucked in enthusiastically, though Marigo seemed nervous at sitting down to table with the rest of them and neither cooking nor serving.

By mutual unspoken agreement, the diners kept away from fraught topics like murder, and Rennie mostly listened rather than talked. But at last, over lime sorbet served in actual frozen limes, she gave the others a somber account of the events that had taken place aboard the ship.

At the end, Prax shook her head and poured herself another iced tea. "How does that even happen?" she demanded. "Again with the murders. You're such a creature of habit...if that's even accurate by now."

Turk grinned. "No, calling her a control freak is accurate. Calling her a creature of habit is understatement."

"*And* with excellent hearing..." murmured Rennie, not looking at him, and he laughed.

Prax shook her head again, exasperated. "It never stops with you, does it. Do you think you'll have to talk to the police?"

"Uh, *yeah*? Since I was sort of there when Sammi Stoyer hit the briny and very much there when Loya Tessman turned up dead in a deckchair. The murders—if the deaths *are* both murders, Loya's sure is, and the ship's doctor was not happy about signing off on an accidental cause of death for the groupie—the murders happened on the high seas, but the ship has a G.P.I. registry and sails out of Palmton, so I guess that makes it a Grand Palm Islands problem."

Turk nodded. "I got a call yesterday from the chief superintendent of police, and yes, it is indeed a G.P.I. problem, and yes, they certainly do want to talk to you.

That was the deal: they'd let me take you home first, get your passport stamped and have you rest up overnight, and I'd bring you back to Palmton tomorrow. In fact, you're officially in my legal control—a strangely pleasing feeling that I could easily get used to. I even have papers on you," he added smugly.

"Oh, you do not!"

"Actually, madam, I do; well, a document vouching for your conduct and holding me responsible for you. Since you are after all an important witness to a capital crime and also a foreign national. Not to mention a meddlesome though talented journalist. So your behavior needs to be impeccable or else I'll suffer for it. Phan and I will run you back over tomorrow afternoon," Turk continued. "I'd have told you earlier but I wanted to give you some time not to have to think about it. Obsess about it."

"And very thoughtful it was of you, too… Will there be lawyers then, my preciousss?" murmured Rennie. "Will there be tricksy shysterses?"

"We retain a fine firm of solicitors and barristers in Palmton, of course, who are already briefed and who will help you in any way in which you may need helping. That's what they're paid for," said Turk evenly. "Does that settle your mind?"

"Not in the least. Was it *supposed* to settle my mind?"

He took a sip of lemonade. "Not in the least."

They discussed it a while longer, then turned to other, more pleasant, topics, Prax wanting to hear all about everything that had happened aboard the ship, especially the performance of "Paize Lee". Only Ares had not commented on her tale, though he talked about everything else, and when Rennie was alone with him on the terrace after dinner, sharing a joint in the warm fragrant sunset air, she taxed him with it.

"Why are *your* lacy pink panties in a bunch, o bear of very little brain? I can tell they are, so don't bother denying it. Because it was rock and roll murder, and you think you could have prevented it if only you had been there which you were not and Pig Blue's security boys were and yet they couldn't and didn't?"

Ares gave her a look, but didn't say anything.

Rennie rolled her eyes. "Oh, right, silly me, it's because *I* was there and you think somehow I had something to do with it, that I do this on *purpose*. Well, damn my perfect timing!"

"No," he finally said. "No, I don't think that. Not anymore, at least."

"Ah. Because that would be crazy thinking."

"It would." He favored her with a smile at last. "But—considering your track record? And don't take this the wrong way, but I do think it somehow finds you."

"How else am I to take it?" She smiled back at him with great affection. "And that's *not* crazy thinking?"

"Nope. It's just...what it is."

"What what is?" said Turk, watching Rennie watch herself in the mirror as she brushed out her hair in their bedroom before turning in. "I know that look. I know it of old."

They were ensconced in the wing that Turk had occupied since his infancy—a spacious sitting room, a large bedroom opening onto a walled-in patio that had been safe confinement for a rambunctious toddler, a study full of books and nooks, a music room that had once been a nanny's chamber, a bath with a sunken marble Roman-style tub, a small galley kitchen in case the prince should grow peckish in the night.

All the rooms had been refurbished in honor of Rennie's arrival, and gleamed with polish and paint; the study now boasted a handsome mahogany table and a brand-new electric typewriter so she could work, and the canopy bed was hung with new double-strength mosquito netting, under the slowly revolving fan. Though, as Turk assured his insectophobe mate, not even a jet-assisted mosquito could make it up that high: the tradewinds that constantly blew across the island swirled them straight into oblivion when they hit the mountain spine, and in any case, Lion Island was notably and strangely unplagued by the voracious little joy thieves. Still, he was taking no chances. Rennie *really* didn't like bugs.

She met his eyes in the mirror. He'd shaved his beard for the tropical heat, and though she preferred him with it on, he was every bit as staggeringly good-looking without it. She just had to get used to his gorgeous bare face again—especially the feel of it. She missed the friction.

"It's nothing new, the look. It's the look of 'Hey, I'm back in solicitor country again.' A familiar place to be. Even if the local law is a tad bit not so."

"Speaking of local law— Before I forget..." He got up off the bed and stood a couple of feet away from her chair, a faint grin on his face. "Up. Come on, up up up. Now kneel."

She looked quizzically at him, but complied, dropping to her knees in front of him, her eyes going to where gray silk sleep pants hung low on his hipbones, right in front of her face, then looked up.

"Um…do you want me to…if you…oh, well, sure…"

Turk snorted. "Not that. Well, not yet." He put his right hand on her left shoulder, serious now. "This is something every citizen has to swear when they come here to live or marry a resident or turn eighteen, so don't get all flustered. We might as well take care of it tonight. There will be something to sign tomorrow at the solicitors'. It doesn't interfere with your current citizenship, I promise. A mere formality. So. Repeat after me…"

In about ten seconds he led her through a pledge of allegiance to the Duke of Locksley as ruler of the Lion Islands, and then held out his hand to pull her to her feet again.

She rolled her eyes, exasperated. "How very feudal. And subjugating. Do you make all your serfs do that whilst kneeling naked at your feet? Or am I just special?"

He smirked a little. "No, you're just special. Everyone else stands and is fully clothed."

"It figures."

"Careful, or I'll order you back down there. Now that I lawfully can."

"Prat. You could have a look too, you know," she added, going back to what she'd said earlier. She picked up the brush from where she'd left it on the bed, setting it down on the nightstand, and joined Turk between the impeccably ironed sheets. "You could have the look of 'Hey, my old lady's back in murder country again.' You could even verbally berate me for it. You'd be well within your rights."

"I could do," Turk conceded, taking her in his arms, the silk pants having somehow vanished. "And I would be. But I would certainly never say so. Especially to a newly sworn vassal of my tropical fiefdom. Besides, I'd rather exercise some of my other rights just now, thank you very much."

"No," said Rennie after a while. "Thank *you*."

Seven

"NOT BAD."

Emerging from their bedroom through the French doors onto the private terrace, Rennie peered out over the lush shrubbery at the stunning view of sea, beach, town, mountains and neighboring islands—some Grand Palms, some American or British Virgins, some Lions. She had just showered after a post-breakfast swim in the eternity pool's top level, and her engagement ring, a Niihau-shell anklet that she'd bought on Maui and the damp towel she was now discarding were the only things she was wearing.

"No," said Turk from where he was lying in the shade beside a tiled fountain, "not bad at all… Oh, you mean the island. Well, British people love to get away to where it's sunny and warm—we don't get a great deal of that sort of thing at home."

"So I've noticed. Not surprising that your family grabbed these islands when the grabbing was good. As you say, very different from your usual island haunts." She sat down on a chaise next to his and unpinned her tangled hair, combing it out with her fingers. "How long has this little shack been here?"

"The house? Apart from the original late seventeenth-century sections and the later Georgian and Victorian ones, it was mostly built in the nineteen-teens. And the Bali-style wing went up in the fifties, when that sort of thing was all the rage. Architecturally, it's a mess. But we like that. The island itself belonged to a pirate forebear of mine three hundred years ago, and he's the one who first built on this spot, his own personal fortress. Privateer, officially, but really he was a pirate. A very good pirate, too."

"And by 'good' you mean—"

"Wildly successful. He married an equally successful, and very beautiful if you can judge by her portraits, lady pirate called Madelon Buckmaster. Together they made the family very, *very* rich, for which we're all still deeply grateful—allowed us to buy half of London. Interestingly enough, he too was a Richard Tarrant, and eventually he became the third duke. Usually known as Ironhand, for reasons perhaps best not gone into, though he did have two quite normal ones. Let's say he's well remembered in these parts. By the people, quite fondly. By figures of authority, perhaps not so much."

Rennie draped her towel over the chaise and stretched out on her front on top of it, flipping her hair aside to let the sun have access to her bare rear exposure, nape to soles. It already felt quite the normal thing to go clothing-optional out of doors, or as often and as near to it as was appropriate, and she was aiming to have achieved at least a nice all-over biscuit color by the time they went home.

"I can imagine. Well, my lord, every time I think I know you, you surprise me. But if Stephen can be descended from a lawyer and a whore—which are the same thing in the minds of many, come to think of it—I don't see why you can't be the descendant of a pair of buccaneers. Or acquisitions specialists, if you prefer. Seems appropriate, somehow."

They were comfortably silent for a while in the warm sun and light breeze, then Rennie had a sudden horrified thought. "This wasn't a *slave* island, was it? Because I would really hate that."

"Christ, no! Rather staggeringly in advance of their time, Ironhand and Madelon didn't believe in slavery. Most of the slaves across the Caribbean were freed in the early eighteen-hundreds in any case, but we never owned slaves here ourselves. I don't know if it was out of nobility of spirit or sheer economic sense, but by Ironhand's decree anyone—black, brown, yellow, red or white—who lived or worked or even set foot here was a free person, and because they were working for themselves as well as for us, they worked ten times harder than any slave would have done. So did the Tarrants—just because we had titles and owned the place didn't mean we could sit back with our feet up and eat bonbons. Quite the contrary: we had to be a shining example of constructive and often manual labor. But make no mistake, everyone here was every bit as ruthless and bloodthirsty as any pirate anywhere; just because Ironhand was a gentleman didn't mean his attitude was a gentle one, on land or sea. As you can probably tell by the name. And nor was Madelon's a lady's, either. Though indeed she *was* a lady."

"Goodness! Not exactly Swiss Family Robinson, then."

"Only in self-sufficiency. Back then, Lion Island was a totally self-sustaining enterprise: the men crewed for the Tarrant fleet and blacksmithed and built ships and houses and cast guns, the women farmed and fished and made clothes and rope and sails and put up food. Even the kids worked, as herds and crop pickers on land or shellfish gatherers onshore. And the family pitched right in."

"And they say communes are a brand-new fad. Well, dang those hippies! But not a particularly *feminist* commune, apparently. The chicks were still doing the cooking and sewing. Slavery, no. Sexism, yes."

Turk laughed. "Only if they *wanted* to cook and sew, or couldn't do anything else. There was one family, the Callows, where all the women were expert swordmakers, and nobody, least of all Ironhand, would rather have seen them making dinner instead of the best blades in the Caribbean. He carried one himself, and so did Madelon, and all their crews. The Callows still make swords, though as the demand for weapons-grade ironmongery isn't so great anymore, they've expanded into jewelry and flatware, very fine stuff—and yes, before you ask, we'll go buy something from them before we go home. But the rule was, everyone here had to do *something*, usually several somethings, from the Duke on down. And quite a lot of somethings wanted doing. The island produced cotton, sugar, pork, beef, fish, shellfish, rice, salt, fruit, flour and rum, among other things—as we still do. That famous ham you so happily pigged, as it were, out on at breakfast was famous even back then. Besides growing food for export, the farmers had to feed the island families and the ship crews, who were the envy of the seven seas for their on-board pantries."

"I see. So how was all this idyllicness financed?"

"Hello? *Pirates*? Loot, of course. Also export, as I

mentioned. Everyone shared, no one starved, and when they weren't out busily privateering all on the salt sea-o they all lived here together, one big happy pirate family. They got married here and raised their children here, and when they grew old or ill, or were hurt in battle, they would be taken care of here, and when they died they'd be buried here. Often at sea, out in one of the deepwater channels. There was quite a touching ceremony, actually."

"I'm sure. But suppose they wanted to leave? While they were still alive, I mean."

"Nothing to stop them. Settlements would be made, according to status and length of service—like profit-sharing or a pension plan. But very, very few went away, though we sent numerous kiddies off to school in England and brought them back educated, as we still do, to run our lawful businesses. Yes, there actually were some, it wasn't all merry marine muggings! Most of the original families are here to this day. There's about a hundred founding surnames, and then all the ones who came later, most of them related in one way or another. As you saw coming in, it's all different colors and all different original nationalities and everybody genuinely equal. It's been like that since the first. We are insular, in the true sense of the word, and apart from a small, steady tide of incomers and off-island marriages—must keep that gene pool from stagnating—that's how we like it."

"How feudally socialistic. Sorry, I mean, what a communally enlightened little paradise. This fascinates me. Tell me more. What did their fellow nobles, not to mention other Tarrants, think about our pirate pair? Were they outraged? None of them could declare *their* own country, after all, so I could see where they might have been envious and annoyed. Put some of this stuff on my back, please?"

Turk opened the bottle of sunscreen, shifted over and obliged. "Well, they weren't very happy about it, as you can imagine. But technically Richard was a privateer, not a pirate, a well-known recipient of royal favor sailing under letters of marque from the Crown, and he kicked in way more than his share to the family coffers, so they had to suck it up. Oh, and we have Madelon's jewels as a giant founding piece of the family collection; you're welcome to go through them and wear anything you like, unless you have scruples about adorning yourself with, well, loot, which yeah right I forgot who I'm talking to. In due course, as I said, he became duke, though it didn't cramp his style a bit when he did."

Rennie flexed her shoulders as Turk rubbed the cream into them, enjoying the pressure of strong musician's fingers as much as he enjoyed pressing the satiny, sun-warm curves.

"Besides wear fabulous jewels, what did Maddy do after they got married? Stay home and pop out baby Tarrants?"

"Sometimes; they had five, after all. One of their daughters married a Danish prince. But Madelon really was a proper pirate; she sailed with Richard, and captained her own ship in tandem with his when they went raiding. They made quite the team in battle, judging from the old records. And, which was incredibly rare for a chick in those times, even rarer than being a lady pirate, she was an actual educated scientist, a biologist; she studied native herbal cures with the island medicine women and even wrote a couple of medical texts that were very highly thought-of. She just very much liked being a pirate captain as well. Apart from that, they were pretty conventional, especially for a pair of buccaneers. As duke and duchess they were of course accepted in the best society, and warmly received at Court in London and Paris and the Continent—they were personal friends of several crowned heads. People pretended a lot better in those days: it was smart to be friendly, and Ironhand and Madelon never attacked a ship owned by somebody they liked."

"I think I like *them*. Where did they keep their fleet?"

He was still applying sunscreen to her shoulders and back and rear end and the backs of her legs, though the strokes were getting longer and slower and deeper.

"At the high point of their careers, they had a fleet of ten ships, which were anchored in Lion Bay—best harbor in this part of the Caribbean, and very well defended. Some of the ships were even lawful, and they were all fast and well gunned. But they always kept their fastest, best-gunned one right here below in Silver Bay, in case they ever needed to get out to sea in a hurry. They even dynamited a reef break so they could scarper out to deep water as fast as possible."

"And the treasure?"

He was using both hands now, and Rennie was just about boneless. "Do you know nothing about pirates? Was stored in secret caves, of course. There's a bunch of them all over the island, I'll show you sometime. They're empty now, except perhaps for some bats or wild pigs. Anyway, when Ironhand died—in his bed at a vast age, surprising everybody including himself—Madelon buried him here, and continued to run their empire with the help of their children. Except for the heir, Miles, whom they had sent back to England to get civilized. When Madelon knew she was dying, she sank their escape ship herself. We can go scuba diving to see her if you want, she's lying on the bottom of the bay below, right outside the reef pass."

"MADELON?"

"The *ship*. Madelon's next to Ironhand in the little church above the town, both of them looking as orthodox in effigy as any upscale English couple of their day; we'll pay our respects before we leave." Turk smiled with unconcealed pride. "If you look very carefully on the tomb ornamentation, though, you'll see tiny skulls and crossbones and ships and cutlasses carved all over the place. That was Miles's idea, their eldest son, the one who'd been so resentfully packed off to Locksley and then Oxford to learn dukeliness. It didn't sink in very deeply, as he followed in his parents' piratical footsteps, ruling the waves with equal profit and success. At any rate, being a big believer in accurate presentation, he had the marble carved in England and sent out here on one of his ships."

"Sounds like something a rock star would do."

"Back then, pirates *were* the rock stars. So were poets."

"A simpler, happier time."

The motion of Turk's hands had ceased, though she felt them cupping her now well-oiled behind. Turning her head and resting her chin on her shoulder, Rennie saw him eyeing her rear curves with possessiveness and intent. *Great minds, or at least oversexed ones, think alike…*

She arched her spine and hips, pushing into his hands, and remarked hopefully, "I always wanted to be ravished by a handsome English pirate."

"I can arrange that, me proud colonial beauty."

"Don't we have to get our asses over to Palmton so I can talk to the cops?"

"Plenty of time for that. I have other plans for our asses just now. Especially yours." He moved over on top of her, lowering himself upon her back and gathering her long hair into one fist. "Stand by to be boarded."

She shifted under his weight. "Too bad you can't clap me in irons."

"That too could be arranged."

"Come on then, shiver me timbers, mate. Shiver them good."

"Arrr."

"Well, *that* certainly managed to take my mind off the murders, for which I'm most thankful," said Rennie after, as they lounged happily entwined on the chaise. "Nice work, Captain Feedback. But in spite of all these charming distractions, I do have to think about them, you know, the murders, and my brain she keeps bringing me back to Loya wanting to talk to me aboard ship. She really did look scared, poor cow. Fear-for-her-life-level scared. I've seen that look often enough to know."

Turk pulled her to lie more comfortably on top of him. "I never discount your slaydar, you know that. But what do you think she wanted to discuss?"

"No idea, and now I'll never know. Plus Luke Woods

said that Hoden really wanted to talk to me too, and he didn't either. So I need to figure that out as well."

"I was watching the local news on Grand Palms TV while you were in the pool earlier. That excrescence Jo Fleet has been oozing his way all over Palmton, accompanying new and merry widower Ted Tessman. The deleterious duo summoned lawyers down from New York, and so did the Weezles. The same ones, actually—the lawyers for Isis Records and Tontine Booking. Keeping it all in the dysfunctional family. I recognized them on the news."

"Makes sense. Fleet was on board the ship with the rest of us, but I only saw him, I didn't speak to him—just as well, he seriously puts me off my feed. The Weezles can use all the help they can get, to get them through the stickiness of two dead bodies on their happy cruise. As for Ted, well...I couldn't stand Loya, as you know, but I wouldn't have wished her dead in such a horrible way. Though I might have killed her myself, given sufficient cause, and God knows she gave me plenty... Did the news say anything about that groupie who went overboard?"

He shook his head. "Not that I saw. Why do you ask?"

"The ship's doctor let slip to the captain and first officer that it didn't look like drowning to him, and I wondered."

"Not drowned? How can they tell?"

"No water in her lungs. They were giving her artificial respiration and nothing came out. So she was dead before she breached the billows. But how she got that way, I do not know."

"Yet."

"Yet."

Eight

After lunch, Rennie and Turk flew over to Palmton in the seaplane, this time piloted by Phanuel. Learning that Rennie's presence had been requested by the Palmton police, the high-priced Weezle lawyers, who had met with their high-profile clients as soon as they'd stepped off the plane down from New York, had immediately demanded a share of her time as well, and the cops had said fine, sure, sit in if you like, more convenient if we don't have to go through this twice. Turk had chivalrously refused to let her go unescorted or unprotected, ringing up the Tarrant family's local legal counsel and having him arrange the meetings at the firm's offices in Palmton. Speaking of protection, Ares had suggested that he should come along in a professional capacity, since there *had* been two murders, after all, and Turk and Rennie had been targets before now; but they had firmly yet gratefully declined his offer and told him to go catch some waves instead.

Landing the elegant craft in the section of Palmton harbor that was reserved for seaplanes, well away from the huge liners, Phanuel leaped out to tie the plane nose and tail to the floating mooring, while Turk stepped from the cabin and onto the boards of the dock as if exiting a royal coach.

He turned, extending his hand to the plane's only other occupant, and regally assisted her out of the cabin. Smiling at him, Rennie alighted and stood beside him, then glanced around with interest at the busy, bright little city; there had been no time to take a good look yesterday, and she was delighted with what she saw. As was Turk, watching her carefully: he'd been nervous for her earlier, but not now. *She'll do fine; and dear old Sir Geoff and the rest won't know what hit them...*

"I love that you have legal representation in every port," she remarked as the three of them headed for the bayfront esplanade in the smart little launch that had come to fetch them at Phanuel's hail. "You never know, do you."

"No, you never do."

Phanuel had errands to run, so they parted company on the esplanade and Turk and Rennie strolled up through the Old Town. In the exquisite eighteenth-century building that housed the law offices of Shipsterns, Glasson, Churching and Knight, all long-established Grand Palm families with a touch of piracy in their own veins, they were greeted cordially by the firm's most junior partner, Will Knight, who would be advising Rennie and steering her through her upcoming session with the police and the Weezle lawyers, which was scheduled to begin in about half an hour.

She was surprised at sight of him. Will wasn't any older than Turk and had dark hair almost as long; otherwise, he was neatly and professionally dressed in charcoal-gray linen Bermuda shorts and jacket, crisp white shirt and narrow school tie. By contrast, his noble patron was clad in a cotton Mexican wedding shirt, board shorts and flip-flops—though Turk had also gone in for the very becoming samurai-style half-ponytail he favored for surfing. Well, he was a marquess and the heir to a major local landowner, he could get away with it. Rennie herself had felt the need to make more of a clothing statement, or a different sort of statement, and so she had put on a pretty sundress, in ombréd shades of brown from cream to deep cocoa, rose-pink sandals and a big floppy straw hat, and pulled her long hair into a nice neat French braid down her back. Couldn't hurt to look like a lady for the legal beagles and the fuzz. Not to mention for any press they might encounter. Which they probably would.

"Who are you for?" asked Will, smiling, charmingly taking Rennie's hand in his and holding it, not shaking it. "You belonger?"

"I *beg* your pardon?" said Rennie, startled, instinctively gearing up to take icy offense and whip her hand away.

Turk chuckled. "The common greeting in these parts. It means who are your people, what family do you claim—or claims you. Being idiomatic, it doesn't even require an answer most times. And a 'belonger' is simply a native Grand Palm or Lion Islander. Will knows perfectly well who you're for. He's merely being irritatingly local."

"Indeed I am. A very great pleasure to meet you, Miss Stride. And to see *you* again, Richard. Even under such circumstances as these." He went on to explain that the other partners sent profuse apologies—the Tarrants not being clients ordinarily fobbed off on juniors—but they were all occupied at the moment and the senior partner would come shortly. The rest would show up when they could.

"Besides, I'm the youngest of the lot, therefore my masters, one of whom is the dear old pater, thought I'd be most relatable to you, being more aware of your situation and more like your own age. His lordship knows the drill. So you get stuck with me for now, I'm afraid," he concluded winningly. "Though I understand that this sort of thing isn't new to either of you."

Turk gave a short, unamused laugh. "You've been talking to King Bryant and Berry Rosenbaum and Shea Laakonen, have you?"

"Lovely people! Outstanding legal minds! Yes, I have. It's good to be prepared, and you two didn't give me much time. Oh, and I understand we need to sign a document or two? Let's do that now, then, shall we, and get it taken care of."

Will gestured, and they sat down at the splendid Georgian cherrywood banqueting table, now pressed into humbler service for conferences and, apparently, document signings.

"Right there, please…here…and here…and Richard signs there. I understand the oath was duly sworn? Yes. Good. Welcome to Lion Island citizenship. Now—may I call you Rennie?—why don't you tell me all about it? Before the coppers and my elders show up. What happened?"

"She died of WHAT? But…how?"

"Heroin poisoning, according to the preliminary post-mortem," repeated Detective Chief Superintendent Edward Meryton of the Grand Palms Police, pleased with Rennie's shocked reaction, which was mirrored to varying degrees all round the table. "We just had word from the coroner's office. A particularly pure sort of heroin, too. We've been seeing a lot of it around the northern Caribbean lately, and I don't have to say that we would all dearly love to put a good solid permanent stop to it."

The splendid Georgian cherrywood chairs around the big table had been gradually populated over the past couple of hours with a dozen or so sober-faced individuals, including the Weezles' lawyers, who had arrived with Jo Fleet, and of course the police themselves, in the main presence of Chief Superintendent Meryton, whose lofty rank reflected the delicate diplomatic nature of the situation. Meaning this was already an international incident, so let's not make it worse, and also no one cared to allow the Marquess of Raxton and his future Marchioness to be handled by lesser personnel.

This diplomacy carried through to the law firm itself. The senior partner, Sir Geoffrey Shipsterns—short, dapper, gray-haired, distinguished of mien—had joined them first, smoothly apologizing for his delayed appearance and inquiring after the health and well-being of Lord Saltire's, beg pardon, Lord Raxton's, ducal parents, whom, he proudly reminded the assembled company, he had known since before Richard, beg pardon, his young lordship was born.

His young lordship had merely nodded distantly, and introduced him to her soon-to-be ladyship. Rennie thought she detected a tiny yet distinct vibe of oh-right-heard-all-about-*you*-young-madam from Shipsterns, and from his fellow seniors as they had trickled in, and she had definitely intercepted a stealthy glance or two at the giant heart-shaped ruby on her left hand. She pretended she hadn't noticed the glances, but she also subtly angled the ring so they could all get a good look. Then she decided she was being paranoid: why would they risk offending the future seventeenth Duke of Locksley's Duchess-to-be? Not to mention offending said future Duke himself.

She had favored the room instead with the sunny smile of one who'd been recently invited to dine with the actual Prime Minister of this actual island nation. *Suck it up, lawdogs! I'm going to be the next Pirate Queen of Lion Island, whether we like it or not, so let's decide we're all going to get along, shall we…or at least pretend we are?*

And then the male secretary, impeccably Bermuda-shorted like all the other men, had come in to announce the arrival of the cops. And then Superintendent Meryton had mentioned heroin.

"It sounds like something out of James Bond," said Sir Geoffrey, shaking his head but enjoying himself immensely—clearly a big change from his usual law diet.

At the other end of the table, Superintendent Meryton shifted slightly in his seat, and everyone who hadn't already been staring at him turned to look. He returned their stares composedly: a medium man—medium height, medium age, medium appearance, medium brown skin. These islands didn't have a big race problem, though of course there was often a bit of friction even at the best of times, but people of all colors held jobs of all sorts and at all levels, part of the reason it was such a pleasant place. Meryton had the typical soft lilting voice and gentle, blurry accent of a Grand Palms native, though his diction was as clear as Sir Geoffrey's, which Rennie attributed, rightly as it turned out, to an off-island education, and a rather superior one too. But his features were sharp, and his eyes were sharper, and his attention, and intelligence, sharper even than that. *Far from medium clever, it seems; I will have to be careful...*

"Yes, very much like that, Sir Geoffrey," said Meryton dryly. "And far too creative for our liking. It seems that the shirt she was wearing had been soaked in heroin, and the drug transferred itself to her skin, causing an overdose even though she hadn't actually taken any of it by more, ah, conventional means."

"She'd been in the sea, though," Turk pointed out. "How could they tell? Wouldn't the smack have all been washed away?"

"Two very good questions, m'lord," said Meryton, after a moment. "Well, we didn't know at first, of course. But it was soon clear even to the ship's doctor that she'd died of an overdose. And when it also became clear that she hadn't shot it or snorted it or ingested it, forensics looked for another means of delivery, and found faint drug traces on every skin surface that the shirt would have covered. Very faint, but there. The ship's officers gave us the clothes she'd worn, and forensics, again, was able to recover traces off the inner surfaces and seams of the fabric, even though it had been soaked in the ocean. She was fatally overdosed by contact before she went overboard." He paused again, and didn't look at anyone. "And beaten up pretty badly, as was the other victim."

"One moment," said Will Knight. "You said earlier, as did Miss Stride in her initial statement, that there was a scream before the victim went overboard. If she was already dead of an overdose..."

"Then how did she manage to scream at all, you mean." Meryton looked impressed, like a teacher at a precocious child who'd questioned a dubious math equation.

"She didn't," said Turk. "She wasn't the one who screamed. So then—someone else was there when she went over. Someone involved but not the murderer, someone who protested what was being done, do we think? Or someone uninvolved, who saw it and was horrified, and registered said protest by shrieking her head off?"

Meryton looked even more impressed. "That, we don't know yet. But we do know that, from the amount of heroin that was present in her body, the victim Stoyer died from the drug, not from the fall. And not from drowning, either—no water in her lungs. It was a corpse, if you'll all forgive the unpleasantness of my saying so, that went overboard."

Rennie's eyebrows had moved upward at the mention of water-free lungs, and now they crept skyward even further. *Huh. You want unpleasantness, cop?* I'll *give you unpleasantness! You have no* idea *the unpleasantness I've seen. Nobody but Jesus and Turk...*

"What made forensics think to do testing on the shirt in the first place?" she challenged. "It seems a bit—exotic a possibility. I mean, perhaps not the sort of thing that would occur to you first."

Meryton transferred a thoughtful gaze from the table top to her. "I expect that would be because we've seen this 'sort of thing' before in these parts, Miss Stride."

Considerable stir at the table, though Rennie and Meryton had locked their gazes like chess players and did not stir an eyelash. "Well," she said after a while, "I suppose that would make it—logical. Any thoughts as to why she would don such a lethal garment in the first place? Unless, of course, she didn't do it voluntarily, before she was precipitated into the Atlantic. Which, since you say how beaten up she was, I would very much think she did not."

Meryton's eyes half-shuttered at her correct guess; this young American about to be subsumed into the royal family of these parts was exactly as her reputation, which preceded her by miles, had made her out to be—intelligent, clever and annoying, holding no brief for man, woman, beast or deity. He'd read all about her previous crime-solving exploits, and had had a hard time believing that the coppers of several major U.S. cities and two different sovereign nations had let her get away with the antics they had. He'd have to talk to the police departments she'd managed to browbeat into submission, just so he'd know exactly what he was dealing with, personally. And he had absolutely no intention of letting her get away with any similar antics here, or allowing the Grand Palm Islands to make that sovereign third. But that was before he'd met her. Abruptly, he decided to jettison the professional condescension and speak frankly, as to a possible source, but nevertheless warily, as to a potential liability.

"Bruises were found on her arms and throat and ribs that would suggest exactly that kind of forcible compulsion, as I'm sure you heard while you were still aboard ship on your way here? Yes... What you wouldn't have heard, because we've been keeping it quiet, is that such evidence is not unlike three other instances that have occurred in these islands. Though no one else was thrown over the rail of an inbound cruise ship; that's new and troubling, and we don't plan on letting people make a habit of it. But, chiefly for economic reasons, we do have a definite drug problem on the rise here of late; and over the past few years, yes, we have found three bodies dressed in similarly treated garments, similarly bruised and similarly dead of overdoses. And found floating in the middle of the channel between here and the B.V.I.s. On past form, we can only assume there are more. Perhaps many more."

"And have you also found any clues to go with these three bodies?" asked Turk, whose attitude had suddenly picked up all the condescension that Meryton's had lost.

"No, m'lord, I'm sorry to say we have not," said Meryton evenly, and turned the discussion back to what Rennie had seen on the ship, which information she was pleased to impart, equally evenly.

The rest of the interview, in Rennie's experienced estimation anyway, was a piece of cake. Well, as cakeish as a murder inquiry can get. Pleasant as he seemed, Meryton was at first encounter nowhere near as personable or perceptive as Detective Chief Inspector Gordon Dakers of New Scotland Yard—for whose dear cynical presence and whose dear pink Sergeant Alfred Plum Rennie felt a distinct pang of fond nostalgia. But she had promised Turk to behave herself, and she was punctiliously obeying her promise, taking a perverse joy in the flawless subservience of her conduct—and in knowing she was exasperating Ampman just the tiniest bit by behaving so, which was always fun.

After the double inquisition by the team of Tarrant lawyers and the cop delegation came a painstaking explanation by Sir Geoffrey of maritime law regarding homicide, the usual polite cop request for Rennie to stay in the neighborhood, and a little ripple of patronizing sexism when the Marquess of Raxton assured them that, being his official betrothed and in his lawful custody, she wasn't going anywhere. Rennie's eyes narrowed as his lordship spoke, but she didn't allow herself to be troubled by the chauvinism, which Turk had obviously tossed out there to exasperate her in turn—again, always fun.

Then, after an excellent afternoon tea had refreshed the participants, came Act Three: the Weezle and Tessman lawyers were shown in, for their turn at bat. They were a typical team of slick New Yorkers, Franz Haran and Larry Mavius, who were lawyers for not only the Weezles and the Tessmans, but for Ted Tessman's giant booking agency Tontine, and for the Weezles' label Isis and its president/owner Jack Holland as well, which all seemed a gigantic incestuous conflict of interest—though few in the rockerverse were inclined to call it so, certainly not publicly.

Rennie gave her award-winning performance all over again, with a different slant to it this time, a slant concerning Loya Tessman and her rather garish end. Mavius and Haran had a considerably dissimilar agenda to the Tarrant solicitors and to the police, naturally, being more concerned with what Rennie could tell them about their star client

Mr. Hoden's involvement. Which had been most minimal, as she made quite clear, and they accepted her word.

Not so much with Loya Tessman. Prior to her murder, she too had been smacked, ha, around—plenty of evidence for that. There was much general speculation as to why she'd been decked out like Paize Lee The Little Hippie Girl, but no real answers. Perhaps the cops were saving the big guns of evidence to fire at other targets, but Rennie merely recounted what she had seen and left them to make of it what they would.

Ted Tessman, the ostensibly sorrowing bereaved, did not show up at all. Which surprised everyone present but Rennie, who thought it was really bad form—*hey, it's your* wife, *you creep!*—but quite typical of the hulking yeti. No doubt the lawyers would fill him in later. When one came to think of it, there wasn't much real reason for him to be there, and his absence was being put down by most of those present to an understandable reluctance to rehash yet again the gory details of his wife's murder. Yeah, no.

More interesting was Jo Fleet's reaction. He had come in with Haran and Mavius, though he'd let them do all the talking, and merely sat in a corner, removed from the table, and just listened. Watched, also: Rennie, glancing at him every now and then, never caught him eyeing her directly, but when she was speaking to the two Weezle lawyers, she could see in a conveniently placed splendid cherrywood Georgian mirror that he studied her very carefully and covertly indeed. Huh. She assumed he had been separately interrogated by the cops, as he'd been aboard the ship himself and was responsible, at least in part, for the fan club activities—hence responsible for Sammi Stoyer's on-board safety. Responsible for everyone's safety, indeed, and a miserable failure in that respect.

She'd never spoken to him, neither aboard the *Excalibur* nor back in New York or anywhere else. It seemed odd, but there had never been any reason for their interaction and their paths had crossed only at a distance, at concerts and press parties and such. She'd certainly *heard* enough about him, though; none of it either flattering or good. Her joking name for him, Mephistofleetles, was not entirely in jest: his Luciferian deals were whispered about in the rockerverse, and the hapless minions who fell under his spell tried to live with their satanic bargains as best they might. You wanted a long spoon, of course, to sup with the devil. But sometimes the only spoon on offer was a short one. Not everyone came out as ahead as the Weezles. If you could call it "ahead."

Nine

AT LAST THE LAW PROCEEDINGS were concluded, with thanks and a bit of mild though quite unprofessional fannishness—nothing serious, just the indulgence of an autograph or two besought, embarrassedly, from Turk for various parties' teenage children, and Turk obliged with his usual grace. Congratulations were proffered to the happy couple on their engagement; then Will Knight courteously saw them to the street, taking en route a few good-humored jabs at Richard, as Cambridge to Oxford, and receiving a few back. Old friends, good friends; not employer and employee. Then the two of them were free, Rennie theatrically and not insincerely mopping her brow and fanning herself with her hat in sheer relief.

"Well, that was—interesting. I especially loved the part where I was declared your legal property. I thought there were no slaves on Lion Island."

" 'Charge'. You're my legal charge. We needed to do that in order to get you over to the island without cop intervention when you arrived in these waters, remember? And I had to be responsible for your conduct because it's, well, *you*, isn't it. Certified foreign journalistic annoyance as well as acknowledged future Tarrant. It's an official thing."

"So it is. Even so, you looked way too pleased, my lord, when they mentioned it back there."

"Did I? Well, now that *you* mention it, 'property' could

be fun...rather turns me on."

"In your dreams, Flash!"

"Maybe...but what do you think about what they know?"

Rennie grew reflective under her floppy pink straw hat. "I think they know a lot more than they're willing to share with us," she said at last. "The cops, I mean. It sounds to me as if there's some serious drug stuff going on around here, and from their questions they seem to think the cruise ship, or people aboard the cruise ship, could tie into it. Two things really stuck out—those other three bodies in the smack-bearing t-shirts, and how both our own victims were beaten up beforehand. I was thinking, maybe punishment of some sort? For serious and as yet unknown infractions?"

Turk looked intrigued. "There's a thought. I could see Loya being brutalized by her brutish husband, as we've all heard the gossip. But why would the groupie girl be so punished? How could she possibly have offended some mysterious drug ring thousands of miles from her usual location?"

"I haven't the slightest idea."

"Nor I. And yes, as Meryton begrudgingly admitted, there is indeed a drug problem, though nobody likes to 'fess up about it. Bad for the holidaying trade, you know; there have been several recent incidents that Phan mentioned to me, before you got down here. Tourists being mugged and robbed, their hotel or villa rooms burgled. All thought to be the work of druggies. Worrying stuff: these islands aren't exactly rich, so you can see where the robberies and thefts would come into it. Race and poverty as well. Wealthy white tourists wandering around, it's a plain temptation to some people who aren't white and some who are, especially when they can't afford to feed their families. We're so much luckier on our island, or rather we were so much cleverer about things, and avoided so many problems. But the Grand Palms depend heavily on tourists to bring in money. Very big money, and if these islands start to get the reputation of a seedy, dangerous place to visit, where the druggie natives will rob and even kill you as soon as look at you, and tourists start staying away in droves, that will affect the whole local economy. Even us, maybe."

He paused to peer into an art gallery window. "But if all this is indeed the case, I don't know how you're going to be able to do that little poking-around thing you usually do. And before you even ask, my deepest regrets, but no, my love, I am *not* going to help you. In fact, I can't. And I'm not wholly regretful, either... It's very different down here, as no doubt you've noticed. It's a foreign nation, and it does not wish to have annoying foreign journalists poking around in its own private murder cases. It's not like New York or even London. And I have to be more...aware of the status quo."

"And you're nothing *but* status here. Yeah, I know, I know. I won't embarrass you. As you said, I won't be able to do very much anyway."

"O me of little faith! I'm sure you'll do your best to prove me wrong, though. As always." But he was smiling when he said it.

They walked for a while in a comfortable silence, hand in hand down the insanely picturesque little brick-paved streets. Rennie looked around with interest. What a charming place Palmton was, at least in these historic touristy downtown parts: very few buildings above two or three stories, most of them either in the colonial architectural style or the native island vernacular. There was little that was grotesquely modern, and Rennie hoped that the advent of such abominations would be long delayed—instead, it was all coquina or brick, light pretty colors, breezeways and interior courtyards that opened inwards from wrought-iron gates. The streets were fully pedestrianized, though bicycles and pedicabs abounded, even the occasional horse-drawn carriage, and full of fascinating little shops and restaurants; there was a suitably impressive and well-preserved seventeenth-century castle, still quite functional, at the harbor entrance, and the streets were full of merry throngs off the cruise ships parked out in the bay or at the quays—the *Excalibur* was by no means the only liner that had recently docked.

But beyond the bright, prosperous, happy-tourist façade, Rennie quickly noticed that there was a poorer reality and an accompanying shabbier quarter of the city, populated by both whites and blacks, hidden carefully away from the visitors who brought their off-island money here to spend. As Turk had said, the island depended on the visitor trade; anything that threatened it would have to be stopped in its tracks. Which could bring about all sorts of unpleasantness. And this being a tourist town, Rennie kept a wary eye out for signs of Turk being recognized by any tourists.

"I'm having a thought, baggage," said Turk presently. "As long as we're already here, why don't we have dinner and stay over at the Palms Inn and head back to the island tomorrow afternoon? Phan has family outside town he can go and crash with, so he won't mind a bit; we can ring up Ares and Prax and let them know we're spending the night and not to worry. I'll take you shopping if you like; I think you deserve a present after all that—you did behave so well in your first official public appearance as a Lion Islander, not to mention as the future duchess. And you totally charmed the firm, which will be ever so useful in future, believe me. After shopping, we can have a nice seafood dinner, real Caribbean style—there's a ton of places where only the locals go."

"Mmm, shopping and food! Two of my three favorite things...and I'm just assuming of course but I do feel quite confident that I'll be offered the third when we get to the hotel? Yes, I thought as much. And I do deserve a reward, I really do, even though you offer it so condescendingly, Dimples. What have they got here to buy besides simple wholesome handcrafts? Not that there's anything wrong with those. Who can't always use yet another woven tote bag?"

"Do the words 'duty-free port' mean anything to you? But I was thinking more of some little shops I know. Home-grown artisans, pearls, coral, carved shell cameos made from local shells..."

Rennie perked up. "Jewelry is never a bad idea. I only hope we don't run into any of my curious fellow voyagers. Or any depraved reporters that might still be lurking about. Or any adoring fans of yours from the other ships. I *can* hope, surely?"

*

A hope forlorn. They were coming out of a goldsmith's studio an hour later, Rennie now wearing a strand of pink coral beads with a carved rose pendant, and sporting a tiny gold enameled conch on her charm bracelet to commemorate her first visit to these parts, when a loud, delighted hail came from behind them.

"Turk! Rennie!"

"Keep walking," she commanded, not turning her head. "It's fans or press or people off the ship, or off some ship. We don't know them. We don't hear them. We don't want them."

"RENNIETURK!"

"Too late." Turk put on the smile he kept for fans and press and people off ships, and turned them both round to face their accosters.

It turned out to be not only people they knew but people they actually liked: Belinda Melbourne and Laird Burkhart, holding hands themselves. And giving off the vibe of being a brand-new for-real beginning romantic item, Rennie noted with pleasure, not merely a shipboard one-nighter. Three-nighter. Well, that was nice to see, if perhaps rather quick work on both their parts. Then again, who was she to judge: she had moved into Turk's Hollywood Hills house—at his invitation—the morning after their first intimate encounter, and see how brilliantly *that* had worked out. Laird and Turk had never met before, but they knew one another by repute and also through Rennie's mutual praisefulness, and they strolled on ahead of the girls, already deep in guitar shoptalk.

"They're just so stunning, aren't they? So tall, so blond, so talented, such fantastic fingering technique..." Belinda glanced hopefully from the two men walking ahead to Rennie at her side, but Rennie wasn't biting. "I heard the fuzz were going to call you over for an interview," Belinda continued, deflated. "Did it go smoothly?"

"A little *too* smoothly, if you know what I mean. I am not to leave town, and we have lawyers in case we need them. Or in case anyone else needs them." She looked pointedly at her friend.

"You mean us? Well, maybe we do. We got a call from the cops ourselves. As did all the Weezles. To come in tomorrow and talk. That's what they always say on TV, isn't it? 'To assist the police with their inquiries.' Laird is in such a state, and so is Buck. We left the ship, you know—Laird was too freaked out to stay on board, and I didn't want him to. We—he got us a suite at the Palms Inn, very nice place. The Weezles are staying there too."

Amused and touched by Belinda's immediate and fierce protectiveness on Laird's behalf, Rennie considered his "state", and that of the Weezles as well. They were all rock stars and quite used to this sort of thing, they would already be girding their loins against police questioning, of course, but maybe... Ever since the beginning of her journalism career, people had been telling Rennie Stride things they would never have told anyone else. And she'd known Laird for years, after all.

"Any chance of me getting my mitts on a Weezle?" she asked. "I wonder if Laird could bag me one? I'd like to talk to it, alone and at length, no publicists or managers present.

Preferably a smart one. Which means Hoden or Luke. Preferably Hoden. It's all along of getting the band off the hook, I promise. And I want to talk to you and Laird as well. We're staying at the Palms tonight ourselves, but you can come back to Lion Island with us tomorrow after you talk to the coppers, and stay as long as you like."

"Well, you're the one who's known Laird since college," said her friend, pleased at the invitation. "Ask him yourself. All he can say is no. Though I bet he won't. Oh, and I accept your kind hospitality on my own behalf and his too. Man, I have *had* it with reporters."

Rennie grinned. "Just hate being on the other side of the fence, don't you, Belinda Starr? I know the feeling."

"I'm sure you do. I may have to change my career. You think forest ranger might be good?"

But Laird didn't say no, when she asked him over huge piles of stone crab claws at the fabulous hole-in-the-wall seafood place Turk took them to, and he promised her that he would certainly try his best to land Rennie a Weezle, though he couldn't make any other promises and everybody certainly understood that. And of course he and Belinda would be thrilled and delighted to be houseguests on Lion Island, and they also gratefully accepted Turk's offer of the Tarrant solicitors.

At around midnight Rennie got a phone call in the hotel suite. She and Turk hadn't gone to bed yet, and Turk took the call. Though he raised his eyebrows in mately reproof as he silently handed the phone over—it *was* kind of late for a chat—he vanished into the bedroom so she could talk in privacy.

A light, unfamiliar, English-accented voice. "Rennie? Is this Rennie Stride?"

"Yes, this is Rennie. Who's this, please?"

"Hoden. This is Hoden. From the Weezles? Laird Burkhart said I should talk to you. I'm staying here, at the hotel, at the Palms Inn. You are too. Can we talk? When could we talk?"

Ten

THE NEXT MORNING, Hoden showed up in the hotel restaurant patio as duly appointed, as Turk and Rennie were finishing a late and leisurely breakfast. He shied like a skittish colt when he saw Turk sitting there, not having expected him, but Turk diplomatically rose from the table and said he was going to pick up Phanuel, who had spent the night with his aunt and uncle in the hills above Palmton, and then go see some people here in town to discuss Lion Island business, he'd be back after lunch. He bent to kiss Rennie and was gone, nodding cordially at Hoden, who still seemed unable to move.

"Hoden. Come. Sit."

Rennie motioned to the empty place on her left, free of breakfast rubble. He came over a bit uneasily and sat, and she studied him from under her lashes. Another Englishman, a North Londoner, a slight youth a year younger and three inches taller than she was, wearing neatly ironed jeans and a touchingly clean new tourist-printed T-shirt; his dirty-blond hair was half-hidden under a floppy bucket hat and his tired hazel eyes were concealed by black Roy Orbison sunglasses, which he now took off in her presence, so as not to be rude.

Trying to be anonymous with the tourist look, she guessed, with sympathy. Fat chance! But she could see why millions of teenyboppers worldwide thought he was the cutest thing in two shoes: he looked like a Muppet. A sexy but non-challengingly-so teenage Muppet, although he had turned twenty-five back in January. Still, for all the unprepossessing and even cuddly air, there was real and keen intelligence in those eyes, and a certain wariness born of weary resignation to the lot of a manufactured idol. Right now he looked exhausted and desperate and living on his last nerve. Rennie immediately felt protective, and ordered him a plate of waffles and bacon and hash-browns and eggs.

"That was Turk Wayland," he said, staring at the seat that Turk had occupied across the table, and absently accepting a glass of chilled orange juice. "*Turk Wayland*. You're with *Him*. You're *His* lady."

Rennie sighed inwardly, hearing the caps and itals. God, even superstars could be groupies, if the idol was right... She saw it all the time: people who were themselves enormous famous huge honking worldwide celebrities being reduced, out of awe and sheer admiration, to dumbsquizzled fannish gibber in Turk's quiet though admittedly far from quotidian presence. Even off-duty, he radiated magic and sparkles and star quality. As a cynical journalist and native New Yorker, she was pretty much immune to that sort of thing; in fact, she couldn't think of anyone who could make her feel like that. Not the Beatles, not the Stones, not Graham or Prue Sonnet, not even Turk before she'd met him—respect, yes, esteem, also yes, adoration of the work, you bet; but mute drop-jawed groupie worship, no. Still, even Turk himself did the awed respectful fanboy thing on occasion, with ancient bluesmen whom few outside the chitlin circuit had ever even heard of, and that seemed right and proper. But she smiled now—as she had learned, as Turk had taught her.

"Yes. Yes it was. Yes I am."

"I didn't know. But—*Turk Wayland!*" He paused for breath, suddenly realizing how rude he sounded, and flustered around disarmingly as he collected himself. "I'm *so* sorry, Christ, I really do have better manners than that. But I didn't know he was with you. I mean, I know he's *with* you, I've read it in the papers, but I didn't...he never said who he was, when he answered the phone last night. Oh, not to suggest you'd be with any other guy! I didn't mean that at all. I just didn't think— And Laird didn't say he was here. I didn't see him on the ship, either. Turk, I mean."

"No, he didn't sail down with us," said Rennie, smiling acceptance of the apology and sympathy for the flusteredness. "He's been staying on his family's island, over on the other side of this one. I only joined him day before yesterday, when the ship docked here in Palmton. Prax McKenna and her boyfriend are there too, and Laird and Belinda are going back with us this afternoon."

Hoden looked relieved, though Rennie couldn't imagine why. "Burkhart. On the ship he got together with that Belinda—Melbourne, is it? Yes—I've read her stuff. She's been really nice to us, on the whole. Like you. Nicer than most. But she wasn't very impressed with 'Paize Lee', was she. No, you don't have to answer. Of course she wasn't. Neither were you. Neither am I, if you must know. But that's not why I wanted to talk to you."

He pulled off the bucket hat, revealing the dirty-blond hair to be smooth, clean, straight and shiny, like a well-groomed Victorian schoolboy's. Rocknroll Christopher Robin. It was cut just below his chin, and brushed his collar in the back; the label or the publicists had made him cut it for the cruise—for a while there it had been as long as Turk's, which was Viking-length. Part of the deal: the Weezles' reputation, the public one anyway, was that they were all squeaky-clean and free of normal rock star vices, and they maintained the front admirably. What went on behind the closed gates of their separate palatial L.A. estates, from Hoden's in the Malibu hills to Matt Cutler's in Pacific Palisades to Luke Woods' in Stone Canyon to Brian Moretti's in Beverly Glen, was quite another story. Many stories, actually. Strange stories. Exceedingly strange stories. Rennie'd heard enough, and seen enough, to know.

But at least here there was no gawking to contend with. The hotel's other guests hadn't batted an eye at either Turk or Hoden; indeed, they seemed quite accustomed to having big giant stars in their breakfasting midst, probably because so many of them were big giant stars themselves, having checked into the Palms Inn for their holidays or board meetings or movie shoots or whatever specifically *because* it was a sanctuary from gawkers.

Quite the guest list, though. From where Rennie sat, she could lob a papaya and hit at least half a dozen movie and TV stars, national politicians from several different countries, some super-rich business and society types, three European royals, a Nobelist novelist renowned for reclusivity and the most famous physicist in the world. Many of them were accompanied by supermodels or other stunning accessories, male, female and indeterminate, some of them lawful spouses, some of them not. Except for a few hyperexcited teenybopper Weezle worshippers being gently chided by their parents not to stare, nobody did any more than flick a politely incurious glance in their direction.

"We can do this any way you want, you know," said Rennie, when the silence had gotten slightly ridiculous and she could see that Hoden didn't know where or how to start. "You can tell me whatever you like, and if you want me to I can take it to the cops for you, or the lawyers, or I can keep it completely off the record and private between us and do my best to advise. Whatever makes you feel most comfortable. Either way, I'm good for it. Seal of the journalistic confessional. Laird will tell you."

He smiled, and it made him look like a totally different person. "Oh, he has. And so has Prax. She rang me up this morning, in fact, so I knew she's staying with you and Turk."

"I didn't know you knew Praxie," said Rennie, a little jealously.

"Years and years," he said, still smiling, reminiscently now. "In London. Before the Weezles. For my first little demo record, I needed a chick backup singer. She'd have to multitrack the vocals because I could only afford one singer, and I couldn't pay a lot anyway. Prax needed even the pitifully few quid I *could* pay her, so she did the session work. I was sixteen, and she was, what, a year older and in England on a visitor's visa. Anyway, we got to be friends, good friends. Then my girlfriend left me for her."

"Oh dear."

"Not Prax's fault. We—Micheline and I—were breaking

up anyway. They spent three months in Morocco and came back separately, and Prax went home to San Francisco. We all stayed friends, and Michie's married now, with a beautiful little boy—I'm godfather. I'm so happy Praxedes has done so well, career-wise; she deserves it. It would be nice to see her again."

"Hoden? *Eat,*" said Rennie gently, pointing at the hugely laden plate the waiter had just unobtrusively set down, and he stared with blank surprise, then began to stuff like somebody who hadn't seen food for days. Which quite possibly he hadn't—too upset to eat, poor lamb.

She watched, and pushed tea and more bacon when his plate was beginning to look rather bare. Well, he'd probably been so worried about the cruise, then freaked about the stupid opera, then even more freaked over the murders, that he'd forgotten about tiny details like eating and sleeping.

"That was *good,*" he said presently, now a happy member of the clean-plate club and looking much more human. Then, suddenly: "Did you know Sammi Stoyer and Loya Tessman?"

Well, at least he knew their names. That's more than most other rockers would have... Rennie looked uncomfortable.

"I did, and I didn't much care for either of them, God forgive me. We had a few run-ins. Stoyer, you may remember, made all those vile and utterly untrue insinuations about her 'romance' with Turk, and Tessman published them in her pestilential little fanrag. Names removed, of course, for libel purposes, but the personal details made it quite clear who was meant. Sammi was stupid and snotty and bitchy, but Loya was cunning and snotty and bitchy. Especially to

Turk, and I couldn't be having with that. Why do you ask?"

"She was jealous that you're with Turk," said Hoden matter-of-factly, and Rennie noted that he didn't answer her question. "They both were." At her look: "Why does that surprise you? I'm sure it's happened before. In all modesty, I've had some episodes not unlike that myself. I mean, my girlfriends have, putting up with that sort of thing. It seems to go with the job. But I'm unattached at the moment. Good thing, too: having a bird around right now would only complicate this nightmare. Though if I could find some really smart chick... Is there any toast, could I—oh, ta."

Rennie had raised a summoning hand, and a waiter shimmered over with a fresh stack. Hoden munched two hot, buttered and perfectly browned slices quietly and efficiently, while Rennie lounged and gave him the space and the silence to feel at ease. Then he leaned back in his cushioned wrought-iron armchair, well under the table canopy's shade, drank some more tea and began to talk.

Generic music biz-stuff at first, then more specifically Weezle grievances: with the label, with the critics, with the fans. Rennie let him rattle on until he felt clearly comfortable, then began to ask the questions she'd had in mind, the ones she'd requested this meeting to get answers to.

"The cruise?" Hoden shook his head until the bangs flew. "No, it wasn't our idea. The record company and Jo Fleet wanted us to make nice with, no offense, critics and journalists, and especially to do the bloody damn rock opera—Christ, I can't even call it that without wanting to heave."

He stared at his empty plate, then took another long swig of tea. "How would *you* feel, being pushed into this bogus group, not being able to choose your own bandmates, not being allowed to play the way you know you can? None of us were; the only thing we were allowed to use were our faces and voices and Luke's and my songwriting skills. They wanted us to be totally dependent on their permissions, for the fans to think we all magically happened—no hard slog, just trippy fairy pixie dust. Not thinking for a minute that I'm Turk or Clapton or Jimi, but I *am* reasonably good, and I only ever wanted to play for myself, *like* myself—not too much to ask, surely. So you go out there and try to play for real, and the rest of your band work like navvies to become real musicians, and all of us are now, and always were really, a hell of a lot better than we get credit for... How would *you* feel, having done all that, for yourself and your bandmates and your fans, trying to be honest, only to find that nobody wants any part of it? 'Just *be* cute and *stay* cute, lads, that's all anyone expects, nobody wants you to be actual artists—not the audience, not the press, not the label, probably not even your old ladies. Nobody cares about your art but you.' Christ, the Monkees didn't know the bleedin' *half* of it."

Rennie wasn't particularly shocked by the strength or the nature of his pent-up anger; she'd seen too much of that sort of thing, far too many artists snake-bit by their own handlers, to be surprised, or to pretend she didn't know whereof he spoke.

"So you chartered the ship because—"

"Because Fleet and Tessman insisted, as I said, and we

caved." Hoden signaled their waiter for fresh tea. "It cost a packet, but as a business expense it was cheap. And under any other circumstances, it might have been a smart idea."

"It *was* a smart idea. Little showcases like that to introduce new music: I bet other bands will be doing that sort of thing down the road. Creedence Clearwater is planning a showcase of their own for December, in fact, at their place Cosmo's Factory in Oakland; I'm invited. It's very effective. We—I'm speaking as a critic now—we liked your old stuff, but your music really has changed, and very much for the better. It's real art, the things on the new album, where before it was just catchy tunes, and you deserve to have it heard. And it *has* been heard. *We* heard it. *Fans* heard it. And *more* fans will hear it, a *lot* more. It'll be talked about and written about, Hoden, I promise you, and it may take a while, but I think you'll find your audience will end up coming with you where you want to take them. Well, except for 'Paize Lee,' maybe."

Hoden looked embarrassed but also pleased. "We wrote that thing years ago, Luke and I, when we were young and dumb. Ted and Jo recently found out about it, and then it all—happened. It was like trying to outrun an avalanche downhill. We couldn't stop it." He took a long beat. "You know? I still think it could have worked, if we'd been able to tinker with it enough. It wasn't a bad idea at first. It didn't start really sucking until Jo Fleet got his crap-encrusted paws on it. It was all about control, of course. As usual with him. We had all this new material we're really proud of, and we wanted to play it for you lot, in hopes you'd write about it, and yet we were forced practically at gunpoint to do that rubbishy thing."

"So, they talked you into the cruise. You did get to play some things you wanted biz people to hear, and very, very good they were; and then you were forced to perform the musical. For—well, for what? Or for whom? Publicity? Is that all?"

"Not for the band's best interests, that's for sure. For their own. To keep us under their thumb. Tossing us a bone or two so we don't bite the feeding hand too hard. What they forget is that *we're* the ones bringing the meaty bones to the dish."

He paused, stared at his plate, then looked up straight at Rennie. "This is what I wanted to tell you: we think they're into some kind of dodgy scheme, and the cruise was something *they* needed, not we needed. Jo Fleet needed, mostly. We had a regular fan club, but he set up this special *super* fan club. 'The Weezle Den', God help us. It's not exclusive, anyone can join if they pay the fee—and it's a *lot*, especially for young fans who don't have much bread—but you do have to be invited in through a current member. It's mostly older fans, or kids with rich parents. The club members get special perks like personally autographed t-shirts and bags and hats, a private lounge at concert venues, photo ops with the Weezle of your choice, parties where we have to show up and mingle. There was even a contest in Loya's magazine, as you know, for fans to come along on the cruise and get to hang with us a little."

"What's wrong with that? More bands should have that kind of thing going for fans, though this one sounds rather posher than most. Maybe Turk should try to get Lionheart to run something along those lines."

"Nothing's wrong with it, not really. And if it *were* only a posh fan club, we'd happily do it. Part of the job, right? But we think it's not all on the up-and-up. We think they're skimming off our take. Some of them. Or all of them. They're up to something, some illegal fiddle, and they're using us to work it."

"That's a serious charge. How do you figure?"

Hoden gave her a look. "We may be a stupid phony rock band, but we're not stupid phony people. Neither are you. I've heard all about you, and not just from Laird and Prax."

Rennie raised her brows. "Ah. Well, you of all people should know not to believe everything you hear."

To her surprise, he burst out laughing. It made him look about twelve, and the sheer delight of the sound made heads turn and people smile all around the terrace. "Very true! Still, we've all been reading you, and reading *about* you, for quite a few years now, haven't we. Prax and the Fillmore murders; and, oh yes, let's see, Baz Potter and that little groupie kid and that ratbag Pierce Hill at Monterey, and that guy at Airplane House, and Turk and Tansy in L.A., and Dandiprat at the Albert Hall with that bastard hanging from the chandelier and Gray Sonnet getting shot, and poor Celandine Vervain, you know she made clothes for us too, and the Stones at Hyde Park with Moggy Barnes, and Cory Rivkin and little Amander Watson at Woodstock, and that studio trip with you clobbering Andy Starlorn, how excellent was *that*, and the rock-critic weekend on Block Island, and probably a few more I've missed—"

"Please. I'm blushing. Okay, we all know murder is my

sideman—what makes you think I can help you here?"

Hoden looked at her with all his good brave soul in his eyes. "If you can't, no one can," he said simply. "Besides, you hated Loya and Sammi. Laird told me. You said so yourself. And *we* hate Jo and Ted. Maybe it's all connected. And nobody's got more connections than you. Wouldn't you like to find out who killed them?"

"So I can give him a bouquet of roses and a medal and a big fat kiss?"

He looked deeply scandalized. "Tessman was *strangled*. Someone pushed the groupie girl *overboard*."

"I know. I'm sorry." She could hear Turk in her head: 'He's just a kid, Ravenna Catherine, go easy on him.' But that kid was her own age and a superstar, even more famous than Turk was, and he had made some desperately serious allegations; going easy on him wasn't going to help anybody.

"Come on," she said gently, getting up from the table. "Let's take a walk on the beach."

Three hours later Turk returned, saw them sitting side by side in the well-landscaped shade beside the hotel pool, looking completely at ease, and detoured over to join them. He dropped a kiss on Rennie's head and a shell bracelet he'd bought for her at a street stall into her lap, and stretched out on the chaise next to her, with Hoden on her other side. They all chatted volubly and professionally for a while, and Rennie was relieved to see that Hoden had overcome his initial shyness and awe of Turk and was behaving like a normal human being. A normal rock star, anyway. And a very nice one too.

He made his departure abruptly, shy again, thanking Rennie for breakfast and their talk, nodding to Turk, and they watched him walk away down the path among the flowering shrubberies. Their relief was short-lived: no sooner had Hoden disappeared across the hotel's broad veranda and gone in at the glass doors than a shadow fell across the terrace. Rennie tilted her head under her hat brim and looked up, and Turk, unusually for him, didn't even bother to rise from where he sat, as soon as he saw who it was.

"Hello, Rennie, Turk," said Jo Fleet, and sat down on Hoden's vacated chaise. "How nice to find you here."

Smiling at them both impartially, Fleet signaled to the hovering waiter and ordered some fancy, fruit-infested cocktail in a giant ice-filled glass. "This is one of my favorite hotels; their chefs are marvelous. But I never get down here enough for my liking. I spent the day sport-fishing, landed the biggest tarpon I've ever seen. Rennie, we didn't get a chance to talk aboard ship…"

Man, not even a cross-fade transition! Just a graceless hard splice… "No," she said evenly, "we never did, did we." She gestured around her. "And then all this came down."

"Which is what I really wanted to talk to you about." He shifted on the padded chaise. "I'd be very interested in what your thoughts were on what—happened."

Rennie leaned back, as he had leaned forward, and shrugged, the effect chiefly in her eyebrows. "You were there. On the ship. You saw everything I saw. Probably more. You were also at the lawyers' office yesterday and heard it all, from me and the cops alike. You didn't have anything to say then. Why ask me now?"

A condescending smile and a sip of the nasty-looking drink. "Why? Because you're Murder Chick, of course. As we all know. Just because we may have seen and heard the same things doesn't mean that the things were the same for the both of us. I didn't want to ask you in front of everyone yesterday. I thought you might have some ideas of your own that you'd want to share privately."

No. "Oh, I've got a few," said Rennie coldly. "But nothing I feel comfortable discussing. What about you, though? Since you kept everything to yourself yesterday? Any insights on the Weezle front you feel like offering?"

When Jo Fleet didn't respond at once, Rennie's eyes went sharply to his face. *What's going on inside that predator brain, Fleet? Because I am sure as hell not going to give you any more ideas than are already buzzing around in there. And did you see Hoden leaving and are you trying to find out what we talked about, or are you just fishing for more than tarpon...*

"I'm worried about those boys," he said at last. "Hoden and the other three. I didn't want to mention it in front of the good detectives, not to mention the shysters, but there's a few things that were bothering me all the way down from New York."

Yeah, I'll bet there were. "Really. What sort of things might those be?"

"You may have heard that the Weezles started up a little fan club a couple of years back? For fans willing to pay a premium for private access to the lads? Nothing tacky, just some parties before and after big concerts, preferred seating at the big arena shows, fan letters and raffles, advance releases, personal letters, Weezles special limited-edition merch, whatever. Pricey, but a lot of the kids have wealthy parents willing to fork out, and older fans can afford it on their own. It's worked very well so far: we get a nice extra income stream to reinvest, not that they need it, of course, but more importantly there's a buzz created. Keeps the band in front of the fans' awareness and keeps the fans interested and happy with the band."

"We're familiar with the club," said Turk in a lazy, drawling voice, eyes narrowed; he didn't like the fact that Jo Fleet had presumed to sit next to Rennie, and was wanting nothing more than to get protectively between his lady and the invader. Lazy and drawling became outright condescending. "It's nothing we'd ever do *ourselves*, of course; but I can certainly see where *you* might want to make something of it."

As Fleet began to bristle in his turn, Rennie spoke quickly, to cover the moment. "It's a good idea, and more bands should do it. There's hardly ever any merchandise around but the odd t-shirt or button, and even those are mostly cheap little things produced by head shops in the Village. Once in a while a label will rustle up something nice, but even those—Jethro Tull t-shirts, Turnstone granite paperweights—are reserved for publicity handouts to critics and writers, not for fans. There was a neat little Jefferson Airplane flight bag that RCA put out a couple of years back—I still have it, in fact, along with Grace Slick's gold lamé shoes that she gave me after a photo shoot. Lionheart's never done anything along those lines, have they, honey?"

Turk saw perfectly well what she was going for, and

played right along, as smoothly as if they had planned it. "Why, no, we never have. Perhaps we should do, do you think?"

Fleet looked at them both eagerly, his annoyance apparently forgotten. "If you ever decide you want to, I can put your people in touch with the guys who handle it for us, or Ted Tessman can. Aren't you with Tontine yourself, Turk? Lionheart, I mean. Yes… Most of Teddy's acts have something like that going on, and it works really well. You wouldn't be sorry."

We're already sorry. "I'm sure it works quite well," said Rennie, with a condescending little smirk of her own. "But getting back to the two deaths, what did you think I could tell you?"

"You being such an observant person, I was wondering if you'd noticed anything…off."

"You mean something I didn't tell the lawyers and the cops yesterday? Are you accusing me of concealing evidence, Mr. Fleet?" Rennie put on a mock-chiding voice, wanting to see how he'd take it.

"No! Of course not! That would be the last thing on my mind," said Fleet, protestingly, but also reluctantly.

"Yes. I can see that."

"Are you going to be down in these parts for a while, do you think?" Turk interposed. Though his expression was carefully, casually blank, Rennie could see exactly what he was thinking: *Oh Christ, what a large nasty blight on my beautiful islands…*

Fleet gazed back at him, calculatingly. "For as long as it takes to sort this out. The boys too. In fact, I need to speak to them. We won't be going anywhere." He rose to leave, leaving the distinct impression he wanted to keep an eye on them both.

"Say hi to them for us," said Rennie as he walked away. "We won't be going anywhere either."

"So, what do you *really* think?" asked Rennie, after they had checked out of the hotel and were in the air again, with Phanuel at the controls of the seaplane, and Laird and Belinda and their luggage tucked into two rear seats, headed out on the short hop back to Lion Island. After their encounter with Jo Fleet, they'd discussed it up in their hotel room as they gathered up the results of Rennie's shopping spree before flying home; she'd filled Turk in on her previous conversation with Hoden, at greater length than before, and now she was eager to hear some conclusions.

Turk was gazing out the window at the passing scenery he knew so well. "About what?"

She hit his arm, and he laughed. "About *Hoden*, of course! What he said to us. And what Jo Fleet said to us. That there's maybe something creepy and bad going on."

"Oh, I'm quite sure there is. And perhaps even to do with Fleet—who can say? But how do you think it connects to the murders?"

Before Rennie could answer, Belinda thrust her face between their seats from behind. "I bet I know! You didn't ask me, your lordship, but I bet I can tell you."

Laird pulled her back into her seat beside him, with a certain proprietorial air. They'd had their own session with the cops and the Weezle lawyers, under the eagle eye of the

Tarrant solicitors and the aegis of the Tarrant name, and now were positively giddy with release.

"Don't be doing that. You're as bad as Strider."

"Did you hear him, Strider?" asked Belinda, mock-outraged. "That was a put-down!"

"Not a bit," said Rennie comfortably, cuddling into Turk's side for the remaining minutes of the flight. "It was a compliment."

Eleven

On the shady side of the beach pavilion in Silver Bay, where she lay reclining on a lounge chair under the vine arbor, Rennie set aside the local Palmton newspaper. Picking up a pair of binoculars from beside her chair, she trained them a quarter-mile offshore, where the waves were breaking on the coral reef. Turk was surfing with Phanuel and Ares, and she smiled to see them. Man, they were so good to look at: a trio of veritable ocean godlings, one dipped in dark bronze, one in glowing copper, one in bright light gold, all with long hair flowing in the surf breeze—brown, black, blond.

She sipped from a bottle of water, cold from the picnic ice chest they'd brought, watching her mate with possessive contentment and a kind of vague nonspecific lust. At almost six-four and two hundred and ten pounds, Turk had always been a tall, powerful man, not tiny and weedy like so many of his fellow Brit guitarists. With Ares' encouragement over the past couple of years—since the L.A. groupie murders, in fact—he'd started working out, and his consort very much approved of the results. Daily surfing here for the past two weeks before she'd joined him hadn't hurt, either, giving him a pleasing bit of a tan and bleaching his hair to solar blond. Thanks to the workouts, his arms, always well-defined from years of playing, not to mention schlepping amps and equipment in Lionheart's long-ago starving-musician days, now looked strong enough to break reefs; muscles rippled across his chest and shoulders, his thighs were like the Colossus of Rhodes, his...

Okay, kitten, cool off, let the man surf the waves for a while, he can surf you *again later...*

Turk was really good on a board, which she had known from their time at the Malibu beach house and, later, the new Maui place. He'd educated her eye for surf: the smoothly breaking waves here weren't humongous or gnarly—Caribbean swells didn't get Hawaii-high, although distantly passing hurricanes could make them pop and stand up double-overhead when they hit the reefs. But today the corduroy was on: the long, clear green, seven-foot tubes rolling in today, one after another, were textbook, and it was pleasant to watch the three tall, well-built figures dropping in and cutting back, in and through and out of the glassy curls. They certainly weren't hard on the eyes, either: hunky guys in swim trunks were never a bad thing. Ares had even been a sponsored semipro: in his UCLA years, he'd ruled the SoCal waves from Trestles to Malibu First Point, before founding Argus Guardians and going into the celebrity bodyguard business instead.

Thinking of the bodyguard business led her, naturally, to thinking of bodies—the shipboard murders. For they were both officially murders now, according to the blaring headlines in that day's Grand Palm Gazette, which one of the housemaids had brought in to Rennie and Turk with their morning tea, and which Rennie had brought down here to peruse more closely. The Palmton crown coroner had confirmed the ship's doctor's statement that bruises not consistent with falling overboard had been found on Samantha Stoyer's throat, face, side and arms; but there had been no mention of the heroin poisoning—apparently it was still being kept back from the public, at least for the moment. And of course there had never been any doubt about Loya's having been deliberately killed—strangled doesn't often happen accidentally, and being tied to a deckchair, with bruises covered up by makeup, invariably doesn't. But who? And why? And what, if anything, did it have to do with the Weezles?

But the bombshell headline lead was that the coroner had found more than bruises and ligature marks and makeup: Loya Tessman had indeed been strangled—crushed hyoid bone, petechiae, all the signs—but under all that, her throat had been slit.

Rennie shivered as she scowled at the story in the light of this hideous new knowledge, trying to read between the lines, but nothing was waving its little hand at her. *God, how horrible.* Though at least Loya wouldn't have suffered much, or for long. According to the newspaper account, it had been an expertly applied wire garrote: she would have lost consciousness almost immediately, and hopefully had never seen it coming. The rest was merely ghastly: her throat had been almost sliced through, and she had bled out. *And you'd think that Detective Chief Superintendent Meryton might have mentioned it to me, wouldn't you! Yes. You would. Since clearly they'd known it for days.*

She tried to remember if there had been a lot of blood on the clothes and deck chair and deck, and on the whole thought not—she would surely have noticed. But she'd been in semi-shock, along with Belinda and Laird, and despite her extensive experience, shock was quite possibly interfering with her accurate recall. If no blood, though, that argued for either post-mortem butchery or the deed done elsewhere, because if it had been done in place before Loya was dead, there would have been blood enough to paint the decks a nice semi-gloss crimson. Only nothing like that had been reported, and even mighty threatenings would not have kept so gruesome an outcome as that apart from public knowledge.

She settled back to read more of the sidebar stories. There was an inane statement from Pig Blue, hired head of security for the cruise, blah blah, nothing there, so typical of that musclebound idiot ex-roadie ex-Hells Angel; a canned comment from Jack Holland of Isis, with the unmistakable stench of publicist all over it; something smooth and smarmy from those well-dressed sharks Haran and Mavius. Ah, here was a bit from Detective Chief Superintendent Meryton, not exactly illuminating, by any means—which was of course his intention. At least Sir Geoffrey Shipsterns was sticking to a terse "No comment" when asked about his client the future Lady Raxton and her involvement. As well he should—discretion was what the Tarrant family paid him so handsomely for.

Rennie scowled some more. *I have* got *to find out more than the pathetic little bit I know, and my sources here are ever so thin and lacking*... Of course, she could always ring up Fitz in New York, at the Sun-Trib—he might be back from the Dordogne by now, the snail-scarfing, wine-swigging little rat—and ask him to have his editor, her old friend and partner in crime reportage Ken Karper, poke into things from that end, as was their usual custom. Still, how many sources could Ken have down here? Not a lot, if any, though he might have some at the mainland end...worth asking, maybe.

She was never going to get anything out of local officialdom, not unless she asked Turk to lean on people with all the weight of his standing in these islands, and she didn't want to do any more of that than they'd already done. Besides, he'd already firmly told her that he couldn't and wouldn't. Oh, if she whined enough, or pulled a Lysistrata and refused to, uh, *accommodate* him, he'd probably oblige her, but he wouldn't be happy about it. It wouldn't be fair on him, and she'd suffer from a sex boycott as much as he would. So best not to even ask. It was becoming abundantly and annoyingly clear that if she was going to find out anything at all, it was going to be serendipitous in the extreme. And maybe she still wouldn't find out a damn thing, and she would have to be satisfied with that.

In rage and despair she flung the newspaper to the sand, then looked around to clear her head. At present she was accompanied in her pleasant situation by Prax, Laird and Belinda, who as one had turned up their noses at surfing or even swimming, preferring to laze and snooze under the palms in the pavilion's sun and shade; after a while, Rennie gave in and nodded off likewise. When the surfers finally hauled out and joined them, and were showering off the salt before sitting down to lunch, Rennie, awake again, had a question—for a change, nothing to do with murder.

"I don't think you ever told me, honey—where the hell

did you learn to surf? England doesn't have a great and long-standing hang-ten tradition, as far as I know."

It troubled no one that, apart from a towel or two, most of them were stark naked. Turk, Ares and Phanuel were the only ones who'd had any clothes on—colorful board shorts to protect their manly bits from the coral reef—and they'd pulled those off as soon as they got under the outdoor shower. Except for inside the house and trips away from the house, or wrapping up if it got a little chilly or to fend off a sunburn, and even then it was a sarong or kurta at most, no one had bothered overmuch with clothes outdoors since their arrival.

Hey, they were on a private tropical island, outside most of the day in private beaches and coves, no one around but them. If they wanted to wear nothing but sunscreen, that was their prerogative. They were, after all, rocknrollers, veterans of festivals and backstages coast to coast, not to mention hanging out at each other's houses and other rocknrollers' houses. Nekkidness was a yawn. Everyone had beheld everyone else in the altogether plenty of times, they'd seen it all before; and the group nudity wasn't in the least bit a turn-on. Clothes would have been a lot sexier. Besides, nobody loved a tan line.

"Where'd I learn to surf? Right out there on that reef," said Turk, smiling at her as he toweled off. "We've been going out since we were, what, six, Phan?"

"Just about," his friend said, flopping down on a chaise in the shade and happily accepting the thick sandwich—brown-sugar-crusted Silver Bay ham, courtesy of the local pigs and cane fields, homemade bread and butter and cheese—and the cold bottle of island beer that Belinda proffered from the cooler. "Every summer and a couple of hols a year. We learned together. Our mothers screamed endlessly at us to stay out of the waves—'Oooh it's so dangerous, barracudas stingrays sharks jellies urchins poison fish reef rash you'll cut yourselves to pieces on the coral, why can't you boys swim in the lagoon where it's nice and calm and safe'—but 'safe' wasn't what interested us. We didn't care a pin, not even when we came home all banged up and bloody from bodysurfing the reef and our mums whaled on our little gremmie behinds and patched us up and sent us to bed without our supper. It was totally worth it."

Turk grinned reminiscently and took a deep hit off his own bottle. "My grandfather finally gave in and bought us boards and hired some of the island watermen to teach us properly. Didn't stop us from getting even chancier. Almost every scar I've got or bone I ever broke—this is where it happened. Good times! Anyway, I stopped counting stitches at a hundred. Phan has more."

"It's nothing to be proud of!" said Belinda, laughing. "But I can see you learned very well. So, you've lived here all your life, Phanuel?"

She and Rennie were passing more sandwiches to the boys, and Rennie fired an orange at the dozing Prax, still snoring daintily in a hammock a dozen feet away, to wake her up.

The islander nodded. "The Shines have been here as long as the Tarrants. We're pirate stock too, but we were never slaves. None of the island families were, thanks to

Ironhand and Madelon, who both must have been a trip and a half. Anyway, my parents made me go to Cambridge when the old Duke offered to send me, for a degree in land economy—there being no courses in it at the other place." He grinned tauntingly at Turk, who grinned back. "After that, I studied in Bermuda and Jamaica and Hawaii, and learned as much as I could about tropical estate management and ocean farming and anything else that could help Lion Island. That's where I met Marigo, in Jamaica, and we got married there three years ago. And then I came home for good."

"Upon which my father promoted his father to new projects and development, and, despite the fact that Phan went to the other place, made him island manager," said Turk lightly.

"Guv'nor put a bunch of noses out of joint when he did, man," said Phanuel.

Turk shrugged. "Not your problem, my friend. Or mine either."

Prax, who had indignantly snorted her way to wakefulness when the missile orange struck her amidships, was now eating it out of one hand and with the other foraging in the cooler for some kind of sandwich besides ham, of which she was not fond.

"How did the island come to be settled in the first place?" asked Belinda, hooking a roast beef on rye with local honey mustard and handing it to her.

Phanuel lay back and draped a towel over himself neck to ankles, against the breeze which blew cool in the pavilion's shade, and assumed a lecturing mode.

"Ironhand came here with his crew, including my ancestor Martin Shine, who was his first officer and closest friend. They were brand-new in the pirate trade, and they needed someplace where they could put in and hide their ship and safely live—a base of operations. When Ironhand found this island, it was totally uninhabited, and he claimed it for himself. He didn't waste any time settling his crew here—whites, blacks, Asians, Indonesians, South Sea islanders, all the people he'd picked up on his voyages, local Indian tribesfolk as well. Nobody gave a damn what color they were, as long as they were good at what they did. As the operation got more successful, there were more ships, and more hands needed to crew them, and farmers to grow food, and docks and warehouses to handle the legitimate trade, and shipwrights and chandlers to build and repair the ships and all the stuff the ships needed. And Ironhand encouraged them all to start families here, or bring them from wherever they had them. Pretty soon we had quite a homeplace going."

Turk nodded, smiling. "He wasn't the duke yet, so he could still play pirate king to his heart's content. Being a second son—therefore 'Lord Richard', not 'Marquess of Raxton'—he didn't inherit the big title until his elder brother died very young without a son of his own."

Rennie shook her head. "I still say it's a horrible way to get a job, waiting around for a close family member to die."

"It's how we do things," he said imperturbably. "Anyway, Ironhand kept up privateering even after he became His Grace, with the enthusiastic approval of the then monarch. Then Madelon Buckmaster crossed his bows—quite literally, she actually fired on him in mutual pursuit of a prize. When the cannon smoke had cleared, they took one look at each other and promptly fell over backwards with love, having decided instantly that each other was the real prize. They got married, and her crew came here to live too. Ironhand made a stupendous payoff to the Crown to make sure the Tarrant claim and title could never be challenged. While he was at it, he also cleverly grabbed Little Lion, Tienda, Vetiver and Springhouse Cay, the four biggest of the small islands between here and the Grand Palms, as a sort of buffer zone, and to hide loot on. Also some small cays sprinkled about over on the Anguilla side. About a dozen islands altogether, all legally his—yes, all right, *ours*—from then on. Officially the Lion Islands."

Movement on the beach path down from the house, among the green leaves and bright flowers and thick tangles of vines: Marigo, barefoot, looking like an island goddess in a colorful cotton shift, her hair turbaned up in a bright scarf and her smooth cocoa skin gleaming in the sun. Everyone greeted her cheerfully, and Rennie pushed sandwiches on her, which she smilingly declined in her lilting Grenadian voice.

"No t'anks, pretty lady, I been cooking for past two hours, sampled more'n cooked, I t'ink. But we have nice rib roast for supper, and fruit pie for pudding... Dere was some phone calls: let us see, two for Lord Richard, t'ree for Lady Rennie, one each for Mistah Laird and Missy Prax. I got deh names, you want hear?" Four heads shook a vigorous negative. "Nah, 'course you don't—well, good for you, den! Now I go in for swim."

She spoke briefly to her husband, then strolled thirty paces to the warm waters of the reef-protected lagoon, unconcernedly stripped off her shift and slipped in like a sleek tropical seal, splashing and gliding through the gentle waves. Turk and Ares put their shorts on again, picked up their boards and went back out to catch a few last sets while the swell was still on, Phanuel lazily declining and stretching out on the chaise next to Rennie.

"I'm glad he found you, sistah," said Phanuel after a long, companionable silence, as they watched the two surfers compete good-naturedly for a wave to drop in on. "I was beginning to worry he'd never meet his match."

Rennie kept her eyes on Turk, amused. "I don't think his lordship ever lacked for female company."

He grinned. "Female company? Maybe not, though he was always pretty picky. But female *companionship*—no, Richard never had that until you came along."

"Not everybody feels as you do," said Rennie, laughing, though his comment had deeply touched her. "In fact, it's been said that I'm the Grim Reaper's groupie and I'll be the death of Turk yet. Or the death of us both. We've both almost gotten killed several times over, you know, because of what I do."

"Almost doesn't count."

Out on the wave, Turk looked majestic and graceful and studly as hell as he carved the glassy face, and they watched him in silence for a bit.

"I didn't feel it the first time we met," she said after a while. "At Monterey, you know, with him? Maybe because Tansy Belladonna had already grabbed him, and she was one of my best friends—though he didn't stay grabbed for long, Tanze being the fickle little hummingbird she was. Luckily for me. But I absolutely thought he was the most amazing guitarist who'd ever strapped on a Strat—as indeed I still do. And of course I thought he was extremely nice to look at. As indeed I also still do. But when we *really* met, just us, seven months later—that horrible night when Tansy was murdered at the Whisky—yeah. That was pretty much it. And then the first night we were together, a week later, after Tanze's funeral, he asked me to move in with him the next morning."

"Did he? I didn't know that. But I'm not surprised. Richard's always known exactly what he wants. Even in the face of opposition. Hell, *especially* in the face of opposition. Look at how he managed to defeat his parents and grandparents to get to do what he wanted with his own life—and let me tell you, that old Duke was one tough bastard. And his mum, the fair Agatha, is even worse. Woman is terrifying. But she fiercely loves her boy, and Richard—he's a real artist. He knew he had no business just sitting around waiting to be a duke himself."

"No... He's also a real guy. And I mean that in the best possible sense. I can't *believe* I'm telling you this... For a chick, I present my energy in a very masculine way, a strong yang way, but he out-yangs me all to hell, and yet he's got this incredibly subtle and gentle and totally non-girly yin vibe going on too, which brings out every last ounce of yin *I've* got. I didn't come up with that on my own," she added, smiling. "My annulled husband's present wife explained it all to me a few years back."

"Sounds like a very wise lady."

"Oh, she is, and a million times better for Stephen—my ex—than I could ever have been, even if I'd stayed with him. Which I was never going to do. And then of course I met Turk, and Stephen and I got annulled, so I'd never been his wife at all, which always seems like some kind of violation of the space-time continuum... But when Turk asked me to live with him, I was so staggered and so thrilled and so happy that I couldn't say yes like a normal person, could I? No, instead I said 'Let's just see how the night goes first.' Here he makes me this gorgeously romantic offer and I put him down for it. I wouldn't have blamed him if he'd kicked me out of bed right there. But that was me trying to save face, to not look too eager or too easy. I was already madly in love with him. I already knew I would."

"So did he," said Phanuel, smiling. "Why do you think he asked?"

They were quiet and comfortable with each other for a while, watching the surfers sitting chatting in the lineup as they waited for a good set to roll in. Then Phanuel: "I know you're probably really tired of talking about it, but what do you really think about the murders? Especially this new information about Loya Tessman having had her throat cut—yes, I read the papers earlier this morning."

She sighed. "I think—I think I don't really know *what* I think? Unlike my usual crime venues, I can't do a lot, maybe not anything, to check it out. Not that anyone ever actually *asks* me to, of course; it just sort of happens, I kind of fall into it. This is a foreign country: the murders happened at sea, but they come under Grand Palm jurisdiction. Except for my friends, I know the people on the ship in only a fairly superficial way and I don't have any personal clout down here but Turk's, by association. I would never ask him to help—I wouldn't do anything to cloud his standing in these islands, or try to trade on it. Besides, he doesn't approve at all of my droll little murder sideline. Being, as I said, that nobody ever really asks me into it."

Phanuel looked at her with respect in his eyes. "But he lets you run it."

"Well, I don't think that 'lets' would really be the word. Permit us to say that he suffers it. Sometimes quite literally suffers." She smiled ruefully. "I'll do what I can, because at this stage I can't *not*. But unless things turn up, I don't think it will be much. I really hate that."

Turk came charging back up the sand, soaking wet, all alive and stoked from his last wave. Pulling his board shorts off again, he doused himself under the freshwater shower, hair too, and saronged himself in a towel. Damp and desalted, he came over to them, twisted his fingers into Rennie's hair and tugged her bare person out of her lounge chair and along the sand.

"On your feet, ye giddy drab! Let's go for a walk."

Twelve

STROLLING ON THE FIRM, WET SAND just within the water's reach, ten minutes later they came to a tiny, hidden cove. Past the point they'd rounded, the dark shore of eastern Grand Palm Island, twelve miles away here, loomed itself up across the channel, the sun going down behind its spiky green peaks in bars of pink and gold and purple, lights twinkling along the shore and up on the hillsides. Beyond those mountains, Rennie knew, in the Palmton Roads on the island's other side, quite invisible from here, the ship was anchored.

"Still too damn close for comfort," she said aloud.

Turk stood behind her, his arms around her and his chin resting on the top of her head as the surfwash came foaming up around their ankles; she'd pulled off his towel and tossed it up the beach, and now they were wrapped in nothing but warm tropical breeze.

"The Good Ship Rock&Roll and all who sail in her?"

"God, you're quick. But yes. And Hoden, and the rest of those poor Weezle bastards."

His voice was neutral above her head. "No sympathy for the late Loya Tessman and Sammi Stoyer?"

Rennie, who had bent over to pick up a large, colorful seashell—a beautiful queen helmet—from the sand at her feet, straightened up and looked uncomfortable. "I'm not going to pretend, you know. They weren't among my favorite people. Or yours either. They hated us both. Well, of course Sammi didn't hate *you*, quite the flipping contrary. But still."

"And we disliked them right back."

"Yeah, but they started it, so who can blame us? And therefore it would be pretty darn hypocritical now to be all bummed about their being defunct."

"So I suppose that would be why you phoned Francher to have him send flowers to the funerals and our condolences to their families?"

He laughed at her how-the-hell expression as she turned in his arms, and ran his hands down her bare back, pulling her against him. "Gotcha! You left your scribble by the phone on the library table, so not hard to figure out. Two wreaths of pink roses, signed with both our names. Tasteful and appropriate. And two more from Lionheart, that you reminded Francher to send, and another two from Laird and Belinda, because they'd never think to send any on their own. You really *are* a lady. I knew I was right about you."

"And you never make mistakes, do you?" She was running her own hands over his back and chest, admiring him as usual; they were both smiling as he swung her around and out of the surf, walking back up past the tideline, his hand cupping one of her breasts.

"I do not. I noticed your great fineness and quality the first moment we met."

"Oh, please! You were all over Tansy. But she was all over you first."

"Our Tanze… She was adorable, if not perhaps the brightest bulb in the chandelier. But I most certainly did notice you and your classiness, in that diner in Monterey, when we were all having breakfast and talking about poor bloody Baz Potter. You were sitting there across from me being all classy, but also batting your eyelashes at that dreadful Irish folkie, with whom you had spent the previous night and who was groping you in full view of the whole table."

"Murdering Irish folkie."

"M'hm, yes, deplorable taste you showed there. And here's me thinking you were brighter than that. Then again, how bright could *I* have been, going for Tansy when you were right there in front of me? What a colossal, albeit temporary, failure of judgment..." He kissed her for quite a long time.

"Nice recovery, Ampman!" She spread the towel on soft springy sea-grass in the shade of a flowering bougainvillea canopy, behind thick screening bushes, and lay back on it, smiling up at him. "But you can continue to make it up to me if you like."

"Did I ever tell you that you were my first erotic dream?"

Turk looked absolutely thrilled. "Well, don't stop there! Let's hear it."

"It was after seeing you play at the Winter Festival at Cornell my freshman year. I was sixteen. And you were lead-guitaristing for that ridiculous little band—"

"Perry the Winkle."

"Yes, well, I was a lot more impressed with Perry's winkie. I didn't even know your name yet and I never got closer to you than twenty feet away, but it didn't matter. I thought you were the cutest thing I had ever seen and I had such a *crush* on you."

"Really!" He was purring like a cat that had just had a gallon of cream poured into its saucer. "Pray continue. And why, I wonder, has it taken so long for you to get around to mentioning it?"

Rennie hit him in the ribs. "Oh, I don't know. Maybe I wanted to keep something in reserve, for future use, in case I—because you're—because you—oh God—I don't—" *Because you make my mind stutter into mute idiot brainlessness every time I look at you. Because you make me melt into my shoes every time you look at me.* "Stop laughing! Anyway, you were wearing the tightest trousers in the history of trouserdom, and you didn't have a scrap of underwear on, and that was all that little virginal jailbait me needed to know. I could even tell that, unlike the vast majority of Englishmen, you were circumcised."

"You could not! Well, perhaps you could—those trousers *were* pretty tight. But circumcision has been the tradition in families like mine for two hundred years—the royals started it, back with the first George, and, like them, most aristo British kindreds still continue it. Prince Charles and I were both done by the same...professional."

"That was really way more than I needed to know. But I can attest to the fact that he did a very nice, professional, aesthetic job." She reached between them to emphasize her point, and he grabbed her groping hand. "I couldn't say about Chuck, of course."

"I should hope not. And no distractions, madam. First I want to hear all about that dream. Tell."

She laughed and lay back on the sand. "It was fairly straightforward, as those things go. You couldn't expect much, what with me being young and maidenly, as I said. Still, I was also hopeful, well-informed and blessed with raging hormones, not to mention an unfettered imagination. I may have been so pure and untouched that I could herd unicorns, but I'd read a *lot* of books. We could go home and re-enact it if you like."

"Not here?" He sounded disappointed. "Selfish, spiteful creature, getting my hopes up. Among other things. Only to cruelly dash them."

"Needs props."

"Home it is, then!"

"You might want to put on that towel first. Just sayin'."

"Well, *that's* a surprise," said Prax. "Or not."

Two days later, and they were all in the dining room before dinner looking at a photo spread in the London tabloid the Daily Intruder, not normally a rag that graced the Falcons Levels breakfast table. Phanuel, over in Palmton on an errand, had caught sight of a certain feature story, and, furious, had brought several copies back with him, in case action of a legal sort or just a beat-the-living-crap-out-of-someone sort needed to be taken, and the jury was still out on that.

Though only just: the four full pages laid out on the dining-room table were pretty good, or bad, evidence of guilt. The photos thereon featured Turk and Rennie in the Palmton streets, Rennie, Turk and Hoden by the pool at the Palms Inn, and Turk, Rennie, Laird and Belinda having dinner at the little seafood hideaway and heading to the seaplane pier the following afternoon.

Typical street photographer grabs, and, though deeply annoying and intrusive, were fairly unexceptionable. But the outrageous and undoubted star of the spread was several grainy but quite recognizable color pictures of all of them together on the beach at Silver Bay. With not a stitch of clothing among the suntanned lot of them.

"I think it's sweet, really," said Rennie, gazing fondly at the shot of Turk and herself knee-deep in surf, laughing, their more serious naughty bits blurred only to the edge of decency, or in some cases not at all.

My, but we look good together au naturel, *if I do say so myself. I wonder if I can call the paper for an unedited print without causing further sensation. Maybe Fitz could score it for me, even though this isn't one of his rags. It would be nice to have when we're sixty-four and still as hot for each other as we are now…though we'll* never *let the kids see it…* She remembered exactly where they'd been when that particular shot was taken. They were lucky the telephoto lens hadn't caught them under the bougainvilleas a few minutes later…well, hopefully it hadn't.

"*Sweet*? Love, it's bloody actionable!" Turk looked more closely at several of the offending photos. "I must call Geoffrey Shipsterns and see what can be done about it. It's clearly too late to keep it away from the Palmton police. And what the hell kind of lens were they using, the bloody Apollo spacecraft's? They had to have been shooting from Little Lion. They couldn't have gotten close enough for pictures like that if they'd been in a boat; we'd have seen them. Maybe Sir Geoffrey can get them for trespass at the least. Though that would mean he'd have to see the photos, if he hasn't already, and being the good sobersided Victorian that he is, he'd probably have a stroke if forced to behold that pretty little fanny of yours. And I mean 'fanny' in both the British and American senses of the word."

"I'm sure you do," said Rennie nonchalantly. "Not to mention Fanny's aesthetic and mighty friend Willy, which I won't mention. I don't suppose Fitz will be too pleased either. If several of his favorite people, and two of his star reporters, are going to appear sans clothes in the tabloids, at least they should have the decency to make it *his* tabloids."

Belinda rolled her eyes. "Well, you have to admit we painted a big old target on ourselves, though a splash of paint might have actually covered some things up. Private tropical island, bareassed rockers and their equally bareassed squeezes. Not to mention Murder Chick and Rock Lordship and two sensational homicides on the high seas, with which most here present are connected. You can't blame them for going for it."

Rennie smiled and tapped the final photograph. "Looking pretty good there, though, my lord."

"Looking pretty good yourself, my lady. I've always said you have the best rack in rock and roll."

"It's been admired," she said with some complacency. "You, however, never said that. Langdale Pikes said that. In his tiresome yet also strangely accurate little gossip column."

"He's as gay as the Spanish flag at a bazaar, what would he know about breasts? Besides, where has he ever even seen their bestness? And I have too said that. Perhaps you've been too busy with Willy when I said it."

"Perhaps. But at Woodstock? You were there yourself; also occasionally topless, as I recall. Not to mention poisoned, as I also recall."

Turk sobered quickly. "I'm not likely to forget."

From across the room, Laird turned and stared. "*Poisoned*? I never heard about that!"

"No, well, we took great care that nobody *should* hear about it," said Turk dryly. "It wasn't as dramatic as it sounds."

"Speak for yourself, axe boy," muttered Rennie. "I was there too, remember?" She nodded at the Intruder, with mostly disgust. "But if you can tear yourself away from the nekkid pics, how is the actual reportage? Any new developments?"

Turk had picked up the paper again and was scanning the story accompanying the frisky shots.

"No news really, though I would not expect to find any here, so amateur a rag is this. It does say the cops're holding the ship another couple of days, so they can poke around some more on board. What *can* they be hoping to find, at this late date? Anyway, the passengers are free to fly home now if they like, or they can stay in a Palmton hotel while the police are searching and then when the ship is released, sail back to New York as planned, the Weezles graciously springing for the extra hotel bills and plane fares. There seems to have been some mild official questioning of many of the passengers, at least according to this. But nothing we don't already know, and from what you lot tell me, nobody else was much of a witness. Just you."

"Is it worth trying to get hold of the U.S. or Brit papers?" asked Laird.

"I doubt there would be much in either that we didn't put there ourselves, Linny and I, being journos-on-the-spot," said Rennie. "Though maybe the U.K. rags would have something more official than this trash, these islands being nominally Her Majesty's patch. At least I was able to talk to Ken Karper and whip something up decent for Fitz. As did yon fair Belinda. An embarrassment of inside dope, as it were. Fitzie seemed quite pleased about it."

She looked suddenly, seriously thoughtful. "I wonder—presumably that damnable photo spread has by now spread itself all over these parts, wouldn't you say?"

"I would very much say," agreed Prax. "What are you thinking, petal?"

"Could it be, oh, a little bit of deliberately planned misdirection, I'm wondering?"

"In what way?"

"In the way of perhaps such exposure, in all senses of the word, might discredit anything any of us might have to say about Loya and Sammi? Being something deliberately planted by whoever is behind all this? I mean, how could a bunch of debauched rock stars and their floozies be the least bit serious or believable about the murders, look at them shamelessly disporting in their birthday suits! And in the papers too. But it could work both ways for us: if doubt is cast upon our stories, that might free us up to find things out."

"You mean free *you* up to find things," said Ares.

"That's exactly what I mean." Rennie began to laugh. "I'd give quite a lot to see Superintendent Meryton's face when he takes a squint at these photos and realizes how they might wreak havoc on his case. Or on his cortex. His eyes, his eyes!"

Turk grinned. "Between him and Sir Geoffrey, should be good. And even though camera chappies with lenses the size of dinosaur todgers managed to snag pictures from a mile away, it is still the case that no journalistic wretches can get over here and make us talk to them. Island, remember? They can try to land, of course, but they'll be repelled in no uncertain terms. That's what that neat little cutter is for. In the old days we would have raised the harbor chains across the entry to Lion Bay and shut the seagates and turned the big guns at the Claws on them. Come to think of it, I wonder if we could still do that—I must ask the harbormaster."

"Rank hath its privileges," said Rennie, conceding his point. "But you'd know all about that."

"Was Turk really poisoned at Woodstock?"

Rennie glanced sideways at Laird, who was sitting beside her on the broad terrace wall, their bare feet dangling over the hillside garden that fell away below, and sighed. It was after dinner that same night; the others had also drifted out to the terrace, and were engaged in spirited conversation, sitting and lounging while Marigo served them drinks and little munchies. The neighbor islands glowed in the sunset, while several pot clouds rose from the terrace to hang in the calm evening air, like the plumes over brooding volcanoes.

"Poisoned? He was. By the same person who killed Cory

Rivkin and Amander Evans. But we got him to the hospital in time, thank God, and then escaped home. Lionheart had already performed, so Woodstock was over for them anyway."

Laird was visibly choosing his words. "That's not the only time that you, well—"

"The only time we've been in peril of our lives?" Rennie gave a short laugh. "You don't have to be so diplomatic about it. No, unfortunately, it is not. We were both nearly gassed to death only a few short weeks after we moved in together, right after Tansy Belladonna was murdered. Then I got shot twice by Tansy's killer, who shot at Turk too. Before that, I was kidnapped by the Fillmore serial murderer, and if it hadn't been for the elements and the goddess Oyá fighting for me, my bleached white ribcage would even now be a windharp in Muir Woods strung with my long golden-ish hair, and I never would have met Turk. Or anybody else, for that matter."

She stared out to sea, and made an impatient, angry gesture. "Oh, yeah, and a bunch of other times too…it's not *safe* around me. *I'm* not safe, not for myself and not for other people. Turk understands this. At least I think he does."

"But you had nothing to do with Sammi and Loya. How could you?"

"How indeed?" echoed Rennie distantly. "But some people think I might have. Like the Palmton fuzz."

"You don't really believe that."

"Maybe not. But I bet I *could,* if I put my mind to it. In any case"—Rennie changed the subject by main verbal force—"despite our proximity to murder on the bounding main, we do all seem to be in the clear for Loya's murder, you and Belinda and I. And presumably Hoden and I, for Sammi's."

"Yeah," said Laird, relieved on several counts. "The cops certainly gave us that impression. Unless they think we're all in it together."

"Hmm... No, I don't get that vibe from them. That Superintendent who came to the law offices to talk to us seems rather to think we're valuable resources and witnesses, not suspects at all."

"And so we are. Well, at least you and Linny are, world-class trained journalists that you happen to be. So what do you think is going on, then?"

Rennie was silent for a while, marshaling her thoughts, and decided to bring him all the way in. "I've been given to understand that there may be something going on with the Weezles." Swiftly she ran down to Laird what she'd learned from Hoden about his suspicions, though she didn't mention where she had gotten the information. "So you see," she concluded.

"Not entirely. You obviously think it all connects down here somewhere, to Grand Palm Island and environs. Drugs..."

"My first thought," she admitted. "Well, pretty much my only thought, neatly confirmed by the coroner's report. Not to mention that Loya Tessman was terrified of something and wanted to talk to me, but she never got the chance. Even Hoden..." She paused, glanced over at Turk across the terrace, raised her voice to carry. "Honey? Are there drug problems here?"

Turk turned to look at her. "Here? On our island? None

that we're aware of. We don't consider weed a problem, of course; it's a part of the culture. Which is not to say there *aren't* problems, over in the Grand Palms, as we were told by Superintendent Meryton the other day. The police are fighting waves of heroin smugglers and local users, and although by mainland standards the problem is not that bad, it's still a lot more pervasive than the authorities would like it to be. So yes, I can see a smack-drenched t-shirt, as was what did for Sammi Stoyer, being a completely valuable indicator to Meryton that possibly the problem isn't as local in origin as might have been thought."

"Huh. You mean maybe it sails in on cruise ships from up north... I wonder—" What she wondered was something she wasn't yet ready to go public with yet. But the name of Jo Fleet swirled around in her brain, as it had apparently swirled in Hoden Weezle's.

"Peace is in the contradictions," said Turk vaguely, getting up to sit behind her on the terrace ledge. Rennie leaned back against him with a sigh, gazing out to sea with the speculative stare of Henry Martin, or indeed Duke Ironhand, assessing a convoy of rich merchant ships and being not at all inclined to let them pass by.

"I have to admit I'm not exactly weeping my eyes out that Sammi and Loya are no more," she said after a while. "In fact, if you must know, my immediate inclination bordered on doing a little happy dance. On their dead faces. Ordinarily I wouldn't dream of horribly rejoicing at the gratuitous loss of human life, but those humans were pretty much gratuitous all round, and though I would probably not have flung Stoyer overboard or slit Tessman's throat, given even half a chance—well, maybe not so much of the 'probably' there—I can't say I'm dreadful sorry they are lost and gone forever."

"Didn't Stoyer use to work in publicity at Columbia? I think some of my friends on the label mentioned her. In quite scornful and sordid contexts, if memory serves."

"M'hm. Phone-answerer, basically. When she actually *did* work and wasn't just mooching off her ex-husband and being a groupie slutbag. Everyone at CBS hated her, thought she was an incompetent piece of trash. *My* friends at the label said she was nothing but a starfucker—when she could even get the stars interested in her at all, which wasn't very often, and her activities were very much frowned on by the higher-ups. She'd been spoken to about the poor work ethic, and had been known to betray friendships to get a shot at musicians she wanted to screw; but the bare-faced, or bareassed, sluttery is what ultimately got her fired. I believe Toy Tyler was the best she ever scored, though he told me one night in his cups that a jellyfish was a better lay than Stoyer. How he might know that, I do not wish to ask."

"I think we all have a pretty good idea of how."

"Very likely." She shrugged dismissively. "Well, if that makes me a terrible person, I don't particularly care. She never cared about other people, so I don't have to care about her."

Turk's voice came quietly from the darkness above her head. "Surely you didn't truly wish her dead, though?"

Rennie was silent for a long, long moment. "No, but… She hurt a lot of people, including us, with that foul spew in Tessman's rag. Out of pure meanness and envy and spite.

So I'm thinking that taking a header into the Gulf Stream, assisted or not, was about the cleanest thing she's done in years. I've never hated anyone before—well, no, that's not true. But it wasn't even so much actual hate that I had for her, because she was far too rubbishy and trifling a thing to waste good honest hate on. She was more like a dead, rotting mouse stinking away under the floorboards of my existence. So you can see where I'm not exactly eager to help track down her killer and I'm not going to pursue it. And as far as Loya is concerned, even less. So! Something new there, Flash."

He put his arms around her, pulled her to him, spoke in her ear. "Well, well, so you're only human after all. And here's me thinking you were better than that."

She laughed, and shivered at the feel of his mouth on her neck. "Sorry to disillusion you, my lord. So, do you think less of me now for feeling that way?"

"Not a bit," said Turk comfortably. "You're so petty and vengeful sometimes, and I love it! In fact, I think all the more of you, for being so honest about it. And you *are* better than that."

They sat on silently for a while as the soft tropical darkness grew; behind them, the others wandered back inside, preparatory to retiring. "Do you want to ask your Powderhouse pal Buck Lai to come over and stay with us for a bit?" asked Turk, out of the blue. "You said he was on the ship, and since Laird's already here..."

She shook her head. "Buck split for New York yesterday. He said it was all getting way too heavy for him and he needed to go home. I think a bunch more people who were on the ship flew home as well, and who can blame them? Still, a lot stayed on and are having themselves a nice little holiday on the island, paid for by the Weezles, before sailing back to northern latitudes, and bless their hearts, why not? But the band is still around. Apparently they have to be here. Why, I couldn't tell you. I haven't heard that any of them are persons of interest, and Hoden's already made his statement."

"I could ask them over too," said Turk, as they walked into the comfortably lit living room. "Get them the hell away from the press maggots. No offense meant, sweetheart." Rennie just waved a hand, no offense taken. "I did call, in fact, and got to speak to young Hoden, and he regretfully told me the band can't leave the jurisdiction of Palmton."

"So?" said Phanuel, from where he sat at a desk at the other end of the room, copying something into a ledger. "Have you forgotten that we are lawfully Palmton right here? That you, as the ducal heir, are a rightful magistrate of the Grand Palm Islands, charged in His Grace's absence with upholding the low, middle and high justice? A legality dating from the days of Ironhand. That's how we managed to get Rennie here before the Palmton plod could grab her. You can do the same for the band as a whole: as a magistrate you're a fully authorized Weezle keeper."

Turk looked exasperated at his own forgetfulness. "Well, of *course*! Right. Let's get them out of it and over here. There's tons of space. Marigo can have the maids get guestrooms ready. I'll call Hoden back and ask them all. Phan, you can ride to the rescue in the seaplane."

Rennie enthusiastically agreed. "Hey, being as *I'm*

already your legal property—I mean, your 'lawful charge'—you might as well make a land grab for the Weezles too. But don't invite any of their parasites: Jo Fleet or Ted Tessman or the rest."

"No fear!"

"You don't really know them, though, Turk, except for Hoden," Belinda pointed out.

He was already picking up the phone. "Doesn't matter."

It really didn't, Rennie considered, watching him verbally charm, or arrogantly straight-arm, his way past several layers of gatekeepers—since that talk with her, Hoden had apparently seen the wisdom of giving orders to telephonically insulate himself. There was a sort of freemasonry of fame: if you were a celebrity, you were on the same footing with other celebritous people, even if you'd never met, so that you could go up to them at airports or parties and start talking and not come across as a stalker. Or, yes, invite them to your private island to escape unwelcome press attention. Besides, Turk and Hoden had already met on friendly terms. Or maybe it was just a thousand years of noblesse oblige coming to the fore.

The Weezles, it turned out, were pathetically eager to take Turk up on his lordly offer of sanctuary, and possibly equally eager to be away from their manager, so Phanuel ferried the four band members and the ladies of three of them—Hoden was solo at the moment—over in time for supper the next day.

Rennie was briefly annoyed—with so many strangers around they all had to put on clothes again for outdoors—but she was enjoying to the hilt the role of lady of the manor: assigning rooms in the guest wings and seeing that the staff swept and aired them, consulting with Marigo as to the menus and the supplies of fresh linens and towels, ordering food delicacies from the home farms and fisheries and from gourmet shops in Palmton, graciously greeting their company when they arrived. She understood by now that the better she played her part, the better things went for Turk, and that was something she always liked to ensure. But she also looked forward to maybe getting to the real bottom of what Hoden had told her, now that he was right there in the house.

Weirdly, once he'd greeted her and Turk with courtesy and cheer, for some stupid reason he was now acting as if they'd never met at all. *Ohhhhkay. If that's how he feels most comfortable, downplaying our little chat in front of the others, or rather* not *playing it…* Well, it was a small island, and potentially a long stay. There'd be plenty of chances, and places, for them to talk. Little room to run. And nowhere to escape to without a boat.

Thirteen

RENNIE GOT HER CHANCE two mornings later, when the day's activities separated the house-party members right after breakfast. Turk, Phanuel and Ares dashed off to a favorite surf break on the other side of the island, not wanting to waste a big swell that was rolling in, and they took Weezle drummer Matt Cutler, another avid boardhead, with them. Everyone else went down to Lion Bay, where they trooped aboard the *Ravenna*, the Tarrants' sleek white hundred-and-fifty-foot yacht, newly rechristened by Turk, for a cruise across choppy waters to the British Virgin Islands, to snorkel in the rocky lagoons of Tortola and have a picnic lunch served by staff on the polished teak deck.

Not up for either double-overhead surf or possible seasickness—that giant swell wasn't rocking the south coast alone—Rennie strong-armed Hoden into a nice lunchtime hack along fresh wet-leaf-dripping tropical trails. In an unguarded moment, he'd mentioned that he enjoyed riding on the Malibu beaches near his home, so they tacked up a pair of horses from the stables down the hill and went thundering off along a path that led to a shell-strewn cove, utterly private. On the way, they surprised a little band of the island's native wild horses, descended from shipwrecked Andalusians of passing conquistadors long ago: graceful, powerful, surprisingly small creatures who turned to watch with interest as the riders went by the salt marshes where they grazed.

Pulling up where the jungle track was edged by soft pink sands, Rennie threw her right leg over the arched neck of her Arabian mare and slid lithely to the ground, grabbing the reins of Hoden's horse with one hand and the sandwich cases off her saddle with the other.

"No one around for miles. So. Right. Let's go. Oh, wait, don't forget your lunch. We can sit over there and eat and talk."

He dismounted, a bit less fluidly than she, and led the horses to a shady, leafy area by a tiny stream where they could munch the seagrass, then sat down next to Rennie under a spreading palm where she had already laid out the lunchboxes. They stuffed themselves for a while, talking about music matters and people they both knew, then Hoden leaned back against one of the man-high, glittery schist boulders that littered the beach.

"Well. It pretty much all began right when the band was formed. You remember?"

Rennie nodded, idly reaching for another piece of fried chicken to help fill in the corners. "Of course. I was still in college, but I remember there was a giant huge publicity-crazed talent search, and your label was spouting a lot of denial in the press about it being just another Beatles ripoff, or even a Monkees ripoff, and at the end of it you four were the Weezles. Even though you were all babies, and half of you could scarcely play a lick, and none of you had ever even seen each other before. You got to do songs by amazing songwriters, and top session cats played behind you in the studio, and you became the kings of television lip-synch. I even used to dance to your singles, in my go-go dancing days."

Hoden laughed, genuinely delighted. "I'm honored. No, really I am. I wish we could have seen you."

"You would have liked me." Rennie looked smug, and took a bite of chicken. "I daresay I did you proud. My favorite song of yours to dance to was 'Vangie'. Though it was tied with Lionheart's cover of 'Peggy Sue', which is a thing of awe and beauty. But getting back to your present issues… To your eternal credit, all that wasn't enough for your artistic wheelhouse. Matt and Brian took lessons from masters to learn how to really play, play as well as you and Luke did, and you all got good. *Really* good. Then most notoriously and publicly you and Luke, though I'm betting it was all four of you, started demanding to be allowed to play like a real band. And that's when the trouble started. As you told me the other day."

"More or less." He smiled, and it was not a happy smile. "We suspected we were being screwed from day one. Business-wise as well as artistic-wise."

"Not an unreasonable assumption. Who did you think was doing the screwing? Jack Holland? Other label vampires? Tontine?"

Hoden took a long pull on a thermos of lemonade. "Them, but more particularly our own personal devil, Jo Fleet. As I mentioned when we talked."

"Ah."

"He was the one who created us, Jo was. Well, you know. You know *him*. He was running a small-time club on the Sunset Strip and not getting anywhere, especially compared to the other clubowners who were scoring hot local L.A. acts like the Byrds and the Doors and Sakerhawk and Buffalo Springfield. Then he had the brainstorm of doing a Beatles ripoff, and set up the contest. We got together right after the Monkees did."

"Blimey, what a coincidence!"

Hoden favored her with a quick grin. "You *think*? Anyway, once Fleet had us all under lock and key, and things had begun to take off, he started the booking agency to take full advantage of our success—Tontine, the very same one Ted Tessman now runs with an iron fist in an iron glove, they have some kind of diabolical deal in place—then another, bigger club, then the deal with Isis, then his own actual label, distributed by Isis. And he contractually tied us to all of them, like some Victorian maiden to the railroad tracks."

He saw Rennie's face change before she could stop it. "Oh, God, sorry, I forgot about that groupie girl in L.A., I didn't mean—"

"No, it's okay. Go on."

Just as he took a breath to continue, something cracked out over the waters of the bay, and almost at the same moment something whined past them like a turbo-assisted bee, clipping a tree trunk not a dozen feet from where they sat and leaving a white blaze across the bark. Another followed almost immediately, zinging off one of the beach rocks. Rennie instantly hit the sand, pulling Hoden with her, and the horses bolted back along the trail, neighing in alarm.

"Was that a *shot*?" he whispered indignantly. "You or

me?"

"Or both! But I'm thinking you, young man. Pop goes the Weezle? See those rocks over there? Now!"

Another three shots as they ran, crouched low, expecting any second to feel the bite of a bullet. They dived for the cover of the rocks and the jungle, and then there was nothing.

"The *fuck*?" asked Hoden sincerely after a long silent moment, staring at her.

"I don't know! Stay down!"

They stayed down for about another quarter hour, and were beginning to think about the long walk back to Falcons Levels without their horses, who were by now undoubtedly back at the barn, when a small, brightly painted jet boat came droning into the cove. Motioning Hoden to keep hidden, Rennie peered around the corner of the rocks to see who was driving the boat, and was more surprised than she liked to see Phanuel Shine at the wheel.

He buzzed in and hovered the bobbing craft, idling, outside the shorebreak, standing up and craning around, obviously looking for something, presumably them. Just as Hoden was about to give a shout, Rennie snaked out a hand and grabbed his arm, pulling him sideways into the sand, shaking her head, shushing him.

After a few minutes, they heard the boat buzz away again, and even then Rennie waited a few minutes more before getting up and nodding at Hoden to get up too.

He did, but his hazel eyes were snapping with annoyance and confusion. "What the bloody hell was *that* all about? That was Phanuel! He could have given us a lift back on the boat. Since the horses have scarpered, as you *may* have noticed."

"I *know* it was Phanuel. I saw him." She gave him a little shove in the direction of the overhanging trees. "I also know I didn't tell anyone where we were riding off to."

He caught her drift at once. "Oh, surely you're not thinking—*Phanuel*? Shooting at *us*? But why would he?"

"I don't know why he would! If he even did! I don't know what I'm thinking! But it's not a bad idea to be cautious… Maybe we'd better not take the trail home after all. If it wasn't him, there might still be someone around. Either way, we're in for a long walk. Good thing we still have some food and water left."

It took them almost four hours of skulking along the beach, keeping to the trees as much as possible, and devouring their meager rations, but at last they emerged from the jungle into Silver Bay cove below the house, hot and sticky and tired, crisscrossed with scratches from the thick underbrush. Rennie held them both back to make sure no one with a gun was hanging around, and then they made a dash for the beach pavilion, to splash off the worst of the sweat and dirt and blood under the outdoor shower and guzzle some much-needed water from bottles in the fridge. But when she saw Hoden longingly eyeing the loaded shelves, she grabbed his arm and pulled him away.

"I'm so hungry, Rennie, so tired, oh please can't we sit down and rest for a few minutes and eat something, there's food right here, look, cheese and fruit and milk…"

"I know, me too, but all we have to do now is get up to the house. They'll take care of us, listen, they'll feed us sherbet, and massage our feet, and fan us with peacock plumes and spray us with ice water and tell us how brave and clever and pretty we are, only a little bit further now, Hoden, do come on..."

She tried desperately not to look at the thick-cushioned chairs calling her name. If they sat down to rest now, even for a few minutes, it wouldn't *be* a few minutes—no, they would fall over like dead things and not wake up till morning. So she grabbed two water bottles and four pieces of fruit, tossed his share to Hoden and inexorably propelled them both toward the path to the house.

Where, to their delighted relief, one of the red-and-yellow golf carts was sitting at the bottom of the hill as if it were a taxi they'd ordered, empty and jaunty under its scalloped awning. They looked around warily, then threw themselves aboard, and Rennie let off the brake and began driving up the hill. Now that they weren't locomoted under footpower and were feeling much more comfortable, they recklessly drank their water bottles dry and gobbled the fruit from the pavilion kitchen, knowing more wasn't far away now and they didn't have to walk another step to get it.

As the cart climbed higher, the switchbacked trail broke out of the jungle from time to time, opening up to a view over half the island, in bright sunlight out above the treetops, and both Hoden and Rennie flinched a little each time they were so exposed. Before they came within sound or sight of the house, he touched her arm, and she turned to look at him.

"Before we go inside: do you really seriously think it was Phanuel who shot at us?"

She stopped the cart in a shrub-screened section of trail and put on the brake. "What do *you* think?"

"I don't know him."

Rennie shrugged. "I don't know him either. I'd never met him till I got here. Turk mentioned him from time to time. They grew up together, they've been friends since they were infants. Turk says he trusts him with his life."

Hoden gave her a long level glance. "I asked what *you* think. You who never met Phanuel Shine till you got here. Do *you* trust him with Turk's life?"

The answer came back in a heartbeat. "I don't trust anyone with Turk's life who isn't me."

"That's what I thought. How about trusting Phanuel with anyone else's life?"

"I can't say," said Rennie after a long while. She looked at him more closely. "Why do you ask this? Why do you ask this *now*? Is there something you haven't told me about?"

"Well—there were those death threats."

"*Death threats*?" She couldn't help it: freaked as she was on so many levels, she relaxed against the cushions, trying not to think about how good it felt to rest, how sore and tired she was. Maybe, if she yelled really loud, Turk would hear, and come down to scoop her up and carry her in his arms the rest of the way… "Okay. Tell. Now."

"It's no big deal. Everybody in rock gets rubbish like that sooner or later."

"No, they don't, Hoden. They really don't. And when they do, they should take it seriously. When did it start?"

He was already visibly regretting he'd brought it up. "I got a couple of letters in New York before the cruise, and a note delivered to my cabin aboard ship before we sailed, attached to a bottle of champers and a bouquet of chrysanthemums. Saying to do everything we were told and not ask questions, or I'd be the first to go and the other guys wouldn't be far behind."

"Please tell me you didn't *drink* the champagne?"

She'd had experience with murderously doctored wine before now, of course. And chrysanthemums were traditionally flowers to be put on graves. But she didn't mention any of that: if he didn't already know, no sense alarming him even more.

He laughed shortly. "No fear! I'm not a complete idiot, you know. I threw it overboard once we were out of New York harbor. Dom Pérignon. It hurt to toss it, but there it is. The flowers went too. I was too freaked out to check them for poison thorns."

"Good thinking. What did the letters tell you to do?"

Hoden shrugged. "Not much. Do the cruise. Perform the opera. Have some fan get-togethers in New York before the cruise. Entertain the winners of the fan-club contest who'd be along on the ship."

"And did you?"

"Bloody right we did! In fact, the groupie who went overboard, she was one of the fans we had lunch with the first day out."

"I see. I know I needn't point it out, but Jo Fleet, Ted Tessman and any other of their minions would have had access to your cabin. The fangirls as well, if they bribed the help. What else?"

"The note that came with the wine and flowers repeated

what the letters had said. But there was more. You were wondering why I stayed away from you aboard the ship, why I hadn't spoken to you even though the other guys did and I'd told Luke I specifically wanted to talk to you? Well, that last note also told me equally specifically *not* to talk to Rennie Stride or I'd be very, very sorry. Well, actually, it said I wouldn't live long enough to *be* sorry and neither would you. So I decided to err on the side of prudence, if you can call it that, for both our sakes. Plus I got a phone call at the Palms Inn, right after I phoned you the night before we met. I didn't recognize the voice. He sounded like a local guy. A Palm Islander maybe, or someone else from around these parts. And he said pretty much the same things. Which, frankly, is why I was so grateful Turk invited us all here. I was too scared to stay in Palmton."

"And yet you called me at the hotel in spite of all that."

"I was too scared *not* to," he said simply. "I figured if anyone could help me, it would be you. The way you helped Prax and Turk and Niles Clay and Sledger Cairns. Sledger's a good friend of Luke's, and she told him all about it."

"Oh, Sledger. Yes, I can imagine. But, of course, it's not a big deal or anything, is it." Rennie looked at him, exasperated, and smacked his arm. "You deserve a good kick in the slats, you know that, don't you. Cast your little rocknroll mind back to what happened when Sledger got those death threats back in December. You do remember that, Weezle Boy?"

"People died," he said in a low voice.

"That's right, they did, and she and I almost did, too. And after you got the warnings, presumably you *did* notice that little Sammi and little Loya both ended up not breathing."

"Well, sure, and it was terrible, but I didn't think that had anything to do with me."

"Oh, *Hoden*… Who knew you were staying at the Palms Inn and not aboard the ship?"

He thought a bit. "Not many people. I couldn't take being on the ship another minute, and that hotel is so nice. But I didn't bring my luggage or axes with me till we came here, only a few changes of clothes for overnight, left everything else in my cabin for the trip home. Anybody could have gone through it in my cabin. The guys in the band knew, obviously. Probably they told the girlfriends. Laird Burkhart knew, and may or may not have mentioned it to your friend Belinda. Jo Fleet, of course. Those lawyers, Franz and Larry. Ted Tessman, who appears to be in a state of uttermost shock and grief at his wife's terrible death, and yes, I am being *deeply* sarcastic. But I hadn't left any orders about phone calls: anybody who rang up the hotel with a plausible story and didn't sound like a crazed groupie would have been put through to the room."

"Especially someone with a local accent. He could have told the operator he was your driver, or that you'd asked him to go collect your stuff from the ship. Since so few people knew you were staying at the hotel, I'm sure his story was taken as true." Rennie brooded for a few moments, then started the golf cart again, and they lurched forward up the hill. "Well. Time to take all this to the lord of the island. And to Ares Sakura, bodyguard to the stars. And after that…"

Resignedly: "To the coppers."

"You got it."

Fourteen

When they reached the house at last, they found that the horses' return to the stable without any riders aboard had caused much alarm. The surfers had gotten back long ago from the reef and so had the yachters from Tortola. Turk had had a phone call from the stablemaster that the horses had come home riderless, and he had immediately sent people out to search. In fact, he had been on the point of dispatching the island's big military-grade rescue helicopter for an aerial search when Rennie and Hoden came staggering dramatically through the terrace doors.

After hugs and questions and water and vats of iced tea and, yes, sherbet, and showers and clean clothes and not a whole lot of answers , not to mention minor first aid for the scratches and cuts, everyone retired to the living room; the Weezlettes and Marigo had gone to the kitchen to fix everybody something substantial to eat. Rennie installed herself leaning back against Turk in the curve of a deep-cushioned sofa, glass in hand; Hoden followed suit alone on the facing one, while the others disposed themselves around the room. *God, it feels so good to sit and put everything in Turk's ever so capable hands…*

"Phanuel is still out looking for you two," said Ares. "They're trying to get through to him on the radio now. Turk sent him out to find you."

"You did, honey?" asked Rennie, not daring to glance at Hoden.

Turk nodded. "Of course. He got bored surfing and went out zooming around on the jet boat. When I heard the horses were back and you two weren't, I went down to the beach and waved him in and told him. He went right off in the boat to look in the north shore coves, thinking to give you a lift and spare you walking all the way back."

"North shore specifically? *All* the coves?"

Turk frowned: he was getting the vibe, loud and clear, of something being not quite right, something that Rennie didn't want to elaborate on in front of all the others, and though he had no idea what it might be, he had long and varied experience of this sort of thing with her, and smoothly changed tack.

"Yes. Joshamee Wilkes down at the stables told me you'd ridden off on the north trail, so it seemed logical to assume you'd be somewhere on the north shore. Those coast trails almost never cross over, because of the mountains. Why do you ask?"

"No reason. We stopped for lunch and stupidly didn't tie the horses. One of them got stung by a bee and they both bolted," Rennie lied blithely. "By the time Phan got there, we were probably on our way home. Through the jungle. He wouldn't have seen us."

She glanced meaningfully at Hoden, and he smiled and nodded and loyally, if non-verbally, backed her up. Then Marigo came in to announce that dinner was served.

"So the next thing he says, oh come on say it with me, the

next thing he says is 'We'd like it if you don't leave town yet, Miss Stride.' Man, if I had a dollar for every time I've heard that—"

"You'd have, what, ten dollars?" scoffed Turk from the other end of the dinner table.

Rennie grinned at her betrothed. "Not that much. But it does get monotonous being ordered to stick around. Especially since I usually want to anyway."

"Well of *course* it does," said Belinda soothingly, who was sitting on Turk's right, with Prax facing her across the table's width. "But Sammi and Loya—"

"No murder talk at dinner," said Turk, with all the authority of the master of the house.

On Rennie's right, Laird Burkhart as his opposite number, Hoden smiled diplomatically at his hostess and changed the topic. "So, I hear there's good eating in these parts. Will someone please pass me some of that much-talked-about ham?"

After they had pretty much exhausted such harmless topics as Rennie and Hoden's adventure, with bullets omitted, and surfing and sailing, and how spectacular the yacht *Ravenna* was and how sweet that Turk had renamed it for his lady, and the Weezles' assorted trials and tribulations staging "Paize Lee" aboard the *Excalibur,* the conversation had veered, inevitably, to their various experiences with the Palmton constabulary, which seemed safe enough to now discuss. Belinda, Laird and Rennie had all been questioned particularly intensively, and each of the four Weezles had also been subjects of interest, so they all enjoyed a little venting over dessert, some splendid profiteroles with chocolate sauce that had them all begging like Oliver Twist for more.

"There's not a lot to go on," said Rennie reflectively, scraping her dessert plate for the last traces of pastry. "We've been over it and over it. Sammi was thrown over the side of the ship. Thrown, not fell. As you all know by now, I was nearby when she was. Though not the only one nearby." Sudden silence around the table; everybody had known what had happened, of course, including the Weezles and their chicks, but none of them liked being reminded. "It was—not very nice. Next day we all heard that there had been bruising and scratches on her arms and face and chest and no water in her lungs, and the coroner confirmed it. As did the cops here. So obviously it wasn't her own idea to go for the big swim. Much as I detested her, she didn't deserve that."

She said not one word about the heroin-laced t-shirt, though Turk of course noticed the omission, and gave her a covert glance.

"As for Loya," Rennie continued implacably, "she was tied to a deck chair and garroted and throat-cut, dressed up in that ridiculous costume from—oh, guys, I'm sorry..."

"No, we wondered about that too," said Matt Cutler, glad to be able to talk openly at last. "Because there was no way she should have been able to get her hands on the Paize Lee clothes, and we all told the cops so. That little red minidress was the costume Penny wore in the first act, and it remained backstage in the dressing room, safely tucked away. Not *locked* away, mind, but still not easy to get at. Or so one would have thought. Why would the woman even want to, for one thing? And she was all made up like the character as well."

Turk had yielded to the unstoppable. "I can see one of the fan-club girls putting the gear and makeup on, for a lark, but Tessman herself? No. It makes no sense. Therefore someone dressed her up for some weird or evil reason of their own, and then killed her. Or killed her first and then put her into the clothes. Could the forensic boys tell?"

Glances turned to him down the table's length: shocked, appraising, interested, impressed.

"You've been spending too much time with your old lady, Turk," said Luke, to turn the moment. "You're even starting to think like her."

Turk raised his wine goblet to him. "A glass with you, sir! As they used to say in these parts, long ago. How kind of you to notice."

"In your dreams, blondie!" said Rennie.

Later, alone in their rooms, she finally told Turk what had really happened, and he hit the ceiling, as she had known he would. They didn't get screamingly angry with each other much anymore; that was mostly a thing of the past for them, when in their earliest times together they had seemed to have a lot more to yell about. But every now and again the volatile old days came back for an encore, as they did now, and the two of them roared epically at one another for a good twenty minutes, Turk shouting at her what the bloody hell was *wrong* with her, she was supposed to *tell* him these things, and she shouting right back at him that it wasn't as if she did these things on purpose, *was* it, and here she'd just fucking *told* him what had happened, hadn't she. At last they both calmed down a bit, and he began to get there himself, as she had also known he would.

"When Phan came in from his run along the north shore in the jet boat," he said much more quietly, not looking at her, "he didn't mention hearing shots *or* seeing you two. Nor did Joshamee speak of a bee sting on Kinch or Aloes. He's a very careful stablemaster, and he knows I love the horses as much as he does—he would surely have noticed and just as surely would have told me."

"Yeah, well, okay, no bee sting. I made that up. The horses bolted when the shots were fired. By the time Phanuel showed up on his zippy little boat, the shooting was all over and we were hiding amongst the rocks. Though if he was close enough, he might have heard the shots. But that boat is really noisy and maybe he wouldn't have. Unless...well, anyway, we didn't come out when he called for fear that the shooter was still there waiting for us."

"And was he? —Rennie, I know what you're thinking."

"So I don't have to say it, do I."

"You think it was Phan who did the shooting, then came in close to shore pretend-looking for you. To see if he'd hit his targets." Turk's voice was dangerously soft. "But why? Why would he shoot at you?"

"I don't *want* to think it was Phanuel, no! Why would it be? But if it was? I don't know. It just seemed...odd that he showed up at a beach nobody knew we were going to. But I was also thinking maybe the shooter was someone from the ship, who thought I knew something and wanted to put the frighteners on. He wasn't aiming to kill, I don't *think*. We'd both be dead if he had been. Or she. It's happened before, as you know."

"I'm hip," Turk muttered. Louder: "Still, the timing's off. Though Marigo—" He stopped abruptly, and Rennie looked at him.

"Yes? Marigo what?"

"—Nothing really," he said reluctantly. "It was something I overheard the other day, before you got here, and maybe I was supposed to. She was talking to one of the housemaids, and it was all about how Phan was spending more time running around the islands than here doing his job, and bringing home all this nice extra money they hadn't had before and ordering her to keep quiet about it, and when she sassed him about it, he hit her. She had a bruise to prove it, too."

"That doesn't sound like Phanuel. Being violent, I mean. Besides, you've always told me his family was quite wealthy, being of Ironhand vintage and prosperity. Not up to Tarrant levels, of course, but as well off as they ever could want or need. Like so many families on the island. This is not a poor place. Not like the other islands round here, and you have the ancestral buccaneers to thank for that. So, again, doesn't sound like him. Does it?"

"No. It does not sound like him at all, which is why I ignored it. Besides, he's *extremely* well paid as island manager, in addition to the family money, so why Marigo is suddenly crying poverty and at the same time boasting about extra dosh I cannot say."

Rennie's mouth tightened. "But she's saying it, and that he hit her. And you thought she meant you to hear. And

I'm guessing that's when a little shipworm of doubt began boring itself into the oaken keel of your long friendship."

Turk was silent for many moments. "I hate to think it did. That I'd be that weak, willing to think that of him. And I *hope* I haven't let it affect me. But—"

"'But' is fine. 'But' is fair. Never mind, my love. Just don't let it get any farther than that." Her turn to be silent. Then: "It's like those horrendous super-atomic Caribbean termites you have here. Even concrete doesn't stop them. So everyone builds their house floors and walls out of greenheart wood from South America, which is the only thing strong enough and hard enough for them to break their little termite teeth on."

He looked at her. "So you're saying my friendship with Phan—"

Rennie gathered his hands in hers. "Solid greenheart, and termites like Marigo may try to nibble at it, but they can't destroy it. House stands."

"Well. I guess perhaps a little bit of pest control might not come amiss. Or at least more trust in the greenheart floor." He visibly shook it off, and returned to what they had been discussing. But he kissed her, hard and gratefully, before he did. "Right...but if whoever it was actually *was* shooting not at you but at Hoden? Because you're right, how *did* they know where to find you? And why were they even looking to begin with?"

"Well, again we must ask all these questions. It could have been anyone and anything. Maybe it's Jo Fleet's heavy mob, trying to terrorize Hoden into signing something he doesn't want to sign. With the death threat letters and phone calls and everything. Maybe it was whoever killed Loya and/or Sammi trying to scare me off. Maybe it's...someone else. Someone we don't know. For a reason we don't know. The heroin—maybe the problem is moving over here from the Grand Palms, which I really, really hope is not the case. But let's keep it to ourselves for now. About the shooting, I mean. You and me and Hoden, and of course the shooter, are the only ones who are aware of it. Nobody else needs to be clued in yet. Except for the cops. I'll ring up Meryton in the morning. As to how they knew where to look for us, not a clue."

"Hell of an acting job we'll have to do." Turk brooded in silence for a while, lying back on the pillows. "Well," he said at last, "I will bet you a bushel of sapphires against a week of bedroom harem games that it wasn't Phan. And you know I'm good for it. I *am* the descendant of pirates, after all."

"Fond as I am of sapphires," said Rennie, "that's one bet I'll be very happy to lose. Though I'd say I win either way, and *I'm* good for it too."

The next day Rennie spoke on the phone to Detective Superintendent Meryton, who was interested to hear of the shootout in Little Shell Bay, and even more interested about the warnings delivered to Hoden aboard ship and at the hotel, but who didn't seem to think it required a personal visit, either her to him or him to her. Rennie, who had been annoyed at the idea of yet another afternoon at the cop shop over in Palmton, was, perversely, annoyed as well to be dismissed so casually, and said so.

A faint sigh came over the phone. "You say there's no physical evidence of the alleged attack, Miss Stride, and I trust your observational powers, so there is really no cause for me or one of my men to come over to look at, well, nothing. If it makes you feel better, I could ask Tenant-in-Chief Hilling to order one of the Lion Island auxiliary officers to go and check the bay out, but according to your own account, there will be nothing to see but sand and surf and a superficial nick on a tree trunk. To which any investigating officer would say 'Oh, yes, look there, some sand, some surf, a little nick on a tree trunk possibly caused by a bullet.' Maybe there might also be a few more bullets buried in the jungle, or in the bay, or in the beach, where no one will ever find them, to which an investigating officer wouldn't be able to say even that much. As for the death threats you say Mr. Hoden received, and I'm willing to take both your and his word for it, there is no possible way I can investigate. No evidence, for one thing, and the incidents occurred well outside my jurisdiction."

"The phone call to him at the Palms Inn—"

"Again, no evidence; nothing but his word as to the threat. I could check the hotel phone records to see if a call was put through around the time you say, but even if there was, that won't prove a thing. I can't really say anything except everyone over on Lion Island should exercise common caution. Perhaps a little more. Neither you nor Mr. Hoden was injured, thankfully, nor were his lordship's horses, so I don't really see what you expect us to do."

"I don't either," said Rennie, unaccountably cheerful again. "But I thought you ought to know. Also I was wondering..."

"If perhaps I had a little fritter of information for you? Right, then. Not for publication, but between you, me, Lord Raxton, and Mr. Sakura as your de facto bodyguard. And kindly don't forget that you are not supposed to be looking into this at all." His voice lowered. "It's definitely drugs, and it's definitely local. Very, *very* local. And that's all I can say."

Rennie felt a chill touch her neck. "You mean Lion Island? *That* local? I don't believe that, and neither will his lordship."

"All I can say, Miss Stride. I just thought *you* ought to know."

Rennie replaced the phone receiver, lost in thought. *Oh, Turk will so very much* not *love to hear this. But Meryton's right: if the problem is connected here, we do need to know. And does that push us back yet again to Phanuel? I so hope it doesn't...* Still thinking, she went to the kitchen for something cold to drink, then took the glass of lemonade out to the tiny covered patio that opened off the landward side of Turk's study.

He had a strange liking for very small, very private spaces that he could burrow away in, like a fox going to ground or a cat with a cardboard box, but which also had sweeping views, where he could see an enemy coming from miles away. He had commandeered or built them into all the places he lived: a glassed-in nook, like a fighter plane cabin, in the Hollywood Hills house, with a view all the way to the Pacific; a high turret in Locksley Hall looking out over the Yorkshire moors; a wonderful space at Cleargrove like the stern of a Tudor galleon, all carved dark oak and leaded windows; a balconied study in Tarrant House, overlooking Regent's Park; a secret lanai in their Maui house; the top floor of the prow house in New York.

This one, lavishly landscaped and hidden from general access, was only big enough for a hammock and two lounge chairs and a small table, and, having been a lookout tower back in Ironhand's day, it boasted a spectacular view over half the island and several neighboring ones up to thirty miles away, with Lion Town and Lion Bay clear in sight far below. She scrupulously refrained from setting foot in this or any of his other bolt-holes; they were his private soul refuges, and unless he invited her in she stayed clear—she had never asked him about his need for them, and she never would. But he had drawn her into this one the other day, when they'd both felt the need of sanctuary, a place for them to hide, together. It was good that he'd shared it with her, because right now she didn't want anyone intruding on either her mood or her thought processes, but she needed to see people at a distance going about their business—it focused her somehow.

Because it was absolutely *maddening* that she could not do more to figure this out; but her hands were effectively tied, by several different sorts of ropes. First and chiefest was her all but total lack of information: okay, Hoden had supplied her with a few vague motives and suspects, but nothing was fixed and she could not go digging for more like clams at low tide. Almost as chief was her inability to ask for Turk's help: that road was well and truly closed; yes, he was endlessly patient and endlessly obliging, but there were some things she could not ask of him and this was most definitely one. There was the note to Hoden and the subsequent death threats and phone calls; and the possibility that Loya Tessman had been likewise threatened, hence the urgent and fearful wish to consult with Rennie. And of course there was the police fiat not to meddle in affairs that were none of her concern. Which edict had never stopped her before, but was doing so here very effectively. Right in her tracks.

She sipped thoughtfully at her drink and stared unseeing at the unreal vista. Something wasn't right here. Something she was missing. But what? And how could she root it out and drag it into the light, where she could examine it at leisure, without giving her game completely away? Only it was no game... Bringing the Weezles over had been, she felt, a smart move as well as a kind and humanitarian one. Though what she might be able to glean from it she really had no idea.

But she would. Oh yes. She would.

Fifteen

After lunch the next day, the Weezle boys went down the hill in two Land Rovers to get the grand tour of the island, guided and indeed chauffeured by Turk and Phanuel. Rennie, knowing they wouldn't be back for hours, shooed the three Weezlettes down to the beach, to which they clattered off giggling and happy. They were real girlfriends and even one wife, not just groupies du jour, so they weren't as unbearable as they might have been. She didn't dislike them, but they were stereotypical drifty pastel lightweight rock consorts and she had very little in common with them, though the wife, Georgie Moretti, spouse of bass player Brian, was actually in grad school for English history at UCLA. So she at least was more or less sound, and there had been a couple of nice academic dinnertime conversations about the Wars of the Roses, to which the Marquess of Raxton had contributed some sensational anecdotes, his family having been particularly closely involved on both sides.

The other two girls, though, had been almost entirely tongue-tied the entire time they'd so far been on Lion Island, except to chatter amongst themselves, and Rennie was suffering greatly because of it. She was unsure if they were tremblingly overawed by his lordship—understandable, if so, and forgivable—or whether they were trying to mess with her head, which was neither. But if this was the way they were going to be for the rest of their stay here, she was going to hit something, probably them. Or possibly Turk, for inviting the Weezles to stay here in the first place. The four band members were all great fun; it was the chicks she was losing patience with.

"Except for Georgie, they're women of few words, all right," Turk had dutifully agreed last night, having listened to her complaints as they prepared for sleep.

"Most of them 'and', 'but' or 'the'. Or else 'Groovy!'."

But at least Rennie had cleared them out of her inhospitable way for the rest of the afternoon, or so she hoped—she wanted them the hell out of the house, and she was relying on Silver Bay to do its thing and charm them into physical and mental torpor until the guys came back. She now gathered Prax and Belinda to her side in Turk's secret patio, where they could be neither overheard nor overlooked, and there she unburdened herself of all that was troubling her, under sworn oath that they would not mention it to anyone, and was much gratified to see the wide-eyed looks of horrified speculation on both their faces.

Prax regrouped first. "So Meryton thinks there might be a connection to here, with the heroin thing, and you think there might be a connection with the Weezles and the ship and Jo Fleet and Hoden's death threats. That's a lot to knit together even for you, twinkle bat."

"As usual, Alice, you have popped down the rabbit hole and put your elegantly beringed finger right on it. And please don't tell me that's exactly what Ares said last night in the sack, because I do *not* want to hear it. But yeah. It is a lot." Rennie's mobile face flickered with several emotional colors. "It all got suddenly much, much bigger than I am feeling quite comfortable with. Usually it's just me and murder. Up close and almost invariably personal. Extremely personal. But this has so much more than that added to it… and I have so much less room to move in. So many fewer resources. So many more lines to toe."

Belinda nodded, with great sympathy. "Well then, let us lay it out like a news story, always remembering our inverted pyramid structure, from most important fact to least. There were two murders on board ship. One of them involving a heroin-saturated Weezle t-shirt, the other a pretty gruesome little staged setup. Smack is known to be moving into the Grand Palm Islands as never before, and possibly over here to Lion Island. The Weezles were aboard the ship and had invited the t-shirt victim as part of a fan club contest that the other victim had organized. And?"

"And Hoden Weezle confides in me his fears and suspicions about what his manager and label and booking agent are up to, though he knows not what it may be, and *says* there were death menaces against both him and my dear little self. The crown prince of Lion Island, who is lord in his own domain and fully capable of commanding minions to my service, has instead flat-out ordered me to stand aside. Even though he is also freaked and fearful for my safety, now that he finally knows what really happened at the beach. And he had quite a lot to say about it, too."

Prax snorted. "Yes, we all heard him saying it. I think that deaf people in Cuba probably heard him saying it. But he's taken that line with you before. Has it ever worked? No, it hasn't."

"Well, it has to work, this time, because the Tarrants are important down here and I mustn't do anything to tarnish that. Nor do I wish to. So, basically, I am forbidden to call on his local contacts."

"And sadly, you have none of your own," said Belinda. "But do not despair! And don't forget we are reporters, you and I. We've dealt with sticky wickets like this before, by the nature of our disreputable profession, and we've always managed somehow. It's why Fitz loves us so much, though he really could pay us better, considering what we do for him. And I do understand why you might have to step more carefully here, given the tricky social terrain."

"You think?" Rennie rolled her eyes. "Yeah... Well, what do you suggest, ladies? Speak. 'My ear is open like a greedy shark, to catch the tunings of a voice divine.' Keats," she added smugly, seeing their astonished expressions. "I did minor in English Lit, you know."

Prax, who'd been busy unraveling a piece of her macramé sash, just because she could, looked up. "I hate to say it, but I think maybe this really *is* one you need to stand away from, even though it irks you. No, wait, stop"—as Rennie began to bubble with protest—"you said it yourself. You've been shot at and threatened. You have no resources at hand and your lord and master has commanded you to lay off girl-detectiving on his island. It can't hurt, surely, to let this one go? And let the cops handle it? You are in a foreign country, literally and metaphorically, and one that belongs to Lord Raxton, not to Turk. It could make quite a mess, even an international one. I'd hate to see you in the legal or personal soup because you stepped on toes you shouldn't have. You don't need to solve all by your own sweet, clever, brilliant self every happy little homicide that prances your way. Obey His Marquessness for once and leave this to the pros."

Rennie gave her best friend a glance that should have sent her hurtling down to the center of the earth, or up beyond the orbit of the moon. Mostly because she knew Prax was right. But—

"Good thing I didn't leave happy little homicides alone when they pranced *your* way in San Francisco, Mary Praxedes. Otherwise we'd be having this conversation on Death Row, San Quentin."

Which was not just below the belt but off at the knees, especially with the waspish tone she'd used, and she was immediately remorseful when Prax bit her lip and took a deep shivery breath.

"Oh, God, I'm *so* sorry, Praxie. I didn't mean it, I'm just feeling so— "

"Frustrated. Angry. Powerless. I know. It's okay." Prax began reweaving the ends of the sash, but she didn't look at anyone, and Rennie knew her friend had been really hurt by the snarly little comment. "But surely you knew that sooner or later you'd get to a place like this one, where you came up against a brick wall you couldn't knock down or get around?"

Belinda, who'd been watching them both and not caring to step between: "Wouldn't that, like, tear a hole in the fabric of the universe?"

Rennie shrugged gloomily. "I always liked to think so."

"So Murder Chick isn't going to ride again in this

particular instance?"

"Doesn't look that way, Lin, does it." Rennie leaned back, with a sigh, in the big wicker chair. "Still, you never know, maybe things will decide to ride my way after all."

"It's so unnatural, though." Prax finished fiddling with her belt, and reached over to pick a violently magenta bloom four inches across from the shrub beside her, smiling—they were friends again. "Every time you give up on solving something, an angel loses his erection."

"Oh, stick it up your jumper, as Turk would say!" But Rennie was laughing.

After they finished their secret crime confab, they moved around with the sun to the main terrace, and Rennie rang for chicken sandwiches on buttered white toast, her favorite, with iced raspberry tea to go with, all of which Marigo soon delivered with a smile.

"Dere now, my ladies, a nice good lunch for you," she said, setting down a handsome mosaic tray that had upon it properly crustless and buttered chicken sarnies and a pitcher of chilled tea and also some salad and a glazed pear tart. "You not been eating so much lately, you don't want get all bony and lose deh pretty figures your mens like. I want see all clean plates when I come back, now."

They thanked her—though Rennie watched her go with a considering look, remembering what Turk had confided—and tucked in, mostly silent while they made short work of the food. Then Belinda leaned back and smiled at her hostess.

"Have you ever met anyone you want to kiss and strangle

at the same time? Oh, wait, what am I saying?"

Rennie snorted a laugh. "Well, not so much. Well, not anymore."

"Was a time, though..."

"Always a time. But in all fairness, Turk is probably the one who's been in that stranglekissy position far more often than I. And who could blame him?"

"Not seriously, though," said Prax. "You just do what you do. As does he. If what you do involves things like, well, murder, that's really no fault of yours."

"Isn't it?" asked Rennie with some bitterness. "I bet if you asked him that, you'd get a very different answer. He'd give you a straight and truthful one too, because of who he is."

"Because of *what* he is," corrected Prax.

Belinda nodded with great gravity. "He's got integrity right out the door. I remember reading how his own family cut him off without a cent when they realized he was serious about this déclassé rock and roll thing, and how hard it was for him to get the band off the ground. Back when the flying saucer first dropped him off on Earth."

Prax chuckled. "Yeah, he really is from some other place. Like Elvis. Or the Beatles. Or Jimi."

"He was homeless, and penniless, and even starving sometimes," said Rennie, quietly but with fierce loving prideful admiration. "He really was. An Old Etonian and a graduate of Oxford and the heir to a dukedom, and he was crashing on people's floors, doing manual labor, driving trucks, busking for money in the street, even being secretly snuck care packages of food and clean laundry by his family's servants, going against his family's orders—and still he wouldn't haul down his flag."

"Son of a pirate! But all he had to do was go home like they wanted him to. Home to a castle. Home to several castles. It can't have been *that* hard. It's a struggle for any artist, but at least he had a nice upper-class cushion to fall back on."

"So it is, and so he had. But he was far too proud and self-respecting to do that. He thought it was too high a price. And he was quite right to think so. They wanted him to give up his music, and that was no price he was ever going to pay. And if you knew what his family was like, back then, you'd have agreed with him. They didn't understand him at *all*: what he was about, what was important to him. It didn't matter to him if he and the band never did any better than playing dank blues cellars; the playing at all was what mattered, not the degree of success. His family never got that: they thought it was a power struggle between him and them, a battle of wills between the ducal order and the wayward heir."

"Which it was," said Prax, "and still is, but not the way they think. And it's not just about him and his music, is it. It's about him and you as well."

"They're better about it now," admitted Rennie, after a pause. "On both counts. We got on very well, the times we've met, and I like them a lot. They've even been to Lionheart concerts, and from all appearances they actually enjoyed themselves. I like to think I've had a teensy bit of influence on them in that area. Or maybe it's just that they want to appease the chosen official broodmare, since said broodmare is not one of their own bony horse-faced kind and must be eased into the correct blueblood ways before she starts popping out the next generation of noble colts and fillies. Especially the heir to the heir. Well, we'll see how *that* goes. But he still has to deal with the expectations of that social echelon. And so do I. He should come with a warning label, really."

Belinda smiled, a little wistfully. "But he does. It's 'rock star'."

Rennie swung in the hammock, broodingly trailing her bare toes along the sun-warm stone. "True enough. Which should be warning enough for anyone. And before you say it, either of you, no, you're right, the warning label didn't stop me. But they really don't get it, his people. They're all supportive, they say they understand, but secretly they still think that sooner or later he's going to see the light as they see it, and toss music on the rubbish heap in favor of his noble destiny as the seventeenth Duke. Well, that's never going to happen. That hard-knock life taught him a lot about the *real* world outside his double set of privileges, and he's going to bend that noble destiny around his own will like a blacksmith bends a horseshoe. He'll do it, the ducal thing, and he'll do it very well, but he'll do it his way, not theirs. It's going to be fun to watch."

"And you'll have fun aiding and abetting," chortled Belinda.

"Damn straight I will! But only up to a point. I can't have *too* much fun: I have to be a lot more careful than he does. He was born to it and with it and in it and amongst it; I wasn't. They'll forgive a lot more from him than they will from me, and I have no intention of embarrassing him or letting him down by not knowing the ropes. And there's a veritable rat's-nest of ropes to trip over. So, homework. But yeah, I'm going to be bending some iron of my own, you can count on that."

"And no doubt bringing it down on people's heads."

"Only when I must, sweetness. Only when I must."

There was a lot of impromptu music going on around the house, now that it was stuffed full of musicians. That was perhaps Rennie's favorite part of living with a guitar god. Well, apart from the god himself, of course. She loved music with a passion, but she couldn't play anything, really, except for a little folk guitar and less piano — too little to ever embarrass herself by playing in front of either her mate or his bandfellows. But it was so nice to have music around, to please her ear and soul.

Like now, after dinner, out on the sea-facing terrace off the living room. Turk was playing banjo, which he loved and didn't get to do very often; Luke and Laird had a nice thing going on guitars, and Matt was really working out on a local folk drum called a keppie.

In her favorite place on the landward terrace, the whole length of the main living room between her and the musicians, French doors wide open so they funneled the sound along with the balmy evening breeze, Rennie contemplated the view, and comfortably listened.

"'Svaha' is kind of Turk's 'Layla', isn't it?"

"Not a bit," said Rennie evenly, turning a smiling gaze on Hoden. He had come through from the other side of the house to join her, and she hadn't heard him approach. "It's more like 'Layla' is Eric's 'Svaha'. Turk wrote it two years ago, you know. Long before 'Layla'. And he wrote it straight. Without the help of heroin or anything else. Unlike some people we could mention."

"But it's about you, yes? Like 'Layla' is about Pattie?"

"It's about *us*. He wrote it to get us back together. I can't say what Eric was writing about, or whom. Though I've heard the same stories you have."

"Well, it worked, didn't it. At least for Turk. Let's hope Eric is equally successful." Hoden smiled, and after a moment so did Rennie, and he went back across the living room to join the jam.

She sat on in the twilight until it was almost dark, and Prax came up beside her. "Hoden been hitting on you?" she said easily, their earlier situational stiffness long forgotten. "He's a tad bit smitten, you know. Just a teensy wee schoolboy crush. Nothing the Marquess would have to challenge him to a duel over."

Rennie turned and stared at her best friend. "You can't be serious! Why would you say this to me?"

Prax shrugged. "Because it's true? I have a pretty good radar for that sort of stuff, as you know. I called Paul Kantner being in love with Grace Slick months before they went public, if you remember, merely from a glimpse of them at a sound check at the Fillmore East. Same with Janis and Jimi's little fling after Monterey, and Stephen Stills and Judy Collins, and Paulie Mac and Linda, and Plato Lars and Sunny Silver, and a whole bunch more rock *ro*-mances. And you will not have forgotten that I knew you and Turk were destined for each other, that godawful night at the Whisky. I even said so."

"So you did. You realize how incredibly uncomfortable you've made me? I won't be able to act naturally around Hoden now, thanks ever so much."

"I'll take that as a compliment to good work."

"As you please."

"I'm glad to see that even Tarrants do manual labor here. There's something really poetically satisfying about seeing a future duke personally shoveling horse poop while little island kiddies are out enjoying themselves on million-dollar Caribbean beaches."

Rennie leaned on the hay rake she'd been using, watching as Turk lifted another forkload of straw bedding out of the stall they were currently working. Pip and Emmy Christmas, two island children she'd often seen around and had had great conversations with, fearless bright spirits the pair of them, had cheerily waved to her as they rode their battered bikes past the stables that Rennie and Turk were mucking out, headed for the nearby beach. She sighed: it would be nice to hit the beach themselves, and they could certainly use it to rinse off the evidence of their morning's hard labors. It was their turn to do some real work around the island, and she had suggested they go tend the horses; it would get a necessary chore done, and also it might take their minds off their worries, at least for a while. The two of them were sneaker-shod for their task: he was wearing nothing but a pair of cutoffs, she was clad in a bikini top and her usual short shorts, and they were both gleaming with honest sweat and covered with prickly bits of chaff.

Turk paused for a short breather, and sneezed as the drifting hay dust got up his nose. "How history doth repeat itself. I remember reading an entry in one of Ironhand's journals where he's complaining bitterly about laboring in the fields with the rest of the men—it was coming up on pirate season, and the harvest had to be gotten in, and he worked just as hard, ashore or afloat, as everyone else did—while the island's strong, healthy kiddies had skived off to go swimming. So unfair, he said. Not much has changed. Besides, both of my grandfathers taught me that you have to put in the work if you expect to have the fun—if you want to have a nice long ride on a nice fresh horse, you have to do the nice old mucking out. Anyway, I rather like doing work like this. It makes me feel useful."

Rennie laughed. "Me too. I learned the same thing when I first fell in love with horses: ride out, cool out, muck out. But I don't grudge those kids one minute of their beach time. They're charming children, and I very much enjoy talking to their dad." As Turk, delighted, opened his mouth: "Yes, yes, I know, Father Christmas, very amusing! But Voel's brilliant, and for an agricultural specialist he knows a ton of all that history stuff I like so much. We've been talking."

"Well, he *would* know all that stuff, as in addition to being the chief agriculturist he's the official island historian." Turk reached up with both arms to pitchfork more straw down from the top of a baled stack, and Rennie's brain briefly stopped thinking in order to pay full attention to the movement. "He's descended from Ironhand's supply officer, you know. In this duller age, he keeps track of all the births and deaths and bridal nights, all the big events. Small ones, too, of course. In fact, I find that those are much the most interesting ones to read about centuries later—the weather and the harvests and who was going to have a baby and who else's son got married and who recovered from a nasty fever and how many bolts of cloth and silver buttons Duchess Madelon ordered to make new captain's coats for Ironhand and herself."

"You lot do plan for the big picture, don't you."

He shrugged. "Have to. We've been going a long time, and there's a good deal to keep track of. You'll come to think the same way, once you're in the book yourself."

"Once I've been assimilated into the fold, you mean. And providing journal material to be read by people three centuries down the road."

"Well," said Turk, "you did promise."

"Indeed I did."

Rennie led the stall's patiently waiting occupant—Aloes, the sweet-natured chestnut Arabian she'd ridden the other day—back into the freshly strawed space and began to curry the mare's dusty coat, thinking about how she, Ravenna Catherine Julia, had ended up here in the first place. That terrible night in L.A., the night their friend Tansy Belladonna would have opened at the Whisky: for some reason Rennie had caught Turk's attention, and he hers, and they had held it even in the midst of the horror of finding Tansy dead backstage. For all his beautiful complexity, when things really mattered to him Turk was pretty much a one-trick pony: he possessed a knack for knowing what he wanted as soon as he saw it and sticking to it, however long it took to get. Not every decision of his was a to-the-death commitment; he made frivolous, for-the-moment choices like everyone else. But not very many, compared to how many he *could* make, and when he saw what he really wanted, that was it. He'd stuck to his choice of Rennie no matter what: from the night they'd looked at each other at Tansy's wake and driven off together into the night, that was it, for both of them.

To Rennie's credit, she had seen it at the same time he had. There had been complications along the way, of course, for the two of them equally. She had had a *very* hard time coming to grips with the realities of his life—both his lives—and Turk and Richard alike had had an equally hard time trying to figure out why she seemed to have such a ferocious need for her own independence, why she hated relying on other people. But blessedly for all concerned, they had sorted that out last year; hence the giant red rock on Rennie's left hand and the wedding plans they'd dumped on their mothers.

She stole another glance at him as he worked, singing softly to himself. At the bottom of everything, it was always music with him. Music was his go-to and fallback, always—his offense, defense and weapon of choice. It was always different, but it was always there: his caveman club, his broadsword, his nine-pounder chase cannon, his AK-47, his forward phaser bank. Music was what attracted people to him to begin with, though there was certainly quite a lot else that quite a lot of people found even more attractive. But he also used music when he didn't know how else to proceed: it was certainly classier than 'Hey, baby, what's your sign?' Not that he'd ever needed to go on the charm offensive; sure, there were females on two continents who'd turned down both Turk Wayland and Richard Tarrant, but there weren't all that many. He didn't ask all that many in the first place, and the ones he'd fended off over the years were legion.

He hadn't needed either defense or offense with her, though. They'd taken one serious, unblinkered look at each other at the Whisky the night Tansy died and had both been slammed by destiny, following in the romance footsteps, apparently, of Ironhand and Madelon. They had crossed paths in the rockerverse before, of course, on several occasions: Monterey Pop, a couple of concerts, a few parties at the houses of mutual friends. But that night, and the night of Tansy's wake that followed a week later, that had done it for both of them.

Fiercely liberated and feministic as Rennie was, she knew that Prax had called Turk her lord and master for good reason, and she didn't mind a bit. In fact, she found it ragingly arousing to defer to him as she did, because she was so resolutely independent and could well afford to. It was kind of like the end of *The Taming of the Shrew*, where everybody thinks that Katherina has been well and truly tamed. Rennie, who'd written a paper on it in college and had gotten an A-plus for it, was not at all sure that Kate had not simply figured out the best and easiest way to manage Petruchio. She was *very* sure that Richard, unlike Petruchio, knew this perfectly well; and she was likewise sure that he found it ragingly arousing too...

She finished with Aloes, having combed out the Arabian's

long silky gold mane and tail, and, leaning against the horse's shining side, she fed the mare a graciously accepted apple. As Turk had said the other day, peace really was in the contradictions: shoveling horse poop and learning how to be a duchess seemed to go hand in hand. It might not always be so, but for now it was, and it was good.

Sixteen

AFTER DOING ALL THE HEAVY LIFTING, quite literally, Turk shamelessly fled, claiming that he needed a quick splash at the nearby beach to get the hay and sweat off himself or else he would die. Rennie jeered after him, but kept on working, not minding a bit but really enjoying herself, really in the groove. She had ridden since she was six years old, and, like Turk's, her instructors had instilled in her from the start that if you were going to ride a horse for pleasure, then you had to make things equally pleasurable for the horse. You had to give him a good active workout, letting him stretch, switching off between walking, trotting and cantering, not too hard or too long—an hour was good, two if you took it easier. Then after, you had to walk him out until he was cooled down, and hose him off if the weather was hot, and walk him out some more until he was dry, and brush him until he shone, and finally blanket him and put him into a nice comfortable stall, with deep, clean straw and cool water and fresh hay and a hand-fed carrot or two. It was the least you could do, and it had to be done.

As she was starting in on the tall bay thoroughbred, Intro, that Turk usually rode when he was here on the island, Voel Christmas passed by, escorting his children back from the beach; they were still on their bikes and riding big loopy rings around their dad. At Rennie's cheerful hail, he shooed the kids up the hill to home, and turned aside to pass the time of day with the new stablehand.

"I hear you had a bit of a misadventure the other day," he said after a few minutes' inconsequential chat.

"Something like that," replied Rennie carefully, reaching under the bay gelding's belly to curry off a few stray bits of straw; gently dodging further questions, she gave Christmas the bee-sting story that everyone took for truth but Hoden, Turk, herself and the shooter.

They talked idly about the island, and its forward-thinking historical practices of non-slavery and profit-sharing as Turk and Phanuel had described them to her, and Voel informed her that that last went on even today. All the land, of course, was in the Duke's name, he said, and they cleared off very little new, instead letting some acres lie fallow or even go back to jungle—it was all carefully managed, by him, Phanuel, the Tenant-in-Chief and Duke Gervase himself, who were intent on keeping Lion Island both productive and pleasant to live on. But in practice the fields were worked jointly and profited from jointly, from crops to cattle-rearing, while each family owned its own house and a few personal acres around it where they could grow whatever they liked or keep a few pigs or chickens for family use, as they'd done for the past three centuries—larger animals were kept in herds on common ground. This excellent and rather kibbutznik arrangement not only supported the families but helped maintain the overwhelming rural charm of the island, where Grand Palm and other places roundabout all looked far more built up and crowded—which indeed they were.

As new families had been drawn to the island and

established families expanded, needing more space, more homesteads and more acreage had had to be carved out, of course; but it had recently been decided that no more jungle was to be turned into farmland, so immigration had been effectively closed off, at least for the time being. They had to take care of the families already established, first; then, down the road, they'd consider a change of policy. The island's population had remained remarkably steady down the years, at around a comfortable, villagey eight thousand—enough to run the place, not enough to feel crowded.

"Really?" asked Rennie, lifting Intro's hoofs one by one to pick them out and then neatly black them. "I did not know it was limited like that; Turk's never mentioned it. It sounds pretty idyllic for whoever's already here, but newcomers not so much."

"Well, if some young person of ours falls in love with an outsider, certainly no one is going to say they can't get married. It's all on a case-by-case basis. There will always be a place on the family farm for them, or in the family business; or if not, and they still wanted to live here, then we would do whatever we could to make sure they had jobs and a home. But anything more large-scale, no. Too many strangers around already, the Duke says. We don't want to end up like Grand Palm, with celebrity incomers or other invaders all over the place. We haven't had trouble over here, but we really should keep a closer eye."

"On?" Rennie's voice was casual as she continued blacking the bay's hoofs.

"On what's ours. As you know, we have four main

secondary islands—Little Lion, Vetiver, Tienda and Springhouse—and about a dozen smaller ones, all uninhabited and sitting out there looking very tempting. The worst that's happened so far is the occasional yacht dropping anchor in one of the little bays, for its inconsiderate trespassers to unlawfully sunbathe and picnic and have a fine old time without asking first for permission. Or worse."

"But how would you know if someone unlawful was lurking about? These are for the most part not teensy little islands. Especially this one."

"We know every face here," said Voel simply. "Anyone around who shouldn't be would be noticed pretty quickly, even if they try to hide or sneak in. It hasn't happened very often, trespassing, but it drives Gervase—the Duke mad when it does. Likewise Phan, as island manager, and Christophen, as Tenant-in-Chief. We're deeply protective of what we have. If you don't nip that sort of thing as soon as you see it, pretty soon there will be ice cream wrappers and beer bottles and abandoned bikini tops strewn all over the beaches."

Rennie laughed and slapped Intro on his powerful, newly gleaming quarters, and he rubbed his face against her front and obediently moved into his large box stall, where he nuzzled her pockets for the carrots he knew she had there for him, and was duly rewarded. Going to the barn's center aisle spigot, she splashed water on her face and over her hands, to remove the worst of the stable dust, and dried off on the towel hanging there.

"Yeah, I can see that happening. You don't go out with a gun to run them off, though, do you? The trespassers?"

Voel grinned, clearly unaware of the full extent of the recent drama. "Not so far as that, no. Though Gervase and Richard are both crack shots. As is Phan. And in all modesty, me."

With the kind of gimlet-eyed suspicion usually directed at brown-paper-wrapped parcels with big block printing and a ticking noise coming from within, Rennie watched Voel Christmas bid her a pleasant day and stroll off home after his children, and she was forced to conclude that, self-admitted crack shot or no, he was probably innocent and could thus be crossed off the list of suspects. The list that still had Phanuel Shine at the top, in forty-eight-point type. *Stop that! Just because Phanuel came in on the jet boat right after we were shot at is no damn proof of anything…*

She was sadly contemplating the long, high, hot climb back to Falcons Levels, and wondering if she could ask Joshamee to phone for a lift, if that wouldn't be too princessy, when one of the house Jeeps came bucketing into the stableyard, with, surprise surprise, Phanuel himself behind the wheel, gesturing her to hop aboard.

Gratefully swinging into the front passenger seat, she settled back as Phan, smiling at her, effortlessly spun the Jeep out of the yard and out into the road that led up from Lion Town to Falcons Levels, two miles away and a thousand feet up, and answered her question with a smile.

"How did I know to fetch you? Himself came in a little while ago, told me you were still down here beavering away with the noble steeds and might be glad of a ride home," he said as Rennie turned her face blissfully into the warm wind of their passage. First thing she was going to do when she got to the house was take a long, long hot shower and then a nice cool soak in that huge sunken tub, with yeah, vanilla and lavender bath bubbles up to her coral-studded ears, maybe she'd drag Himself in with her....

"Oh, you didn't need to come all the way down the hill just for me," she protested with utter insincerity, and Phanuel laughed.

"You looked practically faded away, standing there by the barn; Turk told me you seemed to feel the need to turn out both Aloes and Intro after your ride. You could have left it for Joshamee and his barn rats, you know—there's a bunch of local kids that love nothing more than to hang out at the stables to serve and worship the horses. You're such a good rider, you probably did that yourself at their age—I understand every horse-mad little girl likes nothing better than to sweep out stalls and polish tack and otherwise pamper the equine master race." At Rennie's dismissive but sheepishly confessing little shrug: "Anyway, I needed to pick up some groceries and mail off the boat from Palmton, so it was no trouble. But I would have come anyway."

They were silent for a half mile; then Rennie: "When you were in the boat office, did you hear anything from anyone, about, well, about anything?"

His eyes remained on the rising road, but he shook his head. "Nothing new, sorry. Oh, the ship is being released, but I think you already knew that. I guess they can't find any more evidence aboard."

"I imagine not... I would have thought that most of the passengers wouldn't want to sail back to New York, after what happened, but maybe they will. It's still a free cruise on a very comfortable ocean liner, and the Weezles paid for two-way passage, on the boat hire, so it doesn't really matter to them." She glanced aside at him, paused, decided to go for it. "What's the story about heroin around here?"

"It's a lot more of a story here after that ship you came in on," he said smoothly, though her abrupt change of subject had privately surprised him. "But we've had our share of problems, like everyone else. Not here, thank God, but over in the Grand Palms it's been bad. Can't get away with anything here, though. That's the advantage of a small place like ours, where everyone knows everyone else."

"Or the disadvantage."

"Is there still room at the Phanuel-Didn't-Do-It Hotel? I'd like to check in. Desk!"

The bubbles from the vanilla-and-lavender-scented bathwater had not yet faded as Rennie looked at Turk from under the curve of her damp arm, like a flirty kitten, leaning on the broad flat marble tub edge. She sounded abashed, as well she might.

"The least you could do," said Turk severely, though he was smiling, "is to apologize to him."

"Well, what he doesn't know…" She slid down in the bathwater and watched appreciatively as Turk stripped to join her, inverting her position so that she was gazing up at him, with an air of demure innocence that didn't fool him for a heartbeat. "I never really *seriously* thought he was the one to shoot at us on the beach, you know. It was just that it all fit together so perfectly, at least in the depths of my fevered brain, which was probably suffering from the combined effects of terror and dehydration, not necessarily in that order. If I'd been more rational, I would never have even mentioned it to you."

"Hmm. What has occasioned this road-to-Damascus moment, may I ask?"

"Oh, nothing specific. We drove up from the stable together, Phan and I, thank you so much for sending him to fetch me, and we…chatted. He's not the one. And neither is Voel Christmas, whom I talked to after you split, even though you haven't asked me about him."

"Why *should* I ask you about him?" He carefully stepped down into the tub and slid behind her, pulling her to rest against him, between his thighs, enjoying the feel of her water-slick body and the bubbles and the movement of pleasantly cool liquid sloshing chest-high around them both.

"Because I understand that you, your father, Phan and Voel are all crack shots."

"Ah. And since I was otherwise alibi'ed for, and my father isn't here…"

"Quite so. But, as I say, neither of them. None of you." She shifted in the water, reaching for the bath oil bottle.

"Stop wiggling like that or I will be obliged to do something dreadfully inappropriate in response. Or perhaps dreadfully appropriate."

"Oh? Do tell me some more about this ambivalent something you'd be obliged to respond with, my lord. Or, alternatively, do it."

"Tell me what you think first. Or who you think."

Rennie settled back against him again, letting the bubbles build. "Okay. And not forgetting that there are probably plenty of other good shots on the island, because, you know, pirate heredity... You remember I spoke to Hoden at the hotel the other morning, right? Well, you were there, of course you do. And that he was convinced that Jo Fleet and Ted Tessman and perhaps Jack Holland and the shysters Larry and Franz were all or some of them up to something at the Weezles' expense. Perhaps literally at their expense, like cooking the books."

"Yes, I do recall hearing you mention something of the sort, and did not think it unlikely."

"And you also remember Superintendent Meryton telling us about heroin being rampant, or more rampant than usual, let us say, in this neck of the woods? Meaning Grand Palm and some of the nearby islands."

"I remember that as well. But not, as I recall, this island."

"No. Not this island. Not then. Later he did drop a few crumbs for us to follow the smack trail right to our door. And I wonder now if there isn't a good reason for that, but that's not what I was thinking. I was thinking about those three other bodies wearing heroin-laden shirts that turned up in the neighborhood waters. The ones Meryton ever so casually mentioned at our little parley in the law offices."

"And you being you, a creature who never does anything in moderation—"

"Part of my charm."

"— you jumped lightyears at a single bound to arrive at the thought that because Hoden is suspicious, Fleet is somehow guilty. It does not strike me as an entirely improbable scenario, that he's up to something and the Weezles want to know what it is, but drugs? Why would he take the risk? And how would he do it? And most importantly, again, why?"

"Hadn't gotten that far yet," admitted Rennie, pouring more bath oil into the water and frothing it with her feet. "But as for *why*, well, money, of course. Tontine must be supplying Ted Tessman with a whacking huge percentage, judging by the wails and moans of all you talented folk he parasites upon, but he seems like a notable greedhead and I bet no matter how much it is, it's not enough for him."

"Perhaps not, but I recall hearing that Loya had major family brass of her own. Though maybe she didn't like to share with her husband. And now, of course, he being her widower—"

"—presumably inherits all her goods and chattels and bank accounts. Not a bad motive, right? And Jo Fleet is a glutton and not in the stuff-his-face way." She sighed contentedly as Turk reached his arms around her and applied a silky, bubble-laden sea sponge to her front. "Same with his piggy little friends. Jack Holland of Isis is always looking for a big payout, and what lawyers aren't avaricious weasels? Saving your own pet shysters, of course."

Turk snorted derisively. "Please! Don't let the pretty manners and distinguished bearing fool you; they'd take your hand off at the wrist like a hungry caiman if it meant they could squeeze a few more drachmas out of your hide. Which is, of course, why my father retains them. Dear Sir Geoffrey is the worst of the lot, without doubt."

"Oddly reassuring." She had nudged them both round

in the water and was now employing a loofah on her bathmate's back, her legs hooked around him. "Well, as I say, that was as far as I'd gotten. It's pretty far-fetched, I know. Just Hoden's grievances and my own rampant dislike of the parties involved, Weezles excluded. I have no idea how any of it is accomplished, if indeed it is accomplished, at the other end of the supply chain, and even less idea how they would manage things down here."

"Unless—?"

"Unless they had puppet people down here already, to do the dirty work for them. And I do mean dirty. Like murders. And where there are puppets, there are also puppet masters."

Turk went very still under the loofah's abrasive strokes. "Which brings us back to whom, do you think? Not Phan, but someone else from here? Since Lion Island has managed to remain smack-free?"

"Under the age-old policy of not befouling one's own nest. Maybe." She tossed the loofah and picked up the sea sponge to finish with, watching the clean water run over his gleaming wet shoulders and looking at the sponge with disapproval. "I hate these nasty things. They get slimy so fast and usually right when you're in the middle of using them."

"And you still have to loyally carry on. It's an English thing."

"Be that as it may. As a disloyal ex-colonial, I'm going to buy some nice clean scrubby terrycloth washrags at the dry-goods store in Lion Town tomorrow; that would be 'flannels' to you, Britboy... But no, not Phan. And no one here I can think of. No one I've met, certainly. Or if I have, they're very, very good at concealment."

To her relief, he didn't seem offended or annoyed. "Well, it's an interesting theory. But even I can see that it's going to be nothing you can prove to Superintendent Meryton's satisfaction." He grinned maliciously. "How does it feel to be kept pretty effectively out of the picture, lady mine? Even though you discovered one of the bodies and witnessed the taking-off of the other? Something new for you, isn't it."

"I like your cousin Oliver *so* much more than I like you, have I ever told you that? Yes! I do! He's way nicer than you are, and he even looks like you, though of course he's much prettier, and he's much smarter, and he went to a much better school, and he's got a title almost as grand as yours. So it would not be a big adjustment at all."

Turk pulled her under the water. "Don't even *think* it."

Seventeen

INEVITABLY, THE PRESENCE of so many merry at-leisure musicians had inspired Turk to write, and that had in turn inspired Hoden, and then Laird, and once the rest of the Weezles had shown up, all of them had begun seriously collaborating on the various songs that were being batted out. Amazing songs, too; good job that Turk, much against his family's wishes, had installed a tiny studio in a formerly unused outbuilding, half shed, half cellar—the smallest of his half dozen or so musical facilities, but more than adequate for the current purpose.

Where the boys were at the moment, and Prax with them to contribute peerless vocals. Nobody knew what they would actually *do* with these tracks—the legal ramifications for so many musicians and songwriters on four different labels would be a nightmare to sort out—but they were all enjoying themselves enormously, so objections, at least at this point, were nonexistent.

With her houseguests off on their own pursuits—the Weezle girls had gone over to Palmton for lunch and a day's shopping, driven in one of the speedboats by a friend of Phanuel's who was also employed as an oysterman, and Belinda was writing something on the terrace, actual *work*—Rennie, who should also have been writing, had gotten fed up with everything, so she had decided to go down to Silver Bay, thinking to paddle around in the lagoon and snorkel or perhaps scuba-dive along the reef, where the wreck of Ironhand and Madelon's escape ship, the brigantine *Hades Rift*, forty-two guns, was lying not very far down. She was a strong swimmer, and had done dives before; even so, she knew it was foolish in the extreme to dive alone in unfamiliar waters, and therefore she had told Turk where she was going. He had said fine, but had also asked Ares to accompany her, he being expert in diving as well as surfing.

She was glad of the company; Ares was as deeply bored as she was, the surf being flat as a mountain pond and Prax being busy with musicmaking, and he jumped at Rennie's suggestion that he come along to dive the bay.

"I hear from several people that that reef is amazing, full of corals and fish. We've surfed over it enough, now I'd like to see under it. And I really want to check out that wrecked ship, the one Turk told us about. She must have been one gutsy broad, that duchess."

"Well, she was a pirate too, wasn't she? That was her gig even before she met Ironhand, and by all accounts she was as good at it as he was. It was their ship. She would have known what he wanted her to do with it, after he died. As a sort of memorial."

Ares studied her contemplatively for several moments, and she busied herself assembling sandwiches and drinks for the lunch basket, aware that he was doing so.

"What?" she asked finally, not looking at him.

"It's already started, hasn't it."

She didn't pretend she had no idea what he was talking about. But she stilled her motions, and then sighed. "Yeah. Do you think it's a problem? Or a bad thing?"

"That you're starting to grow into your job? Your *real* job? Your real *life*? As a pirate duchess? No. I don't think it's a problem at all. Or a bad thing either. Not for you, and not for him. As long as you're sure this is what you want. It's not exactly something you can change your mind about later. Well, not without a lot of pain and screaming and yelling and lawyers and really bad publicity."

Rennie laughed. "I'm sure *he's* what I want. Could not in fact be surer. The rest of it comes with the dinner, and I realized that a long time ago. And he says the same." She patted his hand, moved. "But thanks for the concern. If anyone understands—"

"Me. And Mary Praxedes. It isn't the same for us, and it won't ever be. But we can still understand."

"I know. And you do."

The moment was over. They grabbed the lunch basket, then piled into a golf cart and trundled off down the hill to the bay. When they'd parked the cart, they went into the little boathouse, where all manner of aquatic equipment was kept—surfboards of varying sizes, scuba gear, spare towels, wetsuits, even swimsuits, as not every guest of the island was into skinnydipping.

As planned, they splashed around in the shallow, warm lagoon for a while, investigating the tidepools among the rocks, wearing water shoes for safety, then went back to the boathouse and got out the scuba gear. Ares, the more experienced diver, gave her a short, deadly serious course in dive safety, to remind them both, then rigged her up and did the same for himself. No wetsuits, which Rennie totally hated; they gave her major claustrophobia, and you had to *pee* in them, which was completely disgusting. Besides, they weren't going that deep and the water was bath-warm—all they needed was swimsuits, air tanks, masks and flippers. The area in which the *Hades Rift* lay was too inconvenient to swim to, so they took a small motorboat and chugged out to it. Then, setting up a bobbing safety flag, so that people would know they were there and underwater, they checked their gear yet again and tumbled backwards over the boat's side.

Immediately they were in another world, and Rennie felt all her stresses leaving her as they floated down through clear, pure, tourmaline-green water, streams of bubbles from their own passage rising up around them. Shafts of sunlight fell across everything, lighting up her skin, gleaming it like mother-of-pearl in between the halves of her tiny bikini. Shoals of the most improbably colored reef fish wafted by, unconcerned at the human presence: comical puffers, neon-bright parrotfish, brilliant blue tangs, angelfish that looked nothing like the ones she'd had in a tank when she was a kid, needle-shaped and vertically oriented trumpetfish, even a small barracuda or two, with their evilly underslung and toothy jaws.

Watching the incredible aquatic parade, enchanted, she had almost forgotten their destination when Ares swam into view in front of her and tapped his left wrist—time to be moving on if they wanted to get a good look at the wreck. They weren't going deep but they still needed to be careful with their air. He pointed, like a lance, with the efficient-looking speargun he'd insisted on bringing. Well, there was bitey fishy riffraff in these waters, so probably he wasn't being paranoid, and he'd insisted she strap a rather fearsome dive knife to her right calf, just in case.

Underwater, it is by no means serenely silent, as most people think: you have the sound of the regulator in your ears; the thump of your own heartbeat; the whoosh of air coming in from the tank, your life and breath; the bubbling of air going out and rising through the fathoms; odd slaps and smacks and boat noises echoing from a surprising distance; even the clicks and pops of tiny snapping shrimp hidden in the reef, their territorial warning noises sounding like, of all things, frying bacon.

Things look about a third closer, too, as in a rear-view mirror, so you need to adjust your sight references, and you have to turn your whole head like an owl, because of the mask and tank. There was a lot to remember; but it had all come back as soon as she had gone underwater, and she suddenly saw why Turk loved this place, from the jungly hilltops to right down here below the waves.

Leaving the drifts of fish behind, not without a longing backwards glance, she followed Ares out into a deeper channel. There were fish here too, bigger ones, still totally unafraid of them, moving through the water like aquatic buffalo herds; huge slow prehistoric-looking sea turtles; even vast and beautiful manta rays flapping slowly by above her head. But chiefly the landscape now was a coral one: living colonies of every size and shape and color, cup corals, staghorn corals, elkhorn corals, star corals, tube and fan and whip and branch corals, fantastic sea sponges like big floppy barrels, in the wildest colors—hey, pick your own bath sponge! Rennie turned gracefully round and round, balletic, eager to take it all in, and perhaps to find a pretty shell or coral chunk to bring back to Turk—a dead one, of course, she'd never kill a live creature for the sake of its house, and these waters were protected anyway. And then there it was, what they'd come to see: about thirty feet below the surface, the dark timbers of an ancient but still beautiful ship lay on the sandy bottom.

If she hadn't been underwater at the moment and needed to keep the regulator going, her jaw would have dropped. The *Hades Rift* was remarkably intact for a ship of its age and situation. Two hundred and some years ago it had been dynamited and sunk deliberately, at the command of Captain Madelon Buckmaster—at that time, Madelon Tarrant, Dowager Duchess of Locksley. Unsurprisingly, she found her eyes stinging, not with seawater but with tears; the ship had been sunk when Ironhand died, so it was a marker, a token of the duchess's love for her duke, a sign that her pirating days were done with him, and that she ended them gladly in his honor. The ship hadn't gone down in battle, Rennie was thankful to recall, so no hapless crew members were entombed with it; she need fear neither grave nor ghost.

Waving and pointing directionally to Ares, she swam down to within a few feet of the wreck, knowing not to get too close to risk getting caught and stuck, or maybe attacked by a barracuda or moray eel lurking in the dark hull crevices. As Rennie floated over it, she could just make out the great shattered wound amidships that had sent it to the bottom, framed by the remains of hull and decks and copper-bottomed keel. Sheltered by the reef from passing hurricanes, the *Rift* was scattered into giant coral-covered timbers, two centuries of marine growth and drifted sand blurring and softening her splintered outlines, giving her an organic appearance. *What a pretty thing this must have been…*

With the *Ravenna* as comparison, a craft of much the same length and build, Rennie pictured the ruined brigantine she saw before her as alive and above and intact again, running fast before a following sea, her sails like clouds, her midnight blue and claret paintwork—the Tarrant house colors—bright in the sun. She saw Madelon standing on the quarterdeck, in a long coat lavished with silver lace, bucket-topped boots, a leather and feather hat, while behind her stood Ironhand himself, tall, bearded, blond—like another Tarrant guy Rennie knew—his hand on his duchess's shoulder, a Callows sword at his side. *This was their escape ship—but they escaped long ago, together…*

She found herself wondering what the pirate couple would think of the drug smuggling going on in the waters where they had once ruled as king and queen. They would have approved of the profit, certainly; hello, *pirates*? But the nature of the cargo, no; she couldn't think that that was something their honor would have allowed. They would have blown any drug-running ship out of their waters and out of existence, or so at least she hoped.

A shadow ghosted between her and the light; looking up, startled, she saw that it was only another manta. There had been several of the graceful giants that had swum past while she was exploring: they soared through the water like waving silver cloaks, their edges rippling rhythmically, their long whippy tails trailing behind. No danger from one of them, but there were stingrays around too: you had to be careful with their mean little stingers—if you trod on one and it zapped you, it could be really painful, especially if the barb got lodged in the wound, and sometimes even fatal.

For the most part, the rays were fearless of humans, and completely benign; there was actually a cove over on Little Lion where you could feed them, though tourists were strictly not allowed. The creatures would swirl round and round underwater in vertical loops, or they would come into the shallows and gently nibble round your ankles or bump up against your thighs, and you could scratch their backs and feed them shrimp; they seemed to enjoy the interaction. But here they were in their element, so mysterious, so graceful; here she was the awkward one, the intruder.

She swam around to the other side of the ship, her flippers moving slowly behind her as she kicked, wondering if there was anything left inside the hull. Not that she would dream of pillaging or even touching anything: it should all remain exactly as it was. Perhaps Madelon had left some token of herself and Ironhand aboard before she sank the ship, and it remained there even now—the thought pleased her.

A huge dumb-looking grouper lumbered past, and Rennie twisted in a tumbling arc to watch it out of sight. She couldn't see Ares, but she knew he would not let her roam too far out of visual range: it was getting late—the sun shafts were now taking an afternoon angle through the water—and air was tending low on the dial. She rolled over in the water as several other shadows flickered between her and the light, and was relieved to see that it was merely two more of the giant rays.

Getting a little crowded down here...time to go! She pushed off a nearby bit of reef. Harmless as they were, those mantas were moving too close for her liking. She began swimming back to the boat, or to where she thought the boat was. Yet another ray went by, cutting off the light, and then suddenly it wasn't a ray at all but a diver, suited and masked, who had grabbed her around the neck and was trying to tear out the hose to her air tank. A diver who certainly wasn't Ares.

At first stunned, then enraged, Rennie pulled her dive knife off its straps around her calf and slashed backwards through the water at her assailant. *Who the hell* is *it? Where did they come from? Were they lurking in the wreck all the time, and I just didn't see them?* The face behind the mirrored mask was hidden from view, and the black wetsuit covered all bodily identifiers; she couldn't even tell if the athletic attacker was a man or a woman. She kicked off her swim fins to let her bare feet get some purchase on the sandy seafloor. They struggled for what seemed a long, long minute, her breath sounding increasingly raspy in her own ears. Well, she was still getting air from the tank, he hadn't managed to rip out or cut the tube yet, but he was holding it closed enough to interfere with her airflow. Then one of her wild slashes finally connected, and suddenly there was a drifting red mist all round them. *Oh dear, blood in the water,* not *a good idea...*

As she struggled, a silver arrow shot past her face in a trail of bubbles, and she instinctively startled backwards. If Ares was trying to hit the guy, his aim was way, way off. Then a hitherto concealed manta rose up off the ocean floor, silvery and enormous, three times her height across, ruffling angrily and hiding them both with its wings. A stingray, considerably smaller, rose with it, and through a cloud of sand, Rennie thought she saw the stingray jab the attacker right in the ribs with that deadly tail. But before she could confirm this, a shrieking pain shot through her foot; in her shock she almost lost her mouthpiece, and then Ares was there and throwing his arm around her waist, to tow her to the surface.

They broke through to the air, Rennie coughing and choking as she inhaled seawater, struggling to match Ares' haste and power, and once above the waterline they thrashed their way to the boat. Ares heaved her aboard, whooshed himself in as well, and before she could even untangle herself from the gear, he was zooming out of the bay and doubling back toward Lion Town. Gasping for air, she sprawled there for a few moments on the padded stern bench, and then Ares reached back and grabbed her bleeding heel, pulling it down below her waist level.

"Ow! That *hurts*! Was it a ray?"

"Of course it hurts, you stupid girl! Not a ray; you stepped on a sea urchin. I saw the whole thing. Keep it down! So the venom stays in your foot and doesn't spread up your leg. It was lying on the bottom and you didn't see it, and you stepped right on it and now you've got spines in your heel."

"Oh my God, I do, don't I…wow, look at those things. No, no, that's not right at all. There was someone down there, he tried to pull out my air hose. You even fired a spear at him." She looked wildly over the side of the launch. "Where did he go? Is he hiding? He might still be around—"

"There was no one, Rennie. I was shooting at a shark that had come in too close. A little reef one, but still. I didn't want any more of them checking us out."

"He must be hiding somewhere then, the guy who attacked me. I got him with my knife—we shouldn't run away..." She looked around to see where they were. Ares had slung the speedboat around the westernmost point of the island, and now they were flying through the light channel chop, headed toward the Claws and Lion Bay beyond them. "Where are we going? This isn't the way home."

"No—I'm taking you to the hospital in town. You need to get those spines out."

She nodded agreeably, peering with a kind of detached interest at the spines in her foot; she was already beginning to fade from the quite ridiculous pain. "Oh, yeah, right, that's good thinking. We don't want that guy coming after us. Or that ray either. Blood in the water. Turk is going to be so mad at me." She leaned back in the stern of the boat, as if it had been a gondola and she a contessa of old Venice, and closed her eyes.

Ares gave her a quick anxious look, and throttled up the boat's speed.

Eighteen

"OH, IT'S YOU...ARE YOU MAD AT ME? Don't be mad, it wasn't my fault."

Rennie, who had half-risen, disoriented and startled, when Turk came quietly in, lay back down again, curling up around her pillows. After she'd gotten home from the hospital, she'd obediently sat on the edge of the sunken tub for three hours as she'd been ordered, with her injured foot, now spine-free, immersed in water up to her calf—water as hot as she could bear it. Now, foot dry and neatly wrapped, she'd retreated to bed and dropped codeine, her friend as always in pain situations.

"I must say, I've had warmer welcomes. But no, I'm not angry, and I know it wasn't your fault. This time." Turk's voice was gently teasing. He didn't bother to turn the light on, but took off his shirt and sat down on the edge of the bed to pull off his jeans. After the studio session, he had gone to the Tenant-in-Chief's office to check over some papers that needed signing, and so had missed all the drama; as soon as he'd gotten back to the house and been informed of Rennie's watery mishap, he'd dashed to their rooms, anxious but not wishing to disturb her if she was asleep. "How's the foot feeling?"

She beamed up at him. "Excellent well, it is a fishmonger! Voel's nice lady doctor wife pounded all that nice local anesthetic into it, and then I've had it in the really, *really* nice hot water, because that's supposed to break down the venom, and now I could walk barefoot on a carpet of sea urchins. But I'd rather make sushi out of the spiny little bastards. Mrs. Doctor Christmas, that would be. She's outasight!"

Turk was trying not to laugh at her stoned good spirits. "That she is. But you won't be walking on urchins or anything else. Didn't she tell you to stay off it for a couple of days?"

"Yes, yes, no horses, no water shoes. Very sad."

Five hours earlier, Hannah Christmas, one of the resident doctors at the Lion Town hospital, had leaped into action when Rennie was carried in by Ares Sakura. It was a small facility, but immaculately up to date, with forty beds, an E.R., several clinics and even a fully equipped operating room. Really serious cases, of course, were taken over to the big hospital in Palmton, but for most day-by-day purposes there wasn't much the place and its personnel couldn't handle. It was empty at the moment, Lion Islanders being a disgustingly healthy lot, as she was cheerfully told while Hannah, assisted by two nurses, worked on her foot to draw out the urchin spines and clean the wound. The place was staffed mostly by native-born inhabitants who had trained off-island and come back to work and live, and both Hannah and the nurses were of these.

"Could have been a lot sadder, you know," said Turk, trying to get her focused on reality again. "What a good thing Hannah was right there when Ares got you to town."

Rennie nodded cheerfully, and seemed to sober up. "Did the other driver ever show up at the hospital? The one who hit me. Diver, I mean. Attacked me, I mean. It looked as if he, or she, got slammed with the stingray's stinger right in the chest. That can't be good. Though I guess he deserves it for coming after me like that. I got him in the leg with my knife, too," she added with satisfaction.

Turk shook his head and sat half-reclined beside her on the many pillows, drawing her into his arms. "No, sweetheart. Hannah said no one but you came in with an injury, certainly no one with a stab wound or a ray sting. And"—here he looked at her strangely and carefully—"Ares said there was no other person down there. Just you two."

"But there was, I saw him!" said Rennie, with a little flounce of protest; she seemed back to more or less her normal state, but was showing signs of dismay. "Or her. They tried to rip out my air hose, and that was when I stabbed them, with that dive knife Ares made me wear, and then the ray exploded off the reef bottom and nailed him in the chest with the stinger. The guy who attacked me, not Ares. Though he got off a shot with the speargun. Ares, not the other guy. And that's when I stepped on the urchin."

He shook his head again, moving to shut her down before she got unhealthily worked up. "Ares said there was a small shark and that's what he was shooting at. Your air hose got displaced when the ray reared up and you hit the reef, and you were seeing things because your hose kinked and you didn't have enough air. Not ripped or cut or torn. There wasn't anyone else there, only you, the ray, the urchin and Ares. He got you into the boat right as your air was running out, and thence to the hospital. Voel was there, and he came running out to help as soon as he saw you. He and Ares took you into the E.R. and Hannah went straightaway to work on your foot. No one but you came in stung, by an urchin or a ray or anything else."

When she remained mutinously, miserably silent, he wrapped his arms around her more tightly and pulled her close against him, his lips against her hair. "When I was a little boy here on holiday, I saw a man die from a ray sting. Not nice. Don't be doing that, please? Rennie? I'm not angry, but please promise me..."

"Oh...okay. I don't think I'll be diving again anytime soon anyway. It's always something with us—poison, or stingrays, or little aquatic hedgehogs, or some damn thing. But this was no accident."

"Love, it *was* an accident!" He felt her flinch, dropped his voice to its lowest register and pulled out his silkiest tones to soothe. "There, you see? No evil underwater ninja. Only fish. Besides, who knew you were going to be diving to the wreck? You and Ares didn't even decide that until everybody else in the house was away. How could some scuba-diving, mirror-masked assassin know you'd even be there? Was he lurking around underwater, circling the island like a demented hammerhead, waiting for people to come along so he could rip their air hoses out?"

Okay, that's true enough. Even if he is using that damn seductive voice on me... She mulled it all over for a while. "Well, when you put it that way, maybe not, then. No one else *was* in the house..." Her mobile face clouded over, and she moved away a little so she could see Turk's face. "I suppose you're right."

"She admits I'm right! Will wonders never cease? So, dear, what can the matter be? Besides your poor wounded foot. Shall I kiss it and make it better?"

"It'd be a start..."

Turk lifted up said foot and began to kiss her toes, and the high arch and blue-veined instep peeking out of the bandages, and from there, nibbling up the curve of her calf to the soft skin of her inner thigh, and sudden clarity shot through her like fire.

"Oh God don't *do* that—by which I mean yes, *just* like that..."

"Do make up your mind, madam. But what's really got you worried?"

Rennie's reply came in a hesitant, almost shamefaced murmur; Turk's mouth on her thigh was blurring her brain almost as much as the codeine. "I heard at the hospital that there's a big storm, maybe even a hurricane, stomping around farther down the island chain, and it could be heading this way."

"Yes?"

"Uh, *hurricane?*"

Oh. Turk berated himself inwardly; of course she'd be freaked, after that terrifying Agatha Christie episode on Block Island last month. Ten Little Indians, well, ten little rock writers, cut off on the island by an early-season hurricane. Writers on the Storm, all right: about fifty of them had gone up there for a media conference, one of them a murderer. Most of them had managed to get clear of the island before the storm hit, but the ten for whom there had been no room on the last ferries and planes out had been temporarily marooned, and stalked by a killer who struck twice, successfully, before being overpowered by Rennie and the other seven. They'd finally been evacuated by Coast Guard heroes while the effects of the hurricane were still on, but it hadn't been fun. So he could see where she might fight shy of tropical storms and their nastier, larger sisters, at least for a while. Stingrays and urchins were bad enough.

He settled her into his arms again. "Don't worry about it. How are you feeling now?" Actually, now that she knew Turk wasn't cross with her, Rennie was feeling pretty good. The latest slug of drug had kicked in, and the kisses applied to her cerise-toenailed little piggies and regions northward had done their bit as well.

"Me? Oh, I'm fine. Though you could always kiss my foot some more—*I* don't mind if *you* don't."

"That's all you get for free. Anything more, you have to do as I say and get some sleep first."

"Fine, sure, whatever... You should wear peach lip gloss when you surf, Turk, it would be very good for your lips and it would look so pretty with your hair..."

Again he struggled to keep from laughing. "And that's what we needed to know! Why don't you take this, then?" he added coaxingly. "Nice Dr. Hannah sent it over for you, and we can send you off to Happydreamland, shall we? I'll be here when you wake up."

"'We'? Ohhh yeah..." She vaguely recalled all the concerned people who'd shown up on her return from Lion Town like a wounded but triumphant Spartan, Ares and Voel escorting her, all of them with relief on their faces.

Praxie and Linny! Hoden and Laird! The Weezles and their ladies! Phan and Ares! They were all such good people! And Turk! He was gorgeous. He was perfect. He'd come into her life crowned with glitter, cloaked in a rainbow, riding a unicorn. She could surely take another pill for him, you bet.

Now he was holding a glass of water and a Tuinal to her lips; she swallowed obediently and snuggled down into the pillows, and five minutes later was out like a lapsed firefly. Turk sat holding her hand until he was sure she was asleep, then returned to the terrace, where the others had clustered. Seeing him, they fluttered forward with questions, which he fielded with patience and care.

No, it wasn't bad. Yes, she was still in pain, but not so much as before. No, it had never been life-threatening, urchin spines seldom are, unless you are unfortunate enough to get them in a place like your heart, or are allergic. Yes, she'd dropped some pills and was safely asleep. Yes, stoned out of her gourd. Yes, a *very* good thing. Yes, she'd have to stay off her feet for a few days. Yes, they could go see her in the morning when she woke up. Praxedes, would you and Belinda look in on her every hour or so if I'm not around? No, thank you, no tea. After ten minutes of this, Turk collected Ares and Phanuel with a glance and a small, significant nod. They casually withdrew, one after the other, to a far and plant-screened corner of the terrace where they could be private and unheard.

Turk asked first. "So, *was* there anyone else? The way she says there was? Trying to cut her airhose? Because if there was..."

Ares shook his head. "I have to say I myself saw nothing

but that big mother of a manta. Thing must have been twenty feet wide, and it reared right up between us like the Berlin Wall. Stirred up the sand all around and I couldn't see through until the water cleared. Then she stepped on the urchin with nothing on her feet, I did see that. I don't know why she kicked off her fins; I just wanted to get her up into the boat and get the hell out of there. So it's possible I could have missed seeing something. Or someone." He paused, and shrugged helplessly. "Otherwise I saw no humans but us, certainly no humans trying to mess with her tank. She went a little delirious on the way to the hospital; she was worried you'd be angry with her."

"She doesn't have to be worried. I *am* angry with her. Well, I was. What did you both do? Tell me again."

"We went down to the cove and were poking around the surf zone rocks, looking at stuff in the tidepools—you know, anemones and starfish and crabs and small corals, we even saw a tiny octopus. We had water shoes on, so we wouldn't accidentally step on anything, like, yeah, an urchin, or a stinging jelly or something else nasty. Then we had a dive safety review, geared up, got into the boat and went farther out over the reef to the *Hades Rift*, where we went in. That was the whole point: we wanted to see the ship. Nothing unusual: lots of pretty fish, very clear water, wreck was amazing. I went one way around the ship, she stayed by the stern. Neither of us went into the ship or even I think touched it."

"But you fired your speargun." That was Phanuel.

Ares nodded. "Reef shark, maybe six feet long and thirty feet away. It was only a warning shot, not trying to hit it, but that's where I was looking. Then all of a sudden this absolutely enormous ray was standing up on end, flapping its wings, and I couldn't see past it to where she was."

Turk pondered this for a moment or two. "So possibly there *was* someone else there who attacked her just as she says. Who grabbed her airhose and then got hit by a stingray he'd disturbed. And you couldn't see any of it because of the big ray and the sand it kicked up. I can't think where she'd lie about it."

"Of course not, but maybe a hallucination if she was starting to lose air? Still, if he *was* real, he would have had to be very, very quick, or hiding in the wreck. I didn't hit the shark or either of the rays with the arrow, I know that, because I went back an hour ago and looked around. First I checked out her equipment, which had a few small scratches that could have come from anything—coral, reef rocks, being tossed against other gear in the shed. Her mask and tank and regulator were fine, though the hose did look kinked."

"Or meddled with, by someone trying to crush it," said Turk darkly.

"—Well, yeah, maybe. Anyway, thanks to the dive flag we'd put up, I knew where to go back into the water. I found the speargun arrow lying on the reef floor, and her knife right where she'd dropped it, so we know she pulled it on *something*, but there was nothing else around. No sign that anyone else had been there, much less attacked her and gotten stung for his pains."

Turk laughed shortly. "Karma is seldom so instant."

"Let's hope it stays that way."

*

In the morning Rennie was early awake, making jokes about the great Achilles, whom they knew, and cheerful as hell, while Turk, lacking the benefit of her excellent meds, was rather less so. She was facing him over breakfast—one of Marigo's divine omelets, fried potatoes, assorted local fruit juices and the Lion Island variant of a spicy pan-Caribbean concoction called callaloo, which Rennie eyed suspiciously but declined to dare.

Instead, she watched as Turk carefully spread his toast with butter and jam, right out to the very edges, as he always did. Suddenly a memory came flooding back: college, her freshman year—she'd discovered Lionheart when they played the Winter Festival and Laird Burkhart had taken her to the concert. Their first album, folk-influenced but already breaking into complex, hard blues-rock—she had run out the day after the concert to buy it in the town's only record shop—had lived on her turntable for the next three months. Even now she could recall, in order, with perfect clarity, every single track; she hadn't loved them all equally, and still didn't, but she did love them all.

And the memory that had sprung to mind was when, on Easter break and spending the day in Manhattan, she'd been walking to meet friends in midtown and had stopped by two taxis waiting at a red light. And spoiling for combat, seemingly: the windows of the cabs were wide open and the drivers were screaming at one another, one pounding the steering wheel, the other the outside of the door through the open window. She had hesitated to cross in front of them when battle so clearly might commence, and then she realized what the song was on the blaring radios, the song they were both ecstatically roaring, as completely on key and in synch as if they'd rehearsed for days: "Go Down Easy, Come Down Hard". And the band was Lionheart, and the song was from that first album, and the singer was Turk.

"I *said,*" said Turk indulgently, and she startled.

"Sorry! I was just thinking."

"So I see. What about?"

"You, what else?" she said with total truthfulness.

He preened a little, covertly, so she wouldn't notice, and Rennie's mouth twitched. *Underneath everything, he's still such a* guy…

"Anything you'd like to share with the class?"

"Oh…only remembering. What were you saying?"

He laughed, his mood abruptly cleared, and took a bite of toast. "I was just thinking as well, about that ball we went to back in March, for your birthday. You remember, the one at Windsor Castle…"

"Ah, the Night of the Long Gloves! Not likely to forget a ball at Windsor Castle. Especially not with major royals in attendance. Being presented to your godmother Auntie Queen Lilibet not the least of it. Plus that was the hoedown you weren't going to let me wear a tiara for. What about it? I wore that pearl and diamond one your grandmother lent me, and nobody turned a hair. Not even Her Maj. Or if they did, they didn't do it where I could see it turning."

"As I recall, you looked both regal and foxy. Hard to pull off."

"Thank you. But why would you think of this now? Is there a point in here somewhere?"

"Not entirely sure." Turk set down his knife and fork and touched his napkin to his mouth; they were breakfasting privately on the fountain terrace off their bedroom, having balked at sharing the morning meal with the rest of Falcons Levels, both still a bit shaky from the previous day. "Something someone said there reminded me of something somebody else said here, about this whole mess. Or maybe it was something you said someone said."

"Do you think you could be just a *bit* more specific?"

"I don't think I can, actually." He looked briefly vexed. "Something about Jo Fleet? Or the Tessmans?"

"Weren't at the ball, I'm pretty certain."

"No, but there was a particularly noxious baronet who was, and he's the one I'm thinking about."

"Druggie stuff?"

"No... More like—more like... Bloke had been sneaking around buying up rural property in the Home Counties, and had been caught using it for unlawful purposes."

"Again I ask: drugs?"

"And again I say not. Laundering money, chiefly, and engaging in other unsavory activities, prostitution among them. I'm not quite sure what brought him to mind at the moment. Maybe I was just thinking of how the drug ring operates down here. If there is one, I mean. And I don't think either of us has forgotten Balto Wallace and his unsavory companions."

She shuffled her cutlery before looking up at him. "I suppose you're right."

"My goodness, twice in twelve hours! Must be a sign of the Apocalypse."

Rennie kicked his bare shin under the table, using her good foot, and he laughed. "Count yourself fortunate, Ampman."

"Always with you," he said gravely. "But why now?"

"Because if it's really the Apocalypse, I plan on being the Fifth Horseman." Before he could ask: "Retribution."

Nineteen

THE STORM ADVANCING from the southeast had begun to close in, working its slow, ponderous way up along the Windwards. The people who wanted to get off the island—all the Weezles except Hoden, who was eager to stay, and their ladies with them—were flown back to Palmton by Phanuel, to catch a private chartered flight for L.A., and the rest busied themselves securing things at Falcons Levels. When Phanuel got back, early the next day—with half a dozen big boxes of provisions, to be on the safe side—he put the plane in its boathouse hanger in the well-sheltered harbor, loaded the boxes into the Rover and drove up the hill to the house.

"Getting very nasty out there," he reported to the others, who were all in the kitchen drinking tea. "The wind is really kicking up. I almost got blown off the road, coming up from town. The harbormaster says the boats are all safe inside the Claws and the seagates are shut, and I think we'd best be staying shut in here ourselves till the storm passes."

"I've never been in a hurricane," said Hoden brightly. "It's probably very wrong of me, but I'm quite looking forward to it. Dangerous or not."

"Dangerous here?" asked Prax, glancing anxiously at Rennie, who was once again remembering the last hurricane she'd been in, and who didn't look very thrilled about being in another—in fact, she looked a little bit sick. Though that could have been a holdover effect from the urchin venom, or from the painkillers; she'd only been allowed to start walking around the house that morning.

Phanuel shook his head. "Not to worry. We've ridden out plenty over the centuries. We're dug deep into the top of the hill, enough to be well set against the wind. We might lose a few roof tiles, couple of trees, get some water damage, but we'll be fine otherwise. We have battens for the doors and shutters for the windows to go over the special hurricane glass. There's at least five wells and springs within walking distance. The house has three emergency generators and enough food to outlast a siege."

"Which you're now going to tell me has actually happened."

"I am, too." Phan's smile flashed. "You know that this part of the house was the original Tarrant fortress, right? Well, Ironhand was shut up here once for three months, when the French navy blockaded the island, thinking to starve him out. Knowing he had enough ammunition to last decades and no shortage of food or water, he worked out a firing rota to man the big guns at the Claws, then he garrisoned this house and guarded the beach trail and the cove with field pieces. Then he sat back and put his feet up, and he and Madelon hung out and played with their kids, or spent many a happy firelit evening molding bullets with their friends, until the frogs got bored and sailed away. Nobody went hungry and nobody got hurt. Except a few Frenchie ships, of course, which the Claw batteries knocked to kindling."

"Great story. Let's see if we can keep his record intact."

Rennie kept going over in her head the reassuring facts: fortress, check; solid, check; stone-built, check; ridge that sheltered against hurricanes coming out of the southeast, check; food, water, electricity, check. Check check check check check. They'd be fine. Yes, they would.

Turk looked up from his book, hearing the nervous note in her voice. "Not to worry, sweetheart. Hurricanes have blown right through this island with no more damage than a lot of water, *bad* hurricanes; and, sorry, Hoden, but this one is just a tropical storm. The swell will get up down below, but there's nothing there to be washed away. By edict, all permanent structures on this island are above the line of the highest wave ever recorded, and there are stone markers all round the island to make sure people never forget where that line is. Didn't you ever notice them, or wonder why no houses are built directly on the beach?"

"I can't say as I ever did. I don't know, maybe I thought real estate taxes?"

Phanuel shook his head. "Try tsunami. The rule is due to the same earthquake and wave that took out Port Royal over in Jamaica, in 1692. Sank it completely, before Ironhand began building this place, and it did not go unnoticed. Nobody knew quakes or tidal waves could happen here, until they did. So he made the law."

"Earthquake? Tidal wave? There have been *tidal waves*? HERE? You are *so not helping...*"

So it *could* be worse than hurricanes, or even murders: Rennie had a strange, long-standing, almost pathological fear of tidal waves, or, correctly, tsunamis. She attributed it to having gone down with Atlantis in a former life, and she often dreamed about them.

"Hey, Freakout City over here, people! I'm the mayor, you know..."

"No, don't freak. But yeah, there have been both those things," said Phanuel. "A long time ago."

"A long time ago means could be again."

Turk shook his head and put aside his book. He understood her nervousness, but he considered that anything taking her mind off the murders and drugginess, even local seismic antics, was a good distraction.

"Most unlikely, and there's no reason to fear. Anyway, Ironhand put us a thousand feet up here, out of reach of ship cannon and *way* out of reach of tidal waves. I promise you, we're not going to be hit by either. Several islands have serious volcanoes, but only very dead ones nearby, like the ones here. There are big faults around too, but we haven't ever felt but little small quakes, at long intervals; that's a good sign, means the pressure's off. As far as what's coming, the island won't get any worse than downed trees and surf surges. Noisy and wet. Just a big old rainstorm. You'll hardly notice."

Understatement of the year. The wind screamed, the skies ripped, the trees bowed and shredded, the rain came in sideways in slashing horizontal blocks, hitting the house like flung gravel. Below in Silver Bay the reef was roaring: waves three times their usual size boomed over the coral and ran in to swirl around the pavilion porch. All the vehicles had been securely parked in garages, and down in the stables, the horses were safely stalled. In the main house, the storm shutters had been lowered hours ago, the door battens fitted into place, the generators switched on. The house staff had all gone to their own homes and families, sent there by Turk the previous day to make their own preparations.

Before the leading wall of the storm arrived, Rennie had nervously suggested they fort up and go to the mattresses: lug some Beautyrests into the living room and all sleep there together for company and comfort. No one had wanted to admit they were as flipped out as she was, but they were, and everyone was privately grateful she had had the idea.

By the time the storm was actually upon them, the whole thing had turned into a sort of non-slumber party. The girls moved three sofas into a U-shape in front of the big fireplace, the open end of the U toward the hearth, the guys filled the space with mattresses wrangled from the nearest guestrooms, then everybody piled them thick and soft with sheets and blankets and heaps of pillows. They all put on comfortable sweats and old jammies for a potluck supper of leftovers and bacon sandwiches and hot cocoa; Phanuel lighted the fireplace against the sudden and surprising chill; and they settled in for the duration. Turk dragged out acoustic guitars, and he and Laird and Hoden played while everybody else sang and banged away on maracas and gourds. They all shared several rounds of joints and rum punch, and after that they drank more cocoa and took turns reading aloud from *The Wind in the Willows* while the storm raged around them.

It was all very snug and safe and warm, and no question but that the close company and security in numbers made them feel tremendously better than they would have if they'd been cowering alone in their own rooms, probably under the beds. But after a while, in spite of the slamming rain and howling wind, everyone got drowsy—the cozy closeness, the heat and glow from the fireplace, the soothing cocoa, the adventures of Mr. Toad, everything made them feel about six years old again—so they turned off the lamps, only a nightlight left on in the hall, burrowed under the blankets and settled in to sleep.

Rennie, wearing a soft, well-worn pair of sweatpants, thick socks and the equally worn old Oxford t-shirt of Turk's she always traveled with to sleep in, felt sheltered and protected as she snuggled up next to him, with Prax on her other side and Ares on Prax's other side. Laird and Belinda shared the other row of mattresses with Hoden, Phanuel and Marigo. She shifted her pillow under her head, Turk spooning her as he often did when falling asleep, his arm around her, his face nuzzling her neck, his whole frame fitting close against her back, and tried not to worry.

And it must have been a dream, but she seemed to wake to half-consciousness and a breath of chill rainwind, and saw a shadowy form slipping past, outside the sofa barricade, in the shadows beyond the nightlight and the terrace, where the tiled Balinese colonnade led from one wing to another. For a heart-freezing moment she thought she saw, stepping through the dark figure in the hall, yes, *through* it, a tall woman in a long coat and high boots and a hat with feathers, who looked straight at her for five seconds and then was gone.

Oh man, no more ghosts, the one I saw at Cleargrove was bad enough... No ghost, not a ghost, wasn't a ghost, just someone going to pee, how unromantic... She pulled the blanket over her head and drifted off again, into a lovely dream of taking refuge from a blizzard in Badger's homely and easeful underground lair, she and Turk and Mole and Rat and Badger all having tea together in the kitchen, eating hot buttered muffins and happily singing Beatles tunes. A while later—could have been hours, might have been mere minutes—she woke a second time, to a tremendous crash that only she seemed to have heard; everyone else was still sound asleep.

Another dream? No, there was a terrific rain-laden breeze tearing through the room. Why wasn't anyone else awake and noticing? Oh, there was: Phanuel, wrestling with the French doors that opened onto the terrace, they'd blown open. She got lightly to her feet, so as not to disturb Turk or Prax, and hurried over to help him.

"I didn't want to wake up anyone else," he said, as they struggled to pull the doors closed and wedge them shut.

"I think they're all sleeping off the rum and the joints. But I'm a pretty light sleeper."

Once the doors and shutters were firmly secured again, Rennie, face and arms and front soaked from the blast, stared through the rain-smeared windows at the fury beyond. It was still pitch black outside, so she couldn't see much, but the palm trees around the terrace were bent double, fronds snapping like whips; the bay below was nothing but raging white water, clearly visible even in the darkness.

"It'll be over soon. Look, the trees are all whipping the other way now, that means the storm's passing; they move through really quickly," he said, seeing her face suddenly go as white as the water. "Are you all right?"

She shook her head. "I was—remembering. That hurricane I was in, last month. Two people died on another island and I was there and I couldn't do anything to stop it. Real Agatha Christie stuff. Only really real."

Phanuel nodded sympathetically. "I know; Himself told me about it. It wasn't the hurricane that killed them, though. And you saved seven other people and you saved yourself. You did well."

"Did I?" she murmured, still staring out the windows. "Maybe..."

Over on the mattress, Himself stirred and sat up, reaching for her. When he saw her by the windows with Phanuel, he stepped carefully over Belinda and around Hoden and joined them.

"Storm over?" he asked in a low tone. "It seems quieter."

"Eye just passed," said Phanuel briefly. "It's kicking up again from the other way round, unless it hooks into the upper-level winds and falls apart."

"*Eye*? I thought it wasn't a hurricane," objected Rennie, and felt the irrational fear skitter across her skin again. Turk saw it, and pulled her backwards against his chest, wrapping his arms around her and brushing the rainwater off her face.

"It got stronger after midnight," said Phanuel. "I heard it on the Palmton radio when I was out in the kitchen. Not to worry, it's almost over now and bad as it seems, it's only a baby one even so. We haven't had a monster 'cane come through here for forty years, and please God we never do again."

"My grandfather told me about that one," said Turk, peering over Rennie's head out into the howling dark. "He said it was truly terrible. It smashed right through the barrier beaches; that's why Silver Bay is such a good surf break on that side, the hurricane ground the reef right down and changed the bottom. Hundreds of people died in that storm, in the Grand Palms and both Virgins, through to the Bahamas and Bermuda, and even all the way up the Eastern Seaboard to New York and New England. We lost sixteen right here, and counted ourselves lucky among the islands."

"Old Duke was right," Phanuel agreed. "That was one nasty storm. But this is just a big rainy windy blow. Go back to sleep, both you."

Rennie allowed Turk to conduct her back to their little nest of pillows and blankets. But as they cuddled up again, she sat half up and asked, "Phan—nobody else is up here, right? Only, I thought I woke up and saw someone come in along the colonnade."

Phanuel laughed. "Not likely, sistah. Nobody here but us. No one would come up here in the middle of this. You must have dreamed it. Don't worry about it."

Turk gathered her into his arms and lay back on the pillows. "Did you really?" he murmured in her ear. "See someone, I mean."

She found herself oddly reluctant to mention the ghostly woman she thought for an instant she had seen, still more so who she'd thought the woman had been. "Phan said it. I was probably dreaming. But you know, it did seem awfully like."

*

Next morning all was fresh and brilliant, bright blue sky full of dramatically scudding fluffy clouds, a strong breeze blowing away the last of the rain-gusts. Rennie woke with the change of light seeping through her closed eyelids, to see the others still asleep. She extricated herself without waking anyone else, and went to go wash up.

She had started making breakfast when she heard stirrings from the living room, and one by one people started wandering in, cheerfully demanding to be fed. Marigo, scandalized that the lady of the house should be waiting on them, took over at the big double stoves, and in no time the table was loaded with hot food.

The TV stations in Palmton and the U. S. and British Virgins were back on the air, and they watched reports of the storm's progress while they ate. No injury or loss of life, for which everyone was grateful, but there was significant damage—roofs blown off, trees down, roads washed out over on Grand Palm from the storm surge. The *Excalibur* had gotten out of port long before the storm had struck, and was well on its way back up to New York; the hurricane was now wandering west toward Cuba, and probably on into Mexico or south Texas after that, where it would lie down and die.

"I'm glad," said Belinda in a heartfelt tone. "Last thing they need trailing them home is a hurricane."

Prax nodded, agreeing. "Like a wet junkyard dog. But what are we going to do now?"

They all stayed in that day, tired and trying to recoup lost sleep, repatriating the mattresses to the bedrooms and collapsing onto them; but even on the second day after the storm the weather was still sparkling and cool. Feeling the pinch of cabin fever, Rennie, Belinda and Hoden left after breakfast, to picnic at Quince Trunk Bay, a charming cove not far east from Falcons Levels. Ares, Prax, Turk and Phanuel declined to join them: the boys had plans for surfing the leftover hurricane swell at a beach on the island's southwestern end, while Prax announced her intention of doing nothing more ambitious than sunning in a hammock on the terrace, and Marigo was staying in the house to tidy up.

"Be careful," said Rennie, kissing Turk off with his board. "The surf is still huge, and there might be rip currents."

"We'll watch out. You be careful too; sometimes that bay gets sleeper waves, especially after a storm." At her blank look: "Sleeper waves? Giant waves out of nowhere that come without warning and run right up the beach? So don't turn your back on the water. And keep an eye on your lunch basket."

"*Not* funny."

The picnickers had decided against riding to Quince Trunk—the horses could use the exercise, having been confined to their stalls for three days, but they were still a little spooked from the storm, and stablemaster Joshamee had discouraged the plan—so instead they had commandeered one of the golf carts. Rennie was grateful to have her mind taken off not only the storm but the ongoing problem of the murders and the possible drug connections, so she had insisted on doing the driving, along the same north shore trail she and

Hoden had ridden out on, only east this time, not west.

The landscape was much the same, if anything even lonelier and wilder—jungle to the right of them, ocean to the left. It had not taken long to reach the intended beach, a wide stretch of sand edged by the usual rock-rimmed tidepools that were to be encountered all around the island. Parking the cart, they had tumbled off, racing across the beach like little kids. They had had a refreshing, if cautious, romp in the surf right onshore, the waves being considerably bigger than usual, as Turk had warned, and had gathered some splendid shells—the seafloor, roiled by the storm, was tossing up rare treasures, and Rennie was considering getting back into collecting, as she had done in her childhood. They'd just changed out of their wet swimsuits into dry clothes, and were starting to think about lunch, when Belinda looked up.

"Sounds like another golf cart?"

The little red awning came chugging through the trees, and they could see Marigo at the wheel. "You forget dis other basket," she chided them, smiling, as she pulled up, indicating a wicker hamper in the back of the cart. "Be pretty hungry wit'out it."

She turned to lift the hamper out and set it down on the sand, but before she could touch it, as if it had been a signal, five very nasty-looking men burst out of the jungle and leaped across the trail, down onto the beach, like something out of a movie. They had five very nasty-looking guns aimed at the picnickers before the stunned three could even move. Somehow it did not seem even for a heartbeat to be a joke, so nobody *did* move. But to said picnickers' blank and total shock, none of it astonished them so much as Marigo. Not so much as a threatening pinky finger was aimed at the housekeeper. She had strolled casually over to them and was already efficiently tying Belinda up with rope she'd produced from the hamper, and then moving on to Hoden, when a third cart, not from Falcons Levels, came tootling toward them from the opposite direction.

"Keep deh gun on his lordship's woman," growled Marigo, pointing to Rennie, and one of the men shifted his weapon to comply. "She big trouble, I want get t'ese two tied up first so she behave herself."

"What the hell are you *thinking*, Marigo?" asked Rennie, slightly recovered from her shock, as, having secured the others, the Grenadian now jerked her wrists behind her back and began fastening them expertly. "Turk and Phan—"

Marigo slapped her across the face. "Keep your mout' shut, my fine lady. A nuisance you are even now. I meaned it just to be Hoden grabbed by him own self, but you two had be here. Well, now you come wit' us."

Rennie's eyes were blazing. "As I was saying, *bitch*. Turk and Phan and Ares will pound you like a jellyfish. I'd do it myself, but as you see I'm all tied up at the moment."

Marigo laughed shortly. "Say dis for you, you got guts. If you want keep dem inside where dey belong, be quietly. We don't want hurt you."

"But you will if you have to. Yeah, yeah, I've seen all the TV shows too."

The hostages were swiftly bundled aboard the golf carts, one to each vehicle, while Marigo and the tallest marauder exchanged a passionate kiss under the popeyed gaze of their captives. *Well, well...I wonder if Phan knows about this...*

Marigo met Rennie's look with a triumphant smirk, and began gathering up the picnic blankets and swimsuits, so as to leave nothing incriminating behind. "I know you did t'ink 'twas Phanuel," she sneered. "Who be shooting at you t'at day you two was over to Little Shell Bay, not so? Not hardly! Was my real man. Him here. Mell Armatreddy." She gestured to the tall, dark-skinned man now standing with his gun trained on Hoden, and he nodded, grinning at them.

"I don't know who you are, *Mell,* but tell your kraken of a girlfriend that whatever the hell it's about, this is not going to work," snarled Rennie.

"She no kraken, miss, whatever that be, she my wife."

Rennie looked thunderstruck. "Wait, *what*? Your *wife*? Your *actual* wife?"

Armatreddy nodded, apparently still trying to figure out what a kraken was. "I marry her in Grenada, ten year ago."

"So then, she's not married to Phanuel Shine at all!"

Marigo had come up behind them. "Married to Shine? Do not make me laugh!"

"But—he thinks you are. Everybody here thinks you are."

"So him and everybody can t'ink what dey like. I only go before deh judge wit' Phanuel in Jamaica so I can get here to Lion Island and set up my business, as I now have. I be married to my Mell all time."

Still astounded at events and revelations alike, Rennie leaned back against the seat as Marigo and her newly revealed husband climbed into the cart. "You bigamous little she-weasel. I do have to admire your planning. But why would he shoot at us?"

"I tell him to. I want wing him, Mistah Hoden, so I can get on wit' my plan. But you mess t'at up for me. It come better in deh end, even so; Phanuel come to deh cove looking for you, and you t'ink 'twas him shooting. You even tell his lordship you t'ink 'twas Phan, I heared you say so. All which to make doubt, which is what I want. But now I have a new plan. Much more betterer."

"And what plan is that, pray?"

"You'll see. Oh yes, miss lady, you shall see."

Twenty

RENNIE DID SEE, as the three little carts trundled farther east along the trail, then cut abruptly south, down an overgrown, barely visible path through the jungle leading to a small hidden bay on the island's southern shore. Nobody lived on that end of the island: it was all dense and almost impenetrable forest rolling up to the feet of the high mountain spine, as Rennie had noticed for herself when she and Turk had done a circumnavigating tour of the island in a small launch, a couple of days after her arrival. As Voel Christmas had told her, this was the half of the island that had never been cleared for farming or building, the ten-mile extent of which, apart from a few crumbling shoreline buildings dating from Victorian times, had remained pristine and intact.

From what she could judge by their travels, calling upon her long-rusty Girl Scout skills and innate compass sense, they were probably no more than four miles or so east of the farthest settlement, a small village called Bassalonie that she'd seen marked on a map, itself no more than the same again from Falcons Levels. So eight miles from home altogether, say ten for a worst-case estimate: hardly out of reach of a rescue party. The trick would be letting the rescuers know they needed rescuing in the first place. In the meantime, all she could do, all any of them could do, was possess their souls in patience and hope for a chance. Oh, and try not to get killed, of course. But that went without saying.

How the fuckity fucking fuck do I always end up in situations like this? Maybe Turk's right, even though he'd never say it: maybe it is *finally time for me to start accepting my manifest duchessal destiny and retire to Locksley Hall and breed for England...*

Their destination became apparent when the leading cart, carrying Hoden and one of the thugs in addition to the driver, bounced and jolted off the track, heading toward a large, ramshackle structure—an old sugar mill, its wooden sides warped and split, standing near the shore, half-hidden by more jungle surrounding. Beside it, a dock in rather better repair was standing in the clear, shallow waters of a little inlet, and a boathouse connected it to the mill.

"Are we theeeere yet?" Rennie whined in a mocking voice, hoping to divert attention from her scan of the place. "I'm huuuungry...where aaaare weeee?"

"Shut it, you! If you must knows, and I do guess you must, on account of you being you, dis is our way in and out Lion Island, but still not our real secret place," said Marigo, sitting beside Rennie in the second cart with her surprise husband as driver. "Nobody has comed dis way for years and years." She turned in her seat to motion the third cart, with Belinda and the other two thugs aboard, to pull up in the shadow of the mill's loading shed, where the first cart had already stopped, and nodded to Armatreddy to pull in behind.

"Bring dems inside, my boys," she called, and Hoden and Belinda were ungently offloaded and shoved through a door whose gleaming steel was surprisingly at odds with the dilapidations of the rest of the structure. Mell Armatreddy parked the cart and dragged Rennie out, followed by his wife, gripping her gun in her hand and looking carefully around for observers.

Inside, the mill looked long deserted, perhaps since the days of the Victorian Lion Islanders who had built it; ancient, complicated, rusted machines still littered the open floor, and there were some old, half-broken chairs lying about. But over against the wall nearest the dock stood boxes and boxes, new-looking ones, which the well-muscled goons who'd grabbed the picnickers, assisted by a few more goons besides, were now busy ferrying through the open door and out to the boathouse, loading the crates onto the sleek, fast fishing boat that was parked within. The three captives had gotten a glimpse of the craft as they were dragged through into the mill, and they had a bad feeling about it all.

Again, Rennie looked around as fast and hard as she could, taking inventory to set against hopes of escape, and out of the corner of one eye she could see Hoden and Belinda, clearly no slouches at observation, doing the same. This sure looked like a center for the drug-smuggling operations, what with the boat outside and all those suspicious boxes over there, yeah, but it didn't seem nearly big enough or active enough for the scale on which Superintendent Meryton had said that the heroin operations were carried out. A staging area, maybe. So where was the *real* action—the smack laundry? And how did it all tie together?

The dimness of the mill made it hard to see what was going on, but the more Rennie eyeballed the place, the more it seemed like some kind of trans-shipping facility. Nothing much seemed to be getting done at the moment, or maybe they were wrapping things up preparatory to getting the hell out. In which case... *We're going to have to get out of here ourselves, somehow, and back to civilization. But* how? *And who's going to be our local guide? We can't simply follow the beach: it would take hours and hours, and they could just cruise along the shoreline and pot at us from that damn boat. And going into the jungle, the mighty jungle, is out of the question. But getting out of* here *is going to be the hard part...*

Two of the muscle men had wrestled Belinda and Hoden over to a hulking piece of rusted machinery that looked fairly immovable, and now were busy lashing their hands to it, while two more held Rennie in grips of iron. *Well, there'll be bruises tomorrow...and yes, I plan on there actually being a tomorrow. Otherwise Turk will kill me...*

She tried to distract with flattery. "These are not Lion Island people. How the hell did they get here with no one seeing them? Did you manage that? Very clever work. Voel Christmas and the Tenant-in-Chief and the auxiliary police are so careful about strangers getting ashore. Let alone Phanuel."

Marigo looked smug. "Night of deh hurricane. My idea. Dey all take small boat in from Springhouse Cay before deh storm start up. Boat drop dems other side of reefs in Silver Bay; dey paddleboards across and surfs in right over, den come up through gardens to house. Waves were big enough, night was dark, so nobody see dem. Well, you did, I guess. When you waked up in deh middle of deh night and t'ink you see someone in the house? I heared you tell

Mistah Richard. You right. Was Mell. Others too came later. I hide all dems in t'at one guesthouse down nearest to where cars at, nobody else dere, and bring dems here to mill when storm start fading. Still noisy from rain and wind and sea, so no one hear, and no one out, so no one see."

Rennie gave a mock sigh. "I so often am. Right, I mean. It's a curse, really. Let me guess—you drugged us?"

"Sleeping pills in deh cocoa, so none of you be awaking when deh boys come in. Guess you didn' drink enough."

"Guess not. But why did you bring them to the house at all?"

"Safest place for hides dem. Nobody looks, and we need get set for deh grab, and to clean up in here before we leave."

"Well planned you, then." Rennie still felt vaguely unsatisfied. She'd only had a quick glimpse in the nightlighted dimness, but Armatreddy had not been the only thing she'd seen that hurricane night. There was still that shadowy figure wearing boots and breeches and coat and a big plumed hat, that had seemed to pause and look straight at her with a glance sharp as the sword she carried. Rennie knew very well, of course, who she'd thought it was—and she still thought it. Turk would probably believe her, considering that when he was in his homeland he lived with any number of, yes, okay, *ghosts*. Something she was going to have to get used to, being as this was the second family spook she'd met personally since taking up with his lordship. But what did it mean? A warning? A promise of help? Who knew?

But right now she knew she needed to keep Marigo and perhaps Mell talking; she needed information, and they were the ones who had it… "How did you get hooked up with all this?"

Flattered to be asked, happy to boast, Marigo preened, spoke patronizingly. "Oh, did not you know? Some reporter 'tective *you* be! 'Twas Mistah Jo Fleet, a'course." She was looking away, and did not see Rennie's suddenly blank face. "He come down to Palmton four year back, and he set up his outfit, wit' deh special washings for t-shirts and all. I come to hear about it, but I have my own plan, so I go to him and tell him how he can make t'ings easier and safer and more betterer for each of us, if he move all to Springhouse Cay and make me partner. I tell him deh Tarrants own it, which make him laugh and laugh, but I do not know what so funny, not den. He look into it, see it be like I say, and he move t'ings over dere: deh washing, deh shipping, all. Only we keep deh shirts stored here, for being safe. By den I have met Phanuel Shine, and 'marry' him, or so he t'ink I do, and I have come live here. Easy as kiss your hand, miss lady, dere it be."

She laughed, gathering and folding up a few loose shirts lying about. "Duke him always talking about new business chance for Lion Island; well, here one already be, and he don't have to lift a finger, nor he even knows it. T'ree year ago now we set up t'at still, on deh far side Springhouse. Nobody live dere, family never go dere, and we can come and go so nobody notice."

"Using fishing boats, sightseeing boats, diving boats," prompted Rennie helpfully.

Marigo nodded happily. "Even surfboards, windsurf boards, snorkelers wit' waterproof packs. We get shirts here, drop drugs dere; we wash dem into deh shirts, gets dem over to Grand Palm and out of deh country as lawful fan merchandise. Easy as kiss my hand. We pirates, like deh old days."

"Don't flatter yourself! At least the pirates were honest about what they did. Were those three bastards who died just experiments, the ones the cops told me about, or did you and your jolly shipmates kill them on purpose, like Loya Tessman?"

"Maybe little bit one, little bit t'other. What matter to you?" Marigo's eyes narrowed. "Phanuel, he never could see it. He always been Tarrants' lackey, never want be independent, stand on him own. He go away to school, England, Bermuda, Jamaica, all paid for by deh old Duke, den he t'row it all over for be errand boy to deh new Duke and Mistah Richard. T'at how I meet him in Jamaica. I marry him because I t'ink I can use him, no more'n t'at. I not a belonger here, not an islander, so what cares I? Mell he did know, and did not care. He knew I do it for him. For us."

Belinda bristled. "As far as I know, Phan has never been anything but kind and loving to you, Marigo, and the Tarrants really love him. He's their friend, not their errand boy. You're the one who's nothing but a slave—a smack slave, working for your plantation bosses."

The change in Marigo was astounding. "Shut you up, whore, you know *naught* 'bout me! When dis over, I be able to live like a queen. My family Demeray—Shines and Tarrants, we have had history wit', backlong years and years, on Grenada; all dis seem to me damn good revenge."

Rennie grinned. "Oho, so that's how it goes! What,

Ironhand and his crew gave your lot a good smackdown way back when, and you're still stinging? Ooh, maybe your family sold him out and he thrashed them good for it? I see you haven't learned much, you treacherous cow. I guess blood really does tell."

"So much you know, slut." Surprisingly, Marigo didn't seem upset at the aspersions Rennie was casting on the Demeray kindred, but continued clearing away shirts and other litter from the floor and tables, tossing it all into a large cardboard box. "Boys, bring her over here and tie her."

Rennie had been standing so rigidly that she wouldn't have shifted an inch if she'd been clobbered from behind with a tire iron. She was ready for a chance to strike back before she got tied up like the others, because she couldn't not even *try*, because that would be too shaming forever. Her chance, admittedly not a very good one but all she was likely to get, seemed to be here at last: Armatreddy, who had been moving boxes to clear a suitable space to secure her, now had to untie Rennie's hands from behind her so he could fasten them in front of her to the spokes of the huge flywheel Marigo was pointing to.

As he loosed her, in the tiny seconds she had of freedom she lit up with all the rage she'd been denying ever since they'd been grabbed, energetically unleashing a few of the tricks Ares had taught her and Turk years ago. She ripped out of the grip of the two brutes holding her and exploded into fluid movement, getting in a few really solid and painful smackdowns on anyone within kicking range, scything their legs out from under them. It was all in vain, of course; not only did her captors have guns, they were big, strong dudes whom she had no hope of overpowering. But she had to try. A point of honor. She couldn't face Turk, when next she saw him—and yes, she *would* see him again—and admit she hadn't even laid a glove, or a foot, on these creeps.

She was vaguely aware of Marigo looking surprised and impressed at her sudden fury, even barking a short laugh as Rennie roundhoused Armatreddy in the groin, her best and strongest move, doubling him up like a billfold with a ninja-worthy sidewards kick; perhaps such a move was one Marigo had wished to practice on him herself. She got in another on one of the men who had held her, but before she could manage a third, the gorilla who wasn't bent over clutching his crotch grabbed her from behind and held her fast off the floor, despite her slamming into him with both elbows and crushing his instep with a mighty stamp. The guy swore, but didn't loosen his grasp, and when Armatreddy could stand upright again, he backhanded her hard, so that she ended up sprawled over the machinery.

"Nice, but no more heroics, lady," sneered Marigo, kicking her in the side and hip, so viciously that it would leave bruises like stained glass. "Not goin' to do you deh smallest bit good. Stay quiet and it all be done wit' and no one be harm'."

"Promises, promises." All the same, Rennie resisted being wrestled to the flywheel and hitched to it like a recalcitrant mule—*"You said no strings could secure you at the station", and yet here you are, secured; damn you, musical memory!*—and kicked out at every opportunity, but her targets had learned to avoid the length and strength of her legs, and she didn't connect again. Once fastened, she struggled for a bit longer, then gave up and glanced over at Hoden and Belinda, who met her gaze with proud and equally seething ones of their own. "Soooo—exactly what *was* that plan you mentioned, Marigo?"

"No business of you, what my real plan be. But I tell you like I say: I have planned to kidnap Mist' Hoden and hold him for ransom. Dere is big money his side and it an easy grab. I org'nize it all."

Rennie almost burst out laughing at the look on Hoden's face, but she kept it in. "Really? I wouldn't have thought you could organize anything more complicated than breakfast."

"It all me," snapped Marigo. "*Me*. I have 'ranged lot more'n kidnap, you will see. I figure I best not try grab Lord Richard him own self. Not because for Phanuel, stupid man, be fond of him, but because it be so stupider go try for lordship on Tarrants' own island. And plus Phan said you be here sooner or later, and I know all about *you*, what a pest of hell you be, so I think to keep you off. But lordship will pay much for get you home safe, though why I do not know, excepting you must be one powerful good fuck. And Jo Fleet say Weezles pay just as big to get Mist' Hoden back, and Mistah Laird for Miss 'Linda. We already partners, like, from deh T-shirts, so we go partners in dis grab also."

"Really. The t-shirts?" *Keep her talking, keep her talking...*

Marigo seemed gratified at Rennie's curiosity. " 'course! As I says. Deh shirts what gets deh special washing over to Springhouse. In deh drugs, you know. Den, once dey dry, dey gets sent out to deh fan club places, very carefully kep' apart from deh reg'lar ones we send wit' dem to disguise. When dey get where dey going, deh smack is rinse out and dry to powder again, still full strengt', almost no loss. But you have to be so muchly careful—even touching deh shirts, you absorb t'rough your skin and be dead in a few minutes. We lose several workers in laundry who did not wear protection gloves and masks and such. Which is what happen to deh stupid groupie girl."

Rennie nodded thoughtfully. "Ah. She got hold of one of the shirts, she put it on and bingo, heroin poisoning. She got disoriented and fell overboard."

"How you figure t'at?" she asked, frowning. "No, dey put it— Mist' Ted, him say—" But she saw the carefully expressionless attention all three captives were suddenly paying her, and shook her head angrily. "No more talks."

"So, you and Jo Fleet then. Partners." Rennie's contempt was plain as she ignored the order to silence and kept right on fishing.

Marigo nodded, stung all over again. "*And* deh lawyers Mistah Larry and Mistah Franz, *and* Mist' Ted."

"Yes, I see. And now?"

"Oh, we knew soon or late we must pack up and go, and we be ready. We leave now with Mistah Jo and t'others."

Hoden glared at her. "What others? You mean there's more of you than just the apes outside?"

Marigo laughed. "Oh yes, my fine gentleman, more dere be!" Ever since they arrived in the millhouse, her patois had become stronger and more incomprehensible the more annoyed and the more excited she got. "Nah, we doh work for he so much, no more she either not now, we work for weself. De t'ing be, ah t'ing you need know, is dat only."

Rennie ran this over in her head, but it defeated her. She

ventured a leading question. "Does 'she' live in the islands, then?"

But Marigo merely glared, so she tried another tack. "Surely they all have enough money by now, even 'she'?"

Sullenly: "All dems need more cash, all times, and not care how it come."

"No, I don't suppose they do. But what, the clubs and the kickbacks and the bootlegging and the money laundering weren't enough? Not even mentioning the drug laundering?"

Marigo gave a short laugh. "Even your precious Tarrants don't ever t'ink dey have enough money. You going to marry in, you ask Lord Richard if t'at be not so. Mistah Jo say grab be to get money for Hoden from t'other Weezles, won't to harm him none. But then you and your friend gotta get yourselves grabbed too, along wit' he."

"How positively rude of us. It certainly wasn't on our to-do list for today."

"Be not cute wit' me, lady. You best hope your man really do want you back enough to pay for you. I still have not decide if you get bought back in one piece. And why t'at be so? 'Cos 'nother one of us is who attack you diving. Instead, he end up get stung by t'at rayfish, and I hold it 'gainst *you*."

"Is he okay?" Rennie was trying not to feel guilty, and by and large succeeding. *Hey, I was right! There really* was *a guy down there by the wreck! And he really* did *try to freakin' kill me! I can't help but give a bit of a cheer for the ray that punched a hole in him...*

"You do not see him in hospital in Lion Town wit' you,

do you? No, 'cos he *dead*. From sting." Her voice was as venomous as the ray itself. "Was me who send him, you know. Go after you and cut your air."

"Oh please! How did he even know where we were? Nobody in the house did."

"I did," she said smugly. "You forget I be right dere, in pantry. All t'others were out, but I still dere, where no one see. Nobody never notice servants, right? I overheared you in kitchen tell Mist' Ares where you two be going to dive, down round deh wreck, and I tell Mell send down someone cut you airhose, mess you around." She scowled. "Instead, you mess *him* around, like you always do ever'body. He Mell's cousin, and we do not like seeing family hurt or dead. Annoying too to lose a helper at dis time, but so it be. Pity he could not get you drowned before deh rayfish get him."

"Truly a pity, yes," jeered Hoden as he saw Rennie temporarily silenced with sheer fury. "But I very much doubt you were in this for no more than a couple of ransoms, now, were you."

Marigo bridled. "'Course not! You think I an idiot? No, I have much more biggerer plan nor t'at—"

"Keep silent!" That was Mell, in a sharp-edged tone of voice that surprised them all and interested Rennie no end. *Huh. His accent isn't anywhere near as thick as hers. Wonder where he's from...* "Stupid cow, don't *tell* them! Besides, you were supposed to kidnap only Mistah Hoden. Now it all a mess. What we gonna do with them now? They seen us, they know us!"

"Not problem. T'at one, she his lordship's tart," said Marigo coldly, jerking her head in Rennie's direction, "and t'other whore she belong another big famous star. Dere mens will pay serious good money to get dem safe back, like I say." Her voice turned soft and wheedling. "We can *use* it, Mell. No risk, no problem, and even if we did say we would, we do not need share with deh bosses. Well, they t'ink dey bosses. We get extra money for dese t'ree, we sink dem in off Vet'ver Wall, we finish and vanish. Nobody don't cotched us, and dey never find dem. Good and good."

Mell looked at Rennie and the others, his face shadowed with doubt at the idea of tossing them overboard into the monstrous shark cafeteria that was the sea formation known as Vetiver Wall. "Nah, I don't think it. None of them ever do nothing to us, baby, let us stick to the plan. We leave thems tied here and they be found after we gone."

With not even an altered expression as warning, Marigo started screaming at him, hitting him with her fists, with a piece of wood, with a hammer she picked up from a table. Armatreddy tried to defend himself, but it wasn't working, and finally he hauled back and punched her off her feet. She crashed to the floor, rubbing her cheekbone, staring up at him angrily, but no surprise was on her face; clearly this was nothing new.

"I am so sorry, baby, but you have got understand…we too close now to go for distractions. Let us concentrate on what we got planned, yes? We get things packed, we take boat, we leave these three here or over on Little Lion, we are out and away. Yes? Ah now, there's my prettiest girl…" He pulled to her feet, took her face in both hands, kissed her in conciliatory fashion on the site of the punch. She suffered his touch, forced a smile, pulled away.

"It good, Mell, it good. Now, let us get finish wit' deh boxes, t'at right den? Yes, all good."

He turned away to flop down on the floor and tape up several boxes that had burst open, not paying his wife any more attention than he was paying to the three unwilling guests. Rennie, however, kept her attention fixed on Marigo. *She's like a stingray on the reef floor, or one of those damn urchins—you have to shuffle your feet through the sand so you don't step on her by accident, because if you're not watching her every second...*

After a while, Marigo moved across the room with her billowy, gliding island gait, as if she carried a water jug on her head, leading with her hips, back to where Mell was sitting and working. From her position, Rennie could see the boxes' contents clearly: colorful shirts with creepily cheerful Weezle artwork on them, identical to the shirt that Sammi Stoyer had been wearing when she took her death plunge—the untreated shirts that would be taken over to Springhouse Cay to get their heroin bath. With vaguely forming dread she watched Marigo come up behind Mell. He looked up at his wife over his shoulder, smiled and turned back to his work. So he never saw the shining metal wire that she suddenly produced from a pocket and looped around his neck, or the expression on her face as she pulled it tight, as she twisted it cruelly, as his own blood spurted everywhere—sheeting all over himself, over Marigo, over the floor, over the Weezle t-shirts...

Rennie, though she had seen it coming as if in slow motion and couldn't move a muscle to stop it, was voiceless in the moment. She startled violently even so, as far as her bindings would permit. *Jesus, Mary and Joseph! She's fucking* PSYCHOTIC*! I should have called out... But I couldn't. I literally, honestly, could not get a word out. What was I supposed to do, warn the man against his own wife? He must have known her well enough never to turn his back on her. But she got out that wire so damn* fast, *she's so* strong, *I had no* idea *what she was going to do. But maybe – maybe I should have...*

She felt her muscles tautening and tensing as Armatreddy flopped frantically a few more times, like a speargunned grouper, and then slumped to the floor, awash in blood. The underlings looked over, mentally shrugged and went back to their own work; clearly, it was business as usual chez Marigo. Hoden was white-faced, and Belinda looked on the verge of throwing up as the metallic smell of blood hit her. Rennie had no idea what her own face must have shown, but she knew it couldn't have been good.

"Are you out of your *mind*?" she asked, when she felt she could speak again. She'd held no sympathy for Armatreddy, but still. For a brief instant she even wondered madly if somehow Marigo could have been on the *Excalibur*, to have killed Loya in the same swift fashion.

Marigo hand-waved it off. "Tch! He have it coming, long time now, have hit me once too many. Even him lordship notice, deh last time, my face all swellened. You do not know, lady. Just because your man a good one now do not mean all men be like him; or he be like all deh rest in deh end. Or all women too – maybe I did not be on deh ship, but Lawd I did surely see how dat bitch Tessman need killing."

Rennie's slaydar, that had not warned her of Armatreddy's oncoming death, perked right up when Marigo mentioned

Loya Tessman. *So, Loya needed killing, did she? Maybe you weren't on the ship, but could it be that someone on the ship taught you how to use that thing – or you taught them…*

"Maybe so," said Belinda, in a voice, commendably, that shook only a little. "But your own *husband*?"

"No matter," came the indifferent reply. "Now I have got me my share of deh job, and his too, can buy me ten Mells, and much more betterer ones. Phanuel Shine, he should count him lucky it be not him over dere on floor."

"Is that your 'better plan', then?" snapped Hoden.

"Why, I do believe it is," came a familiar but utterly incongruous voice, and Jo Fleet, cool, amused, holding a gun and smiling like one too, strolled into the mill.

Twenty-one

STOPPING TO CASUALLY INSPECT the body of Mell Armatreddy collapsed on the floorboards in its lake of blood, carefully picking his way round, like a finicking cat who does not want to step in a dirty puddle, finding himself the least ramshackle of the scattered chairs to sit in, Jo Fleet raised an eyebrow at the stunned captives and took the chair as if it were set center stage. *Which it pretty much was…*

"It's like backstage at the Fillmore East on an Airplane night! Or perhaps I should say a Dead one." Pleased with his little jest, he nodded at each of them, smiling. "Hoden, Rennie, looking good. Ah, Belinda, haven't seen you since Altamont, what a bummer that was. Loved those pictures in the tabloids the other day, clearly you've all been working out."

Nobody answered; Rennie, glancing aside at the by now incandescent Hoden, thought that he looked about ready to go supernova.

"Oh, come on!" Fleet had a grin tacked to his face. "Not even a *smile*? No? Man, tough room. Well, as Rennie can surely tell you from her vast past experience, this is the part where I as the villain reveal all the dastardly plots to my quite literally captive audience."

"I think we can figure out a few of them on our own, you sodding wanksock!" snapped Hoden. "Especially the one where you've been running drugs God knows where to God knows who, using MY band as a bloody cover. Not to mention murder."

Fleet ignored his artist, studied a paper he'd picked up off the floor and spoke to the impatiently waiting self-made widow Armatreddy. "Really, Marigo, you might have left that till we were done here. Mell, I mean. He could at least have helped carry stuff to the boat. And then we could have chucked him over the side like that little groupie. Before we got to Springhouse, of course."

Marigo dropped the bloody garrote wire to the floor, with a faint smirk. "We must cuts our coat to suits our cloth. Or cuts a throat. But no man no matter who he be does evah lay hand on me like t'at and come away."

Jo Fleet made a noise of derision. "What's done is done. As for what's to *be* done—"

Rennie raised interrogative brows. "Well? Don't keep us in suspense. You did promise revelations. Does that make you the Great Beast, then? Didn't he come from the sea too? Though I doubt he had such a spiffy boat as the one outside."

"Please. It *is* a nice boat, but I hardly aspire to such Apocalyptical heights. Well now, you girls are both reporters. Don't you want the *whole* story? Even if you might never see it in print? It's quite delicious, really..."

Clearly he wanted very much to tell it, so Rennie just shrugged. "Knock yourself out. I mean that literally, of course."

"Sorry, can't oblige. Well. It started out small, not long after I gave those four ill-assorted musical urchins their first paying gigs. Then the Weezles became *THE WEEZLES*."

"Ah, they grow up so fast, don't they?" jeered Rennie. "One day they're little hopeful kindergarten bands, the next they're leaving home and covering unwittingly for a massive drug op."

Fleet grinned, his not so metaphorical predator's teeth showing. "You may say so. We had done well—I say 'we', when of course I mostly mean 'I'—but I wanted to do much, much better. That was when the drug idea dawned. But I didn't have enough capital at the time to make it happen the way I wanted. So I began dipping into Weezle royalties and concert fees, and I was helped along by Jack Holland—when you're a label president, you can do that sort of thing, for a cut of the action, which I was happy to supply—and my little pilfering became much easier once he came aboard. Then, oh, let's say a *backer* picked up the scheme and ran with it, like a Broadway angel. Fallen angel. That was where the real money came from; family millions were now behind the scheme. Not *my* family, but what the hell, as long as someone had it. We—and I mean my other partners as well as myself—were the ones who put up the sweat equity to start, and later Weezle money when it really started coming in."

"And you still had us for cover," Hoden retorted, his wrath undiminished.

"A *literal* cover band, yes." He laughed with real amusement as he heard Hoden growl. "Anyway, the drug op moved along swimmingly. Then we started the fan club. Perfectly kosher on one level, dear boy, you needn't grind your molars so. We serviced your little fangirls and fanboys completely legitimately. And profitably: I never once heard you or the other guys complain about the revenue stream it produced, even though you bitched endlessly about the boring photo ops and tedious meet-and-greets. So—another brilliant idea of mine—the fan club soon spun off the Weezle Den, the inner circle. Drugs and sex included: after all, why have young stupid pretty groupies around and available, dying, as it were, to be of service, if you aren't going to make use of them? The Den members thought so too. And business went through the roof."

"I'd been wondering about that," said Rennie, interested in spite of herself. "There couldn't have been that many little Weezle fans with an allowance on a level for smack and whores, surely."

"Oh, there weren't. Which is why most of the Den inside members, the Denizens as they were fondly known, were considerably older than the fankiddies. You could really see it at concerts, which is the only place where the two echelons, shall we say, of members ever mingled. Like vampires and prey; you should have seen them, hunting and being hunted, everybody having a good time. Anyway, a nice little operation, was the Den," he continued. "I speak in past tense now, of course. A very special fan club for very special people. They paid a stiff membership fee, and they got ID so we knew who they were. They got access to the Weezles and they also got—accommodated. Expensive drugs, gourmet food and drink, the best groupies—all for free. Well, free after their dues were paid and up to date, of course. The squeaky-clean Weezle image only helped: who'd ever suspect those lovable moptop rascals of condoning smack and speed and meth sales, not to mention a hooker stable, right there at all their big venues? We even had our own network of drug roadies to schlep the stuff from gig to gig. All the band knew was that it was a special club, for punters who could pony up, and they were persuaded it was for publicity purposes and incidentally brought in some extra cash to the group bank account. But they had no idea how *much* it brought in."

"Or into whose accounts it was brought. Yours, not theirs, right?"

"Right. They never knew about the drugs. We made sure of that. If they ever found out, the whole thing was over, so we were very, very careful." Fleet scowled at Hoden. "But then our little fair-haired boy here decided to start snooping. Fancied himself another Rennie Stride, I daresay."

"Yes, well, we see how *that* worked out," said Rennie evenly.

"It was camouflage," remarked Belinda, as interested as her colleagues, and every bit as disgusted. "You had the teenies from the general fan club around to make it look all sweet and innocent for the smackhead vampires."

"Clever Belinda! Yes, exactly. And then the Denizens could sneak off into private rooms, with not only the best groupies but the best grass and the best coke and the best Hoden White, as we liked to call it. Laundered right out of those t-shirts over there."

He grinned again as Hoden went apoplectic; if the singer hadn't been securely lashed to a piece of machinery that weighed about a ton, he would have gone for Fleet's throat. As it was, such was his rage that Rennie thought Hoden might pull the huge, heavy steel hulk right out of the floor anyway.

"Branding is everything, lad, and they certainly appreciated it. Don't take it to heart. And let me say this in my defense, again: we never involved you boys personally in the Den activities. Though the cops might not see it that way, of course, when this all comes out. So for the moment, your hands are still lily-white. China white. Snow white. I could go on like that all day."

Hoden didn't look as if he very much appreciated the wordplay. Fleet cast a smug eye over him, and then again over at the door.

"Waiting for someone, are you?" asked Belinda, noticing his wandering attention. She had been the quietest of the three so far, but that was only because she couldn't figure out what to say without her head flying off and rolling halfway to Paraguay. Right now she was wondering if this was how Rennie felt all the time, and if so, how her friend managed to survive—it was like living in lava. "Company? Ah, more minions?" she added, pushing it, and looking over at her, Rennie was *so* proud.

"Now that you mention it, Belinda dear—" he made a show of glancing at his very expensive watch—"I am, actually. They should be here momentarily, and then we can finally get this show on the road. In the meantime, any questions? Ask me anything." He spread his hands and looked at them with an expression of mock generosity. "Anything at all. You're both ace reporters, aren't you? I'm sure you have plenty of journalistic voids that need infilling."

Both aces, and Hoden as well, sent him looks that should have made him melt away through the floorboards. Then Rennie, back in control of herself:

"So who *are* we expecting then, you squinty-eyed tosspig? This mysterious financial angel you mentioned?"

For some reason, that made Fleet react not in annoyance but in laughter. "That—might be difficult. No, I'm waiting for my other two partners in, well, yes, you certainly *could* call it crime."

"Anyone we know?" asked Belinda.

He wagged a chiding forefinger. "Ah-ah-ah! That would be telling. But this was never a cast of thousands, you know. It's always been a little, hmm, boutique venture. One general, several colonels, a few capable lieutenants like dear Marigo and dear late Mell. The rest were merely well-paid boots on the ground, the ones down here running the business at the local level, and the distributors back in the States."

Rennie didn't want to give him the gratification of asking exactly who that general was, but she did want to know. "Just how did you pick Turk's family's islands to infest in the first place?"

"You may recall that I mentioned to you, delightful future Mrs. Wayland, how much I like the Palms Inn? Well, on one of my little r&r trips down here—ah, the stress of dealing with temperamental teenybopper sensations, how often I needed to get away!—I encountered locals who had a little amateur heroin outfit of their own going."

He nodded over at Marigo, who was watching him the way a groupie watches a lead singer. "We had our thing nicely ticking over by then, and these two were doing all right on their own account, but I could see that all they needed was some better distribution and an infusion of cash to really expand. Well, long story short, we realized we'd all do better if we joined forces. One thing led to another, and I began dealing with Marigo and Mell, so very helpful. In fact, Marigo was the one who found us two hidden bases for our new joint operation, as she's probably mentioned: this sugar mill, Tarrant property like the rest of this island and abandoned for about eighty years, and Springhouse Cay, also Tarrant property but uninhabited and conveniently out of the way, on the Anguilla side, out into the Anegada Passage, and completely unvisited because of the very treacherous waters. To secure easy access to both locales, she geniusly arranged a sham marriage—Mell didn't mind, since it was all for profit and meant nothing otherwise—to poor pathetic Phanuel Shine, he being Lion Island manager and able to supply her carte blanche to come and go as she liked, and we finally had our setup free and clear."

Rennie's mouth tightened. "And the family never caught on?"

He shook his head. "The Tarrants never bothered with Springhouse, or even with this end of Lion, actually. Forever wild, or some such ecological nonsense. It was perfect for our purposes, and the fact that we were running a major smack ring out of clean-as-a-whistle Lord Turk Wayland's own backyard was absolutely delicious. It also kept us safe; no bananahead local cop would even *dream* of checking out Tarrant property for smack, and in any case, we had Marigo to tip us off if anyone, cop or family, did start sniffing around." He mock-sighed. "Though now that you three have found out about it, it's a good thing we're winding it up. We all have little retreats to pop off to, of course, with our ill-gotten gains carefully salted away."

"I hear hell is nice this time of year. Oh wait..." said Rennie snipingly, and he chuckled.

"Nice try, but whyever would I tell you where we're headed? It's so seldom anyone ever manages to get Rennie Stride at a disadvantage that I want to savor every last little minute of it. Even though you have no idea exactly how *much* of a disadvantage."

"Do you plan on keeping the operation going?" asked Belinda, in a surprisingly normal reporter voice.

"Us, no. But it may well continue on its own; of course, they'll need a new island to work from now." Fleet stretched and smiled, slit-eyed, a cat having way too much fun toying with its three little cornered mice. "They've been very good, our busy worker bees down here, and we'll see they're well rewarded for the risks they took."

"Care to enlighten us further about the method?" That was Hoden, still snarly and dangerous, like a dog too long chained up who now only wants to bite and bite and bite. "Since you're about to ride off into the nonextraditable sunset."

Indulgent laughter from his manager. "I suppose it can't hurt now—and we seem to have time to kill, if nothing else... oh, sorry, we might actually *have* more to kill than time. We'll have to wait and see how it goes... Well. As Marigo started to tell you, it's simple and efficient. We perfected this process by which we can soak fan t-shirts in heroin solution, to be distilled out and recovered later. The smack comes from Miami or Central and South America and other points round here, sometimes even New York. It lands on Grand Palm, just as the cops think it does. Sometimes it sails in on a cruise liner like the *Excalibur,* in big Vuitton trunks accompanying handsome couples or beautiful well-dressed solo ladies, headed for a holiday in one or another luxurious villa , of which the island has plenty. Or it comes in aboard private movie-star yachts and private planes belonging to captains of industry. We never use hippie types to shift the stuff—the more elegant and classy our runners look, the less chance of being stopped. Remember that for future use when you're carrying through an airport, as you rockers tend to do. Some discreet payoffs here and there, and bingo, customs inspection is something that happens to other people."

"I must have a word with Turk about that; he won't like it at all," said Rennie coldly. She was beyond furious by now, but she wanted to get all the details in her head before two witnesses. For future use, as Fleet said; well, if they managed to survive this.

"Oh, the Lion Island customs officers have proven incorruptible, so far. Though quite a few Grand Palmian ones have not, the little dears. Which is another reason why we had to organize things the way we did. Anyway," he continued, "however they arrived, the drugs are taken from Grand Palm or some other Palm to Springhouse by very much smaller boat—little launches, bareboat rentals, fishing boats, all small and local transport that won't attract attention—and they wait there until we're ready to do another laundry. The t-shirts also come in from Grand Palm, Weezles shirts usually, but other bands too sometimes, to cut our chances of being traced. There's a big tourist t-shirt industry in Palmton, so there's never any shortage of, well, material. Our supplier diverts our shirts here, as you see them right over there in those boxes, and we then send them over to Springhouse, again by small boats like the one outside. That's where we wash and dry them. All with greatest care to avoid touching them. The prepared shirts are picked up and sent out through the special fan club to recovery stills in the States. Or else we sell them as is and let the buyer worry about getting the heroin out. It really does all come out in the wash, one way or another."

"Thus giving 'ring around the collar' a whole new meaning," drawled Rennie. "Pride goeth, Joslin. Pride goeth."

Fleet laughed. "We'll take our chances. If anyone ever does notice us here, we're innocently moving Weezle fan merch. Efficient and safe. Long as no one touches the smacked-up shirts. We keep the stuff itself off Lion, so that if by great bad luck someone does see us unloading shirts here, we can confess to nothing more heinous than trespassing and using the mill for t-shirt transport. Marigo keeps the pipeline clear, and we have local muscle from Grand Palm and Anguilla—well, you saw some of them, the ones who brought you here. Mell runs them: they take care of anyone who gets in our way. And now, oh dear, Mell's gotten in our way and has been taken care of himself. Well, well, live and learn. Or die and learn, I suppose."

"And have *we* gotten in your mustache-twirling way,

then?" asked Belinda, with some boldness. "Going to have them take care of us too?"

He shook his head, and didn't see, as Rennie did and duly noted, Marigo's sudden scowl. "No. No, there's been enough killing, and we're really not stupid enough to off a Weezle and two well-known reporters, one of whom is the fiancée of a member of local royalty. The investigations into the shipboard deaths won't lead anywhere, as we didn't leave any clues; but there would be a never-ending public firestorm about three dead notables like yourselves. Nobody will believe your story anyway, and even if they did, we'll be long gone, to a place where even if they found us they couldn't touch us. We've feathered some very nice nests for ourselves, as you can imagine."

Fleet gestured around at the activity: the three heavy types removing boxes and sacks of things, the others out on the getaway boat stowing the stuff, Marigo watching sullenly from the door. "So, we'll take you with us when we've finished cleaning up here. Few more hours tops. We'll head over to Springhouse Cay, where minions are dismantling and destroying the apparatus even as we speak, wrap up everything else, including poor Mell, and sail off into the sunset, as dear Hoden so lyrically puts it. After burying Mell in Vetiver Channel, we'll maroon you three on one of the other cays—hey, just like the pirates who used to live here, what a link with the past! We'll make sure it's got enough water and fruit to keep you all alive for a few days. Then we'll send a suitable ransom demand to Wayland for him to deposit the payment into our offshore accounts. Might as well get a few dollars for you if we can.

Presumably Burkhart and the Weezles will want you other two back as well. They can all afford it, and I'm sure they'll all be willing to pay."

"This isn't my first rodeo, Fleet," said Rennie, a bite to her voice, and her face was suddenly somber. "And I've dealt with rodeo clowns like you before. You think you can dodge the bucking bull with the horns, because you've got the barrel there to hide in as a last resort. But those horns are pretty long and very sharp, and that barrel is open on both ends."

For the first time that afternoon, Jo Fleet's face flickered with something other than a smirk. Fear? Scorn? Disbelief? Doubt? Rennie couldn't tell, and it was gone almost as soon as it had appeared. But with a carefully impassive countenance, he stood up and walked back out the dockside door, and Marigo went with him.

Twenty-two

"WHAT? WAS IT SOMETHING I SAID?" Rennie called mockingly after them; they didn't seem to hear her. " 'But answer came there none'…" Smiling faintly, she turned back to her two friends. "Touchy, touchy… Right, then."

As Fleet and Marigo left, Rennie had relaxed down into her bindings. She hated this. Usually she was the one to figure things out, not have them imposed upon her. Now, despite having considerably more information to work with than she had before, she found herself blanking out. She resolutely sat up straight again, her face and posture conveying energy and possibility, if nothing else.

"Well, well, isn't this *interesting*! I'm thinking we might have a bit of time now to come up with something clever and effective and potentially life-saving. Any ideas?"

Hoden shifted to ease his muscles. "If either of you has superpowers you've not yet revealed to the world—like being able to shoot lasers from your eyes—now would be a good time. No? Didn't think so."

"I got nothing," said Belinda. "My mind's too busy yelling 'Run'!"

He laughed, not unkindly. "Where to, luv? There's nowhere to go."

"Doesn't care, just keeps yelling get the hell out."

"Well," said Rennie, looking around, "let's see what we

have here."

The packing wasn't yet close to completion. If they were going for broomsweep clean, leaving no clue behind, all was, as Fleet had said, a few hours away from that. Which meant time was getting close but not close enough to remove Hoden, Belinda and Rennie from their current locations and take them aboard the boat. Not to mention removing Mell's body. *No, not gonna think about that. Going to think about getting away. Somehow.*

Low voices outside. Then the dock door opened again, and all their heads whipped round to it as one. Equally as one, they were astonished to see that it was neither Jo Fleet nor Marigo, but two new faces. Only those faces were very familiar ones indeed.

"Oh, oh, look who it is!" said Rennie, hiding her astonishment as best she could. "I was wondering when the other shoe was going to drop. The other two shoes, that is. More like heels, though, aren't you. Add Joslin and it's Larry, Moe and Curly, together again at last."

Franz Haran and Larry Mavius strolled through the door and found seats for themselves, and looked at Rennie and her friends with amusement.

"Ouch! Wounded… Not sure if I'm flattered at being referred to as either a Stooge or a heel," said Haran. "Though"—the Weezles lawyer extended one leg to admire the glamorous leather confection on the end of it—"if I have to be a dropped shoe, at least it's a nice expensive Italian one. There, there, little Ferragamos, don't be sad! She's just a meanie in grotty old Keds. But yes, Miss Stride, we're the next of the surprises. Though there might still be a few more to come. And you *are* surprised to see us, aren't you? All of you?"

Hoden rolled his eyes. "Now that you mention it? No. I'm not. We're not. Who else *would* it be but you knobbers?"

Larry Mavius laughed. "Ready for a couple more shockers? How about Ted Tessman and Jack Holland? Your master at Tontine and your label president. That suit you?"

"Again, from what I've heard since I've been down here," observed Belinda, "those two aren't much of a shock either. You guys really don't know how to construct a decent story, do you? Rennie, what's the opposite of burying the lede? Exhuming it? Let's see: you've got drug-loaded t-shirts with your clients' faces on them and a little fan club to get them out to the masses, plus a select clientele with high tastes of its own—what better way to move everything than a record company with distribution facilities and a booking agency with contacts all over the world? And sufficient weasels all round to facilitate the proceedings. Now whyever in hell would you think that would fill us with even a *smidgen* of surprise?"

"Ah, such a pleasure dealing with a reporter. They always cut right to the chase. But really that's exactly it." Franz Haran had put his other foot beside the first and was admiring both shoes now.

"Quite handsome stomps, yes, I believe that's been duly established," said Rennie impatiently. "Complicated little web you've got going here, boys. And a profitable one too—are you really going to shut it all down now? Just because we've stumbled across it?"

Mavius pretended to consider. "Well, it might be easier—

and personally more satisfying—to shut *you* down instead. All three of you. But I'm sure Jo has already explained to you why we won't be doing that. So yes, Rennie and company, we really are. Going to shut down the operation. Not because of you, you needn't take a bow! These things are self-limiting by nature, like a virus, and even before the cruise we'd decided this would be our last hurrah."

Rennie shot Hoden and Belinda a glance: *Keep quiet and let me handle this, okay?* They seemed to understand, and, more importantly, to agree. "Would that include Loya Tessman's and Sammi Stoyer's last hurrahs as well? Not to mention Mell Armatreddy over there"—she jerked her chin in the late Mr. Marigo's direction—"and that poor bastard who got stingrayed to death trying to, oh yes, *kill me*. And those other three extras who got to wear the Smack-bearing T-shirts of Doom and get tossed overboard couple of months back? Last hurrah time for all of them too, I wonder? Self-limiting lives, were they? How many more?"

For the first time, the two lawyers looked a little uncomfortable. "Cost of doing business," said Haran after a while.

"Really! In what way, pray? And to what extent?"

"Oh, come on, relax, no one's going to get hurt here. As Jo told you, we're going to take you all out in a little while to a conveniently remote and uninhabited little chunk of beach and jungle, leave you there, collect the ransom someplace else and then let Wayland know where he can find you. After we've safely hightailed it out of the Caribbean, of course."

"Nice plan," snapped Belinda. "You're forgetting the

fact that we've seen you, we know you're responsible for the murders as well as the smuggling. You've admitted it. Right in front of us."

"Oh, we know." Mavius sounded unconcerned. "We also know you have no proof. Just your unsupported reportorial and rock-starry words. Nevertheless, to repeat myself, we're not going to be doing any more of this, and we're not going to be dropping you into the drink halfway out to sea, so you needn't worry. No…it's all getting a little too close, and, as Jo has undoubtedly told you, the only thing we want to do now is shut down the operation, take whatever more money we can grab and get the hell out to our nice safe little offshore havens and our nice fat secret bank accounts."

Rennie snorted. "You wouldn't happen to know a dude named Lyon Tavender, would you?"

"Who? We've been running this little op for several years: again as I'm sure Jo's told you, we figured the Tarrants' tight little islands would be a safer bet than anyplace else. The family is seldom here, as is the fuzz, and the locals stick to their own business, though we couldn't persuade any of them to join in, all too damn loyal to their noble masters. There's no surveillance by Palmton authorities, which is a lot more laissez-faire, thanks to those noble masters' noble selves. Plus we figured we could always set up Turk for the hit if we were ever busted."

"Bastards," said Rennie evenly.

Haran laughed. "Even though my parents were lawfully wedded when I was born, I entirely agree. Even you were a plus, in a weird sort of way. If we framed Turk's family, or even Turk, to save ourselves, we knew that would stop you in your tracks and get you off the case. If not, the fact that you were around and were seen to be *on* the case was a perfect cover for us. If Rennie Rock Detective didn't sniff anything going on, other people wouldn't think to look for anything. Worked for us either way."

"If they'd busted Turk or if the Tarrants had been blamed or framed for this," said Rennie without heat, "not only would I *not* have been stopped in my tracks, I would have been on *your* tracks until the Lord God Almighty revoked the rainbow. Though I would have caught up to you long before that. You're not as clever as you think. Though you're cleverer than you look. Which isn't hard to be, I suppose."

"Maybe not," said Fleet cheerfully. He'd come back in to hear the last couple of exchanges, and strolling over to Rennie now, he delivered yet another backhand blow to her face, one that left her dizzy, her lip split and her mouth bloodied. "Been wanting to do that for a while now. Andy Starlorn was one of my best friends; I didn't dig what you and Sledger Cairns did to him. As to your last assessment, we're all quite clever enough to have pulled this off, be sure of that. Still, it's unfortunate that you started suspecting something, Hoden, and even more unfortunate that you brought dear Rennie in on it. Not such a smart lad after all, then."

He sat down, spoke confidingly to Rennie and Belinda, theatrically pretending Hoden wasn't present. "We tried to sound him out, discreetly, about cutting him in on our operation, but he's so damn disapproving about things like crime. Go figure. So before the cruise, I sent him some little warnings about doing as he was told and not messing around and especially not trying to talk to you. Pity he didn't pay attention. He didn't even drink the champagne. Reinforced the message by that phone call at the Palms Inn, delivered by Mell."

"And Loya?" challenged Rennie, her head still spinning from the blow. "She didn't pay attention either, I'm guessing."

"No. She didn't. And look what happened to her." Fleet sighed dramatically. "Still, why prolong the narrative? We're not going to hurt you unless we have to, as I said before. Now do be good children and don't make us."

"Yes, well, forgive me not cheering the cleverness of you. But one thing I'd like to know: why bother with double-shipping the shirts at all? Isn't that kind of risky?"

He shook his head. "Not as much as you'd think. More risky to have the laundry on Grand Palm or back in the States—more populated, more chance to get caught. It's a lot safer to have the shirts come here from Grand Palm, move them out to Springhouse, and then do the actual soak on an uninhabited, privately owned island."

"And how very kind of the Tarrants to supply one free of charge."

Haran laughed. "As you say. That cay is really wild. Our buildings are in deep jungle on the ocean side—they're camouflaged like crazy. And it's really out there: no cruise ships passing by, no drug police coming round. It's the Anegada Passage, as you may have heard, a very dangerous and rough stretch of water; nobody goes out in it unless they really need to, not even the Tarrants."

Belinda gave a scoff. "And yet you have your Batcave secret headquarters right here on their home island."

"Well, it's a *bit* risky, true," said Mavius with a brief chuckle. "But it makes it easier for Marigo to meet us and give us information. Someone would notice pretty soon if she kept going over to Springhouse. Here, she can sneak along the jungle trails from the Tarrants' estate or take a small boat right up to the dock. Little boats are always coming and going along here."

"M'hm. And they haven't noticed your other little minions shuttling to and fro?"

"Not so far," said Fleet. "But this is our swan song, so it doesn't matter now. We have enough money for even our notorious tastes, and the G.P.I. *polizia* is too close behind us, treading on our tail."

Ah... " 'Will you, won't you, will you, won't you, will you join the dance?' I guess the answer is 'Won't.' It all leads back to Alice, doesn't it. Right down the rabbit hole... So you figured to take care of some inconvenient business while we were all still out on the high seas aboard the Good Ship Rock&Roll. Loya, well, being who she was, Mrs. Ted Tessman—maybe I can understand you wanting to get rid of her. Hell, I can understand *me* wanting to get rid of her. But what could that chubby little groupie possibly have done that threatened you?"

"Why, Miss Stride, are you fishing for information?"

"No, I'm flat-out asking for it. Demanding it, actually."

"Well, as for Loya, you might be surprised." Franz Haran shifted where he sat on an old operator's chair, its black leather saddle split along the seams and once-white padding spilling out. "But Groupie Girl was considerably snoopier than she should have been, or was healthy for her. We caught her poking into Jo's cabin aboard the ship. She claimed she was only looking for some special photo album that Hoden had promised he and the other Weezles would sign for her. Naturally, we didn't buy it. Not when we saw that what she *had* found was a very incriminating notebook having to do with drug and t-shirt inventory, hidden away in Jo's briefcase. She wasn't entirely stupid: she instantly realized what was going on, and demanded a job as the price of her silence. With Tontine. Handling Lionheart, you'll be happy to hear, Rennie. Hoping to handle Turk, perhaps, personally."

"What did you do? I mean right then; we know what you did ultimately," asked Belinda, when Rennie maintained a stony silence, refusing to be drawn.

"What did we do? Why, we welcomed her to the team and put her into one of our team shirts, to seal her new allegiance. A treated shirt, of course; you'd think she'd have noticed that I gave it to her with surgical gloves on, but no, she just pulled it happily over her head. Pretty soon she was involuntarily junking out. And then it was only a matter of time before she was dead and we tossed her overboard. We'd hoped the water would wash away the evidence, but it didn't cooperate."

"Will all great Neptune's ocean wash this smack clean from my shirt?" Rennie paraphrased. "But not *all* the smack, apparently. The forensic cops found residual traces on her skin and her clothing."

Fleet laughed with real amusement. "Points to Rennie

Stride for best use of Shakespeare in a tight situation."

She bowed mockingly from where she was tied to the flywheel. "Don't forget it's considered bad luck when *Macbeth* is quoted at you. Kind of like, yeah, a curse... So who was it who screamed when Groupie Girl went brinewards? Turk was wondering about that himself, and he wasn't even aboard the ship. Can't have been her, as you say she was already dead. And I heard the scream myself, as did many others."

"So you would have," agreed Haran. "Well, actually, that was dear Loya doing the vocalizing. We had brought her out onto her suite balcony to watch us get rid of Stoyer—a little object lesson if she didn't toe the line and do as we said. Threatened to do the same to her as we did to the little groupie. And yet she still tried to sneak off to speak to you."

Rennie was beginning to sense something worse than anything so far revealed, which had been quite bad enough. "Loya—she'd told me she wanted to talk. We'd set an appointment for after that damn rock opera was over, on the second night."

"So you did," agreed Fleet. "I saw you talking at lunch the day before. After Ted had knocked her around a bit. I guess that helped her make up her mind to rat him out."

"I know. I noticed the marks of his handiwork under her makeup."

"Frankly, knowing how you both felt about each other, I was surprised you'd agreed to meet with her at all, or that she'd been able to bring herself to ask your help. The other boys"—he gestured to the two lawyers—"weren't aboard; we'd made plans to meet in Palmton once the ship had arrived. Loya was the one for whom we held our little warning demonstration with the groupie. But in spite of everything, she was still going to confess to you and nail us all, hoping in the process to cut a deal for herself."

Mavius picked up the thread. "When she tried to get out and find you, Ted took matters into his own hands. Literally into his own hands. We couldn't take the chance of her getting to you to confess."

"Well, forgive me for asking, but exactly what was she going to confess to me *about*?" Rennie's face was expressionless, while Belinda again looked about ready to throw up and Hoden's was set in stone.

"Oh, didn't we say?" Haran's voice was mocking and his smirk cold. "How forgetful of us... Loya was the one behind the whole drug ring. It was her family millions that got Jo started, and in exchange for the funding she demanded control. She was the one running the whole show."

Rennie felt as if she'd taken a cannonball to her middle and now had a great round neat hole there where it had gone straight through, the way people do in cartoons, and she could see her shock reflected on Hoden's and Belinda's faces. *Oh, you are the Queen of Stupid...how the bleeding hell did you miss* that?

"LOYA? I'm sorry, but... *Loya Mailing Tessman*? Cretin editress of rock and roll? You're saying that that twittering little waste of space was the brains behind all this?"

"Such brains as she had, yes. She was quite cunning in a nasty sort of way. Surprising, isn't it? We didn't like it much. But we had no choice. She kept us on a really short rein, the bitch," said Mavius, grinning at their stunned expressions.

"We needed her Mailing inheritance at first, but once we'd built up enough capital of our own... Well, we'd always planned to kill her eventually. Ted's idea, actually. God, he hated her. We all just needed to figure out how and when and where. The cruise seemed like the perfect opportunity. Jo and Ted were going to throw her overboard, same as we did to that snoopy groupie. But we realized we couldn't all be on the ship when she got offed. Too many people might add it up, including you, dear Rennie, and we only had one chance. If we blew it, she'd go running to you, or to the cops. So we figured to keep it as small and deniable as possible. Only Jo and Ted on the ship. The rest of us would fly down after the fact and hook up here."

Fleet was nodding. "The only thing that really fell in our favor was that after she spoke to you and asked for a meeting, Ted kept her locked away in their suite, and she never managed to get out again to ask you or anyone else for help. We figured we could get rid of the body easily enough, but all you damn rockers were always up at all hours of the night, and we could never be sure of a dark, deserted quiet area from which to heave her over. Especially after deep-sixing the groupie slut. We were lucky in that. So we went the other way—made a big sensation of it. If it's spectacular enough, people are often dazzled by the footwork, and they don't look any deeper. So we had to improvise. Hence Paize Lee costuming and a convenient deck chair and a bit of rope. And some guitar strings for a garrote, all of which went equally conveniently overboard."

Rennie had managed to get her astonishment and her revulsion under control. *Loya! Head of a drug ring! Who the hell would have thought it? Clearly the world is coming to an end. And yet it makes a certain kind of sense, and has a bizarre inevitability...*

"So who was the lucky person who got to do the honors?"

He laughed. "Maybe we should have called you in to help, seeing as you *liked* her so much... Well, Ted garroted her in their suite; in the shower, actually. It seemed to make him happy. Thankfully the shower was big enough to fit them both, and afterwards all we had to do was turn on the water for the cleanup and throw her clothes overboard—Ted was cleverly naked, so he only needed to wash up. Once she'd bled out, we dried her off, put her into the Paize Lee clothes that we'd stolen, painted her face to freak you all out, carried her down to the pool and tied her into a deck chair. Which you two girls and Laird Burkhart obliged us by falling over. Which couldn't have been better if we'd planned it like that."

Grinning at their absolute staggerment, Mavius took up the narrative. "We were going to ice the bitch anyway, of course, but what totally pissed us off was that she really *was* going to confess everything to you, Rennie—tell you all about it and throw herself on the mercy of the law. She figured even jail would be preferable to Ted beating her up all the time, which he did, or in fact killing her, which she knew he'd do sooner or later."

"Plus she treated us like lackeys," added Haran, resentfully.

Rennie stretched to ease her bound wrists, concealing pretty much everything she was feeling. "And you aren't? Lackeys, I mean. I was there for that little Q&A with the

Palmton coppers, remember. Joslin sat there like some kind of evil garden gnome, and you two shysters were the ones who did the questioning. Must have been easy, since you knew all the answers beforehand."

Hoden shook his head in genuine amazement. "I have to say I never thought Loya Tessman would be capable of masterminding a major heroin operation. I always thought she was too stupid to run a whelk stall at the seaside."

"Oh, she *was* that stupid. But she was also shrewd enough in her own little way," said Franz. "She used that execrable teenybopper rag as a cover, with other people doing her editorial work, and spent most of her own time either socializing with phonies at Max's or doing *our* work. It doesn't take much, really, to run a drug op once it's set up. After things are all in place, it's only maintenance. But she was exceptionally hands-on and exceptionally controlling. Which is why she had to go."

"But you've said the operation is finished. Concealment is at an end," objected Hoden. "Why kill her now?"

"To shut her up, of course. The fact that we'd also be stopping her horrible little fan mag is a bonus."

"A service to rock and roll," said Belinda acidly, and the men chuckled.

"I suppose so. Perhaps there's a medal in it," said Fleet. Well, you can't get blood from a Stone, right? Oh wait, you can. At least if you were Rennie Stride at Hyde Park last summer."

Rennie glanced at Hoden and Belinda, to find them equally boggled, and looked back at Fleet, who was sitting in a chair over by the wall, smiling hugely.

"I'd say you had hidden depths, Joslin, but your depths are right out there for all to see, aren't they. I won't be dishonest enough to say I'm not staggered," she observed, "since you can clearly see that I am. But…Loya? *Really*? LOYA?"

He laughed. "Oh, babe, believe me, I was surprised too. But she had a brain like a file cabinet, a malevolent file cabinet; she logged in everything everyone had ever done to her. You were in there, all of you, I promise, and Wayland and Sakura and Burkhart and the rest of your merry little band. All your offenses against her, real, imagined and exaggerated, were neatly categorized and filed away for future use, and sooner or later you would have gotten whatever payback she'd penciled in for you. Which Rennie had already gotten a little taste of, with that stupid groupie slut's slanders about Turk. Believe me, that was nothing to what she had planned for you. So we've actually saved you from her revenge."

"Even that stupid magazine helped her develop a customer base," said Belinda, with some bitterness. "An endless supply of smack clients, all hand-delivered under the guise of interviews and publicity. And she could fill their every request."

"Not like your or Miss Stride's superior roster of upscale bands who turn up their noses at such things, or at least hide it better," agreed Haran. "Her clients were either easily swayed second-raters doing the drugs to seem in or with it, or else real addicts who wanted a clean, accessible source they could trust. Loya, and us too of course, fit the bill either way."

"You said you were tired of her domineering little ways, but what finally made you decide to get rid of her?" asked Hoden unwillingly.

"About a month ago, we were making a cash run to—oops, oh dear, almost gave it away again there!—to the lovely offshore haven where our lovely banks are, with the latest hugely obscene mass of lovely money to put in our lovely secret accounts," said Jo Fleet. "She heard Ted and me talking. Ted had been bugging Larry and Franz and me to get cut in for more of the profits, but he didn't want Loya to know about it. I guess he wanted to get together some serious fuck-you money for when he finally dumped her bony Upper West Side ass and could run away with his dumb blonde secretary with the enormous knockers. Loya controlled the purse-strings in their marriage, thanks to a whopping legacy from her rich-bitch mother, a Jewish-deli heiress, and by all accounts she kept Ted pretty short. Sure, he did very well, legit, from the booking business, but she did a lot better. Maybe he couldn't stand it another minute. Maybe that was why he beat her up all the time. Anyway, we didn't at all mind cutting him in for more; he'd helped us get started in the first place and he has continued to be extremely helpful ever since. We first approached him about three years ago, when he became the Weezles' booker, and he was happy to come on board. So was Jack Holland, your ever so hip and groovy label prez. Between them, they arranged the Weezle tour schedules to our best advantage, meaning less hassle and risk and more money for us."

If humans had the ability to snort fire, Hoden would have been flaming the room. "And less for the band, you worthless piece of garbage. We could have been busted for *your* drugs! Worse, you were murdering people in our name!"

Fleet laughed mirthlessly, and so did Mavius and Haran. "Weren't you making enough not to mind if we lapped a bit of cream off the top? Cream that wasn't even in your own little bottle to begin with? Be generous, Hoden! You can afford it. As for the murderees, you hardly knew them."

"Well, blessed are the morally flexible," snapped Rennie, "for they can tie themselves into truly impressive knots. You *kill* people, you fucking bandersnatches, and I'm not even thinking of those two poor cows on the ship or that guy you dragged out to the pier or the other three the cops told us about. I'm thinking of all the kids you get hooked on your poison. I want to kick you in the googies so hard your grandchildren will feel it. Wearing an iron boot. With spurs. That's on fire. Dipped in poison. What a pity I can't kill you right here with the power of my mind."

Haran grinned and stood to leave; the others already had, scornful of the rants. "If anyone *could* kill by mindpower, it would be Rennie Stride, for sure… Well, think of it as Darwinism in action. Survival of the fittest. Drugs winnow out the weak links and the stupid links. Maybe not to an extent as would really make a statistical difference, but hey, it's a start. As we keep telling you, we don't want to hurt you. We only want to make a nice clean getaway. So you'll stay here for a couple of hours while we finish tidying things up, then we'll bring you down to the boat and sail out into the Passage and maroon you on the first suitable island we come to. No one will notice you there for at least a couple of days, though surely your friends will notice you missing long before that, but by then we'll be well out of here."

He paused on his way to the door that led to the dock. "There'll be plenty of water and fruit; you won't starve or die of thirst. I wouldn't recommend trying to swim back here; it's much too far and the channels are full of dangerous currents, not to mention sharks. But you can always go old-school Robinson Crusoe and light a bonfire or write a message in the sand or put a note in a bottle, if you feel your rescue is unduly delayed. Could be worse."

"Yes, I suppose it could," growled Hoden. "And I'm very much hoping that for you it will be."

"You buying any of that?" asked Hoden, the instant they were left alone. "What they keep telling us?"

"About the nice deserted cay and the nice fruit and water so we won't starve?" Rennie shook her head. "Not for a heartbeat. No, I think it's going to be more like— Out the other side of Springhouse, there's this thing called the Vetiver Wall, that Marigo mentioned earlier. It's a hideous chasm in the ocean floor. Phanuel told me about it. The extremely sudden dropoff is from a nice diveable twenty feet just inside the reef to over six *thousand.* Runs for five miles. Emphasis on the 'drop' and the 'off': you're swimming happily along where you can see and touch clear sandy bottom and then in one stroke you go right over into Atlantis territory, this huge blue abyss. The submarine *Nautilus* is probably garaged there. Even Phan's never dived it. Because it's like Shark Grand Central Terminal. *Really* terminal. Something about the crazy currents bringing masses of fish in, and the fish bringing masses of sharks in. And if we're not out of here before they come back, we're going to be joining the late Mr. Marigo in it, weighted down with coral blocks. And we'll all be snacks before we hit the bottom. So start thinking."

Twenty-three

RENNIE JERKED AWAKE from her brief doze and looked around her. None of their captors seemed to be present, which was either a very good sign or a very bad one—there was no way of knowing. *They're probably still wrapping up operations on the boat. So, bad because that means departure draws nigh, and good because it keeps them out of here for a while longer...* A few yards away, Hoden and Belinda had also nodded out, no more comfortably than Rennie had, seeing the way their necks were cricked. By the feel of the air, she hadn't been out long: maybe fifteen minutes, half an hour at most.

So much for thinking about escape! I know we're all tired, but I shouldn't have dozed off like that. I don't blame them, but I should know better... Still chiding herself, she ran her tongue experimentally over the corner of her mouth, where Marigo and Marigo's late hubby and Jo Fleet had all struck her; yeah, her whole face was really sore, but at least not bleeding anymore—the blood had all dried. Her side, where Marigo had kicked her, hurt a lot more—maybe cracked ribs, oh joy. Then she heard it again, the tiny scratchy sound and whispery voice that had awakened her.

"Miss, Miss Rennie! Oh, hear me, Miss Lady Rennie, please wake up, miss!"

"Pip? Pip *Christmas*? Is that you?" Astounded and appalled in equal measure, Rennie rose carefully to her knees. Stretching over to the side of the millwheel, where the boards of the outer wall were parting company, she peered through the gap to see a small shadowy form, and tried to keep her voice calm. "Oh dear God in heaven… Pip, get away from here, these people are very dangerous, sweetie, go! *Now*!"

"Sure thing, Miss," came the child's confident voice. "But we will get you out first. Only come through here, then we go up the mountain to Captain Ironhand's cave, no problem. Emmy is outside waiting, watching. Miss Marigo and those men are way down at the beach; they pull the boat out and are loading it. Don't see us come, don't see you go."

Rennie breathed a sigh of relief; apparently the kids hadn't noticed just what, exactly, was being loaded onto that boat, or seen how it got that way, but *both* children were here? *God in heaven…* "Do you have a knife, Pip, something sharp? A blade, a cutter? They tied our hands to the machines, we can't manage. Oh, be *careful…*"

Before she had finished speaking, Pip slid through the gap in the broken boards and was already cutting Rennie's bonds with a fearfully capable-looking Swiss Army knife. He put the blade in her hand when he was done and glided back again to stand watch at the opening.

"Cut quick, Miss Lady, come quicker."

Rennie didn't need to be told twice. Like the whirlwind of the desert for swiftness she shook Hoden and Belinda awake, telling them with signals and a hand over each mouth in turn to be silent and follow her lead as she sliced through their cords. They didn't need to be told twice either.

She gave one last fast glance around, then left something on the floor, where hopefully it would be found by—well, not the people outside, anyway. *Same old trick...but it worked last time. The classics aren't the classics for nothing...*

Pip leading, then Belinda, then Hoden, Rennie last, they went like footless ghosts out the back of the mill, where the boy showed them how to let the half-nailed board drop behind them, where not to step on the creaky plank that bridged a ditch. Clearly he knew the place well, probably illicitly; Rennie doubted that his careful parents would let him and his sister hang out there. Outside, Emmy was waiting on the edge of the rainforest, eyes wide and anxious; she was urgently waving them to the mouth of a dark, overgrown, tunnely path through the undergrowth that wound up into the hills, where the crews of the *Hades Rift* and the *Sea Goblin* and the other ships of the Tarrant pirate fleet used to hide out on occasion, when it grew too hot for them out upon the oceans of the world.

Rennie cast a longing glance to the side as they passed the golf carts, neatly parked by the mill entrance, hesitated, then suddenly dashed over to the nearest one. She grabbed two backpacks with uneaten picnic food inside, tossing one to Hoden and slinging on the other herself. *The stuff should still be good, and we may need it. Too bad we can't grab the golf carts as well – but they're way too slow and noisy, we'd have those pigdogs after us in no time. Well, feets it is...* And vanished into the heart of more than darkness.

Climbing up the rocky, muddy, airless jungle track, the two children leading the way, Belinda and Hoden in the middle, herself as rearguard—well, not only was she best qualified to hold off possible attacks from behind but she was the hostess and naturally her guests would precede her, and the kids were the only ones who knew where they were going—Rennie reached automatically for purchase on rock outcroppings or low vines, mechanically digging her toes into the wet dirt until her thighs ached and her calf muscles began to scream with the long pull uphill. Her whole left side, from ribs to knee, was throbbing painfully where Marigo had kicked her, and with each step she tried to stretch the muscles out to ease the soreness. *Man, that hurts like a bitch! Considering it was a total bitch who kicked me…*

She hadn't really appreciated how thick and hot and damp and wild the Lion Island jungles were, not until now. Yeah, she'd seen it all from the air and from the sea as well: apart from the golden agricultural squares of meadows and pastures and terraced fields, and the pale fringing beaches and the few towns, the island looked as if a bolt of deep-green velvet had been tossed over the whole place and tacked down by the mountains and shorelines. But now, deep in the tropical forest, it felt very different. In one of their long, pleasant conversations, Voel Christmas had informed her that of all the islands in that part of the Caribbean, Lion was one of the very few that had retained enormous virgin stands of native forest—over half the island, in fact—and that was due to (a), defending against any incomers who would like to cut it down, and (b), careful management for the past three hundred years.

Of course the Tarrant pirates themselves had needed to mill a certain amount of timber—mahogany, Caribbean pine, teak, cedar and the like—in order to keep their ships in good trim. And to build new ones, though mostly they had purchased their replacement vessels in England or the northern U.S. ports, built of good English or American hardwoods that wore like iron. They'd had their own shipyard in Lion Bay, Turk had told her, where all the necessary repairs and construction were done. Additionally, lumber was needed to build homes and docks and farm structures and make furniture for the increasing population.

So various island managers down the years had worked with various lords of the island, with the result that the rainforest and jungly mountain slopes remained deeply and heavily treeful, not threatened by the fields that produced crops and grazed herds in abundance. It was a point of pride, the island's self-supporting independence, and also a point of economics: certain areas had been set aside to be harvested, replanted and harvested again. When the land got tired, it was allowed to lie fallow for ten or fifty or even a hundred years, until lush tropicality had restored it to its former luxuriant self.

Trails snaked through all this flourishing verdure, but so full and extensive was the tree canopy that you couldn't often see the paths and small farm roads from above. As she trudged in the dancing wake of Emmy and Pip, Rennie found herself feeling increasingly claustrophobed out by the stillness of the surrounding jungle, praying for a breath of breeze, or even a machete. The silence was broken only by strange animal sounds, coming sometimes from deep in the forest, sometimes from close overhead. She knew the creatures she heard were harmless—at least she *guessed* they were harmless, the really dangerous animals here were human, or else lived in the surrounding seas—but the noises were uncanny, and she startled continually, thinking she had heard sounds of pursuit. *'Be not afeared; the isle is full of noises'...hopefully not hostile ones...*

As she doggedly hauled upwards, she distracted herself from the assorted pains by considering everything they'd learned in the mill. Loya Tessman as a drug czarina! Great Caesar's ghost, who would have thought it? But she was still stupid, having remained in the thrall of no-neck Ted until it was finally too late, and *that* was what had gotten her killed... The others, well—she had no trouble believing them on any count, and with the help of the angels neither would the cops and a court of law. All provided that she and Linny and Hoden stayed alive to tell their stories. And anyone who tried to hurt those kids would have to get past the three of them to do it.

After a while the trail emerged into a broad, flat place on the mountainside, a wide, level ledge opening to both fresh air and a distant view. Rennie, pausing with the others, looked out and down, and was astonished to see how far up they had come. *Clever hobbitses, to climb so high...* The quick tropical sunset was now faintest red balefire down in the west. The ocean, rippling slow surflines of foam under the leftover storm wind, showed dark velvet beneath a newly risen full moon huger than any Rennie had ever seen; the nearby islands, looking close enough to step across to, were spread out like relief maps, moonshadowed with silver. Across the straits, beyond the big hills of the Grand Palms, the lambent glow of Palmton could be seen against the sky, and farther away, the fainter glimmer of more islands—flat Anguilla, mountainous Tortola, the other U.S. and British Virgins. Below, patches of brightness showed where the settlements lay—Lion Town and the five or six little villages.

Gazing desperately toward the lights of Falcons Levels in the distance, she could see off to the right the eerie shimmer of Bluestar Bay, perhaps the most beautiful place in the entire island. Tiny microorganisms in the water there left shining trails of bioluminescence in the shallow, calm lagoon, as fish leaped or turtles dived; she and Turk had gone in there one moonless night, their bare bodies outlined in silver-blue spangles as they lazily swam and splashed and floated and made love... She leaned over again, hands on her knees, to catch her breath. They were all nearly done in. But according to Pip, they were also almost there.

Gradually she became aware of a faint, distant sound coming across the deep island quiet; it seemed to have been going on for some time, yet was only now registering on her conscious mind and ears, now that she was up high enough to hear and out of the muffling jungle. Far away below, bells were wildly ringing, the church bells in Lion Town and bells from the villages and farms, and there was the sound of what seemed to be horns blowing. No, not horns—conchs! Lion Island was giving the alarm as it had done in days of old. It sounded like something from long ago and a long way off, from down through time or up from the bottom of the sea. Her heart leaped to hear it. *The horns of the Rohirrim! Rescue! Maybe it really even is...*

Ahead, by a jumble of boulders, Emmy was frantically waving them along. The kids had heard the alarm too, and knew what it meant better than she did: it was for the five of them, alerting the islanders to an emergency, but they would not be the only ones hearing it. Coming round the turn of the path, Rennie saw a double waterfall making its misty way down the mountainside, to cross the ledge's width and bubble into a wide pool, then tumble scenically off into space. *Well, at least we'll have something to drink...*When they reached Emmy, the girl beckoned them to follow her, then slid between two boulders and promptly vanished.

Rennie slid after her through the narrow gap and found herself in the mouth of a cave behind the falls, where Pip was standing, beaming proudly; the shielding rocks, offset so that no casual glance could see inside, were all slick with moss and water and hung with a thick curtain of rather unpleasantly squashy vines, but the ground underfoot, just behind, was bare and dry. She pushed everyone inside, then turned back to lean against the huge angled rock at the cave entrance, to catch her breath and get her bearings. She still had a good vantage out over the island: the towns, both coastlines, Falcons Levels tiny and all lit up, miles away on its hill. Which was somehow reassuring; but more so was the fact that she could see down the trail to where it emerged from the jungle. She would spot any trackers long before they could spot her, and with any luck at all, they wouldn't.

By now, judging by the distant commotion, she and Hoden and Belinda had been found missing, and, it being long after dark, the kids too. Turk and Phan and the other island men knew all Ironhand's old hiding places: being no dummies, they were bound to figure it out, and they'd get to this cave with reinforcements as quickly as they could. Preferably they would get there first, and not waste hours at all Ironhand's *other* hiding places… Her only real concern was that Marigo and her vile cohorts would get there sooner, and they had guns and she did not. Hopefully, the rescuers would not be sidetracked into thinking she and the others had already been removed from the island—and even more hopefully would find them before that actually happened.

Drawing a deep breath, Rennie joined the others, as far back into the twisting and turning cave tunnels as they could safely get but not out of sight of the moonlit entrance. It was a whole cavern system, she realized, awed, not a mere cave: an interconnected labyrinth of alcoves stretching deep into the mountain, well concealed and full of pitchy darkness—pretty unlikely that any of the pursuers knew that it was even there, or would want to go any distance inside if they did. No bats, thankfully, and except for some leafy detritus blown in by the wind, inside the entrance, the ground was sandy, dry and clean.

"Emmy, Pip, who knows about these caves?"

Pip scrambled up to her. "Everyone on the island know them, Miss Rennie. Captain Ironhand, he hid out in them, long time ago, him and his men and their treasure. No more treasure, but the cave still here. For sure Mister Lord Richard and Mister Phan, they know."

"But the others? Does Marigo know?"

"Not nohow! That Marigo, she not from here," said Emmy scornfully; the children's accents had grown more islandified as they had gone on, shifting over from their school-taught British standard into the charming local cadence all the residents used unofficially. "She not a belonger—she just an old cow from Grenada. She know naught."

"Nor she do," said Rennie, smiling and doing her best to keep up with the vernacular. "But she might ask those bad men she was with, they might know to come here."

"Nah, they do not!" Pip assured her. "When we were hiding, we hear them talk—they say they do not know the island and do not care to get themselves lost. They are afraid of the jungle, afraid of the dark, afraid of the water. Scaredy raggedy things. Our dad and Mister Phan and Mister Lord Richard, they will soon be here, you will see."

"I know I will. We'll all see. I should have known you little perishers would hang out around that mill."

Pip grinned. "We are not supposed to come that way," he admitted. "But we followed you to Quince Trunk, this morning, just for fun, and to play. And to share the picnic! So we see Marigo and the others take you. First we hide to watch and see, then we trail you to the mill. Once we see where they put you, we hide some more and wait. To get you out, 'cause we see them hit you and we do not like to see that."

"And then we see *you* hit *them*," added Emmy, eyes wide.

"Very wrong of both of you," said Rennie seriously. "You should both have gone straight home, especially once it started to get dark."

"We think we maybe can help," said Emmy, straightfaced, but her eyes were sparkling as Rennie grabbed her and tousled her hair, one arm affectionately circling the little girl's neck.

"Oh, you did, did you, missy? Well, you were right about that, for sure, even though you're probably going to get a darn good paddling when you get home."

"Maybe you would talk our dad and mum out of that, you think?" asked Pip slyly.

Rennie laughed and hugged them both. "Oh, I suppose I could put in a good word. But listen, both of you, very serious now: if I tell you to run, you *run*, and if I tell you to hide, you *hide*. And you don't argue with me and you don't stop and you don't look back. Do you understand me? Yes? Good. Or else you'll be getting that paddling from me first. Now you two go and stay with Miss Linny and Mister Hoden, okay, and take care of them for me. They're probably afraid of the dark. *You* won't be scared back there, will you?"

Another small joint scoff. "Not we! This an old hideout place of ours, from when we were only little. We know all the twists and the turns."

"Do your parents know you sneak up here?" Rennie asked pointedly, but she was laughing. "Because you really *will* get a paddling. Right. Now go, all the way back, please. If you need me, come and get me. I'll be out here."

She exchanged a serious glance with Hoden and Belinda—*Look out for them*—and shooed them off with the kids into the darker places of the cave. Then she turned and moved quietly to mount guard over the cavern entrance.

"And yet I am not comforted," said Rennie, aloud and dolefully.

It was she didn't know how long later; well after

midnight, judging by the position of the moon. Below, the alarms had fallen silent; she hoped that meant the search was progressing, not that it had ended. She had allowed everyone to come up to the mouth of the cave, one at a time, to drink at the waterfall from behind, scooping the clean cold water in their hands. As for food, they had the backpacks she'd grabbed from the golf carts, and the children had expertly snagged fruit from low-branched trees as the little party had hiked through the jungle. They had all filled their pockets, and now there was a small heap of mangos, papayas, star plums and the delicious local custard apples lying on the cave floor.

The backpacks hadn't contained as much as they'd hoped: apparently the goons had pillaged most of it. Rennie had insisted they carefully ration what was left—a few sandwiches, some cheese and chocolate and biscuits, nothing more sustaining than that—as nobody knew how long they'd have to hide before they were either rescued or recaptured. So they'd given the kids the most substantial stuff, and then themselves had filled up on water, which thanks to the falls was in endless supply, and a piece or two of fruit. Now the children were dozing in the farthest cave alcove reachable, with Belinda and Hoden on guard.

She thought about her talk with Pip and Emmy. Clearly they had not been witness to the murder of Mell Armatreddy by his monstrous wife, because they were cheerful and untraumatized, and thank God for that. It was bad enough what they *had* seen, but that…no. Just no. And there was no question but that the children had saved them; otherwise, they'd still be tied up in the old mill. *Or worse…I did* not *like the sound of that little cruise over to Springhouse. I very much doubt we would have been left on Vetiver or Tienda or any other damn island either. Much more likely we'd have been tipped over the side into that charming shark buffet, along with Armatreddy's body…*

So long and hard had she been musing that she started violently when Hoden crept forward from the rear of the cave, to join her behind the sparkling curtain, placing a hand on her arm just as she had spoken.

"You're not?" he asked uncertainly. "Comforted, I mean."

"Oh— " She was a little embarrassed. "I was only talking to myself, thinking how we're probably as safe as we could be right now."

"But no comfort."

"Well, some. We're here. We're not hurt. We have things to eat and water to drink and a place to hide."

"Again I say 'but'?"

Rennie sighed. "But no guns. No knives except Pip's Swiss Army one. No flashlights—those would be 'torches' to you, Britboy. No way of letting Turk or the cops know where we are. Children to look after. Though they seem to be more looking after us."

"No, well, I guess not much comfort after all." He settled lithely cross-legged and jerked his head rearwards, smiling. "They're telling each other stories back there, Linny and the kids. Pirate legends from local oral tradition versus *The Hobbit* from memory. About evens for mad violence, I'd say, though there's no orcs here. Well, unless you count Jo Fleet. It's very bright out there," he added, peering out of the cave. "The moon has gotten all the way up."

She made more room for him as he shifted position. "Actually, now heading toward setting, though not till dawn, when we'll have real light again anyway, but it still worries me. I have a feeling those bastards waited till the moon was high enough that they could see easily before starting after us, though how they would know to come up here I have no idea, so maybe we'll luck out and they'll be running through the jungle. In the opposite direction. Or maybe they're still tidying things up at the mill and boatshed and they'll *leave*. While the getting is good."

"But you don't think that will happen."

She shook her head. "We're loose ends and we need to be tied off, probably permanently. Just our luck if one of them can track like an Iroquois scout. And we won't see them until they're on top of us. Literally."

From a pocket, Hoden produced a mango, cut it open with Pip's knife and handed her half. "If we can't see them, they can't see us. And we're in a nice dark cave, and once they get out of the jungle, they're walking up a nice bare mountainside in nice bright moonlight. And we're still in a nice dark cave."

"There's that... You know we owe it all to Emmy and Pip, that we're even here."

"Those kids are bloody amazing," he said with conviction, and Rennie nodded vigorously.

"*Oh* yeah. I'm already thinking of what I can give them for this. They didn't do it for a reward, but they deserve a big fat honking one, and Turk and I will make sure they get it."

"I'm in." He looked at her for a long time as they both finished off the mango and washed their faces and hands of the juice, rinsing off the knife as well in the falling water; feeling his gaze, she didn't turn her head.

"You and Turk..." he said after an even longer time, letting the sentence trail off.

"Me and Turk."

"No chance?" he asked quietly.

She smiled and touched his hand lightly. "Sorry. Truly. Absolutely none. Forever."

"Right. Just thought I'd ask. In case we're about to die. Wouldn't want to die not having said. No offense."

"None taken. And we are *not* going to die."

"I'm like that," he burst out after a long silence. "I want what I want, and if I can't have it then I'd rather go without. If you settle for second-best, second-best is all you get."

Rennie touched his hand again, grasping it, shaking it gently. "I promise you, you won't have to. You'll find first-best. Because you *are* first-best. You'll see. I'll fix you up myself if I have to, with all my first-best friends, and those are the only kind I have," she added, smiling, and he smiled too. Glancing out again over the dark landscape, suddenly she stiffened all over, like a gun dog on a pheasant, and he came alert as well.

"What?"

"Down there." She pointed, careful to keep her arm inside the shadow cast by the stones. "I thought I saw something. Flash of light."

They waited a while in silence, then the flash came again, and they heard voices in the jungle below, carrying in the silence.

"Well," she whispered, "I guess even old cows from Grenada can follow a trail."

"So it would seem. Game on, then! Oh, but before whatever happens actually happens, there's one more thing I don't want to die without saying..."

They didn't seem concerned who heard them coming: none of them was keeping their voice low, and as revealed, they had flashlights, and appeared not to care if anyone saw.

As soon as she heard them, Rennie hurried to push Belinda and the children back into an even farther recess of the cave, putting the knife into her friend's hand. It was all but pitch black, but better they were as invisible as she could get them; the kids seemed nonchalant—they'd explored here before—though they huddled against Belinda for mutual comfort. Now Rennie parked herself grimly in the cave opening again, beside Hoden. She could see them approaching, not that far below. It would be terrible bad luck if they could find the cave entrance, well concealed as it was. Perhaps Marigo knew it was there, but Rennie doubted that; the others certainly wouldn't.

She counted seven of them, and her heart sank. *We can't handle seven, and seven who have weapons. Not with the kids. We are going to have to hide as best we can, or failing that, Hoden and I will simply have to give ourselves up; it's us they want anyway, us with our certain hostage value. But I really thought they would have gotten away when they had the chance, and not have bothered to come after us...which only proves, I guess, that they had no intention of dropping us off on any deserted cay. More like dropping us off into those sharky depths. Because we know.*

Marigo, as native guide, was leading, then Franz Haran, Larry Mavius and Jo Fleet; bringing up the rear, three of the henchmen from the mill. Mell Armatreddy, of course, was distinctive by his absence, and the rest had apparently stayed below with the escape boat. The seven were out in the open space now, below the falls, and headed straight for the cave entrance, or so at least it appeared.

I guess they figured, and correctly, that this was the only logical way for us to have gone – into the jungle would have been too chancy, along the shoreline too dangerous. Only other way was the path straight up… Or maybe one of them really was *an Iroquois scout…*

The three non-islanders were limping badly, Rennie noted with malice. *Yeah, what price Ferragamos now, you hammer-toed vulgarians! Bet you're kicking yourselves you didn't wear Keds like us…* They weren't exactly in prime condition, either: she could hear them panting like baby belugas as they struggled up the last yards to the broad ledge in front of the waterfall. Glancing back to make sure everyone had stayed in hiding as she had bidden them, she took a few deep breaths to prepare herself for possible combat. To her surprise, she found it was hard to keep still; her feet and fingers twitched with the irrational impulse of the hunted quarry, the urge to break from cover and either fight like hell or run like hell.

Okay, then. This could get nasty. If it comes to it, Hoden and I can lie and claim Belinda got lost in the jungle, or we sent her off on the trail to Lion Town for help…they don't know the kids are with us. Still, we can't fight them all…and now I think of it, where's Teddyboy? For all we talked about him, he never showed up at the mill...

But amazingly, as she watched with clenching hands and dawning hope, the little group was passing by, not turning aside but walking straight past. Not fifty feet away from her, they plodded to the little stream into which the falls overspilled, squatted by its pooling edge and started noisily slurping the fresh cool water—Haran and Mavius even took their shoes off to bathe their blistered feet. *Oh, you'll never get* those *on again, morons! Clearly you were never little Cub Scouts...* Hoden, crouched beside her, was alive with tenseness that matched her own; she could clearly tell he was bursting to do some revengeful bashing, and Fleet would be only his first target.

As thirst was satisfied, the new arrivals talked amongst themselves. Straining to hear, Rennie and Hoden caught snatches of their conversation—chiefly irritated complaints about why the hell did they have to go *looking* for the fugitives, clearly they hadn't climbed the damn mountain, they'd probably gone through the jungle and were halfway home by now. Marigo, standing apart from the non-islanders, was looking closely at the ground, and the two hiding behind the screen of water tensed anew. But stone holds no footprints, and no one had stepped in the water to leave any marks. Jo Fleet also looked around, and Rennie's blood ran cold all the way down as his gaze rested on the waterfall, and colder still as he began to move toward it.

Then suddenly the gravel and small stones started flying upward, dust and grit in everyone's eyes. Marigo and her henchmen scrambled hastily to their feet, the two lawyers still unshod, all of them looking wildly around, obviously terrified, trying to figure out which way, if any, lay safety. The waterfall was blown aside like a rope of lace, and the trees and vines on the slopes began to thrash in a wind out of nowhere and everywhere.

Shading her own eyes against the violent updraft, finding it hard to catch her breath, Rennie felt as much as heard a throbbing roar that seemed to come from all directions at once, a rhythmic thumping reverberating off the cliffs and growing louder every second. Looking out over the landscape, disoriented by the noise and wind, hair flying around her, just as she started to totally panic she saw a huge black shadow against the moon, rising up from the jungle and coming to hover a few feet above the broad bare slope below the cave, beaming a stabbing white light down at the ground. Rohan had come at last.

Twenty-four

TURK CAME SWINGING DOWN from the open side of the helicopter like Ironhand leading a boarding party, and the look on his face made Rennie startle. She screamed his name in warning, but either he didn't hear her over the rotor noise or he chose not to heed: he'd clearly seen what he was heading into, and equally clearly he didn't care. Phanuel, Ares and Laird leaped down after him, like members of Ironhand's crew—Ares with a terrifying set expression that Rennie had beheld upon his countenance several times before, and she knew what it boded. The four of them totally ignored the police behind them in the copter yelling at them to let the pros handle it, and went straight for Marigo and her cohorts.

It was a battle that could have been more satisfying only if it had been fought with cutlasses. Rennie saw Turk methodically pounding the hell out of Jo Fleet, which gave her a primitive, and quite disgraceful, little thrill, and Ares was savagely grappling with Marigo, who had pulled a Beretta out of her waistband and was trying to fire it. Even as Rennie watched, Ares effortlessly twisted the gun out of the Grenadian's hand, and, not a man to be chivalrous in such case, buckled her knee with one heel and popped her in the jaw, knocking her sprawling to the ground. Phanuel and Laird were off to the side acquitting themselves most manfully, now joined by the cops who'd come with them in the chopper. Rennie dearly longed to do some jaw-popping of her own, but restrained herself from leaping into the fray: the guys had it under control, she'd only cramp their style, and besides, she still had the others to look after, just in case, especially the kids.

It was all good, though. Franz Haran and two of the others tried to escape from the punishments being dealt out by the boarding party, turning to flee back along the trail the way they had come. But dozens of men, with barking, snarling dogs straining at their leads—police from Lion Town and Palmton and local volunteers alike, including Voel Christmas, in terror for his children—were now storming up the hill from below, and blocked any flight in that direction. Down over the rocks the other way wasn't really an option, especially barefoot, but Larry Mavius tried to take it anyway, and made the dogs extremely happy. And all the time the helicopter hung low over the hillside before the moon, like some great baleful dragonfly or pterodactyl or fell beast of the Nazgûl, all spinning lights and blasting wind and roaring noise.

Staring open-mouthed at the astonishing scene in front of them, Rennie and Hoden stood in the cave entrance, with Belinda, Emmy and Pip behind them—the three had all come dashing out, clean contrary to orders, as soon as they heard the ruckus. It was over in what seemed a mere instant: Marigo and Fleet and Haran and Mavius, considerably the worse for wear, were loaded into the copter with a police escort, and the others were manacled and marched down the hill, frustrated dogs barking and leaping alongside. By now Turk had Rennie safely in his arms, Ares stood talking with Hoden, and Laird was gathering up Belinda and the kids. Voel Christmas, his face ghastly, dashed over just behind Laird. When he saw his children unhurt, he closed his eyes in thanksgiving, then grabbed them up and hustled them off to one side for hugs and praise and hardly any scolding.

Rennie looked up at Turk, herself half laughing and half collapsing, her clothes drenched from the waterfall and smeared with dirt from the escape. They were both getting more soaked and begrimed every moment from the chopper updraft still beating against the mountainside, and neither of them cared.

"Well, that was some arrival, Ampman. Pity I don't have any cymbals to clash in your honor. The moment seems to call for it."

"Oh, adoring worship will suffice. As usual."

She managed a shaky indrawn breath that barely passed for laughter, and clung more closely. "And yet again, my lord, you've got me screaming your name. One way or another… That was quite the turn-on, I must say."

He tightened his hold on her, noticed the flinch as he pressed her injured side, and eased off. "Christ, you're a bloodthirsty little thing. I find it strangely attractive. But if you're going to be screaming my name, I much prefer it be for other reasons. We'll have to wait a bit for that, though. Oh, and I'll be screaming your name too. Only *at* you," he added darkly. "We'll have to wait a bit for that as well." He tightened his grip again, more carefully, and kissed her hair. "Is everyone all right?"

She peered around, but everything appeared under

control. "So it would seem. But you'd know that better than I. How the hell did you even figure out where we *were*?"

"Voel Christmas called the house, frantic, said his kids hadn't shown up for tea and no one had seen them all day. We realized that the golf carts were gone and you lot weren't anywhere around, either, so we all drove down the hill to town and organized a search. Perhaps you heard the conchs going off, along with the bells?" he said, pride in his voice. "We did that in the olden days, when rival pirates or chastising navies or other tribulations came in sight. We have the siren now, of course, but we like to go old-school. Anyway, when they heard the alarm sound, everybody knew what to do—we've had drills for this sort of thing—and everyone in Lion Town who could came running to the assembly point. Then we all set out to comb the island, by every means possible, including, as you see, air support. We kept in touch with walkie-talkies and radios—which they didn't have in the olden days, of course, hence the use of conchs. Frankly, we didn't think to find you out this way, not so far. But someone from Bassalonie, the nearby village, came by here and saw the kids' bikes and the golf carts near the old sugar mill down below, not to mention the escape boat at the dock, under a nicely minimal guard. Which guards and boat both alike, I must say, were immediately overrun by angry and superior numbers, and going inside the mill I found a sheet of blood, cut bindings and bales of suspicious t-shirts, with your pendant right where you left it. So naturally I figured that was your handiwork. Nice job, though I have to say that trick is getting a bit old."

"Yes, well, I'll try to be more imaginative from now on."

Rennie bent her neck as Turk fastened the carved coral rose around it, and shivered at the touch of his fingers brushing aside her hair. In the high moonlight and the harsh spotlight from the chopper, the bruises where Armatreddy and Fleet had struck her were plain for him to see, and his fingertips gently touched her face.

He went on, though his voice held a note of fear and now anger that even finding her safe had not entirely vanquished. "The Palmton bobbies had been keeping an eye on Marigo for a while, apparently, and tonight they quietly raided that little facility on Springhouse Cay which I'm sure you know all about by now. Considering it's our island, they never troubled themselves to inform my father or me about it, and we may have to discuss it at a later date. Anyway, that's how we knew to come here, and that thrashing was required, and that all of you were probably hiding up in the caves. Meryton had arranged the raid, which Fleet and the rest clearly were not aware of. The good Superintendent had been keeping a closer eye on all this than any of us knew."

"Damn cops."

"Indeed. Still, there are good things about having a cop on your side, if it's the right kind of cop. If you're clever enough, you can get it to agree to what you want, and after that, if anything goes wrong it's their fault, and you are free of blame. And so we got to provide an actual air strike. Not to mention the fact that I personally own the rescue helicopter and was going to do it with or without their permission."

Rennie buried her face against him. "Rank hath its privileges, as we see yet again."

He smiled into her hair. "Just so, and never was I more

grateful for it. Anyway, from what we heard as we came across on the chopper, Meryton and his merry men had ringed Springhouse with police craft, so that no one could escape by swimming, and had scuba ninjas swim in to disable the small boats hidden there, so that they couldn't get away by boat either. Nevertheless, a surprising number of the smack staff tried, and the boats were instantly shot full of holes. As were those who tried shooting their way out. Otherwise, the plod just waded in, literally—it must have been like the beaches of Normandy—and grabbed them all, and their supplies as well. Anyone who managed to make it off the cay was picked up in the water, before they sank to the depths on Vetiver Wall."

"We know all about Vetiver Wall," said Rennie, with a shiver. "Marigo seemed to think it would suit for our last resting place."

"And so it would have done. Over a mile deep and the corals grow undisturbed to thirty feet high. With untold numbers of sharks converging to dine on the fish."

"Or on snoopy reporters and rock stars plummeting down from above."

"And probably on untold numbers of drug runners who didn't do their bosses' bidding." Turk took a blanket from one of the rescue squad and wrapped her in it as she shivered uncontrollably, this time with chill and incipient shock.

"Yes... Well, they clearly knew nothing about the raid, our little friends here, since they were very confidently planning on heading over to Springhouse, to pick up whatever smack was left, and then setting sail for Neverland, or someplace equally unfindable. And tossing us on the way like unwanted ballast. Or marooning us like Peter Pan. It seemed about evens which way it was going to go. So the Christmas kids managed to spring us, and we ran."

"Shh..." He kissed her hair again. "I know. It's okay. We also found a body on the dock. And, as I said, a *lot* of blood on the warehouse floor. Which I'm thinking you might know something about." He didn't say how he'd felt when he'd seen that, terrified it might be hers, what with the pendant lying nearby.

Rennie leaned into him, both her arms around his waist, ignoring the stabs from her bruised side. "That was Mell Armatreddy, the real Mr. Marigo. She garroted him herself, right in front of us. That is one evil, foul, viperous bitch. The kids had followed us from our picnic place, where we were grabbed by her and her minions, and they were hiding outside the mill the whole time, the little bandits. Thank God they were, but equally thank God they didn't see her kill him. I wish *I* hadn't... But, again, how the hell did you find us?"

"Ironhand used this cave, as I'm sure young Master Philip and Miss Emma told you. Given the evidence of the bicycles and the pendant, we figured that they were with you, and since none of you were being held prisoner on the boat, that you'd all gone up here to hide. They're absolutely forbidden to come here, so of course they do, it being a *pirate* cave, and we thought that they'd hare straight to it, taking you lot with them. Also it's the closest of Ironhand's hideouts to the mill. We just—lucked out."

"No, *we* did."

The other two ex-captives had joined them now, also well wrapped against chill and drinking medic-supplied tea for shock, and Turk let go of Rennie for an instant to hug Belinda and grip Hoden's forearm in manly fashion. When he saw the wide-eyed Christmas children clinging tightly to their father's side, he knelt down and held out his arms, and they threw off their blankets and came running to him.

"Mister Lord Turk," said Pip, awed; the kids had emerged in time to see the cavalry ride in, and he looked at Turk now as if he'd been Ironhand himself.

"You two are heroes, you know," said Turk gravely. "Thank you for helping to save Miss Rennie and my friends."

"They were bad men," said Emmy suddenly. "They hurt Miss Rennie."

"I bet Miss Rennie hurt them right back, though, didn't she?" said Turk, and the little girl grinned and nodded, ducking her head against him. "That's all right, then. And you were both so very brave and smart to get them all out of the mill and bring them up here." He gave each child a kiss on the head and stood up. "Now go home in the chopper with your dad, and we'll see you later, yes? Your mum is worried sick."

The two heroes, reaction fast setting in, nodded sleepily, and Voel, with another unspeakably grateful look at Rennie and Hoden and Belinda, shepherded his offspring a little distance away, to await the return of the helicopter.

Gazing after them, Rennie shook her head in wonder. "What incredible kids. But probably they're too knackered to even enjoy the ride, and they'll fall asleep on the way—

we'll have to take them up again under happier circs."

"We will do that. But what about you? You too knackered to enjoy yourself? We can go home, or we can go over to Palmton to watch them all being gratifyingly tossed into the slammer along with their confederates from Springhouse Cay. Up to you."

"Appealing, but no. Home it is, please."

Belinda, who was standing near, looked despairingly at the trail and then at the lights of Falcons Levels far in the distance. "Do we have to *walk* back?"

Phanuel, who had done his share of bashing—though he'd left Marigo to Ares— shook his head. "No, as soon as the helicopter drops the police and their bagful off at the mill dock, it'll come back for us and anybody else who needs a ride home."

"So what happens to them now?"

"They'll be taken by police launch to Palmton ," said Turk. "No need to waste air fuel on them, it's no time at all by boat and we need the chopper ourselves. It's mine, after all, not Grand Palm's. The sooner they're gone the better, and they can have a nice reunion in stir with the scum that Meryton and his boys corralled on Springhouse."

Belinda moved off arm in arm with Laird and Hoden to join the Christmases down on the broad flat ledge, where the copter had landed and would return to after its shuttle run down to the beach, while Rennie leaned into Turk's side and tried not to tremble too much.

"Do we have to wait for the airlift?"

He shook his head with mock exasperation. "Christ, there's no pleasing you people, is there? But no. We don't have to wait. There are Jeeps, Rovers, golf carts, Harleys and horses at the foot of the hill. All we have to do is walk down and choose one of the above."

"I think I can manage that. Just."

Dawn was full upon them when they finally arrived back at Falcons Levels. Much to her own annoyance, Prax had been detailed to hold the fort, in case calls came in or the missing came marching home, and now she had wildly thrown her arms around rescued and rescuers alike. The entire house staff was awake and eager to take care of them all. To keep busy, they'd been fixing food in case it was needed for refueling; the men of the estate had been out searching with the other male islanders, and everyone had been recalled by another tocsin of conchs and church bells. They would all soon be home and abed themselves.

Rennie was too drained to do much more than hug Prax and thank everyone for waiting up and tell them to go to sleep; then Turk took her to their rooms and ran a hot bath for them both. When they emerged all relaxed and clean and shiny—he had narrowed his eyes at her swollen cheek and bloodied mouth and the huge purple-blue bruises already forming on her side, but had merely applied a hot washcloth and arnica, passed her a codeine pill and said nothing—one of the maids knocked on the bedroom door, bearing a tray with a full teapot and several plates heavily laden with some of the food that had been assembled for the searchers.

Thanking her, he took it and turned to Rennie, thinking she would probably be uninterested in sustenance, only in sleep. But she flung herself on the tray like a ravening wolf on a caribou. He smiled, surprised and amused, and raised his eyebrows.

"I don't think I've ever seen you shove anything into your mouth faster. Well, food, at least. Being abducted at gunpoint seems to wonderfully concentrate the appetite."

"I've had nothing to eat since supper the night before last," she muttered defensively. She set down the steak sandwich she was devouring, suddenly embarrassed at how voraciously she'd been stuffing. "Okay, I had half a mango up at the cave. But that was it. We had a little food in the packs, but we had to ration it. None of us got much, it only made us hungrier; and we made sure the kids got the most. And it was a rather—busy day. Crammed full of incident, if not exactly nourishment. Next time I'm kidnapped I'll make sure I eat a good breakfast first."

Her voice had gone very small and tight and quavery on that last. She sounded pathetic, she knew, but she didn't care. It was weird that after everything that had happened, this should be the thing that was just that one final straw too much—that he was teasing her, however gently, for being so desperately hungry—but it was. Maybe because it came from him. Not trusting her voice at all by now, she folded her shaking hands in her lap, holding herself away from the food and the tea and the tray, clearly on the edge of tears.

Turk's smile vanished. He'd forgotten that side of it: she'd been starving all day and all this night and even the night before, not to mention being injured, exhausted, stressed out and in fear; and here he was mocking her for forgetting her table manners. Feeling horrified and guilty, he reached forward and gently put the sandwich back in her hand.

"Oh, sweetheart. I'm so sorry, I didn't mean to— Eat. Please. I don't want you going to bed hungry. Come on, get that blood sugar back up. I'll keep you company, shall I?" He took a sandwich for himself, surprised to realize that he was almost as famished as she was; well, he'd been busy too. And worried. Terrified. Furious. Clearly foodlessness was putting both of them off their game.

When the plates were clean and the teapot was empty and Rennie was finally full-fed, Turk rang for the maid, who returned almost immediately and took the tray from him. Rennie heard him quietly thank her and send her off to her own bed, before she herself completely passed out in theirs.

Next day, they all gathered for a late brunch, where prodigious quantities of serious food were consumed and war stories were compared. Everybody praised everybody else's bravery and cleverness, and all joined together in marveling at Emmy and Pip. Superintendent Meryton had phoned earlier, saying he would need to meet with his lordship, Miss Stride, Mr. Hoden and Miss Melbourne in Palmton in the very near future, like *now*; and they said by all means, they were fine with that, but could it maybe wait a day or two, as they were all still pretty badly freaked and completely wiped out and Rennie had been hurt, and he wasn't too happy about it but said yes of course.

After the meal, Turk dragged Rennie back to their rooms, where he bestowed upon his betrothed the promised scolding. He wasn't a rock singer for nothing, and his trained baritone could have brought down the walls of Jericho if he'd felt so inclined; but unlike their last squabble, this time he kept his voice low and snapped it at her like a whip. He didn't get angry very often, and even then it was usually with the band, not with his beloved—to be cross with her twice in a matter of days was totally not usual. But fueled by his fear and frustration, he tore into her like an oncoming storm. Everyone else in the house pretended they couldn't hear.

For her part, Rennie felt quite hardly done by: after all, it hadn't been her fault, and unlike several other occasions they both could name, she had been more acted upon than acting. She'd been *kidnapped,* for God's sake, and she had not confronted the criminals as was her wont but instead had fled with the others to prudently hide in a cave and wait for rescue, like some damn damsel. So surely he must be pleased about *that,* at least. She knew that he'd been afraid for her and that was where his anger was coming from. Well, she'd been afraid for her too! And afraid for the kids, and afraid for Hoden and Linny, and afraid for Turk and the other rescuers when they came... Plus it was so unfair of him to yell at her when she was sore and battered and not at her best. So, *again,* not her fault. This time. Turk was being outrageously unjustified and unreasonable and unjust, and so she snapped right back at him, with all the injured virtue and wronged blamelessness she could summon up, and all the puff that her aching ribs would allow.

When the guns had finally fallen silent and they'd first merely glared and then flung themselves at each other in desperate embracing apology, his lordship decreed that the three kidnappees go down to the hospital in Lion Town to be checked over, and nobody dared gainsay him. So off they all went, and were attended to by a grateful Hannah Christmas and her staff. Rennie's ribs were duly X-rayed and found to be thankfully uncracked, just badly bruised and blooming in multicolored splendor, and Dr. Hannah wrapped them lightly, alternately scolding her for taking such risks and thanking her for taking care of Emmy and Pip. She was given more pain meds, coals to Newcastle really, but she believed in topping up her stash whenever possible so she did not turn them down. Belinda and Hoden had a few cuts and dings and scratches, and had been as starved as Rennie, but were otherwise fine.

Which was good, because the Tenant-in-Chief of the island, Christophen Hilling, a large, shrewd, affable sort proudly descended from Ironhand's weapons master, had requested a serious conversation with them on recent events as soon as they were all patched up, and with Turk present too, as island overlord and lead rescuer, and of course it was not a request at all.

"Good practice for talking to the fuzz," offered Belinda hopefully. She was right: it was an easy, though searching, interrogation, conducted on the airy veranda of the official residence just outside the town and accompanied by an excellent tea, which no one declined. Tenant Hilling had been jovial and paternal, though deeply serious about said events, and even more deeply concerned about what they all had to tell him. Afterwards, Belinda, Laird and Hoden thought they would unwind a bit on the nearest beach, and

Turk and Rennie went home by themselves.

Hours later, she woke suddenly and completely, heart pounding, momentarily disoriented. Where the hell was she? Not the cave… Oh, right, she was safe in bed, it was all over, it was fine; thanks to the pills, her whole body was no more than vaguely sore, though also thanks to the pills she was dazed and trippy. Under their influence, she'd slept in fits and starts for most of the late afternoon and into the evening, unrestfully, waking only for yet more food trays featuring all her favorite things, which were delivered to her bedside at regular intervals. She'd gobbled every scrap, feeling like Scarlett O'Hara vowing she'd never go hungry again, and had instantly fallen back asleep before the trays had left the room. So yes, she was fine, for a certain value of "fine"; but Turk, where was Turk? Surely he wouldn't leave her by herself…

Through the terrace windows, she saw that it was nighttime, breezy and moonlit; the room was cool, dim and quiet, and the bed was empty of rock stars. Then, about to panic, through the veiling swags of mosquito netting she saw him sitting before the fireplace. Silhouetted against the glow of low flames, he looked merely thoughtful, or watchful, no particular expression on his face; his blond hair was red-gold in the firelight, and he appeared almost as a stranger.

She slipped out of bed and went to stand behind him; he reached an arm round for her, and she leaned forward to circle him with her own arms, resting herself against his bare back. When he said nothing but merely put a hand over both of hers and drew them to his chest, she murmured in his ear, "Please don't yell at me any more, but in the tropical-island preference stakes, my vote's in for Maui."

She felt his deep laughter resonate through her body as he pulled her down to snuggle beside him, carefully avoiding her battered left side. "I'm sorry I yelled. And I'm very, very sorry I teased you. And I totally agree with you about the voting. For now, at least. But you'll change your mind about this place. Are we ready to go home, then?"

"I'd say so, wouldn't you? Well, once we've dealt with the lawyers and the law over on Grand Palm, that is. What about everybody else?"

He sighed and stretched. "Hoden wants to get out as soon as he can; he knows he'll have to give a statement, but he told me this afternoon that he's had just about as much of the Caribbean as he can damn well stand. He plans on chartering a plane from Palmton to L.A. The rest of us can all fly back to New York or L.A. at our leisure. Unless you'd like to sail back on a cruise ship, just the two of us? Wouldn't that be romantic?"

"Are you kidding me? Not if it was the Ark itself!"

"I didn't think so. He and Belinda also told me you did a very creditable job of smacking those orcs around in the mill. I hear you dropped a few of them before they got the drop on you."

"I didn't do all *that* much," she murmured. "Just a few of Ares' little tricks."

Turk grinned. "Oh yes? Hoden said you were so enraged he thought your hair had turned to snakes. Which I would quite like to have seen, actually. Little Emmy Christmas, who did see it, now thinks you're some kind of warrior princess." He was clearly enjoying the picture, but Rennie moved uneasily beside him.

"Hey, you guys were the war gods, descending from the heavens on the fell beast to save the day."

"M'hm, we *were* rather smitey, weren't we. Thunderbolts right, left and center. It was surprisingly enjoyable. Too bad we didn't have armor."

"Too bad I couldn't join in. Though I guess it's only fair that you get to be the King of Smite for a change. You've only ever had the chance to bat cleanup. You would have looked damn good in armor, though."

She laid her head against him and was still, both of them watching the fire flicker. Her mind was running through images given her by Laird, who of course had seen it all and done some excellent smiting of his own: Turk bursting into the sugar mill like Hector onto the battlefield of Troy, scattering the enemy before him, commanding everyone to tear the place apart until they found her and the others, ordering the helicopter into the dark skies, impatient and furious that he couldn't fly up to her under his own power and had to depend on a machine. *Yeah…Ironhand redux, all right…* She didn't know when he carried her to bed.

They headed to Palmton the next day, accompanied by Phanuel, who had demons of his own to face, and they went straight to Shipsterns, Churching, Glasson and Knight, who were all expecting them. And where Superintendent Meryton greeted them cheerfully. Well, he *should* be pleased, Rennie considered, coolly shaking hands; not only had he grabbed several internationally sought multiple murderers, he and his boys had broken the back of the biggest drug ring in that corner of the Caribbean. With some help, of course; and to his very great credit, he did not now begrudge it.

"I must say, from what I've heard, that I would never have guessed that the late Mrs. Tessman was the brains behind an operation like that," he remarked, as the three adventurers, plus Turk, Laird and Phanuel, sat down with the solicitors at the familiar cherrywood table over the inevitable cream tea.

Rennie snorted. "Yes, the words 'brains' and 'Loya Tessman' very seldom appeared in the same sentence. I'm as astonished as you are. In fact, probably more so."

Meryton continued serenely, "And I suppose she deserved the rough justice she met with, though if anyone taxes me with it I'll deny I ever said so. Still, we generally prefer it when we can do the justice dispensing ourselves."

Ouch. Rennie felt the sting, but she nodded humbly; that had been a very generous, if somewhat begrudged, pardon, and she was lucky to receive it. "What gets me is how each little barracuda thought they were really the boss fish in charge of the whole school of nasties: Loya, Ted, Fleet, the lawyer boys, even Marigo. Though I can't say I was surprised. But at least Sammi Stoyer was avenged."

She felt rather than saw the skeptical look and incredulous half-smile Turk turned on her. "Yes, your lordship, I mean it! Silly bint paid way too high a price for her skeeviness—I would have called it even if I could have just been able to punch her out a bit."

"Always the soul of fairness and reasonability," Turk said, still smiling. "We'll have to make a Lion Island magistrate of you once we're married. I'm sure it would please my father no end to have a good hanging judge in the family. Literally."

She rolled her eyes at him, and turned soberly to Phanuel, who had been sitting there quiet and withdrawn. "Are you ready, then, Phan? When we're done here?"

He stirred and nodded, though he looked at no one in the room. "Yes, I think I am. If you two will come with?"

Half an hour later, they bade farewell for now to Meryton and the solicitors, and went to see Marigo, locked up tight in the Palmton jail. Turk had nobly meant to offer her legal assistance, purely for Phanuel's sake, even though they all now knew she and Phan had never been married and they also knew what she had done to Mell Armatreddy; but he'd changed his mind once he'd learned that she'd not only kidnapped but injured Rennie. Still, again for Phanuel's sake, they accompanied him to pay a jailhouse visit to his never-was-wife.

Their charitable impulse died a quick death: Marigo proved every bit as septic as she had been in the sugar mill, hissing at them through the cell bars like a rabid possum.

"So, Lord Richard, you has got your slut back and all. Be you careful she don't toss you over and lift her skirt for t'at pretty Hoden boy."

Turk was shaken, Rennie could see; not by the venomous comment but by the look on Phanuel's face. But he gave Marigo a glance of dismissive contempt, and when he spoke his voice was like a spear of ice—his duke voice, as Rennie had long ago dubbed it.

"How kind of you to be concerned, Mrs. Armatreddy. But her ladyship won't be lifting her skirt for anyone but me."

Marigo looked as if she were about to continue in the same vein, or worse, but a look at Turk's face apparently decided her otherwise, and instead she shifted her attention to her not-husband.

"You a slave, Phanuel Shine," she jeered. "Maybe your ancestors was not Tarrant property, but you surely is. I just glad you was not being my husband at all. I never care for you but only marry you for get in wit' deh island, get a look-in set t'ings up for what I want do. Every moment wit' you was a pure misery and I could not abear your touch me."

Phanuel was holding on to himself only with the greatest difficulty, and Turk put a reinforcing hand on his friend's shoulder as Phanuel stepped to the bars of the cell. "Marigo. Why?"

Her Grenadian accent, strong enough before, had apparently trebled in intensity since her arrest, and she snarled at them now in the full island patois.

"Lawd, dis is one tiresome topic. What standard you a go use for base dis t'ing? Are we going to wit' best or worst? Which way in dese islands is deh right one to judge by? To judge *me* by. America way, England way, it be not deh way for me. I jus cyaan not see dis. It all some weak excusing! I do hate see us sell ourselfs to whites in ways which in no manner raise us up. So, I make it simple for me alone. I do for myselfs as I cyaan and take for myselfs what I get."

"Selfish and greedy and unlawful, you mean. People *died* because of you, Marigo. You killed your own husband."

Phanuel's voice was strained, but definite. Oh yeah, thought Rennie as she watched and listened, he was already *so* over Marigo's betrayal—as a fact, at least. But he would hurt for quite a while to come. A quick glance up at Turk where he stood beside her, and she could see that behind the arrogant mask he knew it too, and was hurting for his friend.

"Dere be no law for dis," said Marigo in a bored voice. "All some annoy me. You in special. I be so glad I not your wife ever at all. Makes me wanna wring deh air out of my body rahther than listen more. Cyaan not stand to hear dis rant, on and on. No matter. You enjoying dis, ladyship?"

Marigo turned on Rennie, who held her gaze with an expression of purest distaste, as though she were regarding a nasty gross mess which someone should have cleaned up long before she had to look at it. She said nothing, but merely watched Marigo steadily, and the Grenadian woman suddenly backed up into a corner of her cell, making a protective sign in the air with shaky fingers.

"Get her out from here! She put obeah on me!"

"Not she! You cursed yourself all by yourself," snapped Phanuel. He turned and left, unable to endure any more of his unwife's presence; once he was gone Marigo bent her baleful gaze again on Rennie, obeah magic or not, and Turk stepped protectively in front of his mate. But she moved out from behind him, touching his arm reassuringly as she did so, and stood watching Marigo as before, out of calm, contemplative eyes.

But Marigo was by now neither contemplative nor calm, though she stayed as far back in the cell as she could get, apparently still fearing some sort of hex. "So you, bitch!

How it feel you be his lordship's whore?"

"I wouldn't know," said Rennie after a while, and her voice held clean daylight, to flood that noisome place with air and brightness. "I'm just his lordship's slave."

Twenty-five

IT WAS THEIR FIRST FULL DAY at total leisure after the various excitements, and they were all still resting, still trying to get back to normal. Turk was in the little studio, running off dubs of the songs he and the other musicians had recorded, neatly boxing and labeling them, planning to send them off to each of the Weezles, with the masters for Turk and copies for Laird, Prax and Hoden. Those last three, along with Belinda and Ares, were floating lazily in the eternity pool, having been disinclined to run down to the beach—a very good thing, as it would soon turn out. Phanuel was in the main house, doing accounts; it seemed to take his mind off things. It was very still and quiet and peaceful.

Rennie felt it even before it struck. She had been reading in the main sitting room, enjoying the breeze from the terrace, from time to time thinking smugly of Marigo and the others in the *very* unhospitable slammer, when suddenly her head came up as if someone had called her name, or dropped a plate. But no one had, and then it was there, the earthquake, violently shaking the house, the trees, the whole island.

She dashed outside, well versed from her years in California as to correct quake procedure, and the others were there almost as swiftly, popping out like Swiss clock figures on different levels and terraces. Seeing her, Turk vaulted down to where she stood and put his arms around her as she clutched at him; the ground was still madly vibrating. But something was very, very much more wrong than even that: behind his bright head and against the bright sky, she could see a huge, towering black cloud rising up far to the south, over the edge of the world, reaching to what seemed like the borders of space. Without knowing it, she whimpered into Turk's chest and clutched him even closer. But she never stopped staring at the cloud.

He stroked her rigid back and nuzzled her hair, himself watching the billowing distant plume of dark ash. "It's all right, it's all right…it happens sometimes. It's way down the islands; could be La Grande Soufrière on Guadeloupe, but more probably Soufrière Hills on Montserrat. That one's been twitching for the last year. 'Now she puff but will she blow, Trust the Lord and hope it's no', as the locals pray. All those islands down along there have live volcanoes. Either way, it's two hundred miles from here; don't worry, we're solid. Though there might be—well, there might be a wave. So there will be an alarm. Even so, we're still safe as houses. We're all right."

But it wasn't all right, it was very far from all right. For the third time during their stay, they heard the alarm sounded of conchs and church bells, with the more modern touch of a siren added on this occasion. Down below in Lion Town and as far as she could see along the shore, Rennie beheld people moving swiftly and purposefully to gather the children up from the beaches and get the boats inside the shelter of the Claws; as she watched, the giant, rusted-iron seagates were being winched slowly closed across the narrow ingress to Lion Bay, as if to repel invaders.

The gates had originally been constructed to do exactly that. An engineering marvel of their time, they were a harbor boom and chain taken to the next level, or a supersized riverine lock—huge iron panels cleverly hung from the rocky headlands at the bay entrance, shutting off the narrow passage like a great double door. They were not impermeable—water could still pass underneath—but they could shut out attacking ships, and even partly fend off incoming waves as well, either hurricane or tidal. Which had given her a great deal of comfort, when Turk had first explained the gates to her. Yeah, maybe the days were over when the Spanish navy would come sailing up with a few seventy-four-gun carracks, but waves were always possible. Now everything was done. Now they could do nothing but wait it out.

Thirty anxious minutes later, gathered together on the terrace, they all watched with horror as the waters around the island shivered and drained in the initial drawdown, as if some plug had been pulled in a giant bathtub, and then, with a kind of terrible, inexorable grace, the tsunami came flooding back at a deceptively stately pace, though at Lion Town, the Claws and the seagates mostly stilled the rush as it came foaming in. Not until she looked to the distant beaches could she see how swiftly it was really moving. Nothing could outrun it, nothing and no one could survive it.

The excellence of Ironhand's edict forbidding anyone to build homes below the mark of the greatest previous wave now was clearly seen. This one, thankfully, was much smaller, only about seven feet high where the earlier one had topped thirty. Even so, Lion Town's customs docks were swamped ankle-deep, and some little empty warehouses flooded as well; the north shore was mostly spared, though out on the eastern end the old sugar mill and its boathouse collapsed in the second, larger wave, to which Rennie privately thought good riddance. But not a house was lost, not a cottage, not a boat, not even a clamming dredge; and no lives were lost because the islanders had been drilled from birth for the past three centuries on what to do when the earth shook—get to high ground at once, and stay there until reliably told not to, and not for any reason go down to the shore.

So many people died around the world when they mistakenly assumed that tsunami danger was past after one wave, and went back; or, being altogether ignorant, when they went down to the exposed sands to gather up the fish stranded in pools and were caught by the next inrushing monster. The Tarrants had long since made sure that none of theirs would fall victim; everyone on the island was well instructed on what to do and what not, when the ground shook and the waves came after.

Rennie, for her part, stared at the white horror of the tsunami line, and beyond at the still rising pillar of ash, and queasy from the quake movement, ran inside to relieve herself of breakfast, feeling not the slightest inclination for a closer view of either.

"It didn't look like I'd thought it would—the wave," she explained, subdued and still unsteady, to Turk in bed that night. The ash cloud was still hanging over the island of Montserrat, glowing red and shot with lightning, though the earth and sea had finally quieted. She had taken one look out their windows and buried her head in the pillows and in Turk. Suddenly paradise had turned infernal, and she would never so blindly trust in its beauty ever again.

"No... Not a pretty sight. Beautiful and terrible, rather. I've never seen one either. In fact, no one here has; the last one was a hundred years ago. Thank God everybody remembered what they'd been told to do, or not do."

As soon as they were certain that the danger had passed, they had spent the rest of that day going around the island, making sure that no one had been harmed or needed help, and that damage to property was minimal. Poseidon the earthquake god, or perhaps Pele the volcano goddess, had been on their side there, though this part of the world was not their turf—Agallu, then, mighty spirit of earth in the native religion of these islands. Not a severe eruption as those things go; four waves in all, but only the second had been of a size to inflict real harm, and as it turned out, thankfully, it hadn't.

Turk had been tireless in looking after his people, and Rennie had been rapt and respectful, watching his solicitude as he went street to street in Lion Town. Then, driving out to the handful of villages and tiny farm hamlets, he joined the townsfolk where they clustered around the "shade tree", the large, centrally located tree in each village under which locals would gather to socialize or exchange news or huddle in fear of just such events as had transpired. That day they had congregated under their trees for mutual heartening, and it was his job to provide care, asking after everyone's welfare, promising to repair whatever needed it, comforting whoever wanted it.

She had tried her best to emulate his example, following him into the throngs that greeted him, shaking hands, inquiring, reassuring. The women, with or without small infants, came to her instinctively and naturally, "Mister Richard's lady"; the men and the older children went just as unerringly to Turk. In the course of their day's progress they crossed paths several times with Phanuel and the Tenant-in-Chief, who were out and about doing the same thing, but Rennie noticed that the people came to Turk more eagerly and more readily, and were more cheered by speaking to him, and even to her.

Caught up in the busy moments of making sure others were safe, helping hands-on where it was needed—whether it was first aid or moving a fallen tree—she had forgotten her own fears as she reassured theirs. It was all very symbolic and feudal and lord-and-lady-of-the-manor-ish. But it felt right. And she was still more shaken than she'd thought: even now she kept seeing the water in her mind's eye, and she startled at every aftershock.

"I thought a tsunami would be like a big giant breaker a hundred feet high. This was more like—a shelf of ocean. It kept coming in and in and in..."

Turk nodded somber agreement. "If we didn't have such a mountainous coast, it could have been truly terrible. The way it was over on some of the other islands. Here, it was more like a sleeper wave; the reefs helped break it up, and the mountains shut it down. Though where it ran up the streams, it was bad enough. But we came out of it safely." He kissed her hair. "I'm very proud of you. You did so well with everyone; they all said. Talk about a baptism of fire..."

"Maybe." She burrowed closer. "Maybe. But *you* were the one they came to."

So their departure was pushed back again, not for destruction done to them and theirs but because the entire region's energies were switched over to helping out the islands that had been hardest hit; that was how it was done, and they didn't want to leave while they were still needed. The residents of Falcons Levels pitched in with everyone else, working to put up care packages for the devastated folk on Montserrat and other islands: mostly food, medicine and clothing—Phanuel, with a kind of icy focus, contributed every single thing that Marigo had ever owned—but also whatever helpful machines and tools could be spared, or purchased by Turk and the Lion Island authorities. All this was stacked on the docks and on the beaches, and relays of small boats, the cutters and launches and fishing craft, even the seaplane, ferried it over to Palmton to add it to other such relief coming in from all around, and then out to wherever it was most needed.

Lying spent on the terrace after a long day of aid work, Rennie moved over in the hammock as Turk came out to join her. He cuddled next to her for a long time without speaking, and she was content to share his silence. In the house, she could hear Prax, Phanuel, Hoden and Ares softly conversing; Laird and Belinda were splashing again in the eternity pool.

"It would seem that there was a great seismic event on all levels, an eruption and quake and wave," he mused softly, as he held her. "I mean, in the physical plane, obviously, but also for all of us in all our lives. Deaths, and betrayals, and threats, and dangers...even renewals and cleansings...we came to see things for what they really were."

"Evil too: the contraster of the merely normal against the supreme good, as someone once wrote." She hugged him suddenly, hard, fisting her hands in his shirt. "I for one think it will be very nice to get to England and get married and settle down in the castle, and have fat little blond titled English babies and not have to worry about this sort of thing ever again. Other things, sure; but not this."

Turk smiled at the mention of the blond titled babies, and stroked her hair. "It will never be no 'other things'; we both know that. And I really wouldn't want it to be. But otherwise I think that is a very good plan indeed."

One more thing needed seeing to. Next morning, the entire Falcons Levels party flew back to Palmton yet again, so that they might give statements in coroner's court, an ancient remnant of English common law that was still alive in the Grand Palms, at a session that had been postponed for several days because of the eruption and aid effort. Voel and Hannah Christmas came too, with their brave kids also to be questioned, though much more gently and in judge's chambers, not open session. The offenders had been efficiently jailed, trials and sentencing soon to follow; given the nature of the offenses, it didn't look very good for any of them.

Thank God for small favors: the feared blaze of publicity—Island Drug Ring Broken on Local Lord's Island!

Murder! Kidnapping! Rock Star Hostages! Hero Children!—had not materialized as expected. Rennie didn't want to ask how, though she suspected that Lord Fitz might have had a hand in it; and also the volcano had, thankfully, stolen their thunder—a horrible thing to think, but true for all that.

After the police and the medical examiners had spoken, Rennie, Belinda and Hoden gave their own testimony, frankly and unsensationally. Rennie kept her eyes on Turk the whole time, getting through the more difficult parts by thinking of how much delicious front-page jam she was cooking up for Ken Karper and Fitz—it was the only way she could manage it—and trying not to be Shakespearean about it all. *Marry, crowner's quest law indeed...* After that, Ares and Phanuel had a bit to add, and then Turk himself, in his persona as Lord Raxton, calmly filled in the details as he'd seen them to close things down on their end. A few more witnesses, and it was over.

It was pretty much over all round. The trials would come later; this was merely to see if there was enough evidence to take things to trial in the first place. Though there seemed to be very little doubt on that account. At any rate, a verdict of capital offenses was speedily returned by the jury, so trial it would be; no bail had been allowed for anyone, and none had been expected. When the Lion Island contingent, minus Phanuel, whose emotional limits had finally been reached, and nobody blamed him one bit, arrived yet again at the Shipsterns law offices to wrap things up, they were met by Will Knight, who told them with great satisfaction that alleged grieving widower Ted Tessman had been busted as he attempted to bribe himself a flight to a nonextraditable location. He had hid out for a week before he was caught, in a remote villa belonging to friends on one of the private Grand Palms, and now that he had been bagged, he had been charged with the murders of his wife and the groupie, plus the drug stuff, plus a number of major financial miscreancies, and not forgetting complicity in the three kidnappings either.

Rennie raised commenting eyebrows as they walked to the now-familiar conference room. "Well, that solves a lot of problems and raises just as many new ones. To wit, what will become of Tontine now that Ted is no longer booking but booked?"

"For starters, I should think a rather intensive investigation," Hoden remarked. "And not only on our account but everybody else's who's signed to them. Many contracts will be reviewed, to say the least. And in our case, Jack Holland and Isis as well. Perhaps Ted and Jo were the only rotten apples in the barrel, though I rather doubt it. I also doubt that we'll be staying on with Tontine in any case, no matter who replaces them, if anyone; I think we'll be following Lionheart's excellent lead instead, right out the door. And departing from Isis Records, too: I'd make a modest guess that, oh, one or two labels might want us aboard."

Ares snorted. "So modest. Make that one or two dozen."

Hoden shrugged, but he was smiling. "Maybe so, maybe no. But also maybe we could set up our own booking agency amongst ourselves, if some of the other Tontine acts want to break ranks and come along."

"Not a bad idea," said Turk. "Even with just our immediate circle of friends—Weezles, Powderhouse, ourselves, Evenor, Thistlefit, Turnstone, Dandiprat, Bluesnroyals, solo acts like Sunny Silver and Leezil Barnes—we could have a very tidy and influential little outfit to take care of not only us but other bands looking for a more personal and less vile touch. We already have promoters who could step in and take over, not to mention our own publicists...it wouldn't be hard to set up and it wouldn't take long to arrange it. And we could all be partners."

"And perhaps our own label as well," said Prax. "Hey, kids, let's use my dad's barn and put on a show!"

Will was very pleased to see them, and so was Sir Geoffrey Shipsterns. They all sat down around the banqueting table, as they had twice before, and a uniformed maid brought yet another elegant tea service. Turk felt momentarily disarranged by the sheer normalcy: it was as if not even a seismic cataclysm could rattle this outpost of Empire out of its centuries-old routine. But the tea and accompaniments were superb as always.

Shipsterns wasted no time. "Glad to see you all, glad you weren't hurt in the little incidents. Very brave, the lot of you."

They murmured back deprecatingly, and he waved a hand with irritation. "Take it gracefully, my dear young people. Well, now. This isn't nearly as complicated as you think it is, not for you anyway. You needn't even return to the country for the trials; what you attested to today in coroner's court should amply suffice as a sworn statement. and it covers Mr. Ted Tessman's activities as well. When the formal trials come up, all those statements will be entered as evidence. Though of course if you *are* needed, it wouldn't be a matter of more than a day or two, and not for a good few months. There's a great deal still to sort out: at least three murders, all the drug ring unpleasantness...not to mention the several different citizenships involved. I doubt anyone not from these islands will get death sentences for their part, even if murder is proved upon them. But it will all be handled."

"I understand it's usually you, Miss Stride, narrating these chatty little after-sessions," said Will, smiling. "But this time let us handle it, if you don't mind?"

Rennie indicated her perfect willingness to allow it and reached for a scone and the clotted cream. Whereupon the just-arrived Chief Superintendent Meryton drew the attention of everyone at the table by tapping his fingers on the gleaming wood, reminding them all who was really running the meeting. Rennie squeezed Turk's hand, knowing he too was thinking of other detectives, other places, and poured tea for him. But Meryton spoke crisply and concisely.

"Well now. It was quite an elaborate plan, and perfectly brought off. At least up to a point. From what we've so far heard in various confessions confirming our investigations, the drug operation had been going on for at least two or three years. These most recent, ah, developments all started aboard the ship, in New York, and a little before, when Mr. Hoden received several communications warning him not to speak with Miss Stride on the cruise, and threatening both their lives. He admits he got the wind up and followed instructions, even though the two had previously planned to do an interview session at some point during the sail. Miss Stride tells us that Loya Tessman approached her the first day, asking to have a private conversation, which was surprising as the two disliked each other intensely, and in any case the talk never happened. I can only assume that the woman Tessman was planning to tell Miss Stride that there was a drug ring at work and that she, Tessman, was the one who ran it."

Rennie nodded. "That's what Jo Fleet told me, anyway. She was probably desperately afraid for her life at that point, if she was willing to confess to me, of all people, that she was a drug czarina herself. And we see that she was right to be afraid. It was pretty common knowledge in rock circles that he beat her, though they publicly claimed a blissful marriage. Who knows, maybe it was, for them. Until it wasn't. Maybe she thought I could protect her, with all my police contacts and everything."

"Very likely," said Meryton grimly. "But let's take it in order. Miss Samantha Stoyer was killed because she found incriminating evidence in Tessman's suite on board ship and tried to use it to blackmail her way into a job at Tontine. Tessman, Joslin Fleet, Larry Mavius and Franz Haran were of course hand in glove with their associate on Lion Island, Marigo Demaray Armatreddy, as she correctly is, not Marigo Shine."

"How did they manage to cook *that* up right under our ignorant Tarrant noses?" asked Turk, rightly furious, and not for the first time. "I thought we ran a pretty tight ship in our islands, keeping that sort of thing out."

"You do, m'lord," said Meryton briskly. "But this was an

extremely professional operation, no fault of yours that they got away with it for as long as they did. Anyway, getting back to Miss Stoyer, Jo Fleet, realizing that blackmail was in play, persuaded her that she'd be an asset to their organization, as long as she kept her mouth shut—and she being completely stupid, he completely convinced her. Then he took her for a nighttime promenade around the ship, allegedly to discuss her wonderful new job-to-be working for Lionheart and the object of her misguided groupie affections, Mr. Turk Wayland. We presume she was ecstatic."

Turk looked acutely uncomfortable, and Rennie lifted his hand to kiss it consolingly. "Don't worry, honey, it never would have happened. I'd have killed her myself first."

Meryton rolled his eyes as Sir Geoffrey harrumphed and Will Knight snickered. "Yes, well. At the start of their little stroll, he'd also given her one of the special-edition heroin-infused Weezle t-shirts, and she'd happily put it on. She would have begun reacting to it almost once; he kept her in it—probably by force, judging by the marks on her—until she overdosed and died, and then he carried her to the rail and threw her overboard. No doubt thinking the seawater would wash out the drug infusion, and it would look as if she'd drowned. Which, as we know, it almost did. But he didn't know that it wouldn't be viewed as a drowning—being already dead, she had no water in her lungs."

"How come he wasn't affected by the heroin himself?" asked Laird.

"He took precautions. Wore long sleeves, plastic gloves, carefully kept his hands away from the shirt—the drug never touched him, though he wouldn't have been affected by so brief an exposure even if it had. It affected Miss Stoyer because the heroin was leaching into her bloodstream through her perspiration over an hour or so. It was brilliant, really."

"It was evil," said Prax quietly, and after a moment Meryton nodded.

"Yes. It was. And if you recall, there were three other similar murders in these islands; thanks to you lot, we can now close the books on those as well. We have the ones responsible dead to rights."

Rennie wished he'd used some other cliché, but there wasn't much else to say about Sammi—in death as in life—and already he'd moved on to Loya Tessman, who presented much more of interest.

"She was the drug czarina, as Miss Stride describes her: she had gone in on the ring with Jo Fleet and her husband and the lawyers, financed it with her family money until it began to be profitable, when she started pulling revenue out of it, and she had exercised total control over the men involved. The men were deeply resentful at having to be dependent on her backing and having to do her bidding, not to mention having to provide her with such a huge percentage of the earnings, so they hatched a plan to get rid of her."

Rennie gazed distantly at the vast antique mirror in which she had studied Jo Fleet; it seemed like years ago. "When she came up to me in the dining room—she never spoke to me, *ever*, unless she was being insulting—she looked terrified. But then she never came round to see me as we'd arranged. I never even saw her around the ship after that. And then she was dead."

"Her husband had beaten her violently, after he saw her talking to you at dinner," said Will Knight. "He said so. He was quite proud of himself, the bl—I mean, the evil creature," he amended lamely after a glare from his father; no rude language in front of the Marquess or his lady. "That's why you didn't see her again until you fell over her tied to the deckchair: she had been held prisoner in her cabin. Tessman had threatened to kill her if she tried to contact you and your friends. He confessed that she tried to escape and tell you anyway. It wasn't honor that made her do it; she was so frightened of him and the other men by now that she was prepared to blow the whistle on herself and suffer the consequences. Probably she had overheard something of their plans for her, and figured she'd actually be safer in prison."

Turk shifted in his chair. "*Did* Ted kill her, then? The spivs Fleet and Haran and Mavius said he did, but we weren't sure." He glanced at Rennie, but her face was averted, and the cold, cut-glass profile could have belonged to Persephone, queen of Hades.

"Yes, by his own hand, and he's admitted it," said Meryton evenly; he too had noticed Persephone, and he wasn't chancing anything with *that*. "But the rest of them helped plan it and knew it was going to happen and helped with the aftermath, hence they're being charged as accessories. Tessman saw Loya's death as a free pass to those offshore unextraditable banking islands. As her widower, he'd inherit her family money, and he'd be able to run the drug operation from there in peace if he chose to go on with it. Though he did say that Loya had made a suggestion—more than a suggestion—that he'd better toe the line or else she'd blow the gaff on *him*. She knew by then how and why Stoyer had been killed. The threat was no more than bravado and bluff on her part, but another reason to hasten her demise. So he garroted her in their suite and then slit her throat just to be sure."

"She was a truly horrible woman," remarked Rennie, apparently back from Avernus, "but she certainly didn't garrote herself and make herself up like Twiggy and tie herself into a deck chair. So it was always murder from the first. And I am still astounded that Ted managed to pull it off."

"Indeed." Shipsterns' smile was brief. "Well, Tessman subsequently recanted, denying he had anything to do with killing his wife, and now he's blaming the two murders on Joslin Fleet, claims he himself had nothing to do with any of it. Fleet and the others say very differently, of course. I expect they're all lying like flatfish. As are their employees on Springhouse Cay; the surviving ones, at least. Someone will crack sooner or later, with the good Superintendent and his skilled staff at work. Not to mention the Shine woman, or the Armatreddy woman as I must correctly call her, as accessory to most of the crimes and principal in the murder of her own husband. Though that seems pretty open-and-shut, thanks to the triple eyewitness testimony we have here."

"Quite. But the Paize Lee get-up and makeup job?" asked Hoden.

"Tessman's way of throwing random suspicion on

you Weezles and away from himself." Meryton scowled briefly. "Set decoration, really. The face paint was to cover the bruises he'd given his wife; they were discovered, of course, almost immediately, by the ship's doctor—who did amazing work with very few resources, far above and beyond—and confirmed by the coroner here. That would hopefully muddle the trail even further."

Belinda looked up. "Why didn't he just throw *her* overboard too—Loya? So much easier, yes? It certainly worked for Sammi, or it would have, at least, if he'd only waited till nobody was around, middle of the night. Eight bells in the dogwatch or whatever."

"You'd think!" Will Knight poured himself another cup of tea. "No muss, little fuss. Thing is, none of you strange rock and roll creatures ever seem to *sleep*. It was a small ship; there was always someone awake and around. He took his chance with the groupie, thinking that everyone was safely inside the theater watching the opera. Impatience was his undoing: bad luck that so many people, including Rennie, had fled out on deck, and quite a few of them saw or at least heard her go overboard. His only good luck was that nobody saw *him*. As for Loya, he wanted to leave a little message to his partners—that if he was willing to kill his own wife for the sake of the business, they weren't safe either."

"So what the hell *did* she mean by wanting to come talk to me, then?" demanded Rennie of Superintendent Meryton. "Loya, on the ship. Was she just jerking me around?"

"I can't say for sure, of course," he said after a moment, "but I imagine she probably wanted to spike their guns—

Fleet's, her husband's and the others'. She knew it was drawing near its end, her heroin empire, and she wanted to get out with as little cost to herself as possible. If she did get caught, she was hoping to have pre-emptively enlisted you on her side, with claims of abuse and death threats."

Rennie nodded slowly. "Which all weren't completely unjustified, were they. She was building a defense, with me to support it, and scrounging sympathy to help get her off the hook. Even though she was the one running it all. Good plan! I'd probably have fallen for it, too, being the grade-A number-one bleeding-heart that I am."

"You say that as if it's a bad thing," said Turk quietly, and brushed his lips across the backs of the hand he was still holding.

"Isn't it?" she asked with equal quietness, and looked at him with troubled eyes as the rest of the room looked away.

He shook his head slowly. "No."

While all this was going on, Philip and Emma Christmas, under the anxious and reassuring gazes of their parents, were being gently questioned in a comfortable sitting room by a kind-faced woman judge and a paternal attorney, both of whom had kids of their own. Though subdued, they were on their best and shiniest behavior, swelling especially prideful when their interrogator told them they were on their honor as island citizens to tell the strict and unvarnished truth. Turk had told Voel and Hannah to take them home in the seaplane when they were done and then send the plane back for the rest of them. The children were predictably thrilled at being asked to help the police in their investigations: they conscientiously told a tale that jibed with all the others and gave the shuddering horrors, well concealed, to their listeners; and when it was all over their parents bought them each a big ice cream soda to take on the plane with them.

Phanuel flew back to Lion Island with the others, but Turk and Rennie stayed on overnight at the Palms Inn, dining with the Prime Minister as invited. Dinner at Government House was a small, intimate gathering of a mere thirty guests—local dignitaries and other celebrity residents well known to Turk, plus the P.M. and his family, all of them positively bursting with curiosity to meet Rennie, as an assumed future addition to their social circle. They had all heard about her and her betrothal to Lord Raxton, who had been a target of local matchmaking mothers for years, just as he had been in Britain, and it would not be inaccurate to say that most of them were not best pleased at developments. But they were still curious about her.

Now, of course, there was much more sensational homegrown news to discuss than a couple of sordid little shipboard drug murders that had happened hundreds of miles away. How little they knew her, if they thought she was going to supply them with gossip fodder; besides, if Turk himself fought shy of their little coterie, what made them think she wouldn't as well? So she was cool and reserved at first, but with her fiancé's reassuring hand on the small of her back as he introduced her, she soon managed to pull on her superhero reporter costume and charge into things, once more unto the breach, and at moments the breach-charging became extremely entertaining indeed. At least for her and his lordship.

To flatter her and please Turk, she'd even been given the seat of honor on the host's right, across from a rather frightening Dame of the British Empire who'd won her damehood for, apparently, espionage during World War II, though perhaps Rennie might have misheard that part. The P.M. seemed especially taken with his American guest, having monopolized her over the course of the meal, to Turk's private amusement—he could positively *feel* her itching to get the hell out of there. All in all, though, a not entirely unpleasant evening. But they were glad to get away early, and joined Hoden at the Palms Inn for a farewell drink or two.

"Why do people cheat?" asked Rennie, as they headed back to their island the next afternoon in a seaplane taxi.

Before they left, they had seen Hoden off at the Palmton airport, where a chartered jet was waiting to whisk him off home to L.A. Their bon-voyage parting had been flower-filled and genuinely affectionate, all three of them making sincere professions of warm amity and many promises to stay in touch. Happily, Rennie knew they would: in spite of the very temporary mini-crush Hoden had apparently had on her, which all concerned were silently writing off to the stresses of the past weeks and a mild intellectual dazzlement, Hoden and Turk seemed to have begun a genuine friendship. Of which she completely approved: neither man had enough real friends, and both could only benefit from having one who understood the very particular problems each of them faced. Not enough genuine peers, no pun intended.

"Cheat!" Turk turned to look at her, startled. "*We* don't. We never would."

"No, *I* know *that*—but Marigo... And that actor we met at dinner... And look at almost everyone in every band we know. Even some of our own friends. Ned and Melza cheated on each other. Even Graham and Prue. You remember. We all heard about it."

"They don't now. They wouldn't."

"Is it just being rock stars? Or something worse? Who's to say for sure?"

He touched her cheek, curious but not alarmed; they were way past that kind of insecurity in their relationship, and he wasn't troubled now. "What are you really telling me here?"

"Hoden—" She tried to find words that didn't make her sound like a raving egomaniac.

Oh. He looked intensely relieved. "—had a bit of a crush on you."

She stared at him. "You *knew*?"

Turk felt an unreasoning desire to laugh. "My darling, of *course* I knew. Men always know these things. At least where their own women are concerned."

Rennie snorted, but it was a smiling kind of snort. "Oh really? Most men wouldn't know things about their women *as* women if a house fell on them. But God forbid some other guy is interested: it always comes down to a possessional thing—their female is eyed by a rival, then the antlers start rattling in the glen. I give *you* the benefit of the doubt, of course, as I always do. But I didn't even tumble to it that he was feeling like that. Praxie saw it, she always notices all that subliminal attractional stuff; but I was so surprised. Not fishing for compliments, but I'm not exactly Helen of Troy. Or even Helen of Malibu. Guys don't as a rule fall for me just like that. With one notable and completely requited exception. Which is fine with me, I might add. So I just didn't see it."

"You wipe the palace floor with Helen, sweetheart. And it takes an epic hero to measure up to you. A demigod, even. Someone special. Altogether superior. Someone like me. Well, actually me."

She whacked his arm. "Insufferable git. But how could I not notice? And I would *never*—I like him so much as a person, and I thought we were—friends."

"And you are," said Turk comfortably; secure and confident in her choice of him, he could afford to be generous on Hoden's behalf. "I bet you've already promised to fix him up with one of your amazing colleagues? Yes, I thought so. I'd suggest Belinda, but she's already taken. Oh well, you've got plenty of friends... Besides, why *shouldn't* he feel like that? About you, I mean. We should both be flattered. He'd probably never met anyone like you in his life; clearly you hit him for six. And now that you've told him there's no future in it—as I presume you did or you wouldn't be going home with me now? Yes, well, thank you, *that's* a relief—now that he knows that, he will be your friend forever and never sniff around you again. That's how men are."

"No," she said, snuggling against him as Lion Island appeared beneath them and they circled over the Claws for their landing in the bay. "No, that's how *you* are."

Twenty-six

"That guy of yours has balls the size of asteroids," said Laird admiringly, that evening at Falcons Levels. "You should have been here when we realized you three and the kiddies had gone missing. He and Phanuel were berserk to get that chopper in the air, even when the police started screaming that they'd shoot us out of the sky if we took off. Then the cops turned on a dime and asked to come with. So we said sure, hop in, always room for more. It was so exciting, you have no idea. Or maybe you have. Is this why you do what you do? For the rush? Man, I was so *into* it! You should have seen Turk take down Jo Fleet. And that was even before he knew that Fleet had hit you. If he'd known that, he would have torn the bastard's head off with his bare hands."

"I did see it, actually, and very satisfying it was. And speaking of giant brass balls, yours were clanging pretty loudly themselves," remarked Rennie. "I saw you going to town on those lawyers. So did Belinda, which is more to the point—I'm sure you received a very nice thank-you for rescuing her. Hero sex is always awesome. Believe me, I know."

Laird blushed, and was about to say something when Turk came out onto the terrace with Belinda, Ares and Prax close behind, all four of them bearing trays laden with pitchers of lemonade and iced tea, and huge bowls of pasta drenched in Rennie's Italian grandma's signature red sauce with meatballs and pork chops, and home-baked baguettes, and plates of cream wafers and chocolate pie and raspberry squares for dessert. Marigo had baked some lemon bars before going off on her mariticidal rampage, but they all thought perhaps even "Waste not" didn't cover it, so they'd binned them—and they'd prudently tossed out the cocoa tins too, just in case. Setting the trays down on the big picnic table, they each joined their respective mates. Phanuel had begged off dinner, having instead gone to visit his parents in Lion Town, and nobody minded a bit.

Rennie smiled up at Turk. "Ironhand must be very proud of you. You're a credit to his pirate DNA. If I weren't already sleeping with you, I would *so* open my legs."

"And you're an extremely bad influence," said Turk severely, trying to look disapproving but feeling secretly proud and pleased. "God knows I have had my share of brawls in my satisfyingly misspent younger days, but never before have I gone for someone with pure primitive intent to kill. If Ares hadn't pulled me off—"

"Nice, innit?" murmured Rennie demurely, not looking at him. "Maybe now you understand me a bit better? It felt pretty good, I'm thinking, yes?"

"Yes, it did! It felt *damn* good. And that's what scares me so much. Well, no more. From now on, we're both going to—"

"Oh, *what*? We're going to what? You're going to tell me something boring like we need to settle down and start behaving like a future duke and duchess, aren't you. Well, not gonna happen! Listen"—she put down her glass and turned to face him—"when we come to the big title, and may that day be long delayed, we're not going to do it like your parents or grandparents. Yeah, yeah, we'll have tea with your godmum Auntie Queen Lilibet, and with your godbrother King Charles III, if it so falls out—and we'll manage just peachily—but we're never not going to be rock and rollers. You *know* this. I'm aware that there have been some fairly dodgy Tarrants down the centuries, but you and I are probably the most piratical couple who've come along in your family since Ironhand and Maddy themselves, and we're going to be a duke and duchess more like them than like any of your lordly predecessors. That's the way it is, and everybody had damn well better get used to it."

"I know. That's another thing that makes me nervous." He looked at her and started to grin. "So, we're never going to be like normal people then, are we."

"Nope," said Rennie comfortably. "There's progress for you. Have a bikkie."

It had finally come down to the last few nights of their stay on the island. Duties were calling them back to their various homes, and departure couldn't be put off any longer. But no one was feeling guilty: they'd all needed the decompression time, to regroup and recupe in contented idleness, to allow the sun to warm the horror out of them.

Safely home in L.A., Hoden had phoned a few times to check in, proffering assurances that everything was okay on the Weezle front and promises to come visit again in New York or England or the Hollywood Hills once he and the other guys had sorted out their tangled professional lives. He'd even courteously sent Rennie a thank-you gift of diamond earrings as a combined hostess present and token of their shared ordeal, and pearl ones to Belinda and Prax.

Rennie wasn't so sure it was all as okay with him as Hoden claimed it was, and she worried about him; he'd been through a lot. Still, the Weezle future seemed strong and brighter than ever, now that they were free of the Jo Fleet and Tontine slime, and if Hoden was any indication, he and the band would come through peachily, able to do their own thing at long last. Plus she loved the earrings, and Turk had invited Hoden to the wedding. He'd accepted with delight, and Rennie was already combing the list of her friends to find him a suitable date.

Pip and Emmy had been duly rewarded for bravery. A matched pair of small, beautiful palomino horses, of the ancient Caribbean breed called paso fino, would soon arrive in the island stables under Joshamee's care, while two gleaming new bicycles with literally every possible bell and whistle already stood outside the Christmas home, and Shipsterns *et al.* were in the process of setting up all-expenses-paid college trusts for both children. Everything was the grateful and conjoint gift of Turk, Rennie, Laird, Belinda and Hoden—to Voel and Hannah Christmas' staggered, stammering thanks. But Rennie had taken their hands and gently said that the thanks were all due to their incredible kids.

As for Phanuel, instead of spending his time idly brooding, he seemed to feel better and better the more he had to do. Turk reminded his protesting lady that healing came in different forms and doses, and let his friend work as hard as he pleased, or needed to.

As promised, one afternoon Turk drove down with his fiancée in one of the Rovers to the charming white church that stood on its grassy hill above Lion Town. Inside, the coquina-stone walls and high arched windows made the place cool and bright. It was very old, and stunningly plain: a nave and perhaps twenty rows of dark native-wood pews in front of an altar also cut from a block of coquina. There was a small baptistry on one side where island children for the past three hundred years had been christened over a marble font brought from England on a Tarrant ship. On the other side, a tiny chapel that held a double tomb hid itself behind a wrought-iron screen.

Rennie paused with appropriate reverence at the chapel's open gate—she'd even brought some flowers as an offering, an armful of blazing orange lilies picked from along the path—then moved forward to the two effigies lying side by side on the plinth atop the white marble tomb, and gently placed the wild blossoms at their feet.

Well, you couldn't really tell from old effigies, could you, any more than you could from old paintings, how people had actually *looked*. It all depended on the skill, or the honesty, of the artist, and these carvings, as well as the tomb itself, had been done by a sculptor in England and imported here after the fact. But accurate or not, these were very skilled carvings indeed. Duke Ironhand bore a striking and felicitous resemblance to the Tarrant male with whom Rennie was most familiar, though it might just have been the long hair and beard and strong, handsome features, not to mention the hippie-looking clothes. As for Madelon...

"What a lovely woman."

"Indeed," said Turk, but his eyes were not on the effigy.

Rennie laid a gentle hand on the marble fingers of the pirate duchess where they held a carved stone flower, astonishingly detailed, even the rings showing clear. As did everything else: the curve of the marble cheek, the gown's graceful folds and delicate lace ruff, the pendant T on its strand of huge pearls around her throat—as if it had all been frozen rather than sculpted. Though the sword at her side was admittedly a bit unusual. And carved right there, hidden in the ornate floral frieze round the tomb's edges, were the ships and skulls and pirate things Turk had mentioned.

I still think it was you that night, in the hurricane, looking out for us. Thank you, sistah Duchess Maddy! I also think I really *need to get a pendant like that made...unless you're not wearing yours in there and it's in the vaults back at Locksley and I can borrow it...just for the wedding...just until I get a tattoo...*

"So this is how you and I are going to end up." Rennie didn't look at him, it wasn't what she had meant to say. But she felt his surprise, and also his immediate understanding.

"Well—yes. But in the mausoleum at Locksley Hall, though. You saw when we brought my grandfather there. Except for these two, all the Tarrant dukes and their wives are there. And so will we be, eventually."

"Effigies too?"

"Certainly. It's the way my family does things. Still, we can manage something more rock and roll for ourselves when the time comes."

Rennie smiled. "Stratocasters and typewriters? That leather outfit I made you? My favorite Gina Fratini dress?"

"Whatever you like."

Rennie smiled no more. "It doesn't matter, you know. It really doesn't." She looked at him at last. "As I said after your grandfather's funeral: as long as I'm sleeping there next to you, it's all fine."

"You won't be sleeping next to anyone else. Dead or alive."

"You've said that before."

"Just a reminder."

Their very last night, they all dined together on the main terrace. In Marigo's now-permanent absence, Turk had happily taken over the cooking chores, with the others as ad hoc kitchen serfs, and for their farewell dinner on the island he had made many sumptuous small seafoody things, all from local waters: fluffy, snowy lobster rolls, crab cakes and fried oysters and shrimpburgers, conch and clam and scallop fritters, three kinds of chowder; and for dessert a slushy chocolate and blood-orange sorbet that made everyone kneel before him in gratitude and awe.

After, happily stodged into immobility, they sat in lounge chairs or sprawled in hammocks, sipping lemonade or island beer, watching the sun set behind Grand Palm Island; the air was warm and pleasant, the stillness broken only by bird sounds and the slow hoosh of the surf below in Silver Bay. By tacit consent, they avoided discussion of the murders, the drug ring, the hurricane, the volcano, the earthquake and the tsunami—indeed, anything of substance or seriousness—and instead talked quietly about marginal topics, which came as a relief to all concerned.

"Phanuel, will you stay here?" asked Laird after a while, carefully. "I can't imagine you leaving, but with—" Out of tact, he avoided mentioning Marigo's name, but everyone heard it just the same.

Phanuel looked out to sea, his horizon-stare much as his ancestor Martin Shine's must have been. "Not going anywhere, man. There isn't anything or anyone come from outside, or in, that can spoil this place for me. Not with how the Tarrants have been with the Shines for three hundred years. That's too big to leave or lose. Besides, my whole family is here. I'm not done and I won't be alone."

"Partners," said Turk quietly, addressing the others from the double hammock where he and Rennie were cuddled up together. "All in. The way Martin was with Ironhand. Running the island businesses, sharing in all the decisions, making plans for future investments and industry. Total trust. My dad took Phan's dad, Reuel, into full formal partnership four years back. And then he gave Phan the island to run. He was afraid Phan would leave eventually and go be the guiding genius island manager somewhere else."

"Not a chance! But it was your idea, brother," said Phanuel.

"The Guv'nor saw the good sense in it and jumped on it," replied Turk, waving a hand airily. "I merely pointed it out to him. He knew it was the smart thing to do, now that trade is beginning to pick up all through these islands. When we decide to capitalize on the local tourist boom—as we will—there are plans to develop Tienda for the luxury set, on the order of a small, super-exclusive enclave like Mustique, not more than a hundred houses and perhaps one really elegant hotel and restaurant. Plus a casino and resort on Vetiver; it's quite beautiful over there, and, like Tienda, it's far enough away from here so as not to encroach on our peace. When we move on all that, we'll have someone we know and trust to manage things. Someone whose family we've lived with for centuries, with a vested interest in our family doing well because his family will do well too. Also it was the right thing to do, and no one deserves it more. In ten years, the Shines will be a great deal richer than they already are and the Tarrants will be as well. It doesn't stop there: all the rest of our people here will be even more comfortably off than they are now. Works out all round. We're still a commune, after all."

"Somewhere Mr. and Mrs. Ironhand are smiling," said Prax, and Turk laughed.

"I gather Marigo didn't want to wait for that?" asked Ares.

Phanuel shook his head. "No—she never liked waiting for anything. Or working for anything either, come to it. Always with her it was the fast fix and the unearned reward. In more ways than one, I guess. I was so stupid, and I really never saw it. God, I'm so sorry...I still can't believe she kidnapped you girls and Hoden, and was going to—" He broke off, and the silence spoke instead.

"Not your fault, Phan," said Rennie gently. But Belinda, cuddled up with Laird in a hammock of their own, looked thrilled.

" 'Sorry'? Are you *kidding*?" she crowed. "I don't mean to be insensitive, but it's an ill wind and all that, and besides us of course actually being alive, it's already blown some good. In my direction, anyway. I'm getting a *huge* story in Life magazine out of it! My personal account of me and Hoden Weezle and Rennie Stride being kidnapped by rockerverse killers and evil drug masterminds on a beautiful tropical island, and being rescued by Turk Wayland and Laird Burkhart and Ares Sakura and the brave Lion Islander Phanuel Shine. Rock stars and drugs, only the other way round. With photos. Unless you want to write it up yourself, Rennie?" she added belatedly, and deeply insincerely.

Her hostess looked aghast, and shook her head with vigor. "I didn't think so," said Belinda, relieved. "And I promise I'll keep the kids out of it, for their protection. But really, what could be better than that?"

Turk shifted uncomfortably. "Not so much with the rescuing there, missy, thanks ever so. We just rode in with the Palmton cavalry. And I don't think Superintendent Meryton will be too pleased."

"Not the way *I* saw it, pirate boy!" chortled Belinda. "And I was there, don't forget; I actually *did* see it. Besides, whatever I didn't see, Hoden filled me in on. And I very much doubt that Meryton will ever read the story."

"Hoden exaggerates greatly," remarked Turk. "What the hell is that bloke's real name, anyway? I feel like an idiot calling him Hoden Weezle."

Rennie rolled her eyes. "Says the man of a thousand handles... His name is Mark, boys and girls. Mark Hodenhill.

He confessed all to me, when we were up there outside the pirate cave, awaiting death or rescue. He said he didn't want to die with his true name unspoken. Very medieval of him, if a tad bit melodramatic. Anyway, when the group was first fabricated, Jo Fleet, that vile, vile man, thought it would be ever so much cooler and mysterioso if young Mark went by 'Hoden'—no doubt inspired by those single-name wonders Elvis, Cher and Attila—and swore everyone to secrecy about his full name. The promo monkeys at the label, predictably, thought it was brilliant and went right along with it. Morons. Probably too late to change it now. But if he ever leaves the group to do solo stuff—" She looked around at the sudden and very impressed silence that had fallen. "What?"

"He never tells *anyone* his real name," said Laird.

"And I wonder why he told *you*," said Prax.

Turk grinned. "People just tell her things, they can't help it. It's magic or something."

"Well, you can't use it in the story, Lin," said Rennie, with a certain degree of pettishness.

"And if I do?"

Rennie smiled like an angel. "Then I'll tell the world about you-know-what. And won't *you* be sorry."

To everyone's surprise, Belinda blushed. And to no one's surprise, when the story appeared it bore no trace of Hoden Weezle's secret real and rightful name. Not even a hint.

Epilogue

"LETTER FROM PHANUEL this morning," said Turk, late-breakfasting/early-lunching with Rennie on the lanai of the East Maui house—the newly named Halelani, House of Heaven—a couple of months later. "Mostly island business bumf. Love to you, of course. He also says his divorce decree from Marigo is final. He didn't really need it, the marriage having been null and void from the first, on account of that trivial little bigamy thing of hers, but he wanted to be sure. Not that it matters, she being in prison for the next five thousand years or so for killing said husband and kidnapping you lot and being an accessory to the other murders. Not to mention all the drug charges. She's damned lucky she didn't get the death penalty, which we still have down there, and it's hanging, which is not exactly an easy way to go. Even as it is, she maybe got off easier than Fleet and Tessman and the rest, who still have to face murder raps for Loya and the groupie, and all the drug charges of their own. They probably won't end up swinging for it either, as they're U.S. citizens, more's the pity, but it could still happen if they end up with a reasonable and intelligent jury and judge. Christ, I never want us to have to testify about anything like that ever again. Though I know we will. But Phan. It mattered to him."

Rennie heard the anger, saw the sorrow. "Phan will be

fine. You'll see."

"Oh, I know he will. I know. It's just hard for him *now*."

She poured a glassful of fresh lilikoi juice, juice she'd squeezed five minutes ago from fruit pulled off their very own trees five minutes before that, and set the glass and a plate of grilled mahi-mahi and fried rice—both of which she'd actually cooked herself—down before Turk, who was lounging at the wrought-iron and glass table wearing blue surf shorts, no shirt, no shoes, no underwear. All of which she highly approved of, being herself clad in nothing but a flower-batiked purple sarong wrapped around her hips.

If pressed, Rennie would have to admit that she really got off waiting hand and foot on Turk, both of them barefoot and half naked in their tropical paradise; there was an interesting South Sea Gauguinesque retro fantasy vibe to it that deeply pleased them both. Maybe it wasn't very feminist or liberated, but it sure was libera*ting*. He did the same for her, of course, in his turn, and he made a really dishy cabana boy, but they liked it best when she was playing the role, for different reasons. She felt like a fraud otherwise: it seemed that they'd hardly gotten home from Lion Island, and here they were back again in yet another dazzlingly beautiful oceanic Eden. What a lazy, privileged life they led. But not really: they'd both been working like mad, they'd been through a lot, and the timing had just worked out.

Yes, Hawaii was great, as she'd told Turk her vote was in for. She had even managed to keep her mind off the fact that three quarters of the island of Maui was composed of one of the most massive volcanoes on the planet—Haleakala,

House of the Sun—and by no means had it been declared extinct; in fact, their own house stood upon its slopes. Which fact, after her recent volcanic trifecta—quake, eruption, tsunami—was hardly a small consideration. Still, Halelani was very, very nice, even though they were only spending a few days more here, relaxing after the band had gone home.

Lionheart had flown out, of course, to inaugurate the brand-new studio Turk had installed by putting the finishing touches on his solo album and wrapping the recording for the band's tenth, to be released for Christmas. He had gotten his way in other matters as well: true to his plan, there had been no big Lionheart tour this year, just the Far East jaunt after playing at Stephen and Ling's wedding. The only other place they'd been extensively away to was Lion Island, and except for those tracks he'd recorded at Falcons Levels with the Weezles, that hadn't been business at all.

Next major project on their personal agenda was participation in a rock train across Britain, the landbound version of the ship trip, only for charity this time: fifty notable musicians assembled by their good friend Graham Sonnet, most of them also their friends. Then seguéing right off the train, it would be their own wedding in October, at Locksley Hall. It had all seemed so very distant for so long, and now it was mere weeks away, which hardly seemed possible.

Cleverly, they'd managed to escape all the planning: they'd dictated their wedding outfits to Punkins Parker and her little atelier elves, and the menu and the music and the guest list and the honeymoon venues to their mothers and Turk's grandmother, who by all accounts were having a blast. After the wedding trip, they'd go back to New York, hopefully. And stay there for a while. A good long while. A year. Three. She loved traveling, and loved traveling with Turk, and loved that he had all these incredible houses to travel to, but she was at the point where she wanted nothing more than to quietly settle down somewhere for more than a couple of months at a time, didn't matter where as long as she was with him.

Of course, quiet settling still might not be immediately possible. Turk's first solo LP on Lionheart's label, Centaur, would have been released right after their honeymoon, and he'd have to do publicity for it; then there would be the new Lionheart album and the publicity for *that*. And the band would have to start seriously thinking about the next tour, though no doubt their manager Francher Green and their label president Freddy Bellasca were already working on that—and bingo, the precious sabbatical year had already vanished, just like that. But all that was well into the future; for the moment, they could relax.

Once they'd left Lion Island, they'd spent a couple of days in miserable Miami observing Jim Morrison's equally miserable obscenity trial—the real obscenity being not what Jim was falsely accused of doing but the cheap political motivations of the trial itself—and commiserating with Jim and his editor spouse, who was right there at her consort's side. Shaking their heads sadly at the foredoomed Greek-tragedy outcome— which everyone could see coming for a mile away, including the principal—they'd flown home to New York, where Rennie had written a blistering couple of pieces on the trial and the American justice system, or lack thereof; then they'd had themselves a busy few weeks at the prow house, settling some pre-wedding matters, including clothes fittings, and enjoying their city before they had to leave yet again.

In a creative fever of her own, Rennie had batted out enough material to keep Fitz happy until at least Thanksgiving, while Turk—back to being Turk again, not Richard, and both of him were grateful and relieved about it—had spent considerable time at the midtown offices of Centaur, hashing things out with Freddy Bellasca about Lionheart contracts, the new album and his solo album in particular. Then they'd upped sticks and come out here, to Halelani, where Turk had had a very productive time with the band—and she likewise with her own work, having wanted to complete her book before the wedding, and having succeeded.

It had all been very domestic. Lionheart had brought their wives and girlfriends, and their tech support team, producer Leo Hafferty and engineer Thom Courtenay and sound guys Boanerges Rivera and Pudge Vetrini. Centaur a&r guy Gerry Langhans, representing the label, and Francher Green had flown in at different times with *their* wives—though definitely not Freddy, who was cordially detested by all. So it had been rocknroll as usual, only on Maui, and with lilikoi. *Ohana* for real, and she'd been genuinely happy to see the band. Yes, even Niles, which was the first time ever for *that,* for sure. Even the other group wives hadn't been as obnoxious to her as they usually were. Maybe the times really were a-changing. But she couldn't help missing the prow house. New York did that to you...

She glanced down at her right hand. There was a handsome new ring on her middle finger, one she'd commissioned from the swordmaking Callows matriarchs of Lion Town, who as Turk had mentioned were now into jewelry as well. Heavy, heavy silver set with a flashing rainbow moonstone, a skull-and-crossbones carved in relief on each side of the shank. She'd had one made for Turk, too, only the stone in his was a sapphire, his birthstone, cabochon and cat's-eye. The rings were carefully copied from the ones Duke Ironhand and Duchess Madelon were wearing in effigy, on their tomb; it had seemed to Rennie only fitting for the future Duke Turk and Duchess Ravenna to mark their Lion Island adventure with copies of their predecessors' rings. A triumphal commemoration of sorts, from one pair of rockers to another.

"I was thinking how that beautiful girl over at the Grand Palm airport was looking at Phan when we were waiting for our flight back to New York," she said presently. She was idly nibbling at the remnants of her dessert, a fine specimen of the wondrous Hawaiian delicacy called a malasada, the islands' version of a doughnut; traditionally they were unfilled, but a place in the nearby village crammed them to bursting with chocolate or jam or cream, and Rennie was addicted. "You remember, we talked to her? The one who runs the Silver Bay gourmet shop in the concourse, she gave us all that delicious stuff to eat on the plane ride home. She certainly seemed interested in him. Don't you think they'd be fantastic together?"

Turk set down his knife and fork, and looked more

cheerful. "Bonniah Gracen. She's one of ours, a Lion Island girl born and bred. She went to university in the States and she lives in Palmton now. I've known the Gracens all my life. So has Phan. Wonderful family."

"Well, then. I bet she'd go home in a heartbeat, and I'm sure her folks would be thrilled to have her back. Let's fix them up, don't you think she'd be perfect for him—wait, you're the prince of the island, my lord, just command them to get married."

"If only it were that simple, my lady. She *would* be perfect for him, though—she's a born belonger, like Phan. She understands how it is there, none of that outsider thing. *Nothing* like Marigo. God damn and blast her!" said Turk, with sudden violence. "She actually made me think Phan had betrayed me. Even though I only thought it for… And she hurt you, and she threatened my friends and my island, and she worked against our happiness and peace. For that alone, I hope she rots in jail forever. But what does that say about us both, about her and me?"

Rennie reached over to take his hand, forbearing to remind him that she too had doubted Phanuel Shine's loyalty, and far more than he had, however reluctantly, and he chivalrously refrained from mentioning it.

"It says she's a monster and you're just human after all. Hard as that may be for you to believe. Love, everybody doubts sometimes."

"I don't doubt you. You don't doubt me."

"That's different."

And it was.

Interesting Times

When you're buying time in heartbeats
and you daren't make a stand
And it all comes out the same
if you're a woman or a man
The hours not for telling
The minutes not to fail
The now that's not for selling
The past to no avail

But the future is the future
It's patient and can wait
When it gets here it's the present
and it's never out of date
It comes and goes like liars
It brims with new desires
It burns with hidden fires
It cloaks itself with fate
It may feel like time has found it
Yet there's a way around it
Both curse and blessing, free, not always pleasant

May you always live in interesting times
May your days be marked in rhythms and in rhymes
Anything for a quiet life is well and good for some
But they're never gonna hear those midnight chimes

I need to know who wants to come in
before I'll open the door

Step back from the ledge, but live on the edge
You'll find there's so much more
It may look just like a sinner
But it just might be a winner
It's no game for beginners
and the losers hit the floor
Truth and lies are both concealed beneath the mask
You'll never know for sure unless you ask

So hold out for those interesting times
Forego the plain and mortal daily climes
A tomb or catacomb
Is no one's idea of home
But every part of a distant castle shines

[bridge]

You're never gonna live the life prosaic
You'll never get lost to find your way
All the possible bright mosaic
spread out at your feet today
Fight for the rights of one another
Sing the song that the world began
Live in the heart of one true lover
Die in the arms of the family of man

You'll always crave those interesting times
Require them profane and yet sublime
Inner peace most famously
isn't all it's cracked up to be

Still, don't get hooked on interesting times

Throw the door wide on interesting times
But never cross those signals and those signs
Your days may be no better
but don't be heaven's debtor
May the devil damn those interesting times

~Turk Wayland

A preview of the next Rennie Stride Mystery,
Ruby Gruesday: Murder on the Rock Limited:

Prologue

The gleaming steam train stood in the shed being made ready for its journey, like a prize racehorse in the saddling enclosure on Derby day. Usually it had people swarming round it, workers or guests or just gawkers, and today was no exception; being the pampered, and pampering, conveyance it was famous for being, it was well used all to the fuss. It was called the Silver Archer, and it was the pride of British Rail. Every week it made a three-cornered trip from Cornwall to Scotland to London, catering to tourists who were happy to be catered to on the grand old scale, whether it was in their everyday touristical life or as a once-in-a-lifetime occasion.

This particular trip would be a combination of both. Grey Archie, as it was affectionately known to its handlers, had been commissioned for a four-day, three-night private journey—a fairly usual occurrence. But the passengers just now boarding under the deep blue skies of an early morning in October were anything but usual: a hundred carefully chosen aristocrats and courtiers of the rock world, to be carried in luxury and a blaze of international publicity from Penzance in the far southwest to Edinburgh's Waverley Station, playing all the way—a rock festival on rails. All in all, a train of some twenty vintage cars, wood-paneled and picture-windowed, each bearing a resonantly British name like Glastonbury or Caernarvon or Loch Lomond: for this occasion, rechristened the Rock Limited.

It had begun as the cherished brainchild of several British rock superstars: train full of rock superstar friends, with all the music made on board to be recorded and the resultant album sold for charity, once the various permissions among a dozen record labels had been sorted out, and the whole thing to be chronicled by the reporters and photographers invited along and shot for a documentary by film people. There had been a huge free concert on Hampstead Heath over the weekend, to give the enterprise a proper and publicity-laden London launch before the public, and now the main event was about to unfold.

Many of the passengers had arrived in Cornwall a day or two before, staying in nearby country-house hotels or on the estates of friends; some had flown or choppered down privately at the last possible moment, some had driven, or more likely been driven, others had taken rather less resplendent trains down to Penzance to connect with the Limited.

The mode of dress seemed to favor comfort over style, and many people were clad in funkily anonymous rock and roll fatigues. But a prevailing percentage had obviously chosen to treat this trip as the rockerverse equivalent of the Orient Express, and if there were no sweeping sable coats or leashed pairs of white borzois to be seen, there was certainly some eye-poppingly exotic garmentage milling around on the platform getting its compartment assignments sorted out: fringed buckskin, paisley velvets, leather pants, lace minidresses, Cavalier cloaks, highwayman hats, long hair, beards, longer hair. All being madly Nikon'ed by famed rock photogs like Francie Nolting and Baron Wolman and Judson Horn.

On the edge of the happy throng, a man in a stained and wrinkled old Burberry stood watching and smoking a cigarette, a look of contempt and contemplation on his face, which was even more ravaged than the raincoat. He was clearly decades older than the average Limited passenger; stocky, not tall, not attractive, balding under his fedora. Improbable as it seemed, he was clutching a boarding pass and ticket, so clearly he was about to lawfully entrain. After a while he picked up the Forties-vintage rattan suitcase that had been at his feet, and began to make his way toward a sleeping-car down along the middle of the train: the car with Helvellyn, the name of a famous Lake District peak, emblazoned in gold letters upon its scarlet sides.

No one paid any heed to him as he swung the unfashionable suitcase up the boarding steps and vanished after it into the depths of the carriage. His departure three days hence would be rather more populously, and much more sensationally, attended...

Chapter 1

Tuesday, October 6, 1970

"THIS IS *INCREDIBLE*!"

Rennie Stride stood in the train corridor, looking in with tremendous satisfaction through the open door at the sleeping compartment she would be occupying for the next three nights, while the steward labored to stow her deeply laden vintage Vuitton suitcases on the equally vintage, and clearly insufficient, overhead racks. And she gave a sigh of great contentment as she looked. It was all exactly as she had hoped: plush upholstery, polished brass, etched glass, darkly gleaming wood, Art Deco detailing. Even the ceiling fan was from an earlier era.

"Tiny, fusty, dusty, claustrophobic. Just like all those old movies. Yes, it's incredible, all right," agreed guitar god Turk Wayland, who easily tossed up his own battered brown leather luggage onto the brass rack and then lent a sympathetic hand to the steward still struggling with hers. As her consort of almost three years, he was, of course, sharing the cabin with her, and in six days' time he would be her husband and sharing the rest of his life with her.

"Oh no, you're really going to say it, aren't you?" he added, in case she'd missed the sarcasm, and turned to reward the exhausted steward with a lavish tip.

Turk—otherwise Richard Tarrant, former thirty-fourth Earl of Saltire, present twenty-first Marquess of Raxton and future seventeenth Duke of Locksley—did not share his lady's enthusiasm for rail travel. Which Rennie well knew, but she didn't much care. This would never happen again, and she wanted to savor every single minute of it. "This" being the Rock Limited: four days aboard a posh famous old steam train, playing music from one end of Britain to the other, with a hundred or so famous friends, all proceeds from the resultant album destined for charity. With their wedding at the end of it. Turk might not like trains much, but the trip wouldn't kill him, and then they had the ceremony and honeymoon to look forward to.

Rennie shrugged out of her knee-length brown mink and tossed it on the bed, which was for the moment configured as a thick-padded sofa, with lace doilies everywhere one could cling. It had been chilly outside, if perhaps not quite cold enough to warrant fur, but she was headed for her wedding, aboard a fabulous vintage train, and there was no *way* she wasn't wearing a fur coat. So mink had seemed just the thing—though, prudently, she'd opted for the lightest and most casual one she owned.

"Why, yes, Turk, I *am* going to say it. *SO ROMANTIC.* Because it is. Besides, it's not as tiny as all that. I read somewhere that the sleeper compartments on this train are twice the size of ordinary ones. I've seen New York apartments that were smaller than this. I've *lived* in New York apartments that were smaller than this. You're such a snob. And not in a good way, either. This is part of *your* cultural heritage, you know, not mine. Show some respect. Look, the sofa turns into a fold-out double bed, very nice, single upper berth—your lordship will be sleeping up there if you don't watch your step—cute little bathroom thingy, sink, shower so we don't have to use the one down the hall. Just like an Agatha Christie novel... Man, they don't make them like this anymore—oh, you can look out the window from the bed. And a little window seat. Fantastic."

It was late morning on the fifth of October, and they had just taken possession of their luxurious compartment aboard the Silver Archer, Cabin Number Eight in the sleeping-car *Helvellyn*. Which Rennie regarded as a markedly good omen, Helvellyn being her favorite English mountain (she had favorite Scottish and Welsh ones as well). Besides, it was mentioned in a Coleridge poem, and she sure did like her them there Romantic poets. In any case, Grey Archie was now snorting in the gate, working up a head of steam; the tracks would lead it at a leisurely pace through Cornwall and the West Country, up past the Midlands with a little side jog into the valleys of Wales, over the Yorkshire moors and across the border into Scotland, finishing the long, meandering, musical journey at Edinburgh's grand old Waverley Station below the Castle rock, on the afternoon of October the ninth.

But wait, there's more! The excitement didn't stop there. From Edinburgh, Turk and Rennie would immediately head back south by helicopter to Locksley Hall in Yorkshire, his family's ancestral seat since the time of the Vikings, some of whom indeed, had been among those very same ancestors; the next morning, a specially commissioned wedding train would bring the invited guests who'd been on the Limited back down from Scotland to the Tarrants' private train stop, Locksley Halt; and on the twelfth, Richard and Ravenna would be married in the castle chapel, with three hundred guests, including the bridegroom's godmother and distant cousin Aunt Lilibet—known in her more formal moments as Her Majesty Elizabeth II, by the grace of God Queen of the United Kingdom and Defender of the Faith—in attendance.

That was cutting it pretty close, though they had built in an extra day just in case; but they had planned it that way on purpose, and they could always spend that spare day in Edinburgh, which city they both loved. Both of them had wanted to avoid the run-up to the ceremony as much as possible, and so all the actual wedding planning had been left to their mothers and Turk's grandmother the Dowager Duchess, all of whom were only too pleased to have been put in charge. The bridal couple had laid down their requirements and guest list, and then had skillfully managed to avoid doing any actual wedding *work* except selecting their clothes and the music and approving the cake (chocolate, with raspberry filling)—quite enough work, as they thought. In any case, the plans were finalized, the castle was ready, the cake was baked, the guests were wrangled—all the two of them had to do was congratulate themselves on their cleverness and show up on time for the ceremony.

But for now it was the train. Turk—by most reckonings one of the top three or four lead guitarists in the world—and his hugely famous band Lionheart had been among the first to be invited, and in spite of his long-standing dislike of choo-choos they'd all jumped at the opportunity. Their old friend Sir Graham Sonnet, first rocker to be given the accolade of knighthood, was one of the chief organizers, and he was aboard as well; his wife Dame Prunella Vye, first rockeress to be likewise knighted, or rather damed, would join the train that evening at Bath, with the rest of their own band, Thistlefit.

Gray and Prue, than whom few indeed enjoyed a bigger legend and who had been ennobled for their services to musical and economic Britain, had prevailed on some of the mightiest Names around to get on board. And just about everyone that those Names had in turn solicited had also signed on: superstar solo acts and members of first-rank bands from London to L.A., including two Beatles, two Rolling Stones, a Who, Rennie's best friend Prax McKenna and her band Evenor, Ned Raven and Bluesnroyals, pop ballad princesses April Rainers and Swannie Rivers, folk duo Roger and Pamie Hazlitt, folkrockers Dandiprat, Mark Hodenhill, better known to the world as Hoden Weezle, a new singer-songwriter called David Bowie, who'd just hit with a song about some astronaut lost in space, and a whole bunch more.

Rennie had been informed by the proud carriage steward that the Rock Limited was historically the longest passenger train ever to run in British Rail history, and it certainly far outgunned the paltry fourteen cars of the Festival Express, back in July, which had carried a passel of rockers across most of Canada, with Janis Joplin, the Grateful Dead and The Band headlining.

Grey Archie could boast not only more rock royalty (and,

in Turk's case, actual royalty, or at least aristocratic kinship thereto) than the Express, but its rolling stock included two locomotives; three music cars; eight sleepers; two dining-cars, one open all night; a library car, believe it or not; a club car in which music-making, drugs, the drinking of alcohol and the smoking of anything you liked were permitted, indeed encouraged; and an observation car at the very end of the train that strictly forbade all those same things. Hey, you needed *some*place laid back and hassle-free.

The baggage cars were so positioned as to be conveniently accessed if spare equipment or instruments should be needed for recording purposes, with wire-grille cages behind which the luggage and crates were sequestered, marked with the names of the bands they belonged to. All the carriages had corridors through which passengers and staff could walk without difficulty to get to the others, though admittedly it was a day's march from one end to the other. A loooong train.

The passenger manifest of a hundred souls had been carefully and jealously held to roughly half musicians and half support—which meant roadies and techs, journalists and photographers, producers and engineers, film people and assorted other fellow travelers. The catch was, no free and easy riders allowed: nobody who was merely somebody's husband, wife, boyfriend, girlfriend, associate, drug dealer or groupie of any persuasion. Everybody had to have something real to offer the project, or they didn't make it aboard. And of course, given the precious nature of the freight, there were several bodyguards along, dedicated or free-floating both.

There was even a most thrilling rumor going around of a Budgies reunion on the train, since—persuaded by Sir Graham and of course including himself—all five members of that first and most absolutely superest of all supergroups had signed up for the run to Scotland. That fact alone had sent the rock press into a feeding frenzy: the possibility of even just a mere *sighting* had caused them to descend on Cornwall like emmets to a picnic. Even now they were lining the platform, hoping for a glimpse of ever-elusive quarry like Flurry Knox or Snapper Truesdale or Tris Cardin or the amazing Kit Marlowe.

Gray they saw all the time, and he'd been way more than usually public in his relentless p.r. flogging of the train and the charities that the record proceeds would go to, so the journos didn't care so much about *him*. But the other guys seldom ventured out these days, and as far as anyone knew they hadn't played music together for five years; a big dramatic photo or comment or even the ultimate Holy Grail of a bootleg tape would be worth a lot to a lucky photographer or reporter—hence the interest. And the caution.

Janis Joplin and Jimi Hendrix, who'd been scheduled to be on board as well, sadly and shockingly would not be, except maybe in their spirit forms. They had both died of drug overdoses, Jimi two weeks ago, Janis only two days ago, and the entire rockerverse was still reeling. So the train jam would have an unavoidably funereal overtone, but most of the attendees were looking on it as a chance to bid farewell to their friends with a proper rock and roll wake. And, Rennie duly reflected, perhaps that was appropriate.

At least the two superstars hadn't been murdered with her around...for a change.

At last it seemed that everyone was safely stowed, and three long whistle blasts signaled imminent departure. Turk joined Rennie as she hung excitedly out the corridor window, as the occupants of *Glastonbury* and *Snowdon* and *Glencoe* and all the other cars were doing right down the train, everybody waving to friends and fans on the platform as the train began to roll out of the station, smooth as a country stream, not even a lurch to announce its going. Grey Archie did nothing so crass as lurch.

Shortly thereafter, as the train was humming its leisurely way up to the breakfast halt on Bodmin Moor—no or only very slow travel during meals, lest the china and crystal crash to the floors along with the contents thereof, and perhaps a waiter or two with it—Rennie finished ordering the compartment to her liking. She had driven Turk out like Adam from the Garden while she did so, and now she set herself to explore, making her way along the length of the train at a purposeful if swaying pace.

She found her mate in the first music car, up toward the engine end. He was already happily jamming with his old pal George Harrison, Hollywood Hills neighbor Chris Sakerhawk, Rolling Stone Charlie Watts and enigmatic Evenor bass player Bardo on "I Fought the Law and the Law Won"—a song that had a certain degree of appositeness for all five participants, not to mention most of their appreciative audience.

She sat down in one of the overstuffed armchairs to listen,

accepting the joints that flew at her from all directions and passing them on after the obligatory toke. Someone came and sat on the lace-antimacassared arm of her chair and gave a tug to a lock of her long hair, and she glanced up, startled, then grinned.

"You always seem to turn up at the oddest moments."

"I do, I really do."

Laird Burkhart leaned over and casually kissed the top of her head, in purely brotherly fashion. They had been friends since their college days, when they were both undergraduates at Cornell and Laird and his fledgling band Powderhouse Road had played central New York State bars and frat parties and roadhouses, often with Rennie go-go dancing on the side in a fringed black bikini, black thigh-boots and black fishnet stockings. Since every other go-go girl in the land wore demure white boots and bright Day-Glo minidresses, she had looked like Zorro's kinky exhibitionist girlfriend. Which had been just fine with everyone, especially the audience; and no one, certainly not Rennie, had minded at all that perhaps a major percentage of that audience was attending less out of appreciation for Powderhouse's music than out of appreciation for their dancer's mostly-nakedness—Ithaca and the Triple Cities and other nearby environs had never seen anything like it. But now they were all hugely successful and famous, she and the Powders alike, and their friendship was stronger than ever, not least for having been touched by murder and drama and kidnapping related to, or actually aboard, the ocean-liner version of this train, earlier in the summer.

"I can't believe they set up so fast," she said, indicating

the fearsome-looking music-making area—a mass of amps and monitor speakers and microphones and tangles of wires and baffles.

"The roadies have been working nonstop for days so we could start playing as soon as the train started to move. There's a mini-studio like that in two other cars, so everybody gets a chance to play as much as they want, each with a little control booth and board. Very sophisticated."

"Who's doing the engineering and producing? Last we heard, they hadn't decided."

"Yeah, that *was* tricky, since of course everybody's on different labels and of course everybody wanted their own familiar faces. And ears. But the newly besirred Graham Sonnet, being both the head organizer of this little shindig *and* former head Budgie—"

"So, basically, God…"

"Got that right—anyway, our Sir Gray pulled rank and gave the master gig to Jack Straw, who's produced just about everybody. Backed up by Lionheart's guy Thom Courtenay, 'cause not only is he a terrific engineer, he's also English and comes from around here somewhere; likewise Trevor Jones, who did that nice work for Bluesnroyals. Plus Rosie Landers, that chick from Vinylization, four other Brits and three more engineers from the States."

"Good choices. And lotsa people."

"Lotsa music, pretty much rockin' round the clock, so we'll need 'em all once we get going. They've set up shifts so no one gets too wiped out. Plus plenty of us are qualified to jump in and pinch-hit if the need arises: Stevie from our band, some of the on-board Budgies and Beatles, Ned Raven, your old man, bunch more. Even yours truly. None of us is a stranger to the mixing board or the headphones. You're not either, come to think of it; I bet you could moonlight as a producer anytime you wanted, you've got the ear for it. Weird, though," he added, glancing around the room and nodding to friends and acquaintances who caught his eye.

"Actually, not as weird as I'd been expecting, or maybe hoping. But it's early days yet. Oh, and where's Belinda?"

His face and tone instantly sobered. "In California, for Janis's funeral."

"I thought they weren't having one," said Rennie, her expression and voice matching his.

"Well, it's more an ad hoc wake than a funeral. Like Tansy's. She's being cremated in L.A.—today, in fact—and her ashes are going to be scattered privately off Stinson Beach, on the thirteenth. Day *after* your wedding, so at least she won't haunt your future anniversaries."

Rennie shook her head for a long time. "She should have been buried in all her beads and bangles and feathers and the trashy gold pantsuit she wore at Monterey. In a fancy bronze casket in that funky Hollywood cemetery on Santa Monica, with a half-ton stone on top of her to keep her down. That's how blues queens are laid to rest."

"I heard her family didn't want to go that way, whatever she herself might have liked. And since she and that dude she was seeing weren't married or officially engaged, he didn't have any say in the matter." Laird visibly cheered up. "Anyway, Belinda's flying into Edinburgh to meet me when this little engine that could can and does. We'll then head down to Locksley with everybody else aboard who you were nice enough to invite to see you and Turk tie the knot at last. I can't believe he actually ordered up a special train. But I guess that's the way it is when he's being an Englishman at home in his castle."

"*I* can't believe it's actually happening. The wedding, I mean." Rennie gestured around at the plush setting. "This, weird as it is, is real. That? Not so much."

Laird smiled and gave her a quick hug. "Don't worry, sweetcheeks. As your future fellow countrymen say, it'll be all right on the night."

"God's feet! It had better be."

Turk and the other guys looked set to go for the next couple of hours, so with nods and pointings and eyebrow-archings Rennie conveyed to him that she was going to roam around for a bit. He nodded back, never missing a note, and she got up to prowl, snagging herself something to drink to keep her going the length of the car.

Smiling warmly at friends, cordially nodding to acquaintances, icily cutting enemies like a good Victorian—amazing how this environment brought out retro behavior patterns one had only ever read about in books, though it was all pretty much her usual style—Rennie made her way to the back of the train and the lavishly appointed observation car. It was about a quarter full, and she knew every single person there. In the very back, disposed against the windows on a curved velvet sofa and accompanying armchairs, friends Sandy Denny of Fairport Convention, shiatsu guru Pamela Hannay, pop singer April Rainers and rock writer Liz Williams all waved enthusiastically for her to come sit with them, and she started over to join them.

Except that there was this obstacle to be negotiated first, like a troll under a bridge…

Alvy Larrable, short, squat Ozark redneck turned New Yorker who wrote for that despicable rag the New York Pillar, balding and with skin the texture of furrowed sandpaper, at least three decades older than the oldest rocker aboard, was sitting facing the carriage door, and when he saw Rennie enter, he grinned evilly. She moved past him without giving him even a glance, taking great care not to even brush casually against him; then his voice cut through the light chatter.

"Hey there, pretty chick, how did you like reading about yourself and Turk in my Budgies book? Going to give a copy to his dukely parents for a wedding present? Just *wait* till you see my book on Powderhouse Road."

The whole car hushed and people began backing away as Rennie stopped, turned slowly and bent on Alvy Larrable a glance that could have split the earth like an apple, or an atom. His grin died on his face as she contemplated him for a full ten seconds, and then she spoke, in a voice which was more like a fist of stone than anything else.

"Speak to me again, you feculent weasel-dicked man-thing, and I swear I will rip your kidneys out through your ears and stuff them up your festering ass. And I do not swear such swears lightly. You are a malevolent little hobgoblin, and you have got it coming, in spades. So by God do not cross me, Larrable, this day or any day."

Alvy looked as if he were about to say something else, then thought better of it; gathering his ratty Burberry around him, he slunk out the car door, headed toward the front of the train and presumably less hazardous climes. Rennie watched him go, her eyes alight with the balefires of hell, then looked around challengingly at the silent, staring throng.

"WELL?"

Oh no, nothing, nothing, nicely done, well threatened, handsomely sworn, they all said, and turned hastily back to their previous conversations. Rennie continued walking to the end of the lounge and flung herself down next to Sandy and April and Liz and Pamela, who all looked highly amused. She snagged a snifter full of cider off a passing waiter—the hardest liquor going in this particular car—and sipped it as the countryside unspooled outside, her pulse gradually returning to normal.

"One of these days someone is going to stick a dear little knife in his black little heart," she observed to her friends after a while. "Or put a bullet between his eyes."

"Not you, I hope," said Pamela, tossing her butt-length strawberry blonde hair.

"Dearly as I would love to! No. Not I. But that doesn't mean I wouldn't buy a steak dinner and stand bail and provide an alibi in court for the person who does." She signaled for another hit of cider and drew her feet up under her on the velvet cushions. "Now! Who isn't here that we can talk trash about? Because suddenly I am *so* in the mood."

*

Printed in Great Britain
by Amazon